Praise for the works of Melissa Price

Smile Number Seven

A great Hollywood romance novel that goes straight on my re-read list. The book was practically a page-turner with very good pacing…Fifty chapters and 95,000 words led from a fateful encounter in a California desert through a beautiful clandestine 26 years age gap love story with a few twists and turns towards a very satisfying ending. Add to that some drama, a plausible main conflict, grand romantic gestures, an entourage of secondary characters, great dialogue, a nice dose of humor... and you have an awesome read which I could easily recommend to all romance fans.

-Pin's Reviews, *goodreads*

The story is told from both Katrina and Juliette's point of view, which in this case I think was very important to do, especially with the ups and downs from both sides. The pace was perfect and gave enough at the end that I felt the characters got their happy ever after.

This book has a few great tropes but my favourite is the age-gap romance. It really added a lovely extra element to the story. I loved Julia's character best. She was so loving and forthright. The idea of this beautiful creature being hidden in the closet was just damn sad, but don't you worry, she holds her own.

-Les Rêveur

Steel Eyes

… is a compelling read, a book you'll enjoy by the pool or curled up next to the fire. The relationships portrayed, the doubts and hesitations, the hopes and fears—these are the stuff of good romance.

-It Matters Radio

THE RIGHT CLOSET

Other Bella Books by Melissa Price

Skin in the Game
Smile Number Seven
Steel Eyes

About the Author

Formerly a chiropractic sports physician, Melissa Price is a novelist, short story, and teleplay writer. She has coined the term "Lesbianage" to describe her romantic spy novels, *Steel Eyes* and *Skin in the Game*. Her novel *Smile Number Seven* is an age-gap romance. Two of Melissa's short stories can be found in Bella Books' anthologies, *Happily Ever After* and *In This Together.* Her short story, *A Shore Thing* is available from the Bella Books website. She also co-wrote the biographical screenplay, *Toma-The Man, The Mission, The Message.*

Melissa is a lifelong guitarist who is passionate about animal rescue. An avid swimmer, her motto is: Write. Swim. Read. Repeat.

She invites readers to contact her at www.melissa-price.com

THE RIGHT CLOSET

MELISSA PRICE

Bella Books, Inc.
P.O. Box 10543
Tallahassee, FL 32302

Printed in the United States of America on acid-free paper.

First Edition - 2021

Editor: Ann Roberts
Cover Designer: Kayla Mancuso

ISBN: 978-1-64247-234-9

PUBLISHER'S NOTE

Acknowledgment

Thank you to my fierce writing posse, Jacob Shaver, David Carbone, and Oana Niculae, whose critiques have evolved into a contact sport. Thank you to Ann Roberts for her expertise in editorial sculpture. As always, to my readers, I am grateful for daydreamers everywhere.

Dedication

Dedicated to the memories of Nancy and Chick Price who instilled in me a passion for excellence and originality. And for Andrea Price Goldsmith, to whose effervescent artistry I remain beholden.

CHAPTER ONE

If Congressman Dick Peak thought he had a chance in hell to stop the sun from setting, he'd have taken it. He studied the expanse of San Francisco below him from the iconic Twin Peaks and heard his aide lower the window of their limo from behind.

"Hey, boss, we gotta get going," he said. "Your speech at the ROAR rally starts after sundown."

Peak didn't acknowledge him. Instead, he gazed up at the Godzilla-size fingers made of fog that crept toward him while standing in their ominous shadow. He turned and climbed into the limo before the foggy fingers could swallow him whole.

The candlelight from the vigil downtown was not yet visible, but he knew what awaited him. "Goddamn TV cameras will be everywhere, Jimmy," he muttered.

Jimmy lowered the driver's partition. "Take us to the Bill Graham Civic Auditorium," he said. "And drive us past the protesters."

At the protest that was mounting outside the ROAR rally, Creama LaCroppe hurriedly waved her best friend into the VIP section. Former KBCH newscaster Tawny Beige sliced her way through the growing crowd with precision.

"Are you ready, Creama? It's almost time for your interview. "

"I'm a mess. How can I do this TV interview on the heels of…the *stiletto* heels, of Miss Carlotta Cantata's gay bashing last night?"

Tawny whipped out her lip gloss. "Relax your lips. Love the blue gown by the way."

Creama waited for her to touch up her lipstick before continuing. "I had a bitch of a time finding the right heels. How does my makeup look in these lights?"

"You're good to go, babe."

"Hi, Tawny, sorry to interrupt," said the woman interviewer. "We're about to go live."

"Thanks, Dawn." Tawny gave Creama a double thumbs-up and stepped out of frame.

Creama felt the warmth from the glow of a thousand vigilant candles on her bare arms as she watched the outdoor monitor and listened to the lead-in. On one monitor, when she caught the anchorman in the studio patting down his toupee, it reminded her to smooth her long-haired black wig.

"Live from our KBCH studios in San Francisco, this is Action News," said the announcer. The camera cut away to the anchorman as the KBCH theme faded.

"Good evening, I'm Peter Priestly. Our top story tonight is the controversial Right of America's Religious, or ROAR, rally that's underway at the Bill Graham Civic Auditorium.

"While ROAR's organizers have declined live media coverage, we will be airing taped interviews with some of its spokespeople, including tonight's keynote speaker, former Executive Director of ROAR, Congressman Dick Peak."

Priestly paused. "We're going live now to the scene where reporter Dawn Chang is covering the candlelight vigil and protest. Dawn?"

"Yes, Peter, thank you. As you can see, I'm here with a growing crowd of Bay Area citizens who are picketing the event. Thousands have turned out for this anti-ROAR vigil. People are chanting, 'No Hate.' Scores of picket signs read, Ban Bigotry and Equal Rights.

"ROAR, the right-wing religious organization, has come under recent scrutiny for its policies attacking the LGBT community. While still promoting ex-gay ministries and discrimination policies based on sexual orientation, ROAR has outed what they call the Homosexual Agenda. In it, they claim that the LGBT movement is anti-Christian and is infringing on their religious liberty. They've mobilized over a hundred chapters of grassroots churches for their rally tonight."

Creama fixated on the streaks of candlelight that twinkled in the cameraman's lens.

"Diversity Rights Activist Group, or DRAG as it's commonly known, has organized tonight's vigil in protest of ROAR's recent outcry to overturn the Supreme Court's rulings on gay marriage and discriminatory legislation. I'm joined by tonight's spokesperson for the event, female impersonator, Creama LaCroppe. Creama, what is DRAG's mission tonight?"

A light mocha-colored hand adorned with long red nails smoothed the shimmering, royal blue sequined gown. The creamy red lips outlined in lusciousness, the long, black hair, silky and perfect, Puerto Rican Drag Queen Diva Extraordinaire, Creama LaCroppe, absorbed all the light.

"Hello, Dawn," said Creama with her never-let-the-lips-touch smile. "I prefer the title, Drag Queen Diva *Extraordinaiiiire*." Creama's right hand floated gracefully upward and away, her long red nails elongating the word.

"I stand corrected. Creama, what is DRAG's message in a nutshell?"

Creama deadpanned, "In—a nutshell?"

The novice reporter tried to hide her recoil.

"Dawn, we're here to get the message out that what ROAR is preaching is hate. They claim to practice Christian values and they say they're pro-family, but what they preach is *in*tolerance. They hide behind scripture to promote hatred, ignorance, and fear of the LGBTQ community. And now, they're trying to roll back our civil rights as Americans." Creama's shoulders swiveled on her frame to make her point. "We demand the same legal protection for our families as they have for theirs. Tonight we join with our straight brothers and sisters as a community, to let ROAR know that we are one voice against *all* discrimination."

Creama shivered. In a nanosecond, she relived it. The inescapable flashback made her shudder from the horrible moment that was frozen in time. The baseball bat had come crashing down from behind them out of nowhere, a blur from the first blow, until the fatal strike that rendered her cousin Rico lifeless. Victim of a gay bashing, *straight* cousin Rico had died in a pool of innocent red blood.

"Creama, I notice a lot of picket signs tonight targeting former Executive Director of ROAR, Congressman Dick Peak. Why is that?"

Creama gently tossed back the long, black hair and licked her lips, à la 1970's Cher. "*Ay, Chica.* Mr. Peak is a wolf in sheep's clothing—"

"DOWN WITH DICK!" protestors shouted from behind.

Creama continued in her dramatic New York Puerto Rican accent. "He's the driving force behind that pamphlet full of lies called, 'The Homosexual Agenda,' that ROAR wrote and claimed was some kind of official gay manifesto." Creama became indignant. "And, *Mami*, I tell you I never got that memo. I mean if there's an agenda, I'm not goin' to have nothing to wear to the Agenda Party—'cause I didn't know about it—and if it was real, I, Creama LaCroppe, would know about it!"

"Creama, your opponents at ROAR claim that LGBTQ rights are actually special rights. How do you respond to that?"

"That's the lie that ROAR perpetuates, Dawn. What they're trying to do is eliminate our hard-won civil rights. But that's not going to happen because the LGBTQ community is *not* going quietly back into the closet."

Dawn Chang looked around them. "This is a very diverse crowd here. Creama, who are all these DRAG supporters?"

"We're your brothers, sisters, cousins—your parents and your children. We're your doctors and lawyers and military." Creama looked into the camera. "Just your average Americans."

"EQUAL, NOT SPECIAL TREATMENT," yelled the girly contingent off camera.

Creama engaged the camera lens. "Congressman Dick, how would you feel if *you* were gay?"

"Thank you for joining us, Creama LaCroppe. This is Dawn Chang reporting live from the Civic Center. Back to you, Peter."

Hundreds of DRAG supporters had lined up peacefully behind the fixed strands of yellow Police Line Do Not Cross tape. They chanted in unison: "Racist, sexist, anti-gay, born-again-bigots go away."

"Watch your step, cupcake." A muscular woman in a red security shirt smiled and waited to escort Creama up the steps into the DRAG van.

Creama gathered the bottom of her gown and graciously accepted the arm of the security guard. "Thank god for you butches, honey." Then, to the tune of, "You Picked A Fine Time To Leave Me, Lucille," she sang her drag version. "You picked a fine time to leave me *loose wheel*...with four ugly drag queens, in size *THIR-teen* heels."

Creama's drag queen protégé, Miss Coco Puffs, stood and clapped when Creama entered the van. "Brava, Creama. Brava, girl!"

Larry, the DRAG team leader, scratched his burly beard. "They didn't even mention Carlotta Cantata's assault last night in SOMA."

"Don't worry, Larry," said Coco, "it's all over the regular news."

Creama struck a pose. "So, did I look beautiful on TV, Tawny?"

Tawny glanced away from the TV news coverage and answered in a placating maternal tone, "Yes, darling, you were radiant."

"Tawny Beige! I swear I don't know which one of you is a worse liar—my best friend or the lesbian Romeo to my stunning—and I emphasize *stunning*, Juliet."

"Honestly, Creama, you looked just like Cher—post Sonny of course——but not the curly years."

Creama flung her arms up in the air. "Oh! You mean it?" She wagged her body back and forth in sync with her finger. "You better not be taking the name of the queen diva in vain, you lipstick lesbian."

"Stop calling me a *lesbian*! You know I'm not from the Isle of Lesbos. I prefer gay girl. And my pronouns—since we're doing that now—are, Oh-so-she, and very, very her."

"Do *not* get me started on all of my pronouns!" Creama sighed. "I'm glad that interview is over with."

Tawny exhaled hard.

Creama stared at her. "What?"

"Tell her, Larry."

Larry shook his head slowly. "No."

Tawny scoffed at him. "Thanks a lot. Creama, something urgent has come up. There's something else that DRAG needs you to do."

Creama turned to a silent Larry. "Something else. Oh really?" She struck her grandiose hand-on-hip pose. "Maybe I should act like Vanna White and fetch them a vowel…like 'O', as in *Oh really*?" Creama counted her credits one finger at a time on her wistfully animated hand. "I already gave them my name, my fame. I just finished the Dawn Chang interview!"

"Yes," Tawny answered, "and still, you had enough strength left to sprinkle a dusting of drama."

"Tawny, sometimes I swear you're a queen. What do you want now?" Creama turned to the full-length mirror and combed into place a long strand of Cher-hair.

Larry and Miss Coco stood to leave. "We have to take off, but you did a great job, Creama," said Larry. "I'll see you shortly, Tawny."

"Coward," Tawny replied as Larry winked at her and ushered Miss Coco out the door.

"Creama, DRAG needs you to tail Dick Peak to Puerto Rico tonight after the ROAR rally." She winced in expectation of Creama's reaction.

Creama spun around and stared at her dead-on. "Follow him. Are you insane? I have a show tomorrow night at Mecca, okay? I can't go. And don't aggravate me."

"You have to go," Tawny pleaded. "The guy who was supposed to go broke his leg hiking Mount Tam."

Creama rubber-necked her head from side to side. "Maybe he should have kept his legs closer together on the downside."

"Stop it. You're the bitchy queen, not the evil queen. Creama, honey, DRAG needs you. You know all of Peak's quirks. You know what he likes, how he thinks. You're Puerto Rican for chrissakes, you'll blend in."

"You gotta be jokin', *mija*. I was born and raised in New York."

"No joke, sweetie."

"That's crazy! He knows who I am. I'll never be able to get close enough to get the real dirt on Mr. Family Values."

"That's the catch, Creama. You're going as…" Tawny reached to the seat next to hers and held up a man's suit on a hanger, "Carlos."

Creama's eyebrows smacked her hairline. "What?"

"Here's a Canali suit, compliments of DRAG."

"You want me to follow him in drag?"

"No, we want you to follow him out of drag."

Creama swayed her shoulders back and forth like she was on a train. "But if I put on that suit, I *will* be in drag, and what if he recognizes me? Huh? What about that?"

"Don't be difficult. Honey, I'm your best friend and *I* barely recognize you as Carlos. Come on, Creama, it's really important. If you pull this off, you'll be the shero of the gay community. You've always said you wanted to make a difference in this world, well, here's your shot."

Creama fell back into a chair and sighed. "Can I wear a little mascara?"

"No!"

"I can't believe this, *mija*. Give me a cigarette."

"You don't smoke."

Creama huffed. "And you don't have no flair for drama, Miss Thing."

Congressional aide, Jimmy Castilano, snapped open a can of soda and plopped his square frame next to Dick Peak on the couch in front of the TV.

"This is Dawn Chang reporting live from the Civic Center. Back to you, Peter."

Dick lowered the volume and looked away from the TV. He scoffed. "I wish these freaks would just get back in their closets—and lock the doors. I'm so tired of their *equal rights* stomping all over my religious liberty."

Jimmy took the remote from Dick and pressed mute. "I don't know why you insist on watchin' that stuff. You thirsty?" Jimmy offered Dick his Coke.

Dick smiled. "You can always make me smile, Jimmy, since we were kids." He waved away the soda. "I hope my voice holds out till the end of this rally." His smooth boyish face regained its freshness and composure.

The round chocolate-colored eyes and the comic-book black hair made Dick the most freakin' dew-kissed-lookin' farm boy Jimmy had ever seen, even though Dick was more the sharply dressed city type.

"Hey, while it's on my mind, has that congressman from the House Committee on Energy and Commerce returned my call yet?"

"No, that's the second time you've asked me today." Jimmy paused. "Since when do you consult with *Democrats*? Is this important or something I should know about?"

"No. At least not yet."

"Are you sure?"

"Yes! Sorry, I need an answer on an important corporate matter. I'm sure he'll get back to me. I hope he gets back to me."

"I can take care of whatever it is."

Dick shook his head. "No, I'll handle it."

Dick stood, tossed his lucky coin up in the air with his left hand, caught it with his right, and twirled it as he slipped it back into his pocket.

"All you got left is the closing speech, then it's off to the islands. The sun and the sea and the hot little chiquitas, heh?" Jimmy stood and faked a punch to Dick's arm.

Dick leered at him and his eyes darted to the open door. "Shush."

A young woman stood there. "Five minutes, Mr. Peak."

Dick sauntered to the mirror and gracefully smoothed his hair.

Jimmy dusted off the left shoulder of his jacket. "Aw, come on, Dick. You're a single guy. Even the liberal media has called ya good-lookin'."

Dick straightened his tie and caught Jimmy's eye in the mirror. "No, they did not," he said coolly. "They called me charismatic."

"Same difference."

"Jimmy, have you not been paying attention?" he said in a hushed tone. "The whole campaign is based on morals. Christian-right ethics? Is it ringin' a bell, Jim? I have to be careful, you know that." Dick practiced his smile in the mirror. "Nothing, absolutely nothing can get in the way of my bid for the Senate."

Jimmy moved to the door and lit his cigar. "By the time that happens this will simply be the road that was paved with good intentions."

Dick laughed. "Come on, let's finish this thing." He gave his lucky coin a left-to-right toss and left his dressing room.

CHAPTER TWO

Dick took a deep breath and exhaled forcefully while he watched the emcee from the wings.

"Ladies and gentlemen, in a moment we're going to welcome back to the stage the man who planted the seeds of ROAR." The emcee paused to let the crowd applaud. "He has fought vigorously to promote traditional American values and was the driving force behind the defeat of gay marriage legislation. Although the Supreme Court dealt us a blow by making it legal, we finally have new justices who are tipping the court back in the right direction. Our fight is beginning again, and who better to lead the charge than Congressman Dick Peak!"

The audience roared.

Dick lingered a few seconds to breathe in the scent of admiration. The moment he stepped into the lights, the explosive applause charged up the juice that electrified his lanky form. He felt for his lucky coin and bullet in his pocket and gloated over what he had created. With a smile that was better than the one he had practiced, Congressman Dick Peak stormed the stage.

No one in the audience would ever guess that, to him, they were a blur of silhouettes. He capitalized on his branded charisma that Fox

News had so conveniently marketed on his behalf, and then made his audience believe that he was addressing each one of them directly. "Thank you. Thank you," he said, summoning his boy-next-door humility.

"I'll make this quick, folks, because I know you've had a long day here. I've returned to leave you with a few final thoughts." He paused. "First, I want to commend you all in our fight to keep America morally right!" He gazed out at the enormity of his audience as unsynchronized cheers rained down like mortars from the peanut gallery. "Family Values was once a buzz phrase. We have to remember that the history of our great God-fearing nation can, and will, carry us forward. But it's up to you to mobilize voter turnout. Talk to everyone and spread the word. We can take back our country from those who would demoralize our way of life. But, it depends on *you*." His open pastoral palms drew in his flock.

"Don't be discouraged. We're one step closer than we were after the Supreme Court reversed California's Proposition Eight. Can you *believe* the Supreme Court has allowed gays to marry again?"

The collective "Boo" boomeranged back into the audience.

"But take heart. It wasn't long afterward when they ruled that a good Christian shall not be forced to bake a *gay* wedding cake. And while I'm at it, don't get me started on taking a knee at a football game." He waited a beat. "I think the only time someone should take a knee is when they're praying to the Almighty. These are just some of the crucial issues of our time."

Dick's most serious expression fanned out across the abyss. "Gay marriage. What's next, polygamy? How about so-called hate crimes? We already have laws on the books for this. They're called *crimes*. We don't need to single out groups of people. If someone commits a crime, they should be punished. It's so simple. But lawmakers in Washington try to confuse the issue because they think you're not smart enough to see through them, not smart enough to know that they're stomping on your religious liberty. We are in a culture war that we must win!"

This round of applause brought a third of the audience to their feet.

Could've sworn that one would've gotten them all up. Sincere and boyish, Dick shepherded them to the finale. "Traditionally, a family is made up of one man, one woman, and their children. Quite simply, it's my mission to protect that definition of family. But I can't do it without you. Should I get elected to the Senate, I will fight against those who would erode our societal norms. The farther we stray from our Christian roots, the farther we fall as a society." He shook his head. "At least God is back in our schools." He opened his arms wide. "The one thing I'm sure of, my friends, is that without each of your efforts, we wouldn't be the Right of America's Religious! God bless you and goodnight!"

The audience stood and applauded—some whistled. Dick waved as he sauntered off the stage where Jimmy waited for him in the wings.

"How was I?"

"Great, but I really thought more of them would have stood on 'religious liberty.'"

"Right? Make a note of that."

Jimmy nodded. "Senator Tate is waitin' to see you."

Dick smiled wide. "A.C. is here? Really?"

"Dick! There y'are, son," the senator drawled as he approached.

Dick spun around. "Senator, what a…surprise." They shook hands. "I wish I'd known you were coming."

"Well, we didn't want you to feel any pressure." The senator sucked on his cigar.

"We?"

"You've had a good showing here tonight." The seasoned southerner, Senator Tate, placed his arm around Dick's shoulder and leaned in. "It's good to see a young hawk fly. There are too few of us hardline conservatives willing to take the heat for telling the truth… especially in your man-bun generation."

"Excuse me," Jimmy interrupted. "Dick, if you don't leave now, you'll miss your flight."

"I'll let you go, Dick. Oh, one thing before you leave."

Dick shivered with excitement.

"Perhaps after your vacation, we can sit down and discuss your future. When you're ready, I believe you're the right man to lead a few projects in Congress. And you have my full support for the Senate run."

"I'll be looking forward to that, Senator."

"Consider it done, my boy. We'll be in touch." Senator Tate patted Dick on the back and wedged his cigar between his teeth as he left.

CHAPTER THREE

In the DRAG limo on the way to the airport, Larry briefed Carlos Armando Jose Benitez, who, while dressed in a men's Canali suit, much preferred Creama's blue sequins. He gulped half a bottle of Calistoga water and handed it back to Tawny.

"What is all this?" Carlos fanned through a pack of large bills inside the envelope that Larry had handed him.

"Expense account," Larry answered. "There are small bills in there too. We didn't have time to authorize you for a credit card, so spend wisely."

"There's thousands of dollars in here! Hell, Larry, how long am I going for?"

"Cash is better, Creama. It helps keep you anonymous, as long as you don't get mugged." He paused. "Don't blow it in the casinos." He handed Carlos a money belt. "Put this on. There's plenty of room to hide the cash in there. If you need to use any personal credit cards, we'll reimburse you."

"Wait. Did you say mugged? Oh, I don't know about this." Carlos held up the curious-looking belt. "This looks like a rubber cummerbund!" He lifted his shirt and put it on underneath.

"Carlos…Creama…honey, you can do this," Tawny said calmly in his other ear.

"Tawny, I was talking about these shoes. Did a lesbian stud pick these out?" He shook his head in disappointment. "If this isn't a fashion *faux pas*, I don't know what is." He looked up from the shoes. "Make sure that Miss Coco Puffs does my show tomorrow night. My fans are not going to be happy about this."

"They'll survive," Tawny said.

"Oh god." Carlos waved away the thought. "Don't let Coco do 'I Will Survive.' She's no Gloria Gaynor."

"Hey, stay focused." Larry handed Carlos another small envelope. "Inside, you'll find Dick's itinerary and a local contact in Puerto Rico if you need help."

"What kind of help am I going to need?"

"It's a gay contact should you find yourself in a jam."

Carlos twitched. "It better be grape jam…spread all over some good-looking guy. What kind of jam?"

"In case you break a nail, sweetie."

"I'm serious, Tawny. The closest thing I ever did to spying was follow that guy Tommy, who was cheating on me…and I was a nervous wreck if you remember."

Larry remained calm. "Creama, this will be a cakewalk. You'll be checking into the same hotel as Peak. And now you have a contact down there to help you."

"So, why can't *they* follow him? Why do I have to go, Larry?"

"Because no one knows more about Dick than you do."

Carlos and Tawny snickered.

Larry stared at them. "Would you two grow up! Out of drag you can get close to him. If we don't bust this story wide open, trust me, the press never will. He's a bigot, a womanizer, he's slick and we're certain he is up to something illegal. Is that reason enough?"

Creama sighed. "My eyes feel naked. Can't I wear just a *little* mascara?"

"No!" Larry and Tawny sang out.

"Fine! But you are so gonna owe me for this."

"Why so quiet, Dick?" Jimmy asked as the Republican's limo cruised down the peninsula along Highway 101.

"I'm thinking about that damn drag queen, Creama La…LaCoffee."

"It's LaCroppe."

"I know! It pisses me off that that…whatever he is, got such a big interview on KBCH. Did you hear that remark?" Dick mocked Creama. "Congressman Dick what if *you* were gay? That's all I need on my head now," Dick scoffed, "a faggot getting his *biatch* on."

"So what? Your interview will be aired. Besides, nobody knows about that night where you thought she was a real girl."

Dick groaned. "We never did anything."

"Yeah but she had you goin'," Jimmy laughed.

"Not funny, Jimmy. I thought she—*he* was Cher."

"Aw, lighten up, Dick." He smiled mischievously. "I loathe queers and the *gender fluid* as much as the next guy…but that was pretty funny." He was quick to change the subject. "Look, for the next two weeks just forget about everything. You need a break from politics. I've known you long enough to know that you need to get laid. You're too tense, my friend."

"You're right. You know, Jim, you couldn't know me better if we were real brothers."

Jimmy nodded. "I'm closer to you than my real brother." He tilted his head to watch the tinted cloak of night cast its veil upon the freeway. "All's I know is, you can't know everything about nothin'."

Dick chuckled. "We're here," he said as the limo descended under the Departures sign. "I'll call you tomorrow. No sense waking you with the time difference. Besides, I wouldn't want to wake Rita." Dick noticed the chauffeur staring at him in the rearview mirror. When the limo came to a halt, he signaled Jimmy to follow him out to the curb. "The envelope I had you send…" he said in a hushed tone, "it's definitely at the hotel in San Juan?"

"Yeah, Dick. What's the—"

"Thanks, I don't know what I'd do without you, Jimmy." Dick tossed his lucky coin from left to right and dropped it into his pocket. He picked up his briefcase, latched it to his suitcase, and patted Jimmy on the shoulder.

"Yeah, well, when you're the big Senator Peak, make me director of sumthin'. Bing Batta Boom you are on vacation as of now." Jimmy handed Dick his plane ticket and passport. He got back into the limo and waited.

With his itinerary envelope tucked neatly inside his coat pocket, Congressman Dick Peak entered the airport terminal and disappeared among the herd.

CHAPTER FOUR

The blond First Class flight attendant glanced at Carlos's boarding pass. "Good evening, Mr. Benitez, your seat is 3D, aisle, on the right."

Carlos read her nametag and cleared his throat. "Thank you, Kate," he said an octave below normal. He glanced through the cabin, found his seat, and tried to act more like Charlie Sheen than Cher while struggling to stow his gear in the overhead compartment. "Where's Tawny when I need her?" he mumbled under his breath.

He stepped into his row and surveyed the snaking line of passengers as they passed him. He surreptitiously yanked the Canali wedgie out of his butt as he sat, thinking he couldn't wait to check into the hotel in San Juan and wrap himself in his silk kimono.

Scoping out every passenger who boarded, Carlos eagerly awaited his target. He opened to a page in the Spanish fashion magazine and pretended to read it.

"Sir?" Kate said it twice before Carlos realized she meant him. "Would you care for some champagne?"

"Yes, please," he answered. Preoccupied, he took the flute of champagne and leaned into the aisle to peer backward into Coach. *Where the hell is Peak*? At the exact instant he turned back around, the handsome man in the Armani suit sprinted onto the plane last and stood over him.

"Excuse me, I have the window seat," said Peak.

"Oh, sure." *Peak hasn't a freaking clue who I am. I don't know whether to be happy or insulted.*

The PA system crackled. "Ladies and gentlemen, this is Captain DuWitt. Welcome aboard Trans Air Flight 44 to San Juan, Puerto Rico. Everyone has boarded, so sit back and relax. We'll be leaving the gate momentarily and should be taking off shortly."

Carlos tapped his fingers on the armrest, resisting the urge to look at Peak until he felt the plane jerk away from the gate.

"This is Captain DuWitt again. Looks like we're third in line for takeoff, which means we may even arrive a little ahead of schedule."

Once airborne, Peak reclined his seat and closed his eyes.

Carlos studied him. *You're kinda cute, Congressman—at least I thought so that one night.* "It's a shame you're such a schmuck," Carlos said under his breath. Taking his cue from Peak, he reclined his seat, loosened his designer silk noose and closed his eyes. *Pace yourself, Ginger, you don't wanna snap.* He giggled. I'll have to remember that line, he thought before drifting into a twilight nap.

Carlos had no idea how long he'd been snoozing when the twitch in his nose woke him. "Mmm. What's that smell?" He rubbed his eyes and when he opened them, they immediately strayed to Peak's empty seat. The congressman's briefcase lay open with a folder on top. *What if I could get a look at that?*

Carlos averted his stare the instant Peak exited the lavatory, and a minute later Kate served the First Class Coq au Vin. Carlos discovered with each new bite how hungry he was, and then realized he hadn't eaten all day. After dinner, he ordered a coffee, but he couldn't wait another minute to toy with his anonymity. He turned to Peak and smiled. "That was pretty good for airline food, wasn't it?"

"Not bad," Peak answered.

"Excuse me for intruding, but aren't you Congressman Peak?"

"That would be me," Peak replied graciously.

Of the litany of facts Carlos knew about Peak, he knew his ego couldn't resist adoring strokes from his public. He smiled warmly. "This is quite a welcome surprise. I'm a big fan of yours." When they shook hands, Carlos attempted the Kung Fu grip with the Charlie Sheen, not the Cher, eyebrow, accompanied by a firm finite nod of his head.

"And you are…?" Peak asked.

"I'm Cr…" the name Creama almost slipped out, his hand ready to elongate the word 'extraordinaire'. "Carlos Armando Jose Benitez."

"Nice to meet you, Mr. Benitez."

"Mr. Benitez was my father, and not a good guy. Please, call me Carlos."

Dick smiled. "Did you happen to attend the ROAR rally in San Francisco?"

"Actually, yes…I was there, but I couldn't get in."

"Really?" Dick shook his head. "Was it those DRAG protesters that kept you out?"

Carlos nodded. "You could say that, Congressman."

"Please, call me Dick."

Carlos mimicked his friend from the "Debbie Does Drag King" troupe. "Since I missed the rally, maybe you could share some of the highlights."

"If you've followed my campaigns, then you know firstly it was about protecting the American family."

"That's been effective for your career since USC."

Dick smiled. "How do you know I went to USC?"

"Like I said, I'm a big fan." Carlos shook his head in disapproval.

"Something wrong, Carlos?"

"No."

"You sure?"

Carlos waved him closer and spoke in a hushed tone. "Well, it's just those queers that were protesting you."

"They're a thorn in my side." Dick paused and then added, "Especially that Creama *LaCrappe*."

"Oh!" Carlos's octave climbed to the high note of an offended debutante. He refrained from smacking Peak's smug grin and let his voice drop in altitude. "I remember reading about her…"

"You mean *him*."

Carlos winced. "I think the name is *LaCroppe*, drag queen *diva* extraord…"

"Yep, that's the one," Dick interrupted. "We were pleased with the turnout for the rally."

"Only time will tell whether or not gays will gain the civil rights legislation promised to all Americans. You know, the equal protection for gay families thing?"

Dick scoffed. "*Gay* families. How can they call themselves that when it goes against the teaching of every major religion?"

"You mean except for the Reform Jews, right? They don't have a problem with it." He feigned remorse. "How about the Supreme Court reversing the gay marriage ban? But, they *are* the Supremes." Carlos saw himself dressed as Diana Ross, with Miss Coco in the background as Flo, and the baby drag queen from the show as Mary. A Supremes song popped into his head complete with hand choreography. In his mind he sang, *Stop in the name of love.*

"It's good to meet an informed voter. You're really up on this, aren't you?"

"I try," Carlos said coyly. "They're important issues."

Dick glanced at Carlos's crucifix, waved him to lean closer, and spoke in a hushed tone. "I see you're a god-fearing man so I'll let you in on a little secret. The Reform aren't the *real* Jews. The religious ones like Doctor Laura are like us. They condemn homosexuality."

Carlos paused and stared at him. "But isn't that God's job?"

"You have a point there."

The overhead cabin lights dimmed and Carlos wondered if the sentence for killing a man on an airplane was worse than on land.

"That's my cue for nap time," said Dick. With a smile that appeared as an afterthought, he added, "It's really good to meet you, Carlos."

Both men settled back for the long flight in the darkened cabin when Carlos's video screen flickered while he surfed the entertainment. "Ooh, Will and Grace!"

Puzzled, Dick stared at him. "How can you watch that?"

Carlos winked to cover his tracks. "I think Grace is a hottie."

"The brunette is more my type," said Dick.

"Ah, so you've seen the show."

"That crap is on everywhere," Dick muttered.

Carlos's expression rested somewhere between gossip and horror. "I read somewhere that your brunette crush is into AC/DC…and I don't mean heavy metal."

Dick shook his head. "That's a shame."

"Why?" Carlos said innocently. "Lesbians aren't condemned in the Bible."

Dick just stared at him. Carlos put in his earbuds and reclined his seat, using the footrest to stretch out. A couple of hours passed before Captain DuWitt's voice woke him from a dream in which Dick Peak was dancing in jeggings atop the Transamerica Pyramid.

"Folks, there are some fast-moving storms in the area. It looks like we're going to hit some pockets of turbulence shortly, so I'm going to turn on the seat belt sign and ask you to remain seated. We'll keep you updated, but it's going to get bumpy up here for a little bit."

Carlos glanced at an unfastened sleeping Dick. Uncomfortable with his proximity to such a toxic person, he pulled out his phone, leaned toward him and pretended to kiss Peak's cheek while snapping a selfie. *I should let you bounce around the cabin. Maybe it will knock some sense into you.* "La Crappe, indeed. *Mierda*," he muttered. The plane took a small jolt. Carlos tapped Dick on the shoulder. "Dick. Dick."

Peak was out cold. Carlos reached across him to fasten the congressman's seat belt. The plane jerked again, causing Carlos's hand to fall onto Dick's jacket. As he balanced to push himself back into his seat, Dick's eyes popped open. Carlos quickly retracted his hand, hiding a small metal object that he snatched from Dick's coat pocket.

"What's going on?" asked Dick.

"You're either a very tired man or an incredibly sound sleeper."

"I'm a bit of both. What happened?"

"Turbulence. The captain ordered us to put on the belts. I tried to wake you but you were dead to the world, so I put it on for you."

"Why thanks, Carlos," Dick said sincerely.

Carlos nodded. "Don't mention it." It was yet another Charlie Sheen moment.

"Say, Benitez, where are you staying in Puerto Rico…or do you live there?" Dick asked.

"No, I live in San Fran. I'm staying at El Conquistador."

"No kidding, me too. Maybe we'll get together for a round of golf."

"Sorry, it's not my game," Carlos apologized. "Why don't you join me for a cock"— The plane bounced before he could finish the word, "tail?"

"While I'm not in the habit of drinking for sport, I do have the occasional glass of wine." Dick winked.

Carlos smiled. *Oh please! Your drunken orgies are notorious.*

Thump.

"What was that?" said Carlos.

"A little turbulence," Dick replied.

Carlos surveyed the faces in First Class. "Well, the flight attendants don't look too concerned." He stared through Dick's window into the night where he watched intermittent bolts of lightning flash through sheeting rain.

Thud.

"Carlos, I see you're a tapper."

Carlos stopped tapping his fingers on his tray table. "Only when I think about the plane crashing."

Bang!

"Oh God," Carlos said as he started tapping again.

Kate raced toward the cockpit while Carlos and Dick sat at attention, monitoring the situation with quiet intensity.

"Ladies and gentlemen, this is Captain DuWitt again. We thought we could avoid the worst of the storm by climbing to a higher altitude, but it looks like we're going to have to ride out some of it. Remain seated and we'll let you know when it's safe to move about the cabin."

"Looks like we picked one helluva night for flying, huh Carlos?" Dick fidgeted and wiped his hands on his napkin. He reached for a coin that Carlos watched him toss from his left hand to his right.

Carlos nodded. *I can't believe I let Tawny talk me into this!* The pit in his stomach expanded. Dinner had not only not gone down, he felt like it was about to come back up. "Hey, Dick, are your ears popping?"

"Man, are they ever. The captain said we're climbing to a higher altitude to get away from the weather."

"Oh, *Papi*, I hope you're right. I'm thinking maybe we're *losing* altitude."

"You're not going soft on me, are you, Carlos?"

"Nope, I've never been accused of that."

"Don't worry. They've got lots of instruments to fly this baby."

Carlos reviewed the airplane emergency card, checked under his seat for his flotation device, and crossed himself—twice.

CHAPTER FIVE

After leaving Dick at the airport, Jimmy Castilano picked up his girlfriend Rita in the limo and took her down to North Beach for a late supper at Caffe Marconi. On the way, he checked his phone.

"Okay, good. Dick made his flight." He smiled at Rita. "Looks like I'm yours for the night."

"Oh, Jimmy, I just love when you have the limo. It makes you look so important."

He chuckled. "I *am* important. In case you've forgotten, I'm a congressional aide now. You look beautiful tonight, Red."

"Yeah?" She smiled.

"The suite at the Fairmont is paid until tomorrow, you know." He smiled at her and stroked her neck lightly with his fingertips. "So… you maybe wanna order breakfast from room service with me at the Fairmont?"

"*Maybe*," Rita replied coyly.

Tawny Beige kicked off her heels as soon as she crossed the threshold of her upper Castro Victorian. "Hi, Scarlett," she said.

"Hey, sis." Curled up on the couch, Tawny's younger sister held up her bowl and spoon. "Where's our star?" she asked. "I got her favorite celebration flavor. Organic, double-trouble mocha-chociatto-chip, low-fat, frozen yogurt—with the *gay-rainbow* sprinkles."

"Oh, don't ask." Tawny rolled her eyes.

"I'm asking. Everything okay?"

"Last-minute change of plans." Tawny left her shoes where they fell and collapsed onto the couch next to Scarlett. China the cat was fast asleep on her lap. "Creama had to go on a mission for DRAG."

"*Mission*? As in finding the right color shoes?"

"I shouldn't even be telling you this, but Creama is following Dick Peak to Puerto Rico as Carlos."

"What? Why?"

"Because Peak is up to something and we need to know what that is." She leaned back and yawned.

Scarlett flicked her blond bangs from her eyes and handed her big sister the bowl of frozen yogurt with the spoon sticking out. "You've *got* to be kidding. First off, Carlos…as Carlos? Secondly, a congressman! Isn't that risky?"

"Carlos is the best shot we have. He's Latino, knows almost everything there is to know about Peak, and he agreed to go—begrudgingly. But I can't wait to hear from him. Thanks for the sugar, but if you don't mind, I'm going to lie down."

"Make yourself at home, sis. Mind if I stay over tonight?"

Tawny kissed her little sister on the head and stood. "I wish you would. It's been lonely here since Chloe left."

She stopped in the doorway to her dark bedroom and gazed out through the picture window on the opposite wall. The view of the Bay Bridge was best from the bedroom, especially in clear moments like this one. Dazzled by the lighted triangle outlines twinkling across its span, Tawny stared at the headlights inching, creeping like Dayglo ants across the invisible abutments. Coit Tower held its forever vigil over the snaky streets of Telegraph Hill, and she couldn't remember having ever felt this lonely.

"How could you cheat on me?" she asked Chloe's ghost. She sighed away the memories of all the damp nights with candles all over the bedroom, and the fingers of fog creeping up behind them on San Francisco's Twin Peaks. Indelible moments that in Tawny's mind were filled with soft and sultry music. "*You're my favorite person*," the ghost whispered.

Tawny lit only one candle and turned on the TV to catch the late news, grateful that she hadn't run into Chloe and her new flame at the candlelight vigil.

"Oh, damn!" She fumbled for the volume on the remote when she saw Dawn Chang interviewing Dick Peak.

"…America is great because we have a history of moral fiber and Christian ethics, Dawn," the congressman was saying. "We're losing that because our children are so confused. So, if elected to the Senate, I will be that moral compass that our country so badly needs."

"Would you care to elaborate on that?" asked the reporter who had taken over Tawny's live interviews.

Dick straightened in his chair, tilted his chin to reveal his best angle, and waited for the cameraman to take advantage with a closeup. "One way our children are being harmed is by the confusing and wrong messages they're getting about homosexuality. It's sad that kids are forced to learn about homosexuality as an acceptable lifestyle when it's not. Yet, those same students aren't permitted to pray in the locker room before a football game or refer to a copy of the Ten Commandments in their schools. This is the homosexual agenda, to indoctrinate our kids into a life of immorality. And that signals a breach in our Founders' intentions for religious liberty in its truest form."

"Are you saying there's a connection between homosexuality and the separation of church and state?"

"Dawn, don't misunderstand me. I believe that people are free to choose the homosexual lifestyle."

"Choice, my ass!" Tawny balked. "Exactly *when* did you *choose* to be straight?"

"But," the congressman continued, "I believe that to be an immoral choice and I will do all that I can to reverse same-sex marriage and its infringement on Christian faith. To require a good Christian to bake a gay wedding cake is just wrong."

"What about Christian doctors then? Are you saying they shouldn't have to treat gay people?"

"Now I never said that."

"But there is legislation for that and it's tied to you. Would the reverse hold true?"

"I'm not sure what you mean." Peak stared at her.

"In the reverse scenario, could a gay doctor refuse to treat a Christian patient?"

Peak pivoted. "Well, that's not law…yet. So let's stick to the present."

"Congressman, I notice that you keep referring to homosexuality as a choice. What if it turns out that it's a biological variation, like having blue eyes, for example?"

"I've heard opinions that it's a biological error. Even if it is, these people don't have to act on it. That's God's mandate, not mine." Dick smiled. "But there's strong evidence that homosexuality is a choice. Just look at the good results therapists are getting with former homosexuals through Reparative Therapy."

"Perhaps it's a biologic variation rather than an error. But you're referring to the so-called Ex-Gay movement—or what some have called, 'Pray away the gay'—which is now illegal in some places. Let's talk about that."

Dick smiled the boyish, down-on-the-farm smile. "Those questions should be answered by a qualified therapist, which of course I'm not. But several ministries are devoted to helping these people restore themselves to a *normal* life through surrender to the Lord. And people can get that information from ROAR's website."

Tawny stretched out on her bed. "You slimeball. Bet you wouldn't want to be alone in the men's locker room with *any* 'ex-homo' poster boy!" She glanced over at the old wind-up clock, thinking Carlos wouldn't be at the hotel in San Juan for hours yet. She turned back to Peak on the TV. "I feel like I need a shower to wash away your slimy words," she said before turning it off.

Maybe I shouldn't have pushed Creama to go, she thought. The escape of sleep attractively beckoned, where she was free to reminisce about happier times. *Lord knows I haven't seen one of those for a waking moment in way too long.* Her breathing slowed as her head burrowed deeper into her pillow.

The dreary sky clung to the mildew shoreline for the entire drive south on Great Highway from San Francisco. Winter in Big Sur; it was clandestine and cozy in Chloe's arms. They checked into the Big Sur Lodge and received their starter bundle of firewood. Room 25. Chloe spun around straight-faced. "God, I love you, Tawny."

"Sure you do."

"I mean it."

"Chloe, tell me that every day for the next twenty years?"

"Every day." Chloe smiled.

The nightmare jolted Tawny awake. "Damn it. Why won't you go away, you green-haired ghost?" She glanced at the clock. It was only one a.m. Nestled against her, she pulled her cat closer and thought about getting up. Instead, she checked her voice mail, grateful she hadn't missed Carlos's call. The score was, "Nightmare 1, Voice Mail 0."

Mindlessly, she stepped into her fluffy slippers and shuffled through the living room headed toward the kitchen when she saw her sister still on the sofa.

"Scarlett, what's wrong? Why are you crying?"

Curled up in front of the television, her tearful sister looked at her. "I'm watching *Imitation of Life*," she sniffled. "Hey Tawny, remember how we would wait for this movie to come on The Late Show when we were kids? You and Mom and I would stay up all night to watch it and cry our eyes out."

"What I remember is getting up during the commercial to get us all bowls of spaghetti at three in the morning. But, yeah, such a sad movie. I used to think, 'Why doesn't the daughter just be a black girl?' I guess I can't imagine being ashamed of what I was born."

"Really," Scarlett agreed. "I never understood how she could hide like that. A closet black girl pretending to be white. For what? So that she would be accepted in a white world…like that was some prize."

Tawny sighed. "It was a different time and we're tainted with the perspective of white privilege."

"You never were one who longed for the closet. Is it really much different now than it was when you came out?"

Tawny messed up her sister's hair. "Move over and give me some of that blanket." The girls fell asleep before the movie ended, lying opposite each other on the sofa, their feet entangled, exactly like when they were kids.

CHAPTER SIX

"See, Carlos?" Dick said. "The storm has passed and we're fine."

Carlos nodded, his eyebrows arched higher than Joan Crawford's.

"Hey," Dick continued, "you still look a little green around the gills."

Carlos looked out the window and back at Dick. "Yeah well, I'm not convinced we're fine yet but I already ordered wine. I could use it to steady my nerves after that ordeal. Care to join me?"

"Sure. I could use a dose of steady nerves myself."

Carlos smiled. "So you aren't as tough as you appear, Congressman?"

Dick grinned. "I never said I was *that* tough."

The blond flight attendant returned with Carlos's merlot.

"Miss…um, Kate, can you bring one of these for Congressman Peak?"

"Sure." She smiled.

"How long until we land?" Carlos asked.

"About forty minutes."

"Thank God." Carlos downed half the wine like a shot of tequila.

"Feel better?" asked Dick.

"I'll feel better when my feet are on the ground."

Dick smirked. "That makes two of us."

Static filtered through the PA system.

"Folks, this is Captain DuWitt again. There appears to be another pop-up storm cell in the area."

"No," said a man in the rear cabin.

"Not again," whined another.

Carlos focused on the pilot's voice. "We were hoping to avoid it but that doesn't look likely…so at this time I am illuminating the seat belt sign and asking everyone to make sure that their carry-on luggage is properly stowed."

The plastic overhead bins had been rattling intermittently for an hour. As the airplane's coarse vibration intensified in his chest, Carlos sat forward and took a deep breath.

"This isn't funny anymore," Dick said.

"I'd like to know what the hell is actually going on," Carlos added.

"I'm with you," said Peak.

A minute later, Kate dashed up the aisle and disappeared into the cockpit.

Bang!

When she exited the cockpit, she fumbled the microphone to the PA system and pressed the Talk button. Carlos knew by the look on her face that they weren't about to get good news.

"Ladies and gentlemen." Kate's voice shook. "I need your undivided attention. The captain has informed me that we're having difficulty with one of our engines. Due to weather conditions in San Juan, we're being diverted. We'll be attempting to land at an airfield on the southeast side of the island, where our chances are greater for averting the storm and landing safely. We need your full attention and cooperation. While we expect everything to go smoothly, Captain DuWitt has ordered all passengers to put on their life vest. Now. Do NOT inflate it. There's a remote chance that we must make an emergency landing and a water exit."

"Oh my God!" a woman screamed from somewhere back in Coach.

"We're gonna crash!"

Carlos broke a sweat. "Oh, Jesus!"

The flight attendant continued. "I need able-bodied people to raise their hands and identify themselves to assist in the event that we're forced to ditch in the ocean." The cacophony of fearful voices rang out like hundreds of fork tines scraping metal plates.

Carlos raised his hand. He flashed on Bruce Willis's bloodied bare feet bolting across the broken glass while firing on the bad guys in the movie *Die Hard* and steeled himself for what was about to come.

"Please, YOU MUST REMAIN CALM. Do everything we instruct and your chances for egress are excellent. Remove your eyeglasses and put them in a pocket! Give all loose and sharp objects such as pens to the flight attendant coming up the aisle." The plane jerked, throwing Kate into a seatback. The passengers gasped.

"NOW!" Flight attendant Kate shocked everyone out of suspended animation. Every passenger forked over their belongings without a thought.

Kate continued. "When your oxygen mask drops, pull it down and place it over your nose and mouth!"

"Passengers, this is your captain," DuWitt cut in. "We're going to ditch in the water. I'm going to try for the Bay or close to it. Stay calm and do everything the cabin crew instructs."

Kate came back on the PA. "Once the plane has ditched, we'll guide you into the life rafts that are connected to the doors of the aircraft. We'll need you helpers by the exits!"

For all the yelling before, not a passenger made a sound. "Do not inflate your life vest until you are out of the aircraft. Fasten your seat belts tightly, grab your ankles and STAY LOW." The attendant ran to her jump seat. Together, an airplane full of souls awaited the impact.

Carlos could only focus on the droning of the remaining engines, listening intently to make sure he could still hear their drone. Every second felt like minutes to him, and he offered up every prayer he could remember in both languages. "Oh God, save us and I'll never say another bad word about Judy Garland."

"Passengers, stay low!" The flight attendant dropped the mic. The nose of the plane turned upward and Carlos felt the plane's belly slap the water. They were gliding.

Wham! The second impact was more akin to a raw egg smashing into a brick wall. His head slammed into the seat in front and then whipped backward. The lights went out, and he was glad he had drunk the wine. He heard screaming, crying, yelling, and then the voice of the flight attendant.

"Helpers to the exits! RELEASE SEAT BELTS! COME THIS WAY!" the crew echoed.

"Come on, Dick!" Carlos yelled above the din before he bolted into Coach like Bruce Willis's *Die Hard* policeman John McClane.

"*Gracias*," said a flight attendant when Carlos was the first helper to arrive at the exit.

Every able-bodied passenger clamored to get out.

"Stay calm, no pushing!" yelled the flight attendant in the rear cabin.

Kate yanked on the door feverishly. "It's jammed! I can't open it!"

Carlos groped for the armrest of the nearest center seat and jerked it out. Every drop of adrenaline boiled in his arteries as he relentlessly pummeled the window to his right. "Ugh!" He bashed the window until it broke the seal. "Try it now," he yelled.

The airplane door released, and he jumped to the doorway to help Kate slide it out of the way. The rafts inflated.

"What the hell?" Carlos said. As dark as the sea was, through the pouring rain and gargantuan swells, the water in the distance was fluorescent emerald, like Creama's green stage-light gel.

"Phosphorescent bay," yelled Kate. "Get onto the slide!" she kept repeating as each passenger arrived.

"GOOD EXIT!" yelled an attendant from behind. "STAY CALM."

Carlos wondered what had spilled on him during the crash. It wasn't until he felt his wet hair and tasted the liquid that he knew his head was bleeding. Against the current of people flooding the aisle toward him, he leaped over the empty seats toward the rear of the craft.

He pulled an elderly couple out of their seats and passed them off to the attendants up ahead. Crawling along the blackened floor to the back of the plane, he probed his way to the screaming child and peeled him from his mother's rigid arms.

"*Vamos*," he yelled to the mother who was ranting in Spanish. "Come on, *Mami*," he said as he dragged her up the aisle with one hand, cradling the baby in his other arm. Handing the child to the attendant, he lifted the mother, placed her on the slide and handed her the baby. Smoke began to waft through the cabin. Carlos pulled the handkerchief from his suit pocket and wrapped it around his face; the waterproof money belt was making his back sweat.

"Exit!" Kate yelled at him.

But Carlos ignored her command as he again crawled toward the back of the plane. *That felt like a person I tripped over when I had the baby…where the hell was he?* "I've got somebody else! Help, Help!" he yelled.

"Where are you?" an attendant shouted.

"Keep coming! I'm here, right here! Somebody's unconscious."

"Is he alive?"

"*Maricon*! Let's get him the hell out of here." Carlos and the flight attendant pulled the man up the aisle.

The captain clutched Carlos's arm at the door. "Get in the lifeboat!" he commanded. The torrent of rain picked at Carlos's face as it swept horizontally across the airplane's door. He stepped forward, one shoeless foot already on the slide. "Okay let's go," he shouted to the captain.

In a dreadful bolt of lightning, Carlos scanned what he could see of the evacuees. "Dick! Peak!"

No reply.

Captain DuWitt landed in the lifeboat without him. The lifeboat was disengaging from the plane. "Jump! NOW!" the captain ordered. "Kate! I thought everyone was out."

Carlos wheezed from the smoke. "Someone's inside!" he screamed. He coughed violently. The boat rocked in the waves. He dropped to the floor with labored breath and crawled in the direction of First Class.

"Sir! Jump!" Kate yelled.

The airplane drifted in the wave, then took an abrupt slam; the nose was going down. Carlos sprang forward, coughing, spitting out blood, and puking as he spit.

"Oh God, help me!" he cried. He tripped, wedging his leg under a seat. Ripping his pant leg, he howled from the pain as he freed his trapped leg. Two life vests fell on him from under the seat. He tied one around his waist and slung the other over his shoulder as he crawled.

"Ohhh."

Carlos heard the groan.

"Asshole, you would have to be in the front." The plane was filling with water, and the life vest around Carlos's neck was slowing him down. He lunged toward the cockpit. "Dick! Peak!" His hands systematically patted the floor as he swooshed forward. "Six, seven," he said, counting the rows from the door.

"Ah!" Carlos had him. And he felt a life vest around Dick's neck. "*Mierda*! The plane is nosing down." He tackled the semi-conscious congressman and slung the other vest over him.

"One…Ow! Two, *Umph*," he counted as he dragged Peak behind him on the floor. It was getting easier as the airplane sank. Peak was lighter—almost floating. "Four more," Carlos grunted.

A blade of blue lightning pierced the blackness and an ominous crack of thunder echoed off the swells. "Oh, man! We're gonna drown…if we don't get electrocuted first."

Certain that the lifeboat would be right outside waiting for them, he pulled and heaved until he got them to the door. Carlos whipped around to grab hold of Dick, and a shard of fractured fuselage pierced his life vest. He ripped off the torn vest and tossed one of the spares around his own neck.

"What! Where's the fucking boat? Where..." He yanked on the tabs of the life vest to inflate it. It was a dud. "Have to get out fast. Now. Now!" Carlos hyperventilated into one of the vest's inflation tubes. Pulling Peak up against him, he jumped away from the sinking plane into the turbulent obsidian swells of the Caribbean Sea.

CHAPTER SEVEN

Tawny opened her eyes to find her feet tangled up in Scarlett's and China the cat curled up in a ball against her. The flicker from the television caught her eye. What held her there were the words Breaking News. Dick Peak's photo appeared right above the headline.

She dug under the blanket for the remote, squished the cat, and in the process kicked her sister in the ass.

"What's going on?" Scarlett complained.

Tawny turned up the volume and listened to the reporter.

"As of this moment, we have confirmed reports that although the airplane was forced to make an emergency landing, the Coast Guard states that a rescue is in progress. One of the passengers on board may be Congressman Dick Peak, who left last night on a flight bound for San Juan, Puerto Rico. We are still awaiting confirmation and will keep you up to date as this story unfolds."

"Oh my God! Creama! Scarlett, did the phone ring while I was asleep?"

"Duh. How would I know? Wait, that was the flight Creama was on!" Scarlett shot upright. "Doesn't a rescue imply survivors?"

"Who knows! Damn it! I knew I shouldn't have coerced Creama to get on that flight. I have to call Larry."

"Why Larry?"

"He was the team leader who was in charge of the operation."

"Don't you want to wait until we know more?"

Tawny jumped to her feet. "I'm putting on a pot of coffee and calling Larry." Larry had remained number one on speed dial since the late-night calls she had made to him when Chloe had first left. "Come on, Larry, pick up!"

He groaned. "Whoever this is, it better be important."

"It's Tawny, wake up."

"What's wrong, kitten? You okay? Hold on, my eyelids are taking turns staying open." He grunted. "Get. Conscious."

"I take it you haven't heard the news?" she asked.

"Not unless it's old news." His words became muffled.

"Larry, Creama's plane went down in the ocean!"

"What! My eyes are open *now*!"

"It's unfolding right now! Turn on KBCH! They said a rescue is in progress. So that must mean that passengers evacuated—survived… whatever." She shook the nervousness from her free hand. "What do we do? What do we do?"

"Let me call my friend at the *Chronicle* and see if he knows anything. Oh shit, it's two o'clock in the morning!"

"I'm freaking out, Larry. Meet me down at KBCH."

"Now?"

"Why? Can you get there sooner?"

"Grab the line," a coastguardsman yelled to the passengers from the deck of a huge cutter. The crew began hoisting the Trans Air passengers aboard as quickly as possible, urgently taking the children and women.

"It's a miracle that we found you and that no one was struck by lightning," the ensign said to Kate as he shuffled the stream of passengers along the line of personnel. Kate stepped out of line and waited.

"Where's that damn helicopter, man?" asked the ensign.

"The HH-65 Dolphin is on its way for medevac," replied a coastguardsman.

"Good, get these people below."

An agitated Kate pushed her way to the ensign. "You have to go back," she blurted frantically. "There's a man in that plane!"

"Ma'am, we've swept the vicinity twice but a Search-and-Recovery crew is on their way. Our job is to get you to the hospital." He steadied her shoulders and stared into her eyes. "You do realize you were in a plane crash?"

"But you don't understand—"

"You need to go below with the others, ma'am."

"But if it wasn't for this one guy, we wouldn't have gotten so many people out. There are people who did not make it out of that plane!" she yelled frantically.

"Sorry ma'am, I'm following protocol."

"Damn it! Is the congressman on board?"

"Congressman?" asked the ensign.

The sea was rough. And mean.

Yank and paddle.

Yank and paddle.

Rest.

Float.

Carlos had developed a system but he was scared shitless. He flinched from the continuous piercing sting in his leg and on his head. The salt had permeated his wounds; his right leg ached and felt dead in the water. Details of the crash became foggy, and no matter how he tried to stay focused, he couldn't remember everything. Fixated on not drowning in the ocean in the middle of the night usurped every other thought. He was glad that the money belt Larry had given him was rubberized; it helped to keep him afloat once he started to molt the extra life vests that got punctured.

Yank and paddle.

Yank and paddle.

Rest.

Float.

"Damn it! Stop thinking about the opening scene from *Jaws*!" *At least the water is warm and the rain has stopped.* Still, he couldn't get the picture of sharks out of his mind.

He started to cry. The lapping of the waves that washed over them caused him to swallow water. "God, I need your help now," he prayed out loud. "And jus' in case you don't recognize me in Canali drag with the lifesaver necklace—it's Diva Creama." He felt for Dick's head to make sure he was still upright. Peak was out cold and his skin felt weird. "You know…" he said to Peak.

Yank and paddle.

"Being a drag queen does not mean *dragging* your sorry ass out of a sinking plane. And what's up with that stupid bullet shell I took from your pocket, anyway?" Carlos coughed and spit out some saltwater. "I could let you drown…but then I'd be no better than people like you who bashed Cousin Enrico to death. Enrico. Enrico!" *Wait, why can't I picture your face?*

A cascade of silver-blue staccato streaks pierced the night sky and thunder rumbled nearby. On its heels, Carlos saw it; he swore he got a glimpse of bright green when the crest of a swell lifted them above its trough. "The phosphorescent bay I saw from the plane?" His sense of time was so warped. He hadn't a clue how long they'd been out there, but he was queasy, and he gagged again from all the saltwater he had swallowed.

Yank and paddle.

Rest.

Float.

Yank.

Paddle.

Yank…his senses were dulling. But he could see the green getting bigger and then fading away. He shed the last life vest when it became tethered to a plume of seaweed that almost caused him and Peak to sink.

At first he thought he was passing out, but as the gentler current pulled them like magnets through an inlet, the water around them lit up like faerie dust. Psychedelic raindrops tickled the surface green. Everywhere they floated, the green trailed off as their bodies waded through. Faint emerald shadows in the outline of fish exploded around them.

"Oh, *Jesus Christo*, I hope this is the bay and not some kinda fancy flashback."

Yank.

The lightning grew dim.

Paddle.

The phosphorescence faded in and out.

Float.

Carlos's head slammed into something before he gave up and lost consciousness.

CHAPTER EIGHT

Tawny ran a brush through her long waves on her way out the door. There was no traffic when she shot up Van Ness toward KBCH, her travel coffee cup wedged between her thighs.

"Creama, wherever you are, you'd better be alive. Please be alive." Squealing at every turn in the parking garage, her Miata lurched into the old familiar No Parking zone by the elevator. She headed straight for the Security Desk.

"Hey, Miss White, this is a nice surprise," Charlie said, grinning. "Things just haven't been the same since you left."

"That's *Beige*, not White." Tawny and Charlie fell into their old routine. "I need a favor."

"You okay, Miss Beige?"

"No, I'm a wreck. My friend was on an airplane that went down in the ocean tonight, and I need to get up to the newsroom."

Charlie reached under the desk and placed a visitor's pass on the counter. "Is that all you need?"

"I owe you one, Charlie. When a burly guy named Larry gets here, tell him to wait." She was already halfway to the elevator. She knew everyone on the late-night shift when she had worked there until six months earlier. Now, they were Chloe's friends.

Tawny yanked a tube of Midnight Rose from its lipstick holster and blotted her lips before entering the old newsroom. Subdued, only a few desk jockeys worked at their computers and the whole room held an air of stale coffee. She imagined the frontline room was much busier. The rookie in the corner looked up. "Hey, it's Tawny Beige!" Two pierced and tattooed twenty-somethings smiled blankly.

"Hey, yeah, the newscaster," one said.

"Hi," said Tawny. "*Former* newscaster. Where's Chloe?" She used to love that everyone knew her girl, and that she never even had to give her last name. Now she hated it.

"They moved her up to the sixth floor," replied the rookie. "Would you like me to call up there?"

She felt a pit in her throat. "No, that's okay, thanks. I'll head up."

The elevator opened to a muted sixth floor, and all the lights were dim except for the office at the far end of the corridor. Her last two steps were lead-weighted, and she sighed when she saw Chloe tapping away on her computer. Chloe looked the same as she had all those nights when she was ostensibly working late, the same, except for the strips of green hair, which to her eye looked dastardly under fluorescent lighting. Those long clueless nights were still too close for comfort, but Tawny no longer had to wonder if Chloe was working or cheating on her, nope, not anymore. She stood in the doorway until Chloe looked up.

"Oh, Tawny…you startled me. What are you doing here?"

"Look, I really don't want to be here." *Eech, that hair looks even more atrocious up close.* "Creama was on the plane that went down tonight near Puerto Rico…the plane that Dick Peak was on."

"What?" Chloe's eyebrows furrowed. She took off her glasses and dropped them on the desk. "Oh no." She hung her head in her hands and then looked up at Tawny through her fingers. "Please, sit down. Do you want something to drink?"

"No, Chloe," Tawny answered in an icy tone. "I'm here because I need to do something, and I need you in order to get the news firsthand."

"I'm shocked." Speechless, she stared into Tawny's eyes, picked up the phone, and pressed one button. "Yeah, it's Chloe. Get me everything we have as soon as it comes in on the Trans Air crash in Puerto Rico." She hung up. "I heard about the crash, but I didn't know that Creama was on the plane. What's going on?"

"I don't have time to explain…I have to meet someone."

"In the middle of the night? Must be someone special."

"On a need-to-know basis, Chloe...you can't be fucking serious. Thanks in advance for the info. You have my numbers." Tawny turned to leave.

"Tawny, wait. I love Creama too, you know? After all, she did introduce us."

She felt Chloe's words crawl up her spine and choke the blood in her carotid arteries. "Yeah well, I've almost forgiven her for that."

"I wish you didn't feel that way."

"Not more than I do. Look, Chloe..." She felt the rumble of hurt in her abdomen. She wanted to say any one of a hundred other things, although "Fuck you," still topped the list. Instead, she tossed the visitor's pass onto Chloe's desk. "Call me when you have something."

Larry was pacing the lobby when Tawny exited the elevator. "Come with me," he said as he led her by the arm toward the door.

She glanced over her shoulder at the security guard. "Thanks, Charlie. Chloe has my pass."

She latched her seat belt as Larry cranked up his Porsche and made an illegal U-turn on Van Ness. "While I was waiting for you, I called my friend Andy, the reporter," he began. He glanced over at her. "You're too quiet. What happened?"

"Nothing happened, everything is fine. I asked Chloe to call me with any breaking news. I'm consumed with guilt for pushing Creama into this. Where are we going?"

"Andy said to meet him at Joe's..."

"Joe's? Who eats at Joe's?"

"He said he didn't want to talk on the phone. Said he has a piece of interesting information about Mr. Peak." The Porsche hiccupped into second gear on the upside of the hill. Across town, the night was getting foggy again.

They parked almost legally and Larry led the way into the iconic Joe's Diner. "Tawny, there he is."

"Wait. Any idea who those guys are that are with him?"

"No, do you?"

"No. Something's off. I don't like how this feels."

The two beefy guys in Andy's booth sat opposite him with their backs to the door, and one of them turned when the reporter vaulted from the booth. Andy crossed the restaurant and intercepted Tawny and Larry midway. He extended his hand to shake Larry's and shoved a note into his palm. "Leave now," the reporter whispered as he continued on toward the men's room.

Larry put his arm around Tawny, did an about-face, and practically shoved her back out the door.

Her heart sped up. "What the hell was that about?"

"Whatever it was, it was creepy. We're outta here." Larry and Tawny climbed into the Porsche and this time, it screamed back up the hill.

Larry pulled into a No Parking zone, killed the headlights, and handed Tawny the note that Andy had passed to him. The Porsche idled under an old-fashioned streetlamp at the crest of a fall-off-the-edge-of-the-earth street where all the diagonally parked cars gave the illusion of dominoes about to roll over on one another.

"What does it say?" Larry stared at her.

Tawny tilted toward the streetlight. "'Dangerous. Meeting with source.' Larry, just what does your friend Andy cover?"

"Silicon Valley business—Information Technology. He's a garden-variety computer nerd. I mean it's not like he covers the FBI or anything." Larry yawned. "It's going to be a long night. Let's go home, kitten. I'll take you back to your car." He eased off the clutch and the Porsche teetered over the crest of the edge of the earth.

"Lar, did you get a look at those guys sitting with your friend?"

"Uh, no, everything happened so fast…"

"Well, one of them seemed familiar."

"You recognized him from behind?"

"He turned his head for a second, something about his hair." She paused. "Yes, the salt-and-pepper cowlick. I know I've seen him before."

He chuckled. "Always a reporter's eye." He entered the parking garage at KBCH.

She finally smiled. "Promise me you'll call the minute you know anything…"

"Yes…"

"Anything at all, Larry."

"I'm bi-informational so that goes both ways. Do you want me to wait with you at your place?"

"No, it's okay. Scarlett's there."

She kissed his scratchy cheek, got out, and climbed into her Miata, checking her rearview mirror nine times on the way home.

CHAPTER NINE

The captain of the electric pontoon boat navigated back to the shore drop-off point at Bahia Mosquito, on the Puerto Rican outer island of Vieques. The twenty passengers aboard were touring the phosphorescent bay when they got caught in the sudden and violent deluge.

"Captain Sami, are those people out there?" The drenched passenger pointed to the glowing phosphorescent outlines of two bodies bobbing against the shoreline.

The motor hummed as the captain got on the horn and broke in on the military channel. "Come in. This is Captain Sami Juarez from Bahia Mosquito."

"You're calling it into the Navy?" said the First Mate.

"You know I always go by the book, Berto."

"What the hell are people doing out here in the middle of a storm?" Berto asked.

"Strange. Where did they come from is the better question."

Berto aimed the bow floodlight. "I'll say. I don't even see any life vests."

By the time the Shore Police arrived, Captain Sami's bioluminescent bay tour passengers were already safely on the truck dodging the mangroves and jungle-like vines on their way back to the pickup point. Sami waited patiently while the Navy investigated.

Dawn was imminent and all was quiet, the storm now but a memory—for those who were conscious and could remember it.

"He's one of ours," the Navy corpsman called out when he read the laminated ID. "Reserve Lieutenant Carlos Benitez." He then tossed it on top of his instrument pouch and pried the lieutenant's clenched forearm from around the second man's chest.

Captain Sami stood watching nearby.

"What about the other one, Doc?" asked the shore policeman.

"I don't know...but they're both alive. Medevac is ready, sir."

The shore policeman groaned. "They can sort it out in the Emergency Room at the VA Hospital."

The corpsman immobilized the unidentified man. He strapped him to the stretcher, and with the other corpsmen, loaded him into the helicopter—limp. Lifeless.

"Is he going to make it?" Sami asked the medic.

"He's breathing and has an erratic pulse," he said as he rushed past her.

"Oh, man! This guy's face looks like it went through a meat grinder," said another medic.

"Come on, I haven't had breakfast yet," groaned the older shore policeman. "Get these guys outta here." He helped the medics lock Lieutenant Benitez's stretcher next to the unidentified victim.

Captain Sami entered the final fray. "Does the other man have identification?"

"Didn't see any," answered the corpsman. "But he's so torn up, I didn't want to move him more than I had to."

"Let's go!" shouted the pilot.

"Aye, aye, sir."

Buchanan Emergency Room at the San Juan VA hospital was ready and waiting when the helicopter landed on its roof.

The attending physician orchestrated his medical personnel and conducted them through a litany of procedures. Portable X-Ray units gave way to CT scans. Tubes and electrical leads replaced the seaweed.

The nurse was staring at the man who lay unconscious on his gurney when the orthopedic surgeon arrived. "Sir. This is Lieutenant Carlos Benitez. As you can see, the head and facial lacerations have been dressed. I've examined the contusions, and his right leg reveals an obvious compound fracture."

"Do we have the CT results yet?" the doctor asked.

"We should have them any minute. The medics said his heart rate, blood pressure, and respiration have all been within normal limits the whole way here from Vieques."

The nurse switched bags of intravenous fluids.

A different nurse appeared from behind her desk. "That was radiology, Doctor," she said. "The CT scan of the lieutenant's head is normal except for some minor superficial swelling as a result of the lacerations, so he's cleared for anesthesia. They're sending over the films."

"Who sutured the head and the eye?" the orthopedic surgeon asked.

"Doctor Cisneros," the nurse answered. "He and Nurse Puma are already on their way to OR Six for the other victim's surgery."

"Vitals?"

"B.P. 110/70, heart rate 80 and steady, respiration 18," replied the nurse.

"EKG is normal," the doctor said. "Do we at least have static leg films?"

"Not yet, Doctor. Would you like me to call back?"

"I'm heading down to scrub for his surgery. Tell Radiology to get them to OR Four stat. The lieutenant is headed for serious pain and complications if we don't operate on that leg right now." The doctor lifted Benitez's lids and checked his pupils one more time. "Let's do it, people."

In Operating Room Six, the other male victim, listed as Juan Doe, was being prepped for the arduous process of acute post-traumatic reconstruction. Doctor Cisneros and Nurse Puma entered the elevator.

"We're operating *now* with or without a positive ID, Nurse."

"But Doctor Cisneros..."

He held up the sleeve full of X-rays. "Wait until you see these."

When the elevator door opened, they walked at a clip toward the operating room.

"I'm just suggesting that we wait a little longer to see if his paperwork comes through," said Puma.

They entered the scrub area.

"I don't care who this man is, Puma. The area that looks like shattered glass is bone shards from what used to be the man's face! His airway is in jeopardy and that's if he survives infection from the burns."

Sterile and ready, they entered the OR where the team awaited them.

"Okay, everyone," Cisneros began, "a US Navy lieutenant rescued this man. Let's honor his request and keep him alive."

On the mainland, the newswires were already buzzing. Passed out on her sofa, Tawny clutched the phone that rested on her chest. She slid it up to her ear when it rang. "Um-hmm," she answered with her eyes still closed.

"Sorry to wake you, it's Chloe."

"Yeah." She blinked herself awake and sat up. "What do you have?"

"It just came in. The plane ditched in the Caribbean during a storm. So far, there are people still missing, and nobody can confirm that Creama was among those rescued. There's no word on Dick Peak, but they haven't released much."

Tawny sprang to her feet in one breath. "Oh my God, Chloe…is Creama…"

"Dead? They don't know. The Coast Guard is planning their search-and-rescue based on the tide data. It's morning there, so there should be some updates soon. But it's possible that she was rescued and we just don't know it yet. Tawny, you're not alone, are you?"

"Don't go there, Chloe."

She sighed. "I'm asking because I don't want you to be alone through this."

Tawny hesitated. "I might as well tell you. I was the one who persuaded Creama to get on that plane."

Chloe paused. "Whoever is there, Tawny…I'm on my way over."

"No, I don't want you to come."

"I don't care…I'm on my way."

Tawny speed-dialed Larry the instant she hung up. "You sound wide awake," she said.

"Are you kidding?" he replied. "My upper eyelids are glued to my eyebrows to keep them open, I'm using caffeine for eye drops, and I think I can recite all the top stories on CNN better than Anderson Cooper."

"Chloe called…she said that Creama might be among the people missing—if she's not dead, that is. Dick Prick is still unaccounted for."

"Shit. Tawny, I can't believe this. Tell me it's a bad dream."

"It *is* a bad dream. And we're starring in it. I will never forgive myself."

"Hold on there, kitten. Creama's got a lot of spunk, and she may be fine. I haven't heard from Andy, but I'm going to call him again. Put on some coffee and we'll wait this thing out together."

"Chloe's on her way over."

"You're kidding, right?"

"No. She said she doesn't want me to be alone."

"You won't be. I'll be there."

"Are you sure?"

"I'm not leaving you alone with her. Not after the shit that she's pulled. Splash some water on your face and wake up, sistah. Big Larry is on the way."

Tawny wanted to be held and consoled. She wanted to hear Creama bitch about Judy Garland…or anyone for that matter. She flashed on the last time they had gone out dancing.

"Come on, *white girl*, les' go shake what the *mamis* gave us," Creama had said.

Tawny scraped back her hair. *How can I even think of how I feel, when I'm the horrible person who put her best friend on a flight to her final destination? I have* got *to stop thinking that!*

CHAPTER TEN

The knock at the door shook Tawny from her fifth and final alarming vignette. She took a deep breath before she let Chloe in, sidestepped her ex's attempt at a hug, and led the way into what used to be *their* living room.

"Oh, good, I was hoping you were alone. I brought bagels," said Chloe.

"Why?"

"You like bagels."

"No. Why are you glad I'm alone?"

"There's something I've been wanting to talk to you about. Tawny, I know the timing isn't the greatest..."

The doorbell rang.

Saved by the bell! "Hold that thought, Larry's here. Great timing," she said when she opened the door.

Chloe rose to greet him. "Hello, Larry..."

"Save your strength, Chloe, you'll need it." He shuffled through the living room and down the hallway toward the coffeepot. Tawny followed Larry, and Chloe followed Tawny.

The planks of circa 1900 hardwood floors all but pointed the way back in time. The seasoned Victorian kitchen opened into high ceilings, dark woods, and two mahogany antique church pews that met in a cozy "L" under elongated stained-glass windows. Without daylight filtering through them, the brilliant inserts of blue and green remained subdued. The lead windows of the open attached study bespoke an earlier century—a simpler time.

Warm and inviting, the same old coffeepot held its newscaster's vigil on the counter, between the copper sinks and the vintage Wedgewood oven.

"We had a lot of fun Sunday brunches with Creama in this kitchen, didn't we?" Chloe said.

"And we…well… I will again," said Tawny.

Larry leaned against her shoulder-to-shoulder. "You're about as convincing as a toy poodle in pit bull drag. Come on, kitten, this is no time for doubt. We have to put out good energy."

She ignored them both and aimed the remote at the kitchen-size Sony. "Larry, did you reach Andy?" She surfed the channels. "Damn, why can't I find updated news coverage?"

"Because you're not the reporter who's covering it," Larry answered. He stood and fetched the pot of Sumatra and filled all their cups. "No luck yet with Andy." He edged to the back corner of the pew. "I left him messages on his office, home, and cell voice mail. I also left him your number."

"Who's Andy?" asked Chloe.

"A reporter," Tawny said.

"Oh." Chloe's cell phone rang. She glanced at the display and stood. "Excuse me, I need to take this."

Tawny scoffed. "So you can tell *her* you're working late?"

"Tawny…" Chloe began.

"You know what, Chloe? Forget it. Not my circus. Not my clowns."

Larry squeezed Tawny's hand under the table. "I think you mean *monkeys*, not clowns."

"No. I definitely mean clowns."

"It's okay," said Chloe. "I know I deserve that one." She put the phone to her ear as she left the room. "Hello," she answered.

Larry coughed to avoid choking. "Well now, that's progress," he said in a hushed tone. "It may be the first time I've ever heard the mighty Chloe actually attempt to sound humble."

"Me too, Lar. It's scary." She paused. "Don't you think her green hair looks stupid?"

"I'm just glad that when you two split up, *you* got custody of me."

Jimmy Castilano stopped short of entering the Fairmont Hotel and placed the call to the reporter from outside so that he wouldn't wake Rita. He yelled into the receiver. "I wasn't about to tell you anything, Andy! Certainly not in front of that psycho Izzy!"

"You need to tell me now," snapped the reporter, "what campaign scheme is Peak involved in?"

"I told you everything I'm going to, and after that I don't want to be involved. Hey, has your guy at the paper gotten any updates on the plane crash?"

"No, nothing yet."

Jimmy felt his face get hot. "How is it with all your high-tech shit that no one knows if Dick is dead or alive? Call me when you know something."

"Will do, but…"

"What? Hello? Andy! What?" Jimmy couldn't make out what Andy said through static in the line. He looked at the phone after the call failed and resisted throwing it against the brick wall. "Goddamn dead battery!"

Jimmy tiptoed into the hotel room, stripped down to his boxers and climbed into bed next to Rita. Her warmth soothed his ills and shed the damp late-night chill that had seeped through him to his bones. He lay in the dark wondering if Dick was even alive.

As he drifted off to sleep, Rita whispered across the night, "It better not be another woman is all."

Jimmy smiled. "I keep telling you, there ain't another woman."

"Are you saying you had business in the middle of the night?"

"Rita…honey, I'm tellin' you it was business." He sighed. "Dick's plane crashed," he said remorsefully.

Rita gasped and turned over to face him. "Oh my god, is he alive?"

"I don't know nothin' yet. I've called in every favor, pulled every string I could find, but no one knows anything more than I do. But I don't have a good feeling about this. My stomach is doing flip-flops."

She stroked his hair. "Honey, be patient. All we can do right now is wait."

"Not exactly my strong suit," he snarled.

"I'll say," she teased.

He kissed her lips and snuggled against her. "Now let me catch some shuteye while I can."

CHAPTER ELEVEN

Buchanan VA Hospital had seen calmer mornings. The surgeon had worked on the unidentified man's facial reconstruction for hours, and all things considered, he was pleased with the outcome of his exhaustive efforts.

"Congratulations, Doctor Cisneros. He's alive…but I hope your fine work wasn't for naught," said Nurse Puma as she held the door for him. "What makes you think he'll regain consciousness?"

Cisneros pulled off his surgical mask. "I never said I thought he would, Nurse. But, if he does survive and wake up, one look in the mirror at the old face…" The doctor shook his head. "…and he'll have a heart attack. Whichever way this goes, at least he *has* a face now."

Dr. Cisneros entered the ICU, stared at the two inanimate patients, and double-checked the tubes and electrical leads. Broken and torn, the victims were incapable of conscious thought. Devoid of life as they had known it, Dr. Cisneros couldn't guess how long the comas would last, or even if these men would survive. He knew he had done all he could do and silently he asked God to finish the job.

The lieutenant, whose face and eye he had sutured, breathed quietly. Cisneros studied the right leg—how it was pinned, cast and rigged on the pulley at the foot of the bed. The heart monitor beeped a slow steady march. He wondered if the patients could hear him when he told them to wake up—that they were safe—that they could survive this if they tried harder. It was the Juan Doe who garnered his greatest concern for survival.

Lieutenant Benitez's head was bandaged where Cisneros had sutured his scalp, and purple bruises now decorated him from stem to sternum. Cisneros imagined it would be hard for an untrained professional to tell if the right eye had been sewn shut or if it was simply that swollen.

Juan Doe, on the other hand, was mummified. His head and face were entirely bandaged, with openings only at his mouth and nostrils. Under the layers of bandages were hours of remodeling and repair. Cisneros had reconstructed the nose and cheeks with bone taken from the patient's hip, and for now at least, he was breathing and his heart was beating—although he knew there was no guarantee it would stay that way. The skin under the wrapped hip was raw from where he had taken the bone and skin grafts. *That's the least of his worries*. Of one thing the doctor was certain: wherever Juan Doe was, he was there alone.

Nurse Puma entered the ICU and waited patiently by the doctor's side. He turned and nodded at her and almost smiled. "Good work, Puma."

"Your relief is here, Doctor. Come on, I'll buy you a cup of coffee."

It was afternoon that same day before the first few passengers from the Trans Air crash were treated and transferred to specialized medical centers. Most were transported to hospitals and trauma care facilities that had more sophisticated equipment.

Flight attendant Kate sat on the exam table in San Juan General's ER, watching the doctor scribble notes. "So, can I go?" she asked. "I'll be okay."

The doctor holstered his penlight and stared at her. "I know you *think* you feel okay, but you're a flight attendant, not Superwoman. You'll be spending the night here at San Juan General for observation. You went through quite an ordeal, Miss Taylor, and putting aside your sprains and contusions, you're suffering from dehydration. You need to be monitored," he said sternly.

Kate shook her head. "Really, Doctor, I'm fine," she protested. "Do you know where Captain DuWitt is?"

"Probably still with the National Transportation Safety Board in the room down the hall. You need to recuperate and leave the footwork to the authorities."

"But..."

"No buts. Stay here and someone will come to get you as soon as a bed is available. Until then, rest."

Kate reclined on the hospital gurney and watched the doctor leave. She shut her eyes and made a futile attempt to collect her thoughts. The events of the previous several hours had been reduced to random flashbacks that reverberated through her. How could she not have known that the congressman and passenger Benitez hadn't evacuated when she jumped onto the slide? She'd followed protocol! Hadn't she?

Kate groaned, held her ribs and sat upright. She caught her breath, mustered her strength, and snuck out toward the interrogation room to find the pilot. Compelled to join the search for missing passenger Benitez and the congressman, she slinked along the corridor.

"Miss Taylor!" The ER doctor lunged to catch her as she fainted. "Can I get some help out here?"

CHAPTER TWELVE

Tawny slumped in her overstuffed armchair and turned on the living room TV in time for KBCH Early Edition. She recalled a time when she would have cut through metal with her teeth to get this story and report it. Now, the best she could do was not resent the woman sitting in her living room. More importantly, she eschewed the urge to second-guess her decision to leave the newsroom. *Stay in the present! You don't need her to validate you anymore!*

"Now to our breaking news on the Trans Air 44 crash," said the newscaster.

"Make it louder," said Chloe.

"Catch!" Chloe ducked when Tawny chucked the remote at her head.

"While the cause of the crash isn't yet known, heavy storm activity in the Caribbean likely contributed to the reason that the diverted flight did not reach its destination. The National Transportation Safety Board has deployed their rapid response Go-Team to investigate." The newscaster paused. "We can now confirm that Congressman Dick Peak was a passenger on Trans Air 44. US Coast Guard Search-and-Rescue teams have rescued several passengers, and we'll bring you more information as soon as it's released. Elsewhere…" the anchorman's voice droned on.

Larry sighed at Tawny. "So, Chloe already told us that! I want *new* news."

"Don't look at me. I lost custody of the news biz in the divorce. Didn't I, Chloe?"

"I suppose that's my cue," Chloe yawned. "I'm going home for a power nap. In spite of the circumstances, it was good to be here with you, Tawny. You too, Larry." She stood and fetched her jacket from the old hook by the door.

Tawny remained quiet—her defenses still winning by a stingy slender margin—measured in micrometers.

"I'll call when I know something," Chloe continued, "and if you want to reach me, I'll be at home but my cell phone will be on Do Not Disturb." She threw on her leather jacket. "Bye."

Larry nodded at her. "Chloe."

"Larry," said Tawny, "you look like you'll fall over if you stand up. Why don't you crash here for a while?"

"I wouldn't mind going home to shower and get some clean clothes. But I don't want to leave you."

"It's okay. Scarlett will be awake soon. Will you try Andy again before you crash?"

"Sure." He stood and leaned over to kiss her forehead. "You okay after seeing Chloe?"

"Peachy," she huffed. "Why did she have to bring up our Sunday brunches? You'd think she'd be satisfied having ruined all my other good memories. She said she wanted to talk to me about something, but then you rang the bell."

"Have any idea what it was?"

"Not a clue. But then, apparently where Chloe's concerned, I've always been clueless."

At noon, Tawny and Larry stood alongside Miss Coco Puffs as they entertained questions from the press about the missing drag queen extraordinaire.

"Are the rumors true?" asked the reporter. "Was Creama LaCroppe a passenger on Trans Air Flight 44?"

Coco crushed her hankie between her Lee press-on nails and sniffled. "Oh, the thought! I can't bear knowing that Miss Creama LaCroppe, Drag Queen Diva Extraordinaiiiiire, might be somewhere over the rainbow." She dabbed a tear from her waterproof mascara. "Creama, you can't be gone." Coco tossed a puppy dog gaze at the reporter. "You may quote me."

The reporter turned his attention to Tawny. "Miss Beige, with all your news experience, is there anything you can tell us that we don't already know?"

Tawny smiled sadly. "I wish. We've shared with you what we've confirmed so far, but I'll make sure you get updates as soon as they're made available."

When they finished the interview, Larry and Tawny entered the private conference room of the Gay and Lesbian Neighborhood Project.

"It's a shame that Creama isn't here," said Larry. "I think she'd enjoy this."

Tawny looked at him in disbelief. "What the hell are you talking about?"

"Oh, Tawny! I only meant she would love all the media and attention. It's so torchy, you know?"

She shook her head. "I really wonder about you…"

"Well?" Larry asked Chloe the moment she came through the door.

Chloe ignored him. "Hi, Tawny. I was able to get a partial list of patients who were treated in San Juan immediately after they were rescued. Not all are passengers, and the hospitals still won't cough up all the names because of HIPAA regulations and all of that. But I think we'd have heard from Creama by now if she'd been rescued, don't you?"

"Can I see?" asked Tawny. Chloe handed her the list. "What are these codes beside the names?"

"Must you?" said Larry.

Chloe ignored him and lit her cigarette. "They're the various hospitals or facilities where people were treated."

Tawny's heart skipped a beat. "Benitez! There it is."

"Don't get excited. There are two but neither one is Creama. I already inquired." She crushed out her smoke in the ashtray, then placed a comforting hand on Tawny's shoulder.

Tawny's momentary hope collapsed at the end of the list. "If they don't find some kind of evidence soon, I'm going down there myself."

"Don't be crazy," Larry said. "What are you going to find out that the NTSB, local authorities, and Coast Guard can't?"

"I *am* an investigative reporter, Larry."

"And a damn good one," said Chloe.

"I thought you left the news biz, kitten."

Tawny glanced at Chloe. "It's more like the news biz left me."

Chloe squirmed. "So you go down there…then what?"

"Then I'm off to find the Wizard and get some answers."

"Uh-huh, you'd better not let Creama hear you utter a Judy Garland reference," said Larry. "You're serious, aren't you?"

"Chloe, can you get me a Press ID just in case I need it?"

"Sure. I'll have it for you by tonight. But, what if Creama's—"

"Don't say it, Chloe. I don't want to hear it."

Larry's cell phone chirped to the tune of "Follow The Yellow Brick Road." "Hello. Yes, this is he." A long pause ensued. Larry sighed and his shoulders slumped. With furrowed eyebrows and his gaze fixed on Tawny, he listened a little longer. "Thank you for calling me back." He ended the call and tossed the phone onto the table.

"What happened?" asked Tawny.

He exhaled. "That was Andy's secretary. The police found him a short while ago down by the wharf. He'd been beaten and was admitted to UC San Francisco hospital."

"Oh my god," said Tawny. She paused. "Oh my god! We may have evidence of something. The note he gave you is still in my purse." Frenzied, she fished through her purse, flicking away the fringe that kept getting tangled in her fingers.

"Are you joking?" Chloe smiled. "Notes from *me* are probably still in that purse."

He laughed, and Tawny pretended that Chloe was wrong.

"Larry, we need to go back to Joe's. Andy got rid of us at the diner because he knew we weren't safe."

"Why would someone want to hurt a Silicon Valley reporter?" he asked.

"It's a shame we can't ask Mr. Peak," said Tawny. "After all, it is his neighborhood."

"Did you say go back to Joe's? For what?" asked Larry.

"Dessert."

Larry drove around the block twice before finding a spot. As he and Tawny walked toward the diner, he glanced over his shoulder every few seconds.

"Stop it, Lar, you're making me paranoid."

"It creeps me out to think that whoever bashed Andy could have seen us with him. And we don't know who that somebody is."

"My reporter's instincts tell me there's a reason Andy wanted us to meet him *here*."

"Yeah. It's a shame the guys he was with had their backs to us. I couldn't see their faces."

"I told you I got a glimpse of one." Tawny led the way into Joe's and Larry followed her to the booth against the wall where Andy had sat.

"I still don't know what you expect to find," said Larry.

"I'll let you know when I find it." She slid into the tufted Naugahyde booth, opened the menu and peered over it, scanning the customers and the staff.

Larry sighed with periodic ennui.

"I don't see anyone that looks like the men who were with Andy," she said.

"Well that's a relief. What nefarious thing could a geek tech reporter be involved in? When he handed me that note, his palm was all sweaty."

"He stumbled onto something. How badly was he hurt?"

"Dunno, but it ain't good. I'm going to the hospital after this."

"What if his companions from the other night were his warning to back off?"

He shook his head. "I don't think they were his attackers. Why would an attacker be seen with him in public right before?"

"You're right. Still, keep your wits about you when you visit him. I know that you're only here to humor me."

"Thank you," Larry exhaled. "I didn't know how much longer I could fake it."

"Don't *ever* play poker."

He picked at the apple pie on his plate. "How much longer do we have to stay?"

"This is frustrating. What was it that Andy was trying to tell us?" Tawny grunted. "Okay, we'll leave after I hit the ladies' room." Two steps from the booth, she turned back and looked into his eyes.

"What is it?" he asked.

"Humor me some more." She slid back into the booth and felt along the underside of the table. "*Eech!* You've got be kidding me!" She folded in half to look underneath. "What the hell…it's a wad of gum." She lowered her tone and said, "And it's stuck to an envelope."

"What?"

Ripping the envelope from the gum, she folded it twice and tucked it in her pocket. "Let's go. Now."

"You said you've gotta pee."

She grabbed her purse and turned toward the door. "I do, so if you've got a *Q*, let's go make an alphabet."

She looked over her shoulder on the way back to Larry's car.

"Stop it," he said. "Now you're making *me* paranoid." He started the Porsche, jerked it into first gear, and stripped it into second as he headed up the hill to Tawny's.

"Larry, do you think it's possible that Andy knew Dick Peak was into something illegal? And maybe Andy was about to go public?"

He veered right and began the long ascent known as Seventeenth Street. "Or maybe someone was after Peak, and Andy had the story or was trying to warn him? Are you going to open that damn envelope or what?"

"I can't. There's gum stuck to it and me. I'm waiting till we get back to my place to peel it apart."

"I can't concentrate on that until I see Andy," he said. "I'll come over afterward."

"Okay, but I'm opening it when I get home."

"Call me?"

"Sure."

She gave him a kiss on the cheek and hopped out of the car. She climbed the stairs to her purple Victorian and flipped through her keys. As she turned the key in the lock, a deep unfamiliar voice jolted her from behind.

"Ms. Beige," he said.

Tawny whipped around. "Oh my god!" Barely a cinder block of space between them, she came face-to-face with one of the men she'd seen with Andy at Joe's. Trapped, she dropped her purse and everything spilled out. "Get away from me!" Her heart pounded.

The man scurried down the steps—but he didn't seem to be running away. Instead, he chased her bouncing belongings down the hill and gathered them. Holding up a tube of lipstick as a peace offering, he lumbered back up the stairs. Somehow, the scary guy with the spiky cowlick wasn't so threatening when clutching a tube of Matte Crimson.

"May I have a word with you?" he said politely. "I believe we have a very important common interest." He gestured toward her front door.

"Whoever you are, I don't invite strange men into my home."

"Excuse me, ma'am. My name is Jimmy Castilano, and I..."

"*Now* I remember who you are." She sized up the guy that she had only ever referred to as the poster thug of the religious right. "Come in," she said.

CHAPTER THIRTEEN

"*Buenos dias*, Lieutenant, it's Marta again," sang the morning aide when she came to open the blinds in Carlos's barren hospital room. On every other morning, no one had answered.

"Where am I? *Ow*, my eyes. My throat," Carlos mustered with a weak and raspy voice.

Startled, the aide gasped. "Wait, wait. Nurse!" she yelled into the corridor. "The lieutenant. He's awake!"

"Nurse?" Carlos uttered. He tried to push himself up on a right arm that was a droopy noodle and as heavy as a stellar-mass black hole. The nurse raced into the room and took Carlos's pulse. "Lieutenant Benitez. Can you hear me?" he asked the dozing patient.

He fought to open his eyelids, each one a separate burden. "Uh-huh." He wasn't sure what was floating—him or the room.

"That's great, Lieutenant. We've all been waiting to meet you. I'm Nurse Combs."

Carlos opened his eyes. "I must be in heaven," he said, staring at the hunky, blue-eyed man in scrubs.

"No, sir. You're at the VA Buchanan Military Hospital in Puerto Rico."

"Puerto Rico? What the hell happened? How long have I been here?" He tried to get up. "Ow!"

"Don't try to move." Nurse Combs gently eased him back down. "You've been unconscious for three days, sir. Your leg has some pins in it and you're in a cast. Marta, page Doctor Cisneros and tell him the lieutenant's conscious." Nurse Combs slipped the blood pressure cuff around his arm and pumped it up.

"Nurse, what happened to me?"

"I know you're weak, so let's save your questions for Doctor Cisneros. He should be here any minute." While the nurse updated his chart, a marginally awake Carlos barely heard the doctor.

"Welcome back, Lieutenant. I'm Doctor Cisneros. Young man, do you know who you are?"

With his eyes closed, he mumbled. "Cream…ahhh."

"What did he say, Nurse?"

"I think he said the word 'cream,' Doctor. You think he wants coffee?"

The doctor listened with his stethoscope and checked Carlos's vitals. "Ten Hut, Sailor!"

"Huh? Yessir! Ouch!"

"At ease, Benitez, I need you to stay awake right now. Do you know who is the President of the United States?"

"Number forty-five. Don't make me say his name." His parched throat made it hurt to speak. The kind-eyed doctor awaited him behind a fatherly smile.

"Do you remember what happened to you?"

"No, sir." The doctor's face was finally coming into focus until he took his penlight and swung it back and forth between Carlos's pupils.

"You and another unconscious man were rescued at Bahia Mosquito—on Vieques. By all counts, you rescued him."

He concentrated, trying to take it all in. "I-I did? Vieques? What's a Vieques?"

"It's a Puerto Rican island. Ring any bells?"

"No, sir."

"All right, Lieutenant. I'm glad you're awake. I'll be back to see you in a while. Nurse, get him some juice to bring up his sugar and keep him roused."

"Roused?" Carlos asked. "He can do that?"

Doctor Cisneros lifted an eyebrow. "Roused, not *aroused*, Lieutenant. You're obviously weak and with good reason. Perhaps a tad confused." Dr. Cisneros turned to Nurse Combs. "His vitals look good but page me if anything unusual occurs. I'll be back after I arrange for a CT of his brain."

"Nurse?" Carlos's voice was hoarse. "How did I wind up in a Bahia Tostito?"

Nurse laughed. "That's Bahia *Mosquito*. We were hoping you could tell us, Lieutenant."

"Was…I on active duty?"

"I don't know. Are you hungry? This liquid vitamin IV couldn't have been too tasty."

"Not really…wait, do you have any fruit?"

"Fruit, sir?"

"*Sí*, don't tell me there's no fruit on this base."

* * *

Rehydrated and splinted at the wrist, flight attendant Kate left the San Juan hospital two days later than she had anticipated. She bought some clothes at a nearby boutique with the stipend that an airline employee had delivered to her, then checked into the quaint inn where she usually stayed on layovers. Placing one ice pack on her swollen wrist, and a second one under her neck, she propped herself up on pillows to watch the news.

"Congressman Peak, you certainly are big business dead or alive," she said to no one. From what she gathered, the networks had been immortalizing Dick Peak since the crash. Around-the-clock TV preachers canonized their vitriolic poster boy who was missing at sea. And although no bodies had been recovered, they were calling for a memorial donation in Peak's name, to fight for Peak's causes. To make it easy, the followers could send the money directly to them. Kate zipped through the channels until she became dizzy from channel surfing over the speed limit.

She left the TV on CNN and curled up with her pillow. "Four people are now missing and presumed dead," the announcer said in English. The pieces played over and over in her mind—what she could remember of them. *How is it possible that anyone is missing! Every crewmember had followed protocol, hadn't they? Didn't* I? Her thoughts drifted to passenger Benitez again. Seat 3D. "Damn. I should have made him evacuate." It was still eating at her. "Ouch," she shrieked when her wrist collapsed under the weight of the San Juan Yellow Pages. She plopped the ice bag over her sprain and started searching under "Hospitals."

* * *

Tawny wondered if at this moment she was an extra in a macabre play. Jimmy Castilano, Dick Peak's religious right hand, was sitting in her *gay* living room. Although two of her fingers were still sticky from gum, she'd managed to stuff the envelope from Joe's into her purse without him noticing.

"You're right, Jimmy," Tawny said. "This whole ordeal is a nightmare. So, let me see if I have this straight, um, correct. You want to go to Puerto Rico because you're afraid that once the reporters put together that Creama LaCroppe was on the same plane as Dick Peak, they'll think Peak was gay?" Her jaw hung slightly open, not believing what she heard leaving her own lips.

"I'm saying, I think it would be good, when the time is right, if you could confirm that nothin' was goin' on between them two. I saw you on TV and heard that CaCa Puffs."

"*Coco* Puffs," Tawny sneered. "I don't think you should be concerned. You can't get gay by sitting on the same airplane. Tell me, are you afraid you'll be gay by the time you leave here, or do you plan on leaving before that happens?"

Jimmy chuckled. "I'm good."

"Why were you at Joe's with Andy?"

Jimmy fidgeted.

"Don't bother denying it, I saw you there. Why were you with Andy?"

Jimmy ran his stubby fingers through his graying temple. "Andy wanted an exclusive interview with the congressman in exchange for some vital information. I noticed he walked up to you and your friend."

"What kind of information?"

"Why? What's it to you?"

"Mr. Castilano, Andy had something important to tell me, too. But it's not likely I'll find out what it was unless he comes out of the hospital."

"Hospital? What're you talking about? I spoke to him this morning. What happened?"

"He was found beaten."

Jimmy stood and paced across the room. "Is he gonna be okay?"

"I don't know yet."

"Jesus! What the hell is happening?"

"What did he know that was so important that it landed him at UCSF hospital, and do you know who was his source?"

"Miss Beige, Andy and I know a lot of the same people. We was always runnin' into each other, what with him covering the congressman. I don't know what Andy had to tell you, but I'm thinkin' his source was the guy who fucked him up." Jimmy halted. "Excuse my language." He stared at her. "Ya know, I wouldn't a known you were a dyke by lookin' at you."

"Is that some kind of compliment in your diagonal universe? Guess it hasn't occurred to you that this is what gay looks like?"

"Uh, I honestly never really sat down and talked to, you know, one of *yous* before. No offense, but I really wanna make sure the media knows Dick wasn't gay and..."

"Don't even go there. There could never have been anything between Creama and your precious Dick."

"So, is that a yes?" Jimmy asked innocently. "You could leak that to the media...like I said, when the time is right."

"What information did Andy have for you, Mr. Castilano?"

"Sorry, that's privileged." Jimmy smiled. "You fish like the straight broads."

"Excuse me?"

He chuckled. "Give 'em an inch..."

"That's about all I would expect from a guy like you."

"Very cute. Very quick, too."

"Damn it, Castilano! Stop patronizing me. I couldn't care less about how many inches you offer a *straight broad*. My best friend may have lost her life because your boss can't keep his *inch* in his pants." Tawny snorted. "It's six o'clock and we're due for some updates."

Jimmy reached out and handed her his card. "I'm sorry that I startled you. Here's my cell number." He waited while Tawny stared at him. "Don't you want to give me your number, too?"

"No, not really." She turned on the TV.

"Jesus," Jimmy began, "just looking at that wreckage in the ocean gives me the chills."

"I know. How does *anyone* survive that?"

"Grim underwater discovery came today as Search-and-Rescue divers explored the ocean for any wreckage of Trans Air flight 44. Crews focused on the splash point, using ship-based sonar equipment, and underwater robotic cameras. Wreckage was discovered less than half a mile from where the Coast Guard's radar data indicated.

"Divers investigated several suspected sites before they were able to find the plane. Remains of two of the four people missing were recovered. It's not yet known if one of the unidentified bodies is that of Congressman Dick Peak. The Coast Guard has announced that all Search-and-Rescue operations have been halted, as there is no likelihood of survivors at this point."

"Oh, Jesus!" Jimmy scraped back his short hair. He handed Tawny his handkerchief to wipe her tears.

"Mr. Castilano..."

"Call me Jimmy."

"If one of those bodies is Peak's, do you really think his sexuality will be an issue?"

Jimmy hung his head and braced his elbows against his thighs. "Ms. Beige, Tawny, I've known Dick a long, long time. I love him like a brother. I protect him...that's what I do. Right now, all I have left to protect is his reputation. But if he *ain't* dead, he's got some explaining to do. He put me in harm's way without telling me and that's against the rules."

She took the reference to heart. "Harm's way?"

"Let's just say I don't wanna wind up like Andy." He stood and cracked his neck from side to side to ease the tension.

She cringed. "I could recommend a good chiropractor."

"I already have one. Goodbye, Tawny."

"Hold on." Tawny jotted down her number and handed it to Jimmy.

"Thanks," he said, folding the paper and placing it inside his wallet. "I'll be in touch."

As soon as he left, Tawny dug out the gum-ridden envelope from the zip compartment of her purse. She was trying to work around the gum to open it when her phone rang.

"I can't believe you're going through with this," Chloe chided.

"Whether or not Creama is alive, I need to go to San Juan to find out what happened. I won't rest until I do."

"You're not really taking the same Trans Air flight down there, are you?"

"Yes, I am. So, what have you got?" She tried to peel off the residual layer of gum still stuck to one finger.

"I spoke with the hospital in San Juan. I've followed the leads on those two Benitezes from the list I showed you. Unfortunately, that was a dead end. Oh, sorry. Anyway, the name of the person I spoke to was Nurse Mano."

"Thank you. Look, I know I've been tough on you."

"I get it," Chloe replied. "Let me come with you."

Her eyebrows arched. "Come with me?"

"I thought you'd never ask."

"Wait. No. Chloe, that wasn't an invitation. Why do you want to go?"

"To be there for you, and for Creama."

"You're way too late for that."

"Tawny..."

"What?"

"Never mind," Chloe said coldly, from behind a wall that popped up faster than an arcade whack-a-mole. "We'll talk when you get back. Your Press ID is downstairs at Security. Call me from San Juan and let me know you're all right?"

Tawny hung up.

CHAPTER FOURTEEN

Nurse Combs guided Carlos into his wheelchair. "That's it. Easy does it. One last twist."

"You're a good coach," he grunted.

"Attaboy, Lieutenant."

In the days since Carlos had regained consciousness, he'd made great strides both staying awake and learning to maneuver with only one functioning arm and leg. He couldn't wait to get his first dose of sunshine and fresh non-medicinal air. He had bugged the nurse until he finally said yes.

Nurse Combs wheeled him through the double doors into the garden and backed up the chair against the railing. "Here's a good spot to take in the view, sir."

A platoon of tropical fronds fluttered hello, and the balmy breeze blew through his hair, diluting the tug from the stitched patches of still almost bare scalp. Beneath the lapis sky, layers of leaves yawned above him. He squinted—his eyes adjusting to the brilliance of the island's colors. Every hue from the palest shade of lime to engorged forest green depended on the other for contrast.

"Nice, isn't it, Lieutenant?"

He nodded. "Nurse, we really need to do something about this leg cast sticking straight out. I look like a rolling hard-on."

Nurse Combs laughed. "You're a funny guy, Lieutenant. But if that were actually true, you'd be in the Guinness Book of Records. As for the cast, right now it's the best you can do."

"I don't feel like a funny guy. Has anyone located my ID card yet?"

"No, sir. But if it makes you feel better, the medics verified your identity when they transported you from Vieques. That's how we knew your name and your rank. We think the card got lost when you were airlifted." Combs set the brake on the wheelchair.

"That's not good. Hey, would you mind not calling me 'sir'?"

"Yessir." The nurse smiled and pulled a banana from his pocket. "Here, I took it from the mess since you're so fond of fruit."

"Thanks! Tell me something. That guy you think I rescued—who is he?"

"We don't know. The Navy is checking to see if you two were aboard a Trans Air flight that crashed the night before you were found."

"An airplane crash?" He drew a blank. "No way."

"It's pretty unlikely considering how far you would have had to drift—in a really bad storm. You'd have drowned. I think the authorities are just trying to dot their 'i's'."

"So, can I go see him? The guy?"

"You think that's wise, Lieutenant? However it happened, you've sustained significant injuries and you're still weak. You need bed rest. You can visit him soon. Besides, he's still in a coma."

"A coma?" He watched a sparrow land in the bush before him. It fluttered its delicate wings, and balanced on a pencil-thin branch. "Just the same, I want to see him. And nurse, would you at least call me Carlos? I'm not a real formal guy."

"Okay," said Nurse Combs.

"What's your first name?" asked Carlos as he clumsily peeled the banana one strip at a time.

"Manny."

"Manny? Manny Combs?" Carlos paused. "Was your mother a drag queen?"

Manny laughed. "Next best thing. She did hair for the movie studios."

"Ha! I like her already."

"Few people see the irony, Lieutenant Carlos. Do you really want to go see Juan now?"

"Who?"

"Juan—the guy in the coma. We had to call him something, so he's listed as Juan Doe."

Carlos snickered. "The Navy's so original. As splendid as it feels out here, I'd like to see him now before my eyes close again."

Nurse Manny wheeled him down the hall and spun his wheelchair around to back him through the doorway into Juan Doe's room. Carlos quietly contemplated this mystery while he swallowed the last of the banana.

"Manny, it's so lifeless in here—so sterile." Carlos noticed the absence of get-well flowers and personal effects. Everything about the environment was generic, much like his own room before he woke up and animated it.

The only visible sign of life in Juan Doe's room was the delicate margin of luck, or error, between existence and death. That which Carlos witnessed was someplace in between the two. With a language of their own, monitors spoke in life-affirming punctuation. His eyes followed along the tubes and electrical leads from Juan's body back to their sources. This was the language in which Juan Doe communicated with the world.

Nurse Combs parked Carlos a comfortable distance from the side of the comatose man's bed. "I'll check on you, but if you need me, press this call button." He placed it in Carlos's hand.

Carlos observed the void, one imprint at a time. Limbs as limp as leaves on a muggy summer night—the mummy quieter than a dead man at sea. "Hey, Papi, who are you, and how come you didn't wake up yet?" He maneuvered the wheelchair as best he could, and parallel parked his outstretched cast. He leaned on his good arm. "You know, Juan, they say I rescued you…but I don't have a clue from where or from what."

The mummy registered as vacant—like an old prop in the back room on a forgotten Hollywood studio backlot. Except for the monitors' beeps, and the form under the sheet, as far as Carlos could tell, no one was home. He sat there for a few minutes until the respirator and beeps annoyed him.

"Sleep good, Juan, I'll be back tomorrow when you wake up."

He suddenly felt faint and gripped the buzzer. "Sorry, Nurse."

Combs hustled into the darkened room. "You've had enough for one day, Lieutenant." He blotted the sweat from Carlos's forehead with a cool rag, took his pulse, then wheeled him back to his bed. This time, the nurse had to do most of the maneuvering, and Carlos fell asleep watching Manny notate his progress.

Tawny unlocked Carlos's apartment door with the spare keys he had given her and stepped over the growing pile of scattered mail under the door slot. Beyond the hardwood foyer, the ornately elegant patterns on the Oriental carpet invited her in. She slowly gazed around at the stillness that gave the impression that the long Victorian windows eerily watched her every move.

Across the room, lined up in the fashion of a drag queen-museum-display that Creama called Cher "Wigography," a row of Styrofoam heads chronicled Cher's hairstyle evolution in chronological order. The display was a veritable testament to Carlos and Creama's devotion to the many phases of Cher. To the right, a life-size cut-out of Cher in a Bob Mackie gown beckoned from the hallway.

Tawny flipped on the overhead brass chandelier, a leftover from another era. Her heels echoed off the planks in the hall and in Carlos's study. She sat, turned on the desk lamp, and lifted the front of Carlos's antique rolltop desk. Starting with the first of three drawers, Tawny methodically flipped through the files.

"Okay, Creama, where are all your important documents? Maybe a tax return so I can get your Social Security number? Credit cards?" The stagnant air swallowed her questions. When she finished ransacking the top drawer and opened the one beneath it, she lifted out a stack of files and placed them on the desk. Each was labeled by year and appeared to contain mostly documents like tax returns and warranties. When she opened the first file a photo fell out and sailed to the floor. She leaned over and picked it up.

"Sailors? I wonder who these guys were." She tossed the photo with some files and official-looking papers into her knapsack, and lastly opened the final drawer in the rolltop.

An instant smile relaxed her jaw. "So that's where you are! Come to Mama, Mrs. Potato Head." She straightened Mrs. Potato Head's yellow plastic earring. "I've missed you. You must be so confused. Really, how many Potato Heads have two mommies? One *mami* who's a drag queen and the other who's a gay girl? I can't count how many times Creama and I have stolen you from each other. At least we update your accessories." Her eyes filled as she hugged the toy before placing it in the knapsack.

On her way out, she gathered Creama's bills from the floor, grabbed the electric and phone bills to pay them, then climbed over the junk mail and locked up.

An hour later, almost all the papers from the knapsack had been sorted into neat piles on her dining room table. She dropped the phone bill on top of the pile and stared down at it. *Please don't let whomever you've called become your funeral list.* She continued leafing through the last file until she found it. The envelope labeled VISA contained the spare credit card issued to C.A. Benitez. Tawny smiled and heard Creama's voice in her mind.

"'*That way, when I'm in drag, I can use my card 'cause it only has my initials*,'" Creama had said.

Beep-beep-beep.

The third blast of the car horn beneath her window convinced Tawny that Larry was indeed waiting—impatiently. She grabbed her purse and raced down the stairs.

"What were you doing?" he asked. His foot came off the clutch like an exclamation point.

"I've been going through a bunch of papers I brought home from Creama's. I thought it would be helpful to have her social and credit card numbers."

He glanced over at her with knitted brows. "I still can't believe you're going to Puerto Rico. What was in the envelope from Joe's?"

"A note with four words: Strait—as in a narrow passage of water, Bahama, Hold, and Swiss. Strait, Bahama, Hold, and Swiss."

He shot her a glance. "What the hell does that mean?"

"You tell me."

"Probably has nothing to do with anything. Odds are some kid thought it'd be funny to get gum all over someone."

"Yeah. First things first. How's Andy?"

"I couldn't get in to see him when I dropped you off so we're stopping there first."

He wound down the hill on the other side of Seventeenth Street toward Stanyan, then over to University of California San Francisco Hospital. She surveyed the panhandle of Golden Gate Park as they passed by. Dotting the narrow stretch, a panoply of spring flowers in early bloom embellished the usual mixed bouquet of vagrants and dog walkers.

"Creama loves spring flowers," Tawny sighed.

"Yeah…"

"Especially *tulips*!" they sang out together. On cue, they imitated her in stereo and laughed at the inside joke. How Creama had always said *tulips* were better than one. For a split second, life felt almost normal to Tawny. Almost.

They exited the hospital elevator on Andy's floor, where Tawny tried not to glance into the rooms. The sucking sounds and beeps of the life-saving machines spilled out into the corridor and sent a chill through her body as she envisioned the sights that accompanied those sounds.

As though he heard her thoughts, Larry placed his arm around her shoulder like a protective big brother and ushered her forward. He hastened her ahead until he steered her into Andy's room.

They stopped just inside the doorway, staring at the sight before them.

"Hey, Cubby," he said softly. "You look pretty good but purple is *not* your color."

Andy smiled as far as the stitches in his lip would allow.

Larry placed his flowers on the table and pulled a chair up next to the bed. He gently touched the one spot on Andy's arm that looked normal.

"I know it's hard to talk, so just blink twice for yes and once for no. Does what happened to you have anything to do with what you wanted to tell me?"

Two blinks.

"Yes. Does it have to do with Dick Peak?"

"Is he…" Andy mumbled.

"Is he what, who is *he*? Peak?" said Larry.

Andy grimaced.

"Don't try to talk. Just blink. Were you investigating him?"

Two blinks.

"Is it something incriminating?"

Two blinks.

Bleep.

One of the monitors tripped and within seconds, a nurse rushed in. "I'm sorry but you need to leave," she said calmly.

"Of course," he said. "Rest up, buddy. I'll be back to visit."

Andy nodded and Larry escorted Tawny out of the room. They waited in the hall until the nurse left the room. "Is he going to be all right?" Larry asked her.

"He's doing better than he was." The nurse issued the statement like a platitude.

Tawny grasped Larry's hand and led him to the elevator. She saw the tears in his eyes when the fluorescent lights reflected off them, and she reached up to place her arm around his broad shoulders.

"We need to know whatever he knows, Tawny, but what the heck is going on? Could it be a coincidence that Andy wanted to tell me something about Peak on the same night as the crash?"

"I'm wondering if there's more to this than we might imagine, Larry."

"I know. Don't you think it's horrible that a wonderful person like Creama may have met the same fate as a putz like Dick Peak?"

"For now, I refuse to believe that," she sighed. "Come hell or high water, I'll be in San Juan after tomorrow night, and I won't quit until I know what happened."

"Be careful what you wish for, kitten. I really don't get why you're going. This is big news. A lot of people are trying to find out what happened."

"Look. All I know is that they haven't found Creama, and I haven't heard from her. So, until one of those things occurs, I'm going to uncover what everyone else has missed before the trail goes cold."

"You're an even better friend than you are a reporter, Tawny Beige."

"A better friend wouldn't have forced her to go."

CHAPTER FIFTEEN

"Buenos dias, Lieutenant," Marta the aide sang.

"*Hola*, Marta," Carlos answered. "I'll save you the trouble of asking. I'm doing better today."

She opened the blinds and set down a plate of sliced papaya on his bed tray. His mouth watered at the sight of it.

"You're so good to me. But how did you know?"

"The word is out around here."

"What word?"

"Fruit. When anyone sees fruit to think of you."

"Fitting." He used his good hand, but his aim still left something to be desired. The juice trickled down his fuzzy chin.

"You really should let me shave that beard, Lieutenant. I don't know why you would want to hide such a handsome face."

"Maybe tomorrow, Marta. My bruises are still too sensitive."

"Are you ready for your sponge bath?"

"Where is Nurse Combs?"

"He's off today…so, it's me or you stay smelly."

He laughed as he struggled to sit upright in his bed. The kindly endomorphic Marta was round, friendly, and easy to like.

"Come on, Lieutenant, that's right." She raised the bed and helped him the rest of the way.

An hour later, he was parked in his new favorite spot—the garden. He stared out past the vivid magenta bougainvillea and tall manicured palm trees, oblivious to everyone around him.

A salt-tinged breeze shot up his nostrils and nauseated him. The visceral reaction caused his stomach to squeak. Flashes of scenes raced through his mind arranged in tiles—dark dank bursts inside an even blacker jigsaw puzzle. His body flinched or released, depending on the vision. Each visual tile was so fragmented and short, it was impossible for him to see them clearly or to find anything connecting them.

"My mind feels like Swiss cheese. Every time I'm about to chew on a memory, I chomp down on a big old hole," he bitched to the bougainvillea. Once his nausea subsided, he closed his eyes to feel the freedom—to feel the liberation of inhabiting the present moment instead of the Land of the Tile Pictures—whatever and wherever that was. He took some slow deep breaths and saw Tawny's face in his mind. "Tawny! Oh my god! Tawny! Where's Tawny?"

He released the brake on the wheelchair, strained with his good arm and propelled himself in a zigzag pattern back toward the door. An orderly passing by wheeled him back to his room where he urgently bobbled the phone receiver and started to dial. With his good hand, he pressed "1" and froze.

"What the hell is her number?" Closing his eyes, he took another steadying breath. "Okay calm down. She's your best friend...and her name is Tawny. Tawny, Tawny, Tawny...Green. No no no, Tawny Brown. Tawny Brown? No, that can't be right." He took another deep breath and his ribs stung him. "Ow! *Blanca*! Tawny Blanca, that's it. That's it! But how do I find her?" He deflated in his chair. "Maybe Nurse Combs will help me tomorrow." Frustrated and fearful, he dropped the handset back onto the receiver and rang for an aide to wheel him down the hall to visit Juan Doe.

Juan's room was lit barely enough for Carlos to see. "Wheel me next to the bed, please." The systematic bleeps and dings emanating from Juan's monitors formed a discordant rhythmic ensemble, one that served to score Carlos's live-action movie.

"You know what you need, amigo?" He struggled with his one good arm to wheel himself to the window. He yanked back the blinds as best he could. "You need some sunshine and fresh air couldn't hurt. You can't be enjoying that liquid spam they're feeding you. Don't you want to wake up to fresh coffee and pancakes or Eggs Benedict? You like pancakes?" He thought for a second. "Unless of course, you're

Jewish, and then maybe you want lox and bagels. Frankly, I don't know *how* you people eat fish for breakfast."

He dragged himself along the furniture and reached for a paperback that an aide must have left behind. "*The Edge* by Catherine Coulter." He skimmed the Prologue and began reading aloud. "Chapter One, Bethesda Naval Hospital, Maryland." He continued reading until he couldn't anymore and then focused on a vacant Juan. He might as well have read him *Winnie the Pooh*. "So that's the end of Chapter One, Juan."

He tossed the book onto a table and gazed at the electronic life preservers. "We're alive, Juan. Come on, man, if I can wake up outta this thing, so can you. I'm coming back. Every day, mijo, so you'd better get used to the sound of my voice. Then you're going to answer me. I want to know what kinds of things you like to do on a Saturday afternoon." He pondered what he himself might have had once liked doing on a Saturday afternoon.

"Do you like dogs? I love dogs. As soon as I find the right guy and settle down, I'm gonna have me a whole bunch of the furry things." He paused. "I can see that you find me fascinating and that I leave you speechless. So, we're off to a very good start. We both love me." He yawned. "I wish I could remember me. I know I live in San Francisco, that I'm gay, oops, don't ask, don't tell—no wait, that crap's over. Isn't it? I also know I have to call Tawny Blanca. Okay, mijo, get busy because you've got shit to do and life is like, either do shit or don't do shit. Truthfully, I hope you're getting your shit together."

He pushed away from the bed. Feeling lonely, he paused to look back at Juan. "You gotta wake up, man. I'll bet that next to Tawny you're my best friend, and if you weren't before this, well, you musta been if I saved you. I wish I knew if we were lovers, but I can't remember." He wheeled off one-armed, zigzagging like a drunken sailor, humming Cher's, "If I Could Turn Back Time."

Hot and wilted, Tawny checked into the El Dorado in San Juan. She stowed her gear and settled for a hot shower and room service before calling Larry.

"Hi, this is Larry. Can't take your call. If you're worthy, I'll call you back."

"Hi, Lar. I'm at the El Dorado, room 723. It's late here and I want to get as early a start as possible tomorrow, so I'll call when I know something. Tell Scarlett I arrived safely. Love ya."

She hung up and let out a sigh as she leaned back on the pillows she fluffed into a pile. She pulled Creama's folder out of her carry-on and spread out the lists she had organized during the flight to San Juan. It was no use. If her stops were to be geographically correct, she was going to need a detailed map to plan them out. *I have no clue where to start.*

She awoke early, in almost the same exact place where she had fallen asleep. Amid what were no longer three tidy, short stacks of paper, she rolled over to stretch, crinkling the bed of paper beneath her. It felt like the middle of the night because technically it was.

She picked up the phone and hit the Room Service button. "Buenos dias to you, too," Tawny said. "I'm having a coffee emergency."

"Emergencia!" said the man on the line. "Policía?"

No. No police, no *policía*! Coffee—*café*. I need café right now!"

"Ah. *Café ahora?*"

"Yes. *Sí!* Ahora! *Gracias*."

Next, she called the concierge. "Will you please send up a map of San Juan?"

"Would you like it tomorrow?"

"No—today."

"Do you mean *now?*"

"Yes, now is good. Gracias."

Expelling a hard yawn, she shuffled into the bathroom to survey the damage. Her face looked drawn and frightfully white. "I wish I didn't want to put on makeup today." But, no matter how long ago it was, she could still hear her mother's voice. 'There's always time for a little lipstick; no need to leave the house looking like an earth mother,' she would say.

The coffee arrived, as did the compromise of a simple wand or two of mascara, and a swipe of Rouge Rayonnant on her lips. Tawny gulped the last of her coffee while studying the ocean from her terrace. "Creama, where are you? Please be alive...you have to be alive! You just *have* to be." She wiped away her tears and the runny mascara, and then reapplied her makeup.

Tawny took a taxi to the first stop on her list. The liaison at the Trans Air resource location for crash victims and their relatives brought her immediately to a cubicle.

"How may I help you today?" asked the liaison. "Were you a passenger or are you family?"

"Family. I'm trying to get information on my brother, Carlos Benitez," she lied.

"Do you have ID?"

Tawny reached into her wallet and produced the Visa card showing the name C.A. Benitez. "Sorry, I forgot my license." The woman glanced at the card and began typing into her computer.

"Well, Miss Benitez, I can confirm that he was on the flight, but his status is marked 'Missing.'"

Tawny gasped.

"But that doesn't mean he's one of the four lost souls. It may be that he's still in hospital, so we wouldn't have those records."

"Are you saying that Carlos might have been rescued, but the records may not yet show it?"

"Yes, definitely. The storm that downed that flight left a lot of locals stranded, so the medical facilities were terribly understaffed. It'll probably take days or weeks before they can catch up with the paperwork. They were inundated with local citizens who had been injured."

She felt a glimmer of hope. She had the list of facilities that Chloe had given her. "Thanks."

"Would you like to leave your number so that we can update you?"

She filled out the form and checked the first stop of the day off her list. With geographic correctness, she entered San Juan General Hospital minutes later. According to Chloe, she was looking for Nurse Mano, the one with whom Chloe had spoken.

Tawny entered the overcrowded waiting room to a noxious odorous stew of disinfectant and illness. It was obvious to her that the staff was on overload, their local customers sitting and waiting: bleeders to the right, pregnant women on the left. Parents sat along the walls holding their sick children.

Tawny took a shot in the dark as a nurse hurried past her. "Nurse Mano?" No reply. "Nurse Mano?" she asked another nurse who zipped by her.

"Excuse me," said a different nurse as she guided a wheelchair to a woman in labor.

Tawny followed them through the double doors into the treatment area. "Nurse Mano please?" she asked a nurse who was wrapping a wound.

"Night shift," the nurse replied curtly without looking away from her task.

With no luck, Tawny tried to pry information out of the administration department. She took a seat before leaving to update her notes, knowing she'd have to return during the night shift, when the place hopefully wouldn't be a dizzying zoo.

She hailed a taxi, got in and gave the cabbie the name of stop number three. Tawny scanned the list, wondering if she wasn't just spinning her wheels.

CHAPTER SIXTEEN

At Santa Ana Medical Center, flight attendant Kate Taylor fixed her gaze and tapped her foot at the receptionist. "How much longer do you think it'll be?"

"*La doctora* soon," the receptionist answered.

"That's what you said half an hour ago." Kate sighed, picked up a Spanish edition of *People* magazine and pivoted to take a seat. Her foot landed on a shoe behind her. When she turned to the woman with the long auburn hair smiled politely.

"Oh! I'm sorry," said Kate.

"It's okay," the woman said when she cast a wide net and stepped around her. "Buenos dias," she said to the receptionist. "Do you speak English?"

"A little."

"Do you have any patients here from the Trans Air plane crash?"

"What means 'tranzerplencrash?'"

"I am trying to locate someone from the Trans Air plane crash that might have been treated here. The name is Benitez."

"Airplane?" said the receptionist.

"Yes," the woman replied. She lifted her arm, curving her hand in a downward arc as she mimicked a crash, complete with the *boom* at the end.

"Excuse me, miss." Kate approached her from behind. "Hi, can I help? I speak Spanish." Kate recognized her immediately when the woman turned around. "I thought you looked familiar. You're Tawny Beige, right? The newscaster?"

"Former newscaster, who'd gladly accept some help if you wouldn't mind." Tawny glanced at Kate's arm.

"Did you just ask about someone named Benitez?"

"I did."

Kate's eyes trained on the man approaching from behind Tawny.

"Excuse me," the man interrupted. "I'm Marco Rodriguez from Administration. You were asking about a possible patient we've treated here?"

"Yes." Tawny fumbled with her Press ID card. "My name is Tawny Beige, and I'm from KBCH television in San Francisco."

"I'm sorry, I can't give official statements, and due to HIPAA laws I can't give you any personal information."

"No, wait…I am trying to find my…"

"I cannot help you, miss. Please refer your questions to the airline." He dipped his head politely and slithered back into the staircase he'd crawled out of.

"Damn it," Tawny mumbled. She sat on a vinyl bench, pulled out her map of San Juan, and spread it out next to her.

Kate followed her. "Forgive me, but I was a flight attendant on Trans Air 44. Are you a relative of passenger Benitez?"

Tawny glanced again at her arm splint and sling, then gathered up her map. "Please sit down. What's your name?"

"Kate Taylor. I'd shake your hand but…"

"Are you okay, Kate?"

"I'm a little worse for the wear, but part of my charm is that I never stay down for long."

Tawny smiled. "Then someone's not doing it right. It's nice to meet you and I'm glad you made it. Yes, I'm looking for Carlos Benitez. Do you have any recollection of someone with that name?"

"If you're with the press, why are you asking only about him? Is he your boyfriend or something?"

"Hardly. He's much more than that."

Kate raised her eyebrow. "Oh?"

"He's my best friend and I'm desperate to find out anything I can." Her eyes welled and Kate lent a delicate sympathetic pat on the shoulder with her good hand.

"*Señorita* Tyler?" asked the nurse, as she stood there holding a medical chart.

"That's Taylor." Kate smiled at Tawny.

"Wait," said Tawny. "Can we speak when you're done here or later on?"

"Where are you staying?" asked Kate.

"The El Dorado, room 723. Would you consider being my dinner guest? I need to ask you a few questions, if you wouldn't mind."

"How is seven o'clock?"

Tawny nodded. "Seven is good. I'll meet you in the lobby."

Carlos awoke to the aroma of supper.

"Hey, Lieutenant, it's chow time," said the orderly as he placed the tray onto the table and rolled it up to the bed. "Navy chow, served up piping hot."

"Watch your hand," Carlos said. "I'm so hungry I might eat it."

The orderly smiled. "I made sure they gave you an apple."

"Thanks."

"Yes, sir. Word's out in the mess that when they see fruit, to think of you."

"Aye, I've heard this before. You're a good man." Carlos dug in and was devouring dinner when Dr. Cisneros poked his head through the door.

Cisneros smiled. "I'm happy to see you have such an appetite, Lieutenant."

"Hey, Doc! Sorry I can't snap to attention."

"Hmm, is that because of your pinned leg in the cast, your injured arm, or is it that your good hand is too busy shoveling in that chow?"

Carlos put down his fork. "I'm glad you're here, Doc. I wanna ask you something."

He peeled his stethoscope from his pocket and hooked it around his neck.

Carlos continued. "How did I get here and why can't I remember things? Simple things. Like I went to call my best friend...and I know her first name and what she looks like, but I'm not sure of her last name or phone number. Am I brain damaged?"

Dr. Cisneros stepped closer. "Frankly, I'm happy that your brain is working as well as it is. The good news is that your latest CT scans show your brain is normal. What you're experiencing, son, is called Post Traumatic Amnesia."

"Which means?"

"Due to whatever trauma you suffered, you have no recollection of what happened after your trauma or even the trauma itself. You do, however, recognize yourself and some of the past, although some of it might be sketchy right now. With head trauma, pieces of memory may be lost, and whether that's emotional or organic, no one knows when, or if, it will return. But keep your chin up—the loss may well be temporary. Your brain scans look good and you're progressing well—which is a miracle compared to the man I first saw."

"But how do you know if I'll get my memory back?"

"Call it intuition, Lieutenant. While I can't say for certain, if all goes well, at some point pieces of your memory may return. Think of it as a jigsaw puzzle that's halfway complete. Each time you get a new piece, you examine it, try it in a few places, look to see where it fits."

"So, does anyone know what this trauma was?"

"At first we thought you were aboard a Trans Air flight that crashed in the Caribbean. But there was some confusion since the corpsmen who brought you here misplaced your ID. They filled out the forms, which is how we knew your identity." The doctor paused. "I have no clue how you wound up where you did. Unlikely that you drifted that distance from where the plane ditched. And in that storm without a life vest?" The doctor shook his head. "That's not possible." Cisneros unwrapped Carlos's arm and checked the wound.

"What about Juan Doe? Is he gonna wake up?"

"I don't know. But I know that the time you're spending with him helps." Cisneros carefully redressed the wound. "Finish your dinner. Tomorrow, we'll talk about your future so that you can strengthen up and go home."

"I sure hope you know my address, Doc. That's one of the pieces that's still missing."

Doctor Cisneros turned toward the door.

"Doc, wait. If I ship out, what will happen to Juan?"

"Relax, Benitez, you're not going anywhere for a while."

"Thanks for everything. You're my hero, sir."

Cisneros smiled. "Goodnight, Lieutenant."

CHAPTER SEVENTEEN

Tawny checked the time and then tried on every shade of lipstick in her toolkit before committing. Dressed in a skirt and heels, she knew she could have gotten away with any shade of lipstick, but Sea Coral would've been really bad form given the circumstances. She settled on Romantic Rose and entered the elevator to the lobby.

While sitting and reviewing her notes from the local KBCH affiliate, Tawny looked up the instant Kate came through the door. Her blue eyes sparkled from across the room. *They really are that blue.* Stuck in that moment, she only had time to notice the woman's full lips curve into a welcoming smile. She stood and met her halfway.

"Hi," said Tawny. "I really appreciate you meeting me."

"Before we talk, I need to know that this is off the record," said Kate.

"I'm not an official member of the press any longer. Besides, touting myself as one backfired on me at the medical center."

Kate grinned. "Don't sweat it. I was able to find out that they don't know anything anyway. The nurse who examined me today knew I had worked that flight, and so I told her I was trying to find someone from the crew by the name of Benitez. As a courtesy, she told me that no one from the flight with that name had come through there."

Tawny reminded herself to check that off her list and led the flight attendant into the nicest of the three restaurants in the hotel. Aside from the award-winning rating, she had chosen it as much for its softly lit ambiance as its open-air soundtrack. She thanked the maître d' and followed him to the table she had reserved.

By the time they reached their table, Tawny was hypnotized by the sight of the endless azure frontier. "I feel like we're dining on a postcard." Directly before her, the sun dripped into an indigo floor on the horizon, and a velvet breeze pacified her underlying agitation, such that it slowed her heart rate for the first time since Creama's disappearance.

"Thank you," Kate said when the maître d' held her chair and placed an open menu in her good hand. She looked at Tawny across the table. "It smells great in here. I'm hungry."

As subtle as an amateur sleuth, Tawny peered above her menu to peek at her dinner guest.

Kate's eyes continued to scan the different menu pages. "Does anything here appeal to you?"

Tawny closed her menu and observed the striking woman in the wrist splint. "Definitely."

They ordered dinner and Tawny politely made all the small talk she could until she ran out of things to say. She took her opportunity once the dinner plates were cleared and they waited for coffee. "So, Kate, dare I ask what happened up there?"

Kate slipped the fallen spaghetti strap back onto her bare shoulder. "It was a rough night. So many storms and however the pilot tried to avoid them, he couldn't." She gazed across the room and took a breath. "It seemed that no matter how we altered course, the storms kept chasing us. One of the engines was hit and we had to descend. Thankfully, Captain DuWitt was flying or the outcome could have been way worse."

Tawny observed her body language—the way Kate's eyes darted and her fingers trembled as she spoke. She waited patiently for her to continue.

Kate stared out to sea before meeting her gaze. "It looks so calm and beautiful from here. But Tawny, in the middle of the night, with swells washing over you as you hold on to a raft for dear life—along with all those people who are injured and freaking out—it's not so inviting."

Tawny felt another stab of guilt about Creama. "I'm sorry, Kate. As much as I want to find out what happened, perhaps this is too painful for you to talk about yet."

Kate continued as though she hadn't heard what she'd said. "If the Carlos Benitez that was my passenger was your friend, you should know he was a brave man. *Very* brave. He was my passenger in First Class."

Tawny choked on a sip of water. "A-Are you sure we're talking about the same Carlos Benitez?"

"Well, according to the manifest, there were two Carlos Benitezes on the flight...one in Coach, and one in First Class. There were three passengers total named Benitez."

"Three! Nobody said anything about two Carloses. Are you certain?"

"Definitely. I remember because at first I thought the one in First Class was related to a woman named Benitez who was sitting in the second row of Coach. She had asked if there were two seats available together so that she could sit with her husband Carlos. I was going to see about an upgrade for her when she told me that the Carlos Benitez that was her husband was a different man, in Coach. And since you didn't mention your friend having a wife..."

"What did he look like? The one in First Class."

"Thin build, olive complexion. Nice looking with thick black hair and doe-shaped dark eyes, slight Latino accent, suit...and how do I say this—a bit on the dramatic side."

"Oh my god, that's my Carlos!"

The waiter brought dessert and refilled the coffee cups. Tawny leaned back in her chair. "I'm afraid to ask about the details, Kate, but I'm desperate to know anything you're willing to share."

Kate wrestled with her splint and managed a bite of pie. "Your friend Carlos was the one person who kept his cool. He was solely responsible for getting the airplane door unjammed and he bravely evacuated several passengers single-handedly."

Tawny sat up straight. "I'm shocked...I-I don't know what to say."

"He even carried a woman and her child, and an unconscious person. Now I remember. He had a gash on his head that was bleeding."

"I've known him for years and I never knew..." She leaned forward propping her elbows on the table. Sweat trickled at her hairline.

"Mr. Benitez had been instrumental in evacuating compromised passengers—older people, that young mother and her baby, and several others." Kate sighed. "I thought everyone was out of the plane. Benitez was standing next to the captain, and they were both about to jump onto the slide when your friend pulled away. The captain landed in the raft without him. When we yelled to him to jump, he went back into the plane, shouting something—I don't remember what it was.

The rafts were already disengaged." Kate's eyes swept the floor, tears visibly escaping. "That's when the plane's nose started going down. In the storm, we couldn't see much after that. We were out there drifting for a long time before the Coast Guard cutter *Southern Storm* picked us up."

"Didn't anyone go back to look?"

"When we got aboard the *Southern Storm*, I insisted they go back for him and the congressman."

"Are you saying, you're sure that Congressman Peak never made it out of the plane either?"

"That's what I'm saying. Were you all good friends?"

Tawny's eyes opened wide. "What? Friends with the congressman?"

Kate stared at her, waiting for her response.

"No, we were not friends. Why do you ask?"

"Your friend and Congressman Peak were chummy during the flight, so I just assumed they knew each other pretty well."

Tawny issued a nervous giggle as she tried to digest the story. She cupped her hands over her eyes and massaged her forehead. She tried to envision this whole scene. No matter how hard she tried, she couldn't conjure Creama LaCroppe, Puerto Rican Drag Queen Diva Extraordinaire, in a Canali suit, playing Wonder Woman…*and chatting up Peak*? "Kate, may I ask you a personal question?"

"Uh-huh."

"Do you live here?"

"No. I live in San Francisco. That's how I recognized you—I used to watch you on the news."

"Why are you still down here?"

Kate waited before answering. Her eyes darted away and then back to Tawny. "Honestly? I've been trying to find information about your friend. I feel terrible for not forcing him to evacuate. No one I've checked with from the airline has been able to locate him. I fear he didn't make it out…"

"Don't say it. I can't go there."

Kate smiled. "An optimist, eh?"

Tawny flashed on Chloe. "There are those who would claim I'm delusional." She scraped back her hair. "If you think *you* feel terrible, I'm the one who insisted he get on that plane."

"I like you, Tawny. You and Carlos must be very close if you're going through this kind of agony to find him."

"I like you too, Kate. You just used present tense."

CHAPTER EIGHTEEN

"Buenos dias, Lieutenant."

"Hola, Marta. *Cómo estás?*"

Marta flitted across the room with her usual verve, opening the blinds and cleaning up. "It's a beautiful day, Lieutenant."

"That's because you're a ray of sunshine, Marta." Carlos fluffed his blanket.

"Oh, stop." Marta blushed. "When are you going to let me shave off that beard?"

"Maybe tomorrow."

She stood her ground, hands on her ample hips. "You've been saying that since you woke up. I hardly recognize you. You look like a mountain man."

"Join the club. I don't recognize me either." He picked up his little mirror and stroked his beard. "You know, Marta, I don't believe I've ever had one of these before. I kind of like it."

Wiping the table with one hand, she used the other to shake her finger at him. "*Oye*, Lieutenant, if you're keeping it, you need a trim."

"Okay, okay. Do it. But I'm sponge-bathing myself today."

"My," Marta teased, "aren't *we* a little feisty?" She held up the scissors and snipped the air twice.

"Fine, Marta, I'm all yours."

"There you go, Lieutenant. What do you think?" Marta asked when she finished.

Carlos smiled at her in the mirror. "This looks good, Marta! I like the haircut too—it's a little bit punk." He took a leaf from the aloe plant that Nurse Combs had brought for him and rubbed its sticky nectar on his head and facial scars, then spiked the patch of crew cut that was growing over the scar on his head. He sang the chorus to Sonny and Cher's, "I've Got You Babe" to Marta.

"Now there's a happy song," she said.

He maneuvered into an improved wheelchair that Dr. Cisneros had ordered to accommodate this more streamlined leg cast. His attention shifted to the news playing on the TV in the background. He heard people being interviewed about an airplane crash they'd survived. The piece ended with an update that some congressman named Dick Peak was presumed dead.

"Dick Peak," Carlos mused. "Why is that name familiar?" *I guess that's what Dr. Cisneros meant by jigsaw memories.*

Soon after, he entered the corridor to find Nurse Combs standing with his arms folded across his broad frame.

"Where do you think you're going without your wheelchair, Lieutenant?"

"Busted," Carlos groaned.

"Your arm and leg aren't ready for crutches."

"Aw come on, Manny. I already used the new chair and I'm only going down the hall to sit with Juan. How am I supposed to get better if I don't push myself?"

Nurse Manny raised a skeptical eyebrow.

"I'll be really careful…I promise."

"Don't let Doctor Cisneros catch you."

Carlos laughed. "If he does, I'll tell him it was your idea."

Everything in Juan's room was almost exactly as Carlos had left it at bedtime the night before, except for one stunning distinction. "Wow, Juan, congratulations. You have a face." He fell back into the armchair with a grimace and propped his crutches against the wall. "I was beginning to wonder if there was an actual person under that mummy gauze. The doctor removed most of your facial bandages."

Carlos studied the face, trying to assemble the puzzle pieces in his mind, like Dr. Cisneros had instructed him to do. He had hoped he would recognize Juan. "You're not ringing any bells, Juan, and I think you're getting far too comfortable with this one-sided relationship we're having. Even the divas shake up their routine once in a while.

What's that, Juan? You want to know what I mean? Take Cher, for example. She evolved from Cherilyn, to Cleo of Cesar and Cleo, to Sonny and Cher, and eventually to the tattooed electronic diva. Not to mention her amazing acting talent." Carlos reflected for a moment. "How come I know so much about Cher?"

The harder he tried to remember, the easier it seemed to forget. *Swiss cheese*! *My memory is filled with more holes than Swiss cheese*! "I'll bet I know all about Cher 'cause I'm gay—and Cher is like a prerequisite to Homo 101. She's on every gay test." Carlos sighed away his aloneness, fidgeted in his chair and surveyed the dim hospital room. He concentrated on Juan's new face. "You know, my friend, I'm getting too used to your heart monitor beep.

"Listen, you really gotta wake up soon. Doc says he may ship me off to a rehab, which means I won't be able to come read to you no more. So, you have to wake up, it's as simple as that." Carlos paused. "Juan, I think you like it when I read to you from the tabloid, *The Insider*. All that juicy jazz is very entertaining, doncha think?" He turned the page and read aloud. "I was a teenage fetus." He raised his eyebrows. "Now that's a cute trick."

Carlos read *The Insider* out loud until he hit the back cover, pausing only to ogle a photo of Ricky Martin. "*Tsk*, that Ricky Martin is too cute. I shall call him *Rrrriqueno* Martin. I wish this picture was in three-D so I could pinch those cheeks." For the first time, he bit down on the cheese instead of the hole. "Three D. Three D? Why does *that* sound familiar? Three Dee, 3D. Hmm.

"All right, Juan, we're done with *The Insider*. Any questions? No? Then let's move on and tackle your other favorite tabloid, *The National Reporter*."

In his mind, he kept repeating Three D. Then he stared at Juan. *Who are you, and more importantly, who are you to me*?

Juan had not shifted a millimeter on his own since Carlos had been coming to visit him. His only positional changes were medically orchestrated to prevent bedsores and the like. The monitors' beeps had grown repugnant to him—seemingly the antithesis to life itself, and he found that lifelessness depressing.

"It's too dull in here, Juan. Let's see if we can get a little salsa rhythm into those beeps today." With the steady hum of CNN playing softly in the background, Carlos began reading the tabloid *The Reporter* out loud.

"Check out this story, Juan. 'I Was Abducted by an Alien Transvestite.' Like...how would you *know*? Renew my subscription to

Vogue *Alien*, so if we're ever abducted we'll *totally* know which ones are trans. Hmm," he mused as he searched for his next story. "I wonder what aliens wear." He flipped to the middle of the paper. "'Man Born Old, Ages Backward to Childhood.' Pictured above, smiling on his twenty-ninth birthday."

Carlos had remained mostly oblivious to the hum of CNN until that moment.

"Congressman Dick Peak of California is now presumed dead," the announcer said.

"Ahhh."

Carlos turned his head to see who entered the room.

"*Ugh.*"

"What the…?" Carlos jumped onto his good leg, letting the arm of the bed break his fall. He blinked hard and stared at Juan. "Juan!" He thought he saw an eyelid twitch. "Oh my god, he's waking up!" Carlos squeezed Juan's buzzer using the Vulcan death grip. "Nurse! Nurse! Hurry up, get in here! Juan groaned!"

A nurse raced into the room. A monitor spiked. Next, its alarm beeped—the beeps percolated, revving up to a stutter. The nurse spoke into the intercom. "He's in tachycardia. I need a team." She placed her stethoscope against Juan's chest. "You have to leave, Lieutenant."

"Like hell! He's waking up! Isn't he?"

CHAPTER NINETEEN

In a meticulously choreographed medical ballet, the rapid response team scrambled into Juan's room and orchestrated his revival.

Carlos squinted against the sudden harshness of bright light, leaned on his crutches and swung himself to the corner of the room. He eyed bags of fluids and listened to each team member call out life and death statistics—blood pressure, respiration, EKG results.

"Get the paddles ready," the doctor said.

Watching the surreal scene play out before his eyes thinned the breathable air in the room and made the walls shrink around him. Then a nurse held up one of the long skinny stainless silver needles that made Carlos sweat at the sight. "Maybe I'll just wait in the hall." He executed his new spin-on-a-crutch exit, sat on a folding chair in the corridor, and chewed three plastic straws to shreds. Dr. Cisneros raced past him without a word.

"Hey, Lieutenant," said an orderly, "I brought your wheelchair. Would you like me to take you back to your room?"

"My heart is pounding. I wish I knew what the hell is going on in there."

"Unfortunately, sir, I can't help you out." The orderly steadied the wheelchair for Carlos and waited for him to shift into it.

"Would you mind taking my crutches back to my room? I'd rather wait here until I know how Juan is. I'll go nuts alone there."

"Sure. Let me know if you need anything."

While he had no idea what all the beeps meant or what the medical banter that spilled into the hallway signified, Carlos decided to sit vigil until he found out. Too fidgety to stay in one place, he found a way to pace in his wheelchair using only one arm, weaving like a drunken sailor.

His good arm grew tired and sore, and he'd lost count of how many laps he'd done to the nurses station. He rolled back and forth. Back and forth. Time slowed like an endless desert and each passing second became a single grain of sand to be counted. He thought he'd counted half of the Mojave by the time the team left the room. The last to exit, Dr. Cisneros, waited for Carlos at Juan's doorway.

"Lieutenant, you're the first person I've ever seen who can pace in a wheelchair with one good arm." The doctor's lips settled into the paternal smile that comforted Carlos.

Carlos zigzagged back to him from the nurses station. "You're killin' me, Doc. I can't read your expression."

"Your friend is awake, Carlos, but he's incredibly weak."

"Is he gonna make it?"

"One thing at a time. It's a miracle we got him back at all. We're running some tests now, but I know you had a lot to do with him waking up."

"Me?"

"Yes. In all probability, reading to him and speaking to him facilitated his return." Cisneros stepped behind Carlos. "Would you like to meet him?" he asked, wheeling him into the room.

No longer a mausoleum, Juan's room was brighter and larger now that some of the machines were absent and others silent. Carlos sat quietly—plastered to his chair, staring. With his mouth agape, he wondered about the stranger he almost knew.

Juan's bed was tilted upright; the only tube that remained attached to him was oxygen. His lips were no longer gray, but his eyelids bobbed, heavy still from weeks of hibernation. *Juan Doe is…conscious.*

"Go figure, Juan," said Dr. Cisneros. "The man comes and reads and talks to you for weeks, every single day…for hours. And now you're awake, and the lieutenant hasn't anything to say to you." He laughed. "Don't stay too long, Carlos. He doesn't need the excitement."

"Yeah, yeah, sure, Doc."

"I'll be in to see you later," he said to Juan before leaving.

Juan stared at Carlos long and hard before uttering a word. "Who… am I?" Juan asked in a feeble voice. "Are we friends?"

"I was hopin' you could tell me, amigo." Carlos smiled. "Yes, Juan, we're friends. I just don't know nothin' about you."

"My name is…Juan?"

"Well," said Carlos, still in shock that the mummy was mostly unwrapped and talking back. "We had to call you something, and since the Navy is so original…"

"Navy?" He coughed. "I don't feel so good. What did you say your name is?"

"I'm Carlos. Juan? Juan?" Before Carlos said his name the second time, Juan's eyes closed. "Get some rest, Juan. I'll be back to see you soon."

A nurse entered the room. "Tomorrow's another day, Lieutenant. By the way, we all had bets on whether or not Juan would wake up for you."

"Bets?" Carlos said haughtily.

"We decided at the outset, that whoever won or lost, all the proceeds would be given to you both for your recovery."

Carlos smiled. "Really? That's so thoughtful and kind."

Sheltered by palms and embraced by an alcove of white bougainvillea, Carlos witnessed the most stunning sunset yet from his spot in the garden. As the sun sank lower in the sky, he wondered about Tawny. "Tawny, Tawny, Tawneee, where are you? What the hell is your last name and what does it have to do with lipstick?" He continued to speak in order to hear the sound of a familiar voice, even if it was his own. "Tawny…not her lipstick shade. Tawny Brown? No, that's no shade of lipstick. I give up!" He flagged down an orderly to wheel him back to his room.

The day's events had used up what little energy reserves Carlos had banked, and now as his adrenaline dissipated, he grew exhausted from the unexpected turn of events. "Whadya know—Juan is awake." *Now what?*

By night, Carlos entered a land filled with images of dark, broken picture-tiles, populated with composite places and people. He tossed and turned, straining to free his leg in the blackness, water washing over him. Eerie dreams, buried so deep in a subconscious cavern, they might as well have sunk fathoms below the surface of a turbulent sea, never to return.

Anxious and lonely, he was up and gone before Marta could come to open the blinds. He shielded his eyes in the crass fluorescent hallway, then wheeled through the dead quiet of pre-dawn to Juan's door.

The man was lying on his side facing the window when Carlos arrived. The window through which daybreak had yet to efface the void. *Juan's window to the world and a new life.*

On a blank slate devoid of instructions, Carlos observed Juan Doe design his rebirth, on this his first sunrise.

"Good morning, Juan," Carlos said in a low tone. He waited for Juan to acknowledge him before wheeling himself into the room.

Juan turned to him with a distant stare. "Hello..."

"Carlos."

"Thank you. Hello, Carlos."

He wheeled up to the bed. "What are you doing up so early?"

"I've been up most of the night. I'm afraid to sleep." Juan sniffled as tears stained his cheek.

"Hey, mijo, it's going to be okay." Carlos gently cradled his hand. "You're alive. You woke up. But there's no doubt that you've had your fair share of beauty sleep. I know—I was here."

"Why *are* you here...Carlos?"

"We—you and me, that is—were found in a bay the morning after some tropical storm. We were both unconscious." He sighed. "We're lucky they found us, Juan."

"What happened to us?"

"Hmm, that's the great mystery of the universe right now."

"Do you have a mirror?" Juan asked.

"There's one in that little drawer in your bed table. I'll get it for you." He lifted the top of the tray table vanity combo and pulled out the small handheld mirror. He placed it in Juan's hand, and wrapped his fingers around the stem. Carlos strained to reach the string that turned on the light. "Ugh," he groaned, expelling the pain.

Juan held the mirror while staring at Carlos, then, slowly his eyes drifted front and center. He stared at himself blankly, then delicately ran his fingertips over the scars on his face. He laid the mirror in his lap and turned to Carlos. "I can barely feel it when I touch my face."

"You had reconstructive surgery by that nice older doctor you met—Dr. Cisneros. We're really lucky he's our doctor. He's the best on the base."

"Base?"

"We're at the VA Hospital, amigo. They treat Navy personnel."

"I'm in the Navy?"

"I don't know, Juan. I didn't even remember I was Navy until I woke up and they told me. I remember now, though. If it makes you feel any better, I've lost a lot of my memory, too. But a little has already come back. So what do you think? Did the doc patch you up good?"

"I don't know, Carlos." Each time Juan said "Carlos," it rolled more readily from his lips. "I don't recognize me."

"I don't recognize you either, Juan."

"What if this isn't what I really looked like before? How will I know who I am?"

He pondered the question. "Do you have any idea how much people pay for plastic surgery in San Francisco? Wait. How do I know that? Forget it, forget it. Juan, what if this face is a vast improvement over the other one? Heh? Huh? You didn't think about that, did you, my friend?"

Juan chuckled. "I guess there's a lot I need to think about. If only this fog in my head would lift."

"Aye, mijo, I know *exactly* what you mean. I felt that way too for the first few days after I woke up. You, my friend, were out way longer than I was."

"Carlos, I was dreaming of food. I know I miss the smell of coffee, and pancakes sound really good for some reason."

"I figured you for the pancakes type. Say no more, Juan. It's still very early and I got connections down in the mess… you know, the kitchen. Get ready. I'm going to make sure they bring you a feast!"

Carlos wheeled himself to the door and turned to look at Juan. "I'm glad you're awake, Juan. Really glad."

"I'm so grateful that you're here, Carlos. The only thing I'm sure of is that I can't do this alone."

"That makes two of us."

CHAPTER TWENTY

Tawny and Kate met for breakfast again at a sidewalk café in San Juan.

"What a perfect day," Kate sighed. "I swear that the ocean and the sky are competing for the truest shade of blue."

"The morning sun feels so warm on my back," said Tawny.

"Is that good?"

Tawny laughed. "I live in San Francisco, too. What do *you* think?"

"I think that was a waste of time talking to the local authorities yesterday, don't you?" Kate took a sip of coffee.

Tawny's gaze landed in Kate's Persian-blue eyes. *I think your eyes win the competition for the truest shade of blue.* "I don't know what to think. So far, they've confirmed four unaccounted-for passengers. The one they found in the ocean wasn't Carlos or Dick Peak for that matter. But, if Carlos isn't one of the above, and people are still missing, what the hell happened to him and Peak? Did they just wash out to sea?" The gravity of Tawny's own words sunk her. "Oh my God—I didn't just say that!"

Kate reached across the table and touched her hand. "Are…are you okay?"

"Whew." Tawny fanned herself with her menu. "I panic at the inference that Carlos is gone."

"Tawny, we're getting in that car right after breakfast and we're driving up to Mayaguez. I managed to find the other Carlos Benitez that was on the flight."

"How?"

"The manifest."

Tawny slumped in her chair. "What good will that do?"

"Think about it. Even if he's not your Carlos, he may know something we don't. And if we don't ask questions, how will we ever find out? You already know that—you're the reporter."

"Stop trying to cheer me up. Besides, do you really want me to tag along?"

"Tag along? I feel like that's what I'm doing to you. Tawny, finding you was meant to be. Before we met, I didn't have the faintest idea how I was going to find out what really happened to your friend, the hero of this tale."

Tawny smiled. "Me either. I took a lot of grief from my friends for coming down here. Meeting you makes me believe that coincidence is God's way of remaining anonymous."

"I can hardly believe we've just met. In some ways I feel as if I've known you for a long time. Besides, you'll have to drive. No way I can shift gears yet for that distance wearing this." She held up her splinted wrist.

Tawny smiled. Looks like I'll be your right-hand gal today."

So beautiful. This drive to Mayaguez could have been perfect had it been our honeymoon, you damn green-haired ghost! Tawny pulled over at a vista, took a deep breath and exhaled the thought. She turned off the Jeep and glanced over at Kate. "As much as I adore the California coastline, this turquoise Caribbean is intoxicating, isn't it?" She drank in the panorama of the sapphire bay below. Downing it like a shot of solace in too small a glass, she let it spill all over her.

"By the time this is over, Tawny, do you think we'll stay friends?"

"I would like that, Kate. Maybe one day we'll have the luxury of getting to know one another outside of a mad chase for the truth about the most awful situation."

"Maybe we could start now. My little story is easy to follow. One night I returned home unexpectedly when we had a flight cancellation due to fog. I found my squeeze in bed with my best gal pal, and ever since, I've been on sabbatical from relationships *and* gal pals."

"Eew, nasty. I'm so sorry."

"Tell me you would never do that to me, Tawny."

Tawny placed a reassuring hand on Kate's forearm. "I'm a pretty safe bet…I'm gay."

"Really?" Kate said in a disbelieving tone.

"Please don't insult me by saying I don't look gay."

"Well, you don't."

"Honey, this is what gay looks like." Tawny winked.

Kate laughed. "So…you must be what, a lipstick lesbian?"

"Impossible. I'm not from the Isle of Lesbos nor can I locate it on a map. But if it's a label you need, how about lipstick-gym-queen girl—or femme top. She-stud?" She paused. "High-heeled tomboy?"

"I haven't a clue what any of that means."

"Me either. *Gay chick* works for me."

They shared a laugh.

"Does it matter what any of us are, Tawny? I mean, everyone's *something*."

"That's profoundly vague." She yawned and stretched the kink from her neck and stared at the panorama of water and foliage.

"You're a real lifesaver."

"If that were true, Carlos would be with us right now."

"Are you always this hard on yourself?"

Tawny nodded. "Yep, pretty much."

"So, what about you? What's your story?" Kate asked.

"The other woman wasn't my friend, but it was pretty much the same scene except I didn't walk in on them. Chloe——that's my ex——cheated, and then lied about it—for months." She groaned. "I don't know what offends my sensibilities more, a cheat or a liar. Pathetic right? That an investigative reporter could be so clueless?"

"Charming choice but a trick statement."

"How so?"

"Cheating, lying, it's all the same thing."

Tawny nodded and glanced at Kate's mischievous grin. She cranked up the Jeep and headed down toward Mayaguez.

Steeped in Spanish colonial history, the word, *Mayaguez*, Land of Clear Waters, was the one remnant of the indigenous peoples. Now a bustling mango-rich town, Tawny slowed the car when they drove around the Spanish-style *Plaza Colon* and its ever-present cathedral, *Nuestra Señora de la Candelaria*. The ornate pink building on the corner of the square with the arched second-floor windows and doors caught Tawny's eye as she passed it. Pigeons rested on the statue of Christopher Columbus, whose left arm stretched out to welcome them. Tawny took in the large human sculptures with the setting of City Hall behind them.

"It sure is a pretty town, isn't it?" Kate handed Tawny a slice of the mango she had bought from the street vendor they'd asked for directions, and then she called out the turns to get to *Casa* Benitez.

"I think this is it on the right," she said, a few minutes later.

Tawny parked and stood behind her when she knocked on the door.

"Hang in there, Tawny," Kate said a second before the woman with the neck brace answered the door. Kate exchanged some words with her in Spanish, and the lady smiled and gently hugged her.

"It's the woman from Coach," she said to Tawny. "Come, she's invited us in."

The man sitting in the parlor was not Tawny's Carlos. "Ah, señorita," he said to Kate. "I am happy to see that you are all right."

"Señor and Señora Benitez, I'm relieved you both made it through that terrible ordeal. This is Tawny, a friend of the other Carlos Benitez that was on the flight. Unfortunately, he was not as lucky, and we're trying to find out what happened to him."

"Aah, sí," the Benitezes said in reverent unison.

"Your friend," Mr. Benitez began, "was a very brave man. If it wasn't for him, I wouldn't be here. He pulled me out of the airplane."

Tawny still couldn't conjure Creama, out of drag, acting heroic. *Was there a whole other side of him that I never knew about?*

"Señor Benitez," said Kate, "what happened where you were treated?"

"They treated me for some cuts and bruises, and the doctor told me I had a mild concussion. My wife had sprained her leg and neck so they took X-rays and kept us overnight. Then, the officials interviewed us in San Juan and we were released the next afternoon."

Tawny sighed with a heavy heart. "Nothing unusual about that," she said, standing poised to leave.

"That was all, señor?" Kate said.

Mr. Benitez rubbed his cheek. "Actually, no. Some official kept asking me where I was stationed in the Navy."

"The Navy?" Tawny repeated.

"Sí, sí, the Navy. I kept telling him that I never served in the Navy, but he insisted that I did. I remember thinking, 'Is this guy trying to start a fight about Vieques and the Navy bomb exercises that people protested?' So I told him we would all like to see the Navy pollution stop, and then he calmed down. Señorita Tawny, was your Carlos Benitez in the Navy?"

"No."

"The Navy," Kate said. "Did you tell this to anyone during your interviews?"

"No, because I figured they had me confused with someone else."

"I wouldn't be surprised," added Mrs. Benitez. "Everyone was confused—about everything. So many people and so much going on! I was in shock myself."

"I didn't think much about the Navy thing until I started getting telephone calls from people asking me crazy questions like, where in New Jork did I live. I never lived in New Jork."

"New Jork, uh, York? *My* Carlos is from New York."

"Señor," said Kate, "I know this is an odd request, but would you trust me with some personal information like your date of birth and anything else that might help us to distinguish your records from the other Carlos Benitez? We're working very hard to find this man, and I promise you that anything you share will stay between us."

"That's the least I could do," he replied. "Especially for *that* man."

Tawny tried to think of something to ask, but Kate was doing fine on her own.

"That man? You mean, that hero," added Mrs. Benitez.

Tawny sat and politely watched Mrs. Benitez jot some notes on a piece of paper while she spoke about her ordeal. She handed the paper to Kate and then turned to Tawny. "Señorita, I'm sorry we can't help you more. I hope you find your Carlos. Tell me, were you to become Señora Benitez also?" She gave Tawny a warm, almost familial grin.

"No," Tawny laughed. "He is…or was, my best friend. *Muchisimas gracias* for all your help. I wish you both a full recovery." She smiled before she turned and followed Kate out the door.

The heaviness of the Benitez's wooden door closing behind her echoed her sentiment of every roadblock she had hit so far. It haunted her all the way back to the Plaza Colon. She had yet to speak another word.

"Are you still breathing?" asked Kate. "Why so quiet?"

"I'm sorry, but I'm beyond disappointed." They neared the Mayaguez Resort, the glitziest place in town. "Though my Carlos is from New York, I can just see the drag queen diva incarnate of Cher in the Navy! Yeah, right."

"Drag queen?" Kate said.

"Oh…" She bit her lip and pulled over to the side of the road. "I suppose it's time I told you that Carlos Armando Jose Benitez's alter ego is none other than the legendary San Francisco Puerto Rican Drag Queen Diva Extraordinaire, Miss Creama LaCroppe—spelled with two 'p's" and an 'e'."

"What? Get outta here! Are you serious? I've seen Creama LaCroppe's show! She's amazing." Kate shook her head. "That guy *couldn't* have been a drag queen. *Could he*?"

"What do you mean? Of course it was Carlos on that plane."

"But...but you didn't see *this* guy in action. He was—well—downright macho."

"That's the part I'm having a *very* hard time visualizing. Every time you recount his actions, I'm floored by it. Stunned, actually. Hey, are you hungry? I could use something to eat."

"I could use a drink! Come on, Tawny. Park the car. This is a great place for lunch."

Parched and hot, Tawny and Kate entered the Mayaguez Resort's lobby. "See about a table while I grab a newspaper, Kate."

"Okay, grab a pack of gum for me? Anything peppermint."

She crossed the lobby and entered the hotel's gift shop. She was bending down and reaching for a newspaper when the now familiar voice came from behind. "Ms. Beige," the man said.

"Oh!" The newspaper dropped to the floor as Tawny stood and whipped around. "Your stealth greetings are beginning to piss me off, Mr. Castilano."

"I really wish you wouldn't be so formal, Tawny. Please, call me Jimmy." He picked up the paper and handed it to her.

"How did you find me?"

"I just happened to be in town."

"Yeah, right. Do you think all women are that dumb—or only me?"

He smiled. "Who's your friend? She's cute."

"Mr. Castilano..."

He pointed his finger at her. "Hey."

"Fine. Jimmy. She's Miss None-of-Your-Business, and you still haven't answered my question. How did you find me?"

"I followed you."

"What? From where? How did I not see you?"

"I have a local guy driving me around. He did some checking, found out you and your friend were headed this way, and batta-boom, we caught you comin' into town."

She could tell by the way he crisped his collar that he was proud of himself. "Well, I honestly don't know why you're following me. Now, if you'll excuse me."

"Wait a minute, Tawny. Since we're both here, maybe we could join forces and find out what happened to your friend and the congressman."

She pierced him with her stare. "You and I. Us?" she scoffed. "You have some sense of humor and a lot of nerve following me." She paid and left the gift shop, looking for Kate, with Jimmy following her.

"Tawny, I was wondering where you were..." Kate began.

She flicked her head to indicate Jimmy's presence behind her. "This is Congressman Peak's..." she turned to Jimmy, "what exactly are you?"

"Hello, ma'am, nice to meet you." He shot Tawny a disapproving glance. "My name is Jimmy Castilano, and I'm Mr. Peak's congressional aide and personal assistant."

"Since the congressman is among the missing," Tawny began, "Mr. Castilano thinks it wouldn't be a complete, total, and utter disaster for him to join us in our search." She saw Jimmy's disapproving glance and raised him a glare. "I think he's sadly mistaken."

The insult seemed to roll off Jimmy's back. "Tawny, you're at the El Dorado, right?"

"You should know since you've been following me."

"I didn't intend to disrupt your lunch. I'll be in touch when you get back to San Juan. I think you should consider my offer," he said before he left.

"What was that about, Tawny? He's really Congressman Peak's assistant?"

"Poster-thug of the religious right is more like it. Ugh, I loathe Peak, and by proxy anyone connected to him."

"What does he want with you, and how did he know you were here?"

"What he wants is a long story. I can't believe he followed me."

"That's a little creepy, don't you think?"

"A *little* creepy?"

CHAPTER TWENTY-ONE

Carlos sat up on the exam table and wiggled his toes with newfound freedom. "Hey, Doc, this cast is the snazziest one yet."

"I thought you'd like it." Dr. Cisneros grinned while making a notation in Carlos's chart. "While it's called a walking cast, if you overdo it, I'll put you back in the other one."

"Aye, aye, sir."

Cisneros pocketed his pen and looked up. "Except for orthopedic follow-ups, my job here is done. You're almost ready to ship out to a rehabilitation facility—someplace more homelike——where you can become seaworthy again. In addition to administering physical therapy, they're also equipped to provide in-depth psychological therapy."

Carlos lowered his gaze then looked up at the doctor. "Does that work? Will it help me remember?"

"I've heard good things about the work they're doing with that, and it's certainly worth a try. The sooner you get the proper care, the better."

"What about Juan, Doc?"

"He'll be processed as indigent by the civilian social workers, and if there's a bed, they'll admit him to a public facility."

"And if there are no beds available, what will happen to him?"

Dr. Cisneros remained silent.

"You mean I should leave him behind?"

"Yes. He has a long road ahead of him, much longer than yours, and you need to focus on *your* recuperation. You've already done more for Juan than you know."

"Oh, I don't think I can do that—leave him." He maneuvered with his splinted wrist and buttoned his shirt.

"Carlos, your loyalty is commendable but it's time for you to take care of yourself."

He hopped off the examination table and onto his good leg. Dr. Cisneros handed him his crutches.

"No," Carlos said emphatically.

"Excuse me?"

"No, sir. No, I'm not abandoning Juan. If I leave, he leaves with me. Besides, what if he's the key to my remembering?"

"Are you disobeying an order, Lieutenant?"

"Yessir, I suppose this is mutiny minus the Bounty."

The doctor sighed. "All right, I'll see what I can do."

"Thank you, and not only for this, Doc. Honestly, I know I wouldn't be alive if it hadn't been for you."

"I'm not promising anything. I just said I'd try."

"Understood, sir."

On his way back to the ward, Carlos stopped for his usual afternoon visit with Juan. His heart pounded at the sight of an empty room. He pivoted on the heel of the walking cast and hobbled straight-legged down the hall as fast as he could—swinging forward on his crutches. At the end of the corridor, he halted and stared through the glass doors. The tableau before him, though pristine in its orderliness, sustained the breezes of its tropical heritage. Fronds swayed, flowers swelled beneath the sun, and a few people milled about.

Carlos zeroed in on the broken man across the garden who sat alone on the oversize bench under the sweeping shade tree. Thin, pale, and hunched over, Juan appeared frail to him behind the long black hair. Carlos limped toward him, watching Juan stroke the patchy stubble around his facial scars. "Mind if I sit down?"

Juan shook his head.

"It's good to see you out here in the fresh air." Carlos leaned awkwardly in his new cast and sat next to him.

Juan's eyes drifted to him. "Why did you rescue me?"

"I don't know any more than I've already told you, Juan."

"I've been driving myself crazy for days trying to remember. Forget remembering everything. I'd settle for remembering *anything*. I want to know what I like and what I don't. I don't even know what my favorite color is."

"Juan, look around you. Pick one!"

He stared out at the water and thought for a moment. "Blue. It's definitely blue."

Carlos chuckled. "As of today, my friend, blue is your favorite color."

"What if my favorite color really isn't blue?"

"Whatever your favorite color used to be, it's literally history. Blue is your favorite color right here, right now. Who knows? Tomorrow it could be green."

"If you say so, Carlos. But—but I don't think green could ever be my favorite color." He sighed. "I want my memory back!"

"Be careful what you wish for, Juan. You need to give it more time. We both do." He patted Juan on the shoulder. "How do you feel?"

"Stronger today, but I still can't eat very much, and I have to be careful with the sun until my scars heal more."

Carlos looked around and leaned in. "If I could get us into a rehab together, would you go?"

"Why?"

"Dr. Cisneros said he wants to transfer me out soon, and—"

"Carlos, you can't! You're the only friend I have and maybe my one chance to find out who I am." Juan cowered like a little boy, his pale knuckles clutching the bench. "Don't leave me."

"Don't worry, Juan. Calm down."

Juan's fearful gaze distracted from and overshadowed the beauty Carlos witnessed surrounding them. "Hey. Look at me. Juan. Hey!"

Juan stared at him.

"I'll take care of it, mijo, okay? I've got your back."

"But how will you do that?"

He exhaled hard. "Good question."

After dinner, Carlos and Juan spent the evening playing Five-card stud in Juan's room.

Carlos shuffled the deck. "Juan, it's pretty clear to me that you were once very good at *this*. Do you realize how many hands you've won? For a grand total of..." Carlos pointed to Juan's bounty and his lips moved as he counted. "Ten grapes, twelve orange sections, a banana, and a papaya. I can't believe you have all of my fruit! Man, all I have left are two measly slices of pineapple for an ante and a bet."

"I share," Juan said. He picked up the remote control and changed the channel to the news. "Carlos, I keep hearing about that plane crash you had mentioned after I woke up. Didn't you tell me the Navy checked to see if we were on that plane?"

Carlos dealt the hand. "Yeah, but they said we weren't because we had no life vests—and we were found too far away. It's strange, though. Last night on the news, I thought I heard my name but then they interviewed a survivor, some *Puerto Riqueno* with the same name as me. Dr. Cisneros said they're still investigating, but in case you didn't know, the Navy is a bit of hurry-up-and-wait."

Juan tapped his cards together at the edge, and fanned them out staring at the hand he'd been dealt. "I like this game you taught me. Poker, right?"

"Yes, and you play it a little too well."

Juan swiped the long black wave out of his eyes and glanced up at the TV. "Who is that congressman they keep talking about?"

Carlos rearranged his hand. "He's a religious fanatic." He paused. "Why do I know that! It's not like I've had much success with any micro particle of memory I actually *want* to remember."

Juan met his eye. "Who knew that memories could turn to dust?"

"I can kind of remember that congressman guy, and I know I can't stomach him."

Juan looked up at the TV when Carlos lowered the volume.

"Wait," said Juan, laying his cards on the table. "Turn it up. I'd like to hear this."

"Speak of the *devil.* They're airing Dick Peak's makeshift memorial." He scoffed.

"No need for sarcasm, Carlos. However you felt about him, a life was lost."

"Who are you, my freaking mother?"

The station cut to file tapes of the Coast Guard Search-and-Rescue boats. "The young congressman from California is presumed to be dead and lost at sea, in the literal wake of the Trans Air Flight 44 crash."

Carlos placed his cards on the table and turned his attention to the TV. The report traced the congressman's recent rise to fame through social conservatism and controversy, and it ended with a patriotic testimonial from a televangelist with a glued-in-place bad comb-over and a polyester smile.

"Hey, Carlos, can I ask you something?"

"Sure."

"Why do you think people liked that Peak guy? From everything I've heard, it's no mystery why *you* don't like him. I don't like him either."

"Beats me, Juan."

Juan picked up his cards and Carlos followed suit. "I wonder what he was so scared of."

"What do you mean?"

"I don't want to be disrespectful to the dead, but where does a guy like that come off telling everybody else the way they should live and what they should believe?" He thought for a moment. "Have you ever heard the phrase, 'Thou who doth protest too much?'"

"Bravo, Juan. You've remembered something."

"I'll bet he was hiding from something. America is not a theocracy, you know?"

Carlos's eyes opened wide. "Wow, Juan. That's pretty deep shit for a guy who doesn't know his name or his favorite color." He smiled. "Besides, the religious right isn't called that because they're conservative. They're called that because they insist that everybody else is wrong."

Juan sighed. "I'm pretty sure I don't like self-righteous people—and yes, I know what that means." Juan traded for two cards from the deck and rearranged his new hand. "Raise you your last slice of pineapple."

"I'm with you. Don't get me started on self-righteous bitches." Carlos ate the pineapple slice and tossed his cards onto the table. "Sorry, Juan, seems I ate the ante *and* the wager. I'm done for the day. Buenos nachos, pal. See you *mañana*." He reached for his crutches and grunted when he stood.

Juan waited until he reached the doorway. "Carlos, catch!" Juan tossed him the papaya.

Carlos limped down the corridor under the crass fluorescent lights, entered his room, and pushed the door closed with a crutch. He was lying down when the night nurse entered.

"Evening, sir. I was asked to bring you your personal effects since you'll be shipping out soon." She placed the small box on the bed.

"I have personal effects?"

"Don't get too excited, Lieutenant. There's not much there. G'night."

He stared at the box for several minutes, wondering if he really *wanted* to know what was inside. What if the key to his past turned out to be an ominous vision of his future? What if he found something upsetting? Or unexpected?

Everything is unexpected! He tilted the bed until he was upright and tentatively peeled back the flaps of the lid as though the carton was a Jack-in-the-Box, already primed to spring out at him—maybe to punch him in the nose. One item at a time, he would examine the sparse remnants in the small box, searching for who he might have been. Objects, he thought, that were once important enough to be on his person.

He reached in. The gold chain he draped over his fingers felt so familiar, and at the end of it hung a crucifix befitting a person much smaller than him. Cradling it gently in his palm, he let the chain slip through his fingers. "Thanks, Mama," he said, tilting his head down to put on the necklace. "You've been gone a long time, and that's one memory I wish I *didn't* have." In that moment, he wiped away the tears of a little boy.

The next item he fished out was a belt. He twisted it and let it drop onto the bed next to his good leg. "What kind of belt is that?" Something else rolled around in the box when he picked it up to place it on the table. "A bullet shell?" Carlos studied it briefly and tossed it into his drawer. Then he leaned back and picked up the belt, drew it to his nose, flinching from the scent of brine that sent a bilious wave of nausea rumbling through his abdomen, up into his stomach and then his esophagus.

"*Mierda*. That sucked." When he sat up to roll the belt and drop it into the box, he felt the thickness in the middle that made it hard to coil. He pulled at the tight seam along the inside edge. The first bill came out alone; the second bill was stuck to several others. Behind that bill were layers of hundred-dollar bills. "Oh my god, look at all this money!" He broke a sweat and leaned back onto his pillow, his head swirling from the sight.

He stashed the bills back inside the belt without counting them and stuffed the belt back inside the box. "Did I rob a bank?" His right eye twitched. In a nanosecond he had a flashback—heard the roar of a crowd—saw bright blue stage light anointing Goddess Cher. Then, in another flashback—money—on that very stage.

"What the hell?"

Is that Cher? No, it's a drag queen dressed in a gown and wig. It's a performer imitating Cher, and the audience is throwing money at her feet.

Tips. "That money is her tips!" Carlos scrunched his forehead to think harder. "Tips? Whose tips? Who is '*she*'? No. This is too much money to be tips." *Wait! I know a drag queen? No. No way. I'm a US Naval Officer. Where would I know a drag queen from?*

He ripped the little mirror out of his drawer and stroked his beard like a professor might do, then tried to decipher the code out loud. His head sunk back into his pillow. "I'm an officer in the US Navy… who…who knows a drag queen? No, I must be confusing myself with someone else." He dropped the mirror onto the bed. "Goddamn jigsaw puzzle!" He pulled the pillow over his head and fell into a sleep that rivaled his coma.

CHAPTER TWENTY-TWO

While the ride back to San Juan from Mayaguez seemed shorter than the trip to get there, the oppressive humidity had permeated every pore in Tawny's skin, making it feel like wet paste. The instant her hotel room door closed behind her, she peeled off her clothing. Under the immediate stream of her shower, she rinsed off the day and her upset. Not knowing Carlos's fate stuck to her like the paste no matter how hard she scrubbed.

Wrapped in the hotel's lush terry robe, she lay back on the bed and returned Larry's call while waiting for room service.

"I'm so glad to hear from you," Larry said when he answered. "How're you doing?"

She sighed into the receiver. "My emotions are spinning like a gyroscope. I can't sleep, I'm talked out, and I've had a long, hot day of dead ends." She nestled against her pillow. "I feel like a pinball that keeps bouncing between two flippers, avoiding going down the chute but not really scoring any points. What's new there?"

"No surprise to me that you're burning out." He paused. "I saw Andy today and he's coming along. He told me that he was attacked while trying to verify the facts of a big, and I'm talking *big* story."

"A story about Dick Peak?"

"Not just any old story, baby. Someone is alleging that Peak was involved in illegal corporate activities. There's probably serious and credible implication here—not that it matters for Dick Peak. He's been officially pronounced dead."

"I didn't know that; I haven't seen the news today. Did you ask Andy who he was supposed to meet when he got mugged?"

"He never found out. Someone got to him before his contact showed."

"This doesn't make sense, Larry. Seriously, why risk that when you're at the top of your game and in the public eye? Why would he do that?"

"Why would he do that?" Larry asked rhetorically. "Can you say campaign money? Lobbyists? Religious hypocrisy? Take your pick."

Tawny rolled over. "I'm on overload. At this moment, I don't even care."

"Yeah, right."

"I don't. I only want to know what happened to Creama."

"You need to eat, don't you?"

"Is my low blood sugar showing?"

"Knowing you, I'd go with guilt."

"You're right. I'm a big gooey blob of guilt."

He paused. "Get some food and sleep. Things will look brighter afterward. Has Chloe been in touch?"

"I've only gotten as far as your message today, but I haven't spoken with her. Why?"

"She called earlier. Told me to tell you to take her calls."

"I've been avoiding her, but we all need to be on the same page right now. Chances are she'll have the most accurate information sooner than we will."

"Call me when you can?"

"Sure, Larry. Thanks for checking on me."

He chuckled softly. "Where else would I be? You're my kitten. I know you're down there being your relentless self, but I wish you weren't doing this alone."

"I'm not, exactly. I met one of the crew from the flight, and *she's very…*"

"*She*? I haven't heard you say 'she' with that inflection in a long time."

"I'm here to find out what happened to Creama and that's all. As for Kate, she's straight. Cute, but hetero. I promise I'll update you as soon as I know anything. And, Larry, watch yourself. Someone may know your connection to Andy."

"Ain't it ironic that Chloe would turn out to be the one person we *can* trust?"

Tawny turned toward the knock on her door. "Hey, my room service is here. Talk to you soon." She hung up and gathered her robe. "That sure was quick," she said flinging open the door.

"Surprise!" said Kate.

Tawny cinched the thick terry robe even tighter and ran her fingers through her wet non-hairdo. "Kate!"

"I hope it's okay that I'm here." The flight attendant leaned against the jamb. "Would you mind some company?" She paused. "I really don't want to be alone tonight."

Tawny sighed and then smiled. "Come on in."

Early the following morning, the peal of the phone pierced Tawny's sleep, and woke her at the end of what would be KBCH's night shift.

"Hello," she mumbled.

"Oh, good. Finally."

"Chloe?"

"Have you forgotten my voice already?"

Tawny didn't answer.

"I wasn't able to confirm it but there's speculation that your contact Andy was chasing down a Dick Peak story when he was attacked. I take it you've heard the news that Peak was pronounced?"

"Yeah, Larry called and told me both of those things last night."

"The word right now is that Peak's henchman, a guy named…" Tawny heard Chloe shuffle some papers.

"Jimmy Castilano?" she offered.

"Yeah, that's right. Anyhow, rumor has it he beat up Andy as a warning to stay away from the congressman."

"No."

"No, what?"

"He didn't do it."

"How do *you* know?"

"I have good reason to believe that Mr. Castilano might be looking over his shoulder as well." Tawny stroked back her hair.

"What makes you think *that*?" Chloe's words popped like a balloon.

"He told me so."

"You know this thug?"

"Let's just say we've crossed paths. He's down here doing the same thing I am—looking for answers." She yawned again.

"Tawny, obviously news is still in your blood, but I should be there with you. It's dangerous for you to be doing this alone."

"Good morning," Kate called out as she exited the bathroom.

Chloe scoffed. "Wow, really Tawny? Well, I hope you find time to look for Creama."

"That's all I've done!" Tawny protested. "Wait a second, I really don't care what you think."

Click.

She scoffed at the phone when Chloe hung up on her. She placed the handset back in its cradle and glanced over at Kate, who stood watching her from across the room.

"Everything okay?" Kate's smile was fresh, untainted by bad energy phone calls or strips of green hair. "Thanks for letting me stay over."

"Sure. But next time, you get the sofa bed." She stretched against the kink in her neck. "I'm ordering coffee to the room. Would you like something to eat?"

"Coffee's fine. And after that?"

"I'm going to look for Carlos."

"Can I…?"

She smiled. "You have to ask?" She pulled her list from her purse. "Our first stop today is the US Coast Guard."

CHAPTER TWENTY-THREE

"You can lean on my wheelchair, Juan, but don't send me flying down the hall."

"Okay. I saw Nurse Combs and told him we're ready." Juan steered Carlos out to the garden, stopped, and leaned forward to sniff the white rosebush. "I'll miss these beautiful flowers. I think we should wait here until they transport us to the rehab."

"Fine." Carlos fidgeted in his chair. "I know it sounds weird but I'm gonna miss this place. I'll miss the ocean." He panned the landscape and pointed to the west wall. "And the bougainvillea and the sunsets that set them on fire. Sometimes they look like hot pink boas. Maybe they should rename them *boa*gainvillea."

Juan remained silent. Carlos looked over his shoulder. "A boa, Juan. It's a joke."

"Oh. What's a boa?"

"I can't believe a hip guy like you doesn't know what a boa is. It's a long feathery scarf that strippers and performers wrap around their necks and shoulders."

"Maybe you could show me a picture of one sometime. Hey, is this new place going to help us remember?"

Carlos spun his wheelchair around. "Not only that, they're going to help us get strong again."

"How do I pay for it?" Juan asked innocently.

"Don't you worry, Juan, I got it all worked out."

"You're the best friend a guy could have." He wheeled Carlos into the shade. "Carlos?"

"Yeah."

"I don't think my name is Juan," he said apologetically.

He suppressed a grin. "What makes you say so?"

"I don't have an accent like yours, and gee, it's just not me. I think I look more like a...like a Guillermo or a Ricardo maybe."

"Don't sweat it, Juan. Lots of people have an identity crisis at some time or another. But don't confuse my accent—it's New York Puerto Rican."

"What's an identity crisis?"

"At some point, all smart people question who they are. From something as simple as 'does my name really suit me?' to questions about their life's purpose, or even their gender. In an effort to stand out, people are always looking to fit in."

Juan raised his eyebrows.

"You okay?"

"Yes, I think so. In a strange way, it's all very familiar."

"What is?"

"Purpose. Gender. You know...fitting in."

"There's this performer named RuPaul who says, 'We're all born naked, the rest is drag. Any questions?' Pretty cool, huh?"

Carlos looked up when Nurse Combs came through the door. "Lieutenant. Juan," he said. "I suppose this is goodbye. Don't take this the wrong way, fellas, but I've never been happier to see anyone discharged. But it'll be pretty boring around here without you."

"Lieutenant?" said Carlos. "I thought I told you to stop calling me names." He extended his healed arm. "Check it out, Manny." He bent his arm and twisted it back and forth.

"Looking strong, sir." Nurse Manny smiled and shook Carlos's healing hand. "It's been a real pleasure. You kicked up some dust around here and inspired a few of us along the way, Lieutenant." He stood tall and saluted.

Carlos saluted back. "You know what we say in the Navy. No one likes to fight, but someone has to know how. Manny, are you sure this place we're goin' is the best one for me and Juan?"

"Yessir! It's the best around, and in that part of San Juan you'll recuperate faster."

"How?" asked Juan.

The nurse laughed. "You'll have incentive. There's a whole world of fun to be had right outside your door, whenever you're ready for it. A couple of cool guys like you should have no trouble finding the action."

"Juan," Carlos said, "did you remember to thank the staff for getting you into the rehab and for their collection to foot part of the bill?"

"Thank you," said Juan. "Thank everyone for me, Manny."

"We had thanks enough at your going away party." Nurse Combs patted Juan on the shoulder. "Seeing you conscious and on your feet is good enough for me." He held Juan's gaze. "You've got this, Juan."

Juan grabbed him and hugged him.

The orderly came through the doors with a wheelchair and parked it in front of Juan. "Hospital policy. Free ride out the door, courtesy of the US Navy."

He took a long last look around and then eased into the wheelchair. "I'm glad you're with me, Carlos. I'm a little scared. This is the only home I know."

"Don't worry," said Carlos. "If we do the right thing, the right thing is bound to happen eventually."

"What is the right thing?"

"I have a feeling we're about to find out, Dorothy."

"Who's Dorothy?" Juan asked, wheeling along next to Carlos.

"Judy Garland from the *Wizard of Oz*? 'Somewhere Over the Rainbow'?"

"Sorry," Juan apologized.

"You don't know the legendary Judy Garland?"

"Is she good?"

"Judy was wondrous."

Riding in the van through the crowded streets of San Juan, Carlos's heart sped up. At times his hands became clammy, even in the air-conditioned van. But Manny had said it wasn't too long a ride and that he and Juan would be at Santa Clara Rehabilitation Center in no time at all.

Waves of unknowns rumbled in his belly like a bowl of rotten seawater. Down some dusty mental corridor, with cobwebs clinging to his gray matter, he knew there were questions that had to be answered, and they had to be answered by *him*. Questions about who he had been and was he any different now? Soon, he would be walking and moving better, and he could investigate to find the missing pieces. He glanced over at Juan who contentedly stared out the window, daring life to present itself for the first time. *Why am I so attached to him?*

The aide placed his radio back in the cradle and turned around. "We're here and they're ready for you, Lieutenant."

Lost in thought, Carlos snapped back to the present when the driver spoke. "Thanks." He hadn't told Juan, but he too, had fears of his own. While he couldn't remember why, he understood that the phrase, "being afraid of the unknown," never had greater meaning for him or higher stakes. This next adventure was about to begin, and Carlos felt the hammer of the starting pistol cocked—in his gut.

"Ready, Lieutenant?" The corpsman guided Carlos out of the van and then Juan helped him into the Santa Clara Rehabilitation Center.

Once checked in, Juan waited for Carlos every step of the way to and from the elevator.

"This place is pretty modern, huh Juan?"

"Yes, and the staff was nice enough to have our apartment ready for us." He inserted the key in the lock, opened the gray door, and stepped through the living room. "Hey, Carlos check this out. We have our own private terrace." Juan pulled back the blinds that partially covered the sliding door. He frowned. "I already miss the bright flowers in the hospital garden." He turned and walked past the dining table into the kitchen with Carlos following close behind. "This fridge is big enough to hold plenty of fruit for you."

Carlos limped to the sofa and sat. "Ah, this is so comfortable. I forgot how good it feels to sit in something other than a wheelchair or hospital chair."

Juan passed back through the living room, on the other side of which was a short hallway that led to the two bedrooms and bathroom. "Which bedroom do I get?" he asked with childlike excitement.

"Whichever one you want."

"This is better than staying at the Conquistador. I'll take the bedroom on the right—no, wait, make that the one on the left."

Carlos hobbled into the hallway and laughed. "You got it, pal. Wait a minute, Juan…What did you say?"

He pointed. "I said I'll take the one on the left."

"No, just before that. You said, 'this is better than the Conquistador.'"

"What's the Conquistador?"

"Beats me. I was about to suggest we stow our gear, but I suppose we'd better buy some gear to stow."

"Right now?"

"Sure, why not?"

They turned toward the knock at the door.

"I'll get it." Juan stepped toward the door and Carlos sat back down.

"Lieutenant Benitez?" asked a woman.

"No. That's him on the sofa."

The young, dark-haired woman entered. "Then you must be Juan. I'm Sonny LaMatina, your Care Coordinator. It's my job to orient you and answer any questions you may have."

"Sonny LaMatina, you have good timing," said Carlos. "Juan and I need to buy some things. You see, we only have what we're wearing, pajamas, toothbrushes, and some disposable grooming items. I need a good razor."

Juan snickered. "As if you'd really shave off that beard."

"Yes, we were apprised of the situation, so I brought you gentlemen each a pair of hospital scrubs and shoes to get you started," Sonny said. "The scrubs will fit over your cast, Lieutenant."

"I only need one shoe, and the scrubs only long enough to go shopping for something more…form-fitting," Carlos added.

Juan giggled.

With the congeniality of an entertainment director on a Disney cruise, Sonny neatly placed two folders on the table and laid the clothing packets next to them.

Carlos stood and held up the tropical blue scrub top to assess the size. "Thanks, you guys are great. Do you know when we'll be evaluated?"

Sonny pulled two sheets of paper from the guest portfolio on the table and read from them. "Lieutenant, you have appointments tomorrow morning with the chiropractor and the orthopedic surgeon for your legs and spine, and a cognitive evaluation will follow. And Mr. Doe, you'll undergo psychological evaluation with Dr. Heiligenschein."

"Dr. Heili-who?"

"The neurologic tests will be scheduled after that. In this portfolio are maps of the neighborhood with listings of local businesses. And since you're considered convalescing, you're free to come and go, but curfew is nine p.m. for now. In the event you can't get back in time, please inform us. You can check in and out at the desk. Meals are served in the dining room adjacent to the lobby and the hours are printed on this page. Is there anything else you'd like to know before your full orientation tomorrow?"

"What about the rest of today?" Juan said.

"What about it, mijo?"

"There's no schedule?"

"No, Juan," Carlos answered. "We're out of the hospital. It's all up to us now."

"Thank you, Miss LaMatina," Juan said politely.

"You're welcome, Juan. If there's anything else you need, call the desk and they'll page me. Otherwise, I'll see you gentlemen in the morning," she said before leaving.

After Sonny left, they both changed in their rooms and met back in the living room.

"Hey Carlos, we look like a couple of twin doctors," Juan laughed. "You look very doctor-y with that beard—you know, smart."

"I am smart—I think. You know, that's the first time I've heard you laugh, Juan."

"It feels good. I must remember to do that more."

"Just say the word. I'm always up for a good laugh. In fact, at the VA I read a holistic medicine journal that said laughing massages your liver."

"So, we want happy massaged livers?"

"I guess so. But right now I could use a happy stomach."

The balmy afternoon breezes barely mustered enough strength to send a ripple across a puddle. Moisture trapped inside Carlos's cast tickled him as it trickled down the sides of his ankle, inside of which metal screws picked at his tibia when he put weight on it. He hobbled along on his crutches, and Juan slowed, patiently keeping Carlos's pace.

"Let's go in here!" Juan already had his hand on the door of the shop with the window display of sexy clothing. He held the door for Carlos and followed him into the small boutique. Carlos watched Juan take in the array of erotic objects.

Juan tentatively approached a display case and stared down at it. "What are those metal rings for?"

Carlos wiped the sweat from his forehead, breathed in the air-conditioning and then pointed Juan away from the cock rings and sex toys.

"Juan," he whispered, "that's…well, they're…Juan, we're in a sex shop."

Juan's stare remained blank.

"Don't tell me you don't know what sex is."

"No…I mean yes—I definitely know what sex is."

"Come on, let's get out of here."

"Why are you so uneasy, Carlos? It's only sex."

"Sounds like you know a little something about this."

Juan stood tall and grinned. "Yes, it does, doesn't it?" He raised his eyebrows. "I hope I'm as good at it as I am at poker." After a long satisfied look around, he started for the door. Just short of the exit, he reached up and let the fluffy feathers slip through his fingers. "Is *this* a boa?"

Carlos laughed. "Yes, *that* is a boa."

"I like it. Maybe…I like it a lot?"

CHAPTER TWENTY-FOUR

Driving past the walls of Old San Juan, Tawny downshifted and turned onto *Calle La Puntilla* where she parked in front of the Coast Guard Station San Juan. The azure bay did little to distract her. She prayed that GANTSEC, the Coast Guard's Greater Antilles Section would be able to tell her something she didn't already know. "Something is bugging me, Kate. Ever since we saw Mr. and Mrs. Benitez yesterday, the Navy thing keeps coming up for me."

"Why?"

"I've been thinking about what I took from Carlos's apartment. I went there to gather identifiers…credit card numbers, pictures and stuff like that. While I was rifling through his desk, a picture of three sailors fell out."

"Who were they?"

"I was so busy searching for important things, I didn't take the time to look. The photo may be in the portfolio I brought with me or it may be on my dining room table. In the latter case, my cat has likely decorated it with a hairball."

"Maybe it's a picture of an old boyfriend or something," said Kate.

"Who knows. Carlos knew all kinds of people. It's probably coincidence about that Navy thing with the other Benitez, don't you think?" she asked as they entered the building.

"May I help you?" asked the clean-shaven coastguardsman who adjusted his District 7 GANTSEC ballcap.

Kate lifted an eyebrow at the young man in uniform. "Hi, I'm Kate Taylor, and I'm trying to find information on the rescue of the Trans Air Flight 44 passengers."

"I'm not at liberty to discuss that, ma'am."

"Forgive me, I'm a crewmember—one of many people who was rescued by your brave unit."

"Oh, why didn't you say so?" The young man smiled proudly and his demeanor softened. "You'd probably like to speak with the Officer In Charge. He was on duty here that night and directly involved with the SAR."

"SAR?" asked Tawny.

"Search-and-Rescue."

"Yes, that would be great if you could arrange for us to meet the Officer in Charge."

"Please wait here." He knocked, waited a moment and then disappeared behind the door with a name plate that read Lieutenant Commander Harvey Swift. He returned a minute later. "Lieutenant Commander Swift would be happy to see you now." He held open the door for the women to enter.

At first glance, Tawny sensed there weren't a lot of civilian women who called on Lieutenant Commander Harvey Swift. Seaworthy and handsome, he fit the uniform well, and his presence was stark and authoritative. Swift's eyes darted between her and Kate, finally coming to rest on Tawny.

He stood. "Please come in, ladies. What can I do for you?" he asked, welcoming them into his orderly office.

"First of all, sir," Kate began, "I'd like to thank you and your crew for rescuing us all from Flight 44. My name is Kate Taylor and I'm a crewmember."

Lieutenant Commander Swift smiled warmly and walked around his desk to greet her, his right hand outstretched in salutation. "It's nice to meet you, Miss Taylor. We don't often get to meet up after the fact with those we rescue. I'm glad to see you're all right."

"Hi, I'm Kate's friend, Tawny. My best friend was also on that flight but he's still unaccounted for."

"I'm sorry to hear that."

"Lieutenant Commander," Kate began, "my friend and I are trying desperately to find out what happened to that passenger."

He shook his head. "Those records have already been shipped off to the District Commander. Please, have a seat." Swift leaned on his desk with his arms crossed. "There was a lot going on that night. We had the cutter, *Southern Storm*, that was responsible for the SAR, a Dolphin Helicopter that transported the emergency medical cases, and the HH-60 helicopter that searched the ocean for those passengers who didn't make it into the lifeboats. Yep, that was quite a night."

"Were there any other rescues made by your people that night? Perhaps passengers who were rescued and whose identities may not have been matched with those from the plane?" Tawny asked.

"Miss, personnel who weren't out at sea were helping to shuffle victims to different facilities around the island. Some of the roads were washed out. In addition to sustaining property damage, the medical centers and hospitals overflowed with people who needed treatment. That caused us to have to transport the crash victims to various locations. So, exactly which rescue would you be talking about?"

Tawny glanced at Kate, at a loss for where to go from there.

Kate picked up the ball. "So, are you saying that with all the different locations the passengers were taken, that it's possible for either someone, or someone's records to have been misplaced?"

"I'm no expert on the policies of civilian hospitals, but if you had been on this end that night, I wouldn't have blamed you for not knowing which end was up. We barely had response time. Luckily, we were able to get to you and your people, Ms. Taylor."

"Is there some kind of master list with all the medical assignments?" asked Kate.

"Yes, but you won't find them here. We try to be accurate in a disaster scenario. I want to reassure you that I personally saw to the follow-up search, but as you know, there were those few who were unfortunate…who were unaccounted for."

"Would you know if a Carlos Benitez was on that list?"

"Benitez." Swift pondered the name. "Wasn't he the one who was thought to be missing, but then he turned up?"

"Actually, there were two men aboard with that name," Kate replied. "One survived. The other one is the man we're trying to locate."

Swift wagged his head. "I'm sorry, I wish I could be more helpful."

"One last thing, Lieutenant Commander. Would it be possible to speak with anyone who was on the radio that night?"

"Off the record?"

"Of course."

Swift picked up his phone and pressed two numbers. He stood and jingled the coins in his pocket while he waited. His eyes brightened when they met Tawny's, and he held her gaze and smiled until he spoke.

"Bill, when is Greene back on duty? Uh-huh, I see. Thanks." Swift hung up the phone and looked at Kate. "You're in luck. Oliver Greene will be on duty here tonight after ten o'clock. He was the radio operator on the *Southern Storm* the night you were rescued. I'll leave permission for him to speak with you. Is there anything else I can do for you?"

"I'm very grateful, Lieutenant Commander," Tawny said. "We've been searching for information everywhere, and you've been more helpful than the last three places combined."

"It's part of the job. Tell me, Miss…I'm sorry I didn't get your last name."

"Beige, Tawny Beige."

"Miss Beige?"

"Yes," Tawny said tentatively.

"My timing is awkward but…would you like to have dinner sometime?"

Tawny raised her eyebrows. "Thank you for the invitation. I'm flattered. Really. Sorry if I gave you the impression that I'm straight… oh, sorry again, is this supposed to be one of those 'Don't ask, Don't tell' situations?"

Kate remained stoic while Swift's jaw dropped and his eyes opened a little too wide to feign indifference.

"Uh no. No, no…the 'don't ask, don't tell thing'…that's done and over. But when that was the rule, it only applied to people actually *in* the armed services." Harvey Swift stepped to his office door and opened it.

"Thank you again and thanks for the dinner invitation," Tawny said.

"I'm so grateful to you and your crew," said Kate when she shook his hand.

Kate snickered the moment they reached the car.

Tawny held back a grin. "Stop it," she said under her breath.

Kate suppressed a laugh.

Tawny poked her arm. "Stop it!" A giggle escaped.

A guffaw escaped Kate when she fell into the passenger seat. "Did you see his face when you apologized for appearing straight?"

Tawny finally allowed herself to laugh. "No," she snorted, "what did he do?"

"First off, he was looking you up and down from the minute he saw those long legs of yours."

"You've noticed my legs?" Tawny teased.

"Uh, yes."

"Swift is a good-looking guy. I thought he'd be your type."

"Not even close," said Kate. "That laugh felt good."

"I know, right?" She started the Jeep and fastened her seat belt . "So, what questions do you think we should ask the radio operator?"

Kate expelled a long sigh. "I'm calling a timeout. How about a walk on the beach? I think it will do us both some good. You've been on worry detail twenty-four-seven since the crash, and I know I could use some breathing room. Did you know you talk in your sleep?"

"How do you know I talk in my sleep? Were you eavesdropping in yours?"

Kate chuckled. "Since we're free, let's take a walk on the beach near here and decompress."

"A walk on the beach? Gosh, I've been so focused on Carlos, that hasn't even occurred to me." Tawny cranked up the Jeep and drove down the road. "Did you know that the healing ocean vibes people talk about are due to negative ions present by the water?"

"No, but I do know that we have hours to spare in a beautiful place. I order you to enjoy it."

Tawny threw her a sidelong glance and pulled into the entrance to Luquillo Beach. "One visit to the Coast Guard and you're already giving orders."

She and Kate meandered barefoot through the tassels of palm trees that rode side-saddle on the crescent shoreline. With each step, Tawny dug her toes deeper into the warm white sand. They strolled in silence for a few minutes, occasionally passing each other a polite smile.

"Carlos was such a passionate person, Kate."

"What do you mean, *was*?"

"Come on, the leads are thin," Tawny's voice trembled. "Surely there would be some sign of him had he survived. I can't imagine that we wouldn't have heard if he were alive." She stopped and steadied herself with a deep breath. "God, has air ever smelled this good?"

"Stop making yourself crazy. Tell me about Carlos. What's he like? What are his hobbies?"

Tawny turned to face the ocean and stopped. Allowing the bathwater-warm foamy sheet of water to lap across her feet, she reached down and picked up an open clamshell as the tide rolled back out. "Look at this."

Kate focused in on the tiny plants embedded in the sand inside the small shell. "Wow, there are minuscule sea creatures in there! It's like an itty-bitty universe inside."

"Exactly. A random and delicately balanced ecosystem, an entire micro-universe inside a seashell. Life that no one would ever notice or care about unless they happened to look." They observed the pin-size crab burrow down until the sand obscured him. Tawny carefully placed the shell back at the water's edge and continued strolling.

"My friend Creama, whom you know as Carlos, was one of the funniest, most passionate and socially-conscious people you could ever meet. He grew up in the streets of Spanish Harlem with way too many odds against him, and he worked hard to get out. His mother died young, leaving him and his father, a macho alcoholic who had absolutely no tolerance for a gay son."

Kate strolled through the ankle-deep water. "Did his father abuse him because he was gay?"

Tawny nodded. "Carlos didn't have any brothers...but he did have a straight older cousin named Enrico who had tried to protect him on several occasions. One night when Carlos's father had been drinking, Enrico took Carlos out of the house for safety. They were walking through Greenwich Village when they were gay-bashed. Carlos was bruised but okay. Cousin Enrico died in the hospital from the blunt force trauma of a baseball bat. From that day on, Carlos decided to become as *visibly* gay as possible." She paused and turned to Kate. "He was a class act all right. He once spent all his vacation money rescuing stray dogs." She started to cry.

Kate put her arm around Tawny's shoulder. "Hey, come on now, it'll be okay."

"Kate, I was responsible for convincing him to get on that plane. I will never forgive myself...never," she sobbed.

Kate hugged her. "It's going to be okay. You're going to be okay. Breathe and take it one minute at a time. You're not alone in this. I'm right here—with you."

CHAPTER TWENTY-FIVE

Juan lugged the five bags of merchandise that he and Carlos had bought on their neighborhood sojourn. Carlos trailed behind him down the covered outside hallway to their apartment, stepped in front and unlocked the door.

"Man, I'm hungry! You hungry, Carlos?"

"Yes, and they start serving dinner downstairs soon." Carlos flung open the apartment door. "Thank god for air-conditioning. Mind if I clean up first since it takes me longer?"

Juan laid the bags on the coffee table. "No. I'm going to try on my new clothes and decide what to wear."

"I'll try to hurry." He took one of the bags from the table and closed the bathroom door behind him. He soaked in the bathtub with his casted leg hanging over the side, thinking it was a vast improvement over the hospital sponge baths—except when Nurse Combs had given them.

He trimmed his beard, shaved the edges with his new razor, and admired the haircut he'd gotten from the barber down the street. Hints of citrus in the cologne he and Juan bought smelled so inviting that he splashed on a little extra. While not nearly his first choice, dressing in crisp khaki shorts was a minor concession considering the ease with which they slipped over his cast and kept his leg cooler. Looking in the mirror, he thought the royal blue silk shirt spoke a flattering contrast against his olive complexion and deep brown eyes.

While Juan got ready, Carlos stepped out onto the lanai and took a deep breath. For the first time since he'd awakened to his new vacant self and the ordeal he now faced, he felt more normal than not, given what he had to compare it to. While he couldn't be certain, he'd have bet that this was the worst thing that had ever happened to him. At least he hoped it was, because anything worse would be something he'd never wish to remember. He glanced away from his newspaper and then did a double-take when Juan joined him. "Wow, look at you!"

"What's wrong with me?"

"You clean up great, man. Can you believe this is the first time we've seen each other dressed in real clothes instead of those ugly hospital duds?"

"Cool, huh? I'm glad you talked me into letting that barber style my hair."

Carlos reached for his crutches and followed him to the mirror in the hall.

Juan nodded approvingly. "I like it. The man staring back at me is a vast improvement and a much better fit than the one I'm used to seeing." He smoothed the slick wavy black hair with his hand and positioned the long bang to better hide the scar that still made his forehead itch.

"Those long sideburns give you that 'bad boy' edge."

Juan turned from the mirror. "Maybe I was an artist…I think I look like an artist. Or, maybe a rock musician."

Carlos chuckled. "You actually do look a little like Elvis with the sweeping bangs and long sideburns. Let's eat. I'm famished."

"Who's Elvis?" Juan mindlessly took a quarter from his pocket. He flipped it into the air with his left hand and caught it with his right, twirled it between his knuckles, and then slipped it into his opposite pocket. "Seriously, Carlos. Really? Elvis? What kind of name is that!"

"Elvis—the king of rock-and-roll?"

Juan paused. "A king? I like that idea."

"Hey, I've seen someone else do that thing with the quarter."

"Oh yeah? Who?"

He frowned with frustration and pursed his lips. "Damn if I know."

After dinner, Carlos meandered back in the direction of their apartment.

"Hey, Lieutenant."

He halted and turned. "Juan, you did not just call me Lieutenant."

Juan smiled.

"Oh, so you *do* have a sense of humor. What do you want?"

"Do we have to go back to the apartment right away?"

Carlos looked at his new Timex with the Indiglo face. "No. We have an hour 'til curfew. But remember, we have a busy day tomorrow and we're going to need all the energy we can get. Is there something else you wanted to do?"

"I want an ice cream cone...and I saw this little place around the corner."

He smiled. "Come on Elvis, les' find out what your favorite flavor is."

Juan raised an eyebrow. "Chocolate."

"But there are so many other more interesting flavors!"

"Chocolate."

Tawny woke from her early evening nap foggy but relaxed. She walked onto her terrace, inhaled the peaceful tropics, and welcomed the nightly serenade of the coqui that slowed her heartbeat and made her breathe a little deeper. *Such a welcome change to feel so calm even if for only a minute.* She called Kate and told her she would pick her up in half an hour and then got ready and left the hotel.

For most of the ride back to Coast Guard Station San Juan, she felt Kate's eyes on her. Had she not been so relaxed, the stares might have even made her feel like a laboratory subject. "What's this guy's name again?" she asked, even though she knew the answer.

"Oliver Greene. He was the radioman. You want to take the first shot or shall I break the ice for you?"

She parked the Jeep, set the brake and turned to Kate. "I'll start."

All was serene at GANTSEC when the coastguardsman escorted Tawny and Kate to the Communications Center. The uniformed man in the government-green swivel chair spun around to greet them. "Hello, I'm Oliver Greene. Lieutenant Commander Swift said you have some questions regarding the Trans Air SAR?"

Tawny observed him with a reporter's eye. Straight out of central casting, he was the picture of a man born to follow procedure. She surmised that not much ever got by Greene, not even a stray blond hair on his head.

"Thanks for taking the time to speak with us. I'm Tawny Beige and this is Kate Taylor, one of the Trans Air flight attendants." Minus her film crew, Tawny still strived to demonstrate the presence of an experienced reporter—unlike the ball of emotion she had displayed elsewhere on their search.

"Wait. I'm from San Francisco. I know you," said Greene. "Aren't you that newscaster?"

She nodded. "Former newscaster. But I'm here on a personal matter, so anything you tell us stays right here." Her serious gaze held his long enough in an effort to convey accountability.

Kate broke the Tawny-trance with her gentle smile. "May I call you Oliver?"

"Yes, ma'am."

"Oliver, I want to express my deep gratitude for your brave rescue. Without you, I wouldn't even be here." Tawny watched Kate's eyes fill when she stepped forward and shook Greene's hand.

Greene smiled a hero's smile and then looked down as though embarrassed by the compliment. He slowly raised his head and looked at her through golden brown eyes. "You're welcome, Miss Taylor. What can I do for you?"

Tawny began. "Can you walk me through the highlights of the night of the Trans Air crash?"

Greene nodded. "I was on duty in the cutter *Southern Storm's* combat information center when I received a transmission from the Seventh District Command. My orders were to proceed to the last known position of Trans Air 44. The message from the Search-and-Rescue Watchstander said we were the closest and needed to get to the coordinates ASAP." He paused. "I know that our cutter's search lights came up empty on their first sweep, though I'm not surprised with the height of those swells. I'm told they saw the lifeboats shortly thereafter."

"Do you know when the helicopters arrived or what the pilots saw or recovered?"

Greene stroked the square of his jaw with his thumb. "They didn't find anyone after the *Southern Storm* rescued the lifeboats. There was debris but no victims." He looked at Kate. "As you know all too well, it took us a long time to locate and lift you all aboard the cutter. I was down below, still glued to the radio but I was in communication with the Dolphin helicopter that transported the medevac patients. From then on, we were in constant contact with everyone who had a hand in the operation."

"Were there any other transmissions? Any that mentioned victims who didn't make it onto the *Southern Storm* or the helicopter?" asked Tawny.

Greene's steno chair squeaked as it flexed back under his muscular torso. He thought for a moment and sprung forward, reaching for his notebook. "That's a good question. You know…I forgot about that," he added.

"Forgot about what?" Kate asked.

"After we rescued the passengers on the *Southern Storm*, communications from all over the region broke in for hours. We coordinated several response teams that night." He shuffled through the pages of his notebook as he spoke. "One of the helicopters searched and searched, but came up empty. Then, later…it was right before I went off duty in the morning, there was an odd transmission. I think I picked up a civilian call into the Navy on Vieques. I can't really tell you what it was about because as I said, I was busy doing my job."

Kate fixed her gaze on his. "Is there anything else, anything at all?"

"Sorry," he paused, "no, wait a minute." Greene set the notebook aside. He riffled in his desk drawer for his wallet and fished out a scrap of paper that was riddled with doodles. He flipped it over, turned it around, and then upside down. "There it is. In the corner, I scribbled Bahia and then drew this picture here." He held up the paper and pointed to the corner.

"What is that?" asked Tawny. "It looks like…" she squinted and leaned closer. "Like a bug."

"It's a mosquito," Greene said with the deflated air of a man who couldn't believe his doodle didn't boast an obvious likeness. "Really? You can't tell that's a mosquito?"

"Is there something we're missing here?" asked Kate.

"Yes, don't you get it? Bahia is Spanish for Bay. It means Mosquito Bay. I remember it now—one of the weirdest distress calls was civilian—from Mosquito Bay, but the Navy took it."

"Where is that—Mosquito Bay?" asked Tawny.

"It's the phosphorescent bay on Vieques," Greene replied. "I doubt it has any relevance, but someone must have said something about Bahia Mosquito. I wish I could tell you what was said, but that's all I know."

"So, why would the Navy get involved?" asked Tawny.

Greene looked at her. "Because that's protocol."

She nodded. "We really appreciate your time."

Kate shook his hand. "Thank you so much for the work you do, Oliver."

Greene saw them out. "I'm really glad you made it, Miss Taylor." He smiled. "You're the reason I do what I do."

Tawny led the way out of the station. "How about a late-night snack?"

Kate yawned long and hard as she slid back into the Jeep.

Tawny nodded and caught the yawning bug. "Never mind, me either. You need to take tomorrow off?"

"No, I just need an uninterrupted night's sleep."

"Atta girl."

She dropped Kate at her hotel and ruminated over their interview of Oliver Greene. *A civilian call into the Navy. But he thought it was unrelated to the Trans Air crash because it came from Vieques. Still, as a reporter I need to know for sure.* She sighed. "I'll start by looking up this Bahia Mosquito on the map when I get to my room."

She parked, lifted the brown paper bag of snacks she had bought on the way home and got out. As she crossed the desolate garage, she listened to the echo of her heels ping off the concrete. She stopped abruptly, but the echo of flat-footed steps behind her persisted.

She shook her head and exhaled but didn't turn around. "Yes, Mr. Castilano?"

"Hey! How'd ya know it was me?" he said, closing the gap between them.

"You're currently the only stalker I have." She turned to face him. "Don't you know how to use a phone...like a normal person? You lurk. That's what you are, you're a lurker."

"You sure about that?"

"Sure that you lurk?"

"No, are you sure that I'm the only one following you?"

She resisted the urge to scrutinize her surroundings. "Now why would anyone in their right mind want to follow *me*?"

"Hey, is that a dig?"

"It's late. What do you want, Jimmy?"

"I told you. I want to join in your search. I thought maybe we could commiserate. You know, compare notes."

"Commiserate means to sympathize."

"Yeah okay, that's good too. I'll be honest with you. I could use a little sympathy."

She continued on toward the elevator.

He followed. "What, you think I have no sympathy for what you're going through?"

She spun around and raised her eyebrow at him. "Yep, pretty much. You could go search for the congressman without me."

"I have been, but I keep turning up more questions than answers. And you been doin' pretty good so far." He reached out to take her grocery bag.

"That's okay, I'm quite capable of carrying a bag of junk food."

He held both hands up in retreat. "I was being polite."

She smiled.

"Aha! I saw that. I saw you smile. Admit it, I kinda grow on you, don't I?"

"You mean like a wart grows on a—"

"Why are you so rude to me?"

She continued on toward the elevator, and he took an extra stride to keep up.

"As I was saying, it doesn't add up that there's no actual news—*at all*—about the two people we're looking for."

"Are you going to start with that, 'Oh Jesus, don't let anyone think Dick Peak was gay' routine again? I cannot believe I'm having this conversation with you."

"Would you like to join me for a drink before you go back to your room?"

"Not really."

"Why? Because you think I'm some hateful bigot from the *religious right*?"

She laughed at his candor. "Yep, that pretty much sums it up for me."

"Would you be interested to know what I know about your past?"

He followed her into the elevator. "What past? And why would I care?"

The elevator door closed and he pressed 7. "Does the name Ellie Brisbane mean anything to you?"

She scoffed. "What? Not anymore it doesn't. How do you know… Why are you bringing *her* up?"

"You really don't know, do ya?"

"I'm tired and losing my patience. Know what, Jimmy?" She pressed 7 again, hoping it would make the elevator climb faster.

"You sure you don't want that drink?"

"I'm sure. Now what about Ellie?"

"Your ex-girlfriend…" Jimmy paused and straightened his pinky ring. "…is Dick Peak's half-sister."

She dropped the bag, and Jimmy's lightning reflexes kept the jar of bean dip from crashing to the floor.

"You're joking. Aren't you? Please say yes."

"Nope."

"No, that can't be."

"Yes, it totally is."

"You win, Castilano. *Now* I could use that drink." The elevator door opened and closed at the seventh floor, and Jimmy pressed L for Lobby—just once.

CHAPTER TWENTY-SIX

They sat on the leather stools at the sleek modern bar where Tawny downed her first vodka martini in three long swallows. She held up the empty glass and waved it at the bartender. "Bartender. Hey. Hey, bartender—another one."

"You seem to be taking this rather hard."

"Why didn't she ever tell me? How could I not have known? It was obvious to me that she had connections she never spoke about…but she hated anything to do with politics. That was one of the reasons we broke up." She shook her head slowly in disbelief. "Shit, now it all makes sense."

"The congressman had called in a few favors to keep things quiet back then." He swirled the lemon twist in his J&B-and-water and took a sip. "He didn't take it too well when he first found out she liked girls. He was afraid it would affect his support network."

"You mean the fundamentalists wouldn't back a dyke's brother? How very *Christian.*" She reached into the paper bag and pulled out a pack of American Spirit cigarettes. She unwrapped the cellophane, peeled back the paper and took one out.

Jimmy lit it for her. "I didn't know you smoke."

"I don't. I mean I haven't smoked in five years." The first puff was delicate and she barely inhaled, holding it just so between the index and middle fingers of her left hand. "I always thought it was odd that she wouldn't go home to visit. Not even on the holidays. She said she was afraid her family would pressure her into joining an Ex-Gay ministry to 'pray away the gay.' I never would have guessed that she was Peak's sister. Ha!" She laughed. "Could you see Dick Peak having me as his sister-in-law? That alone would have made him destroy marriage equality!"

Jimmy laughed. "This is kind of fun, isn't it? Who'd a ever thought that the two of us would wind up…" he stared into her eyes to make his point, "…*commiserating*?"

"Oh good, you've learned to use it correctly in a sentence. You said there were some things that weren't adding up. Like what?" She took a gulp of the next martini.

He looked around and then spoke so quietly that she had to lean closer to hear him. "Before Dick left for Puerto Rico at the San Francisco airport, he asked me for the fifth time if I'd sent an envelope he'd given me to the hotel where he was supposed to stay. It was addressed to him. When I asked him what was in it, he changed the subject. Then, the day before I flew down here, I got an anonymous phone call." Jimmy took another sip of scotch. "It sounded like a woman's voice disguised, but it happened so fast that I'm not really sure. Anyhow, this person said they had evidence that Dick was guilty of illegal corporate activities and that made me think of the envelope."

She nodded. "That rumor is about to come out in the press. The sixty-four-thousand-dollar question is, is the rumor true, where is that envelope, and what's in it?"

Jimmy pulled back the lapel of his jacket to reveal his inside coat pocket. A white envelope was sticking out. He let the coat fall closed.

She took another puff of the cigarette and crushed it out in the ashtray. "I take it that's the envelope?"

He nodded. "I haven't looked inside yet. I tracked it down in a pile of unclaimed mail at the hotel right before I drove here."

"Isn't the curiosity killing you?"

"Tawny, I'm afraid my curiosity might in fact do just that." Jimmy downed the last of his scotch, his glance darting around the bar. "I don't know if I wanna find out what's inside."

She sized up his slumped shoulders and serious expression. "You act tough but you seem a little nervous to me. Maybe we should take this conversation up to my room."

He smiled. "I thought you'd never ask."

"Yeah well, don't get any ideas, pal."

"Don't worry. I already got a girl. A nice *straight* girl."

"Really. Let me guess. She's home, barefoot and pregnant, pining for you. No, waiting at the door with a scotch on the rocks."

"Now, now, have I made any dyke jokes?" He crisped his collar. "I think you have a distorted view of me."

She took a tipsy step when she first stood and Jimmy caught her. She snickered. "I know…I'm skewed. Thanks for the save. Let's get out of here." The elevator door closed with only the two of them inside. On martini-time-delay, it took three floors before she asked. "What dyke jokes?"

"Okay, you asked. Why can't lesbians diet and wear makeup at the same time?"

"Why?"

"Because they can't eat Jenny Craig with Mary Kay on their face." He laughed in the way that made his shoulders heave.

She closed her eyes and shook her head. "Do you know how old that joke is? You're a piece of work."

"*Wha*?" he said with his palms outstretched. "You don't think I have a sense of humor?"

"Not nearly the sense of humor your girlfriend must have."

He scoffed. "Very funny, very freakin' funny."

Once in Tawny's room, Jimmy sat on a chair and held out the envelope.

"Aren't you going to open it?"

"You open it. Please." He let the envelope slip from his sausage-shaped fingers into her palm.

She moved toward the terrace door while staring down at the envelope in her hand. She pivoted to face Jimmy. "Why me?"

"Like it or not, Tawny Beige, we've been tossed together by a cyclone of circumstance. Our best friends met a terrible fate together. Andy wound up badly beaten while attempting to pass both of us information and I keep getting the willies. Besides, I think we're a lot more alike than you care to admit."

Her eyes opened wide. "How's that?"

"Like me, you're a very loyal friend and loyal people can be trusted. We live by a code." He loosened his tie and sank back in the floral armchair.

"What makes you think I can be trusted, Mr…?"

"Hey!"

"Right. Jimmy."

"You have what you call, integ-ri-ty. And you got a set a balls on you, I'll give you that."

"Ovaries."

"Huh?"

"That awesome sense of power I exhibit? It's ovaries, not balls."

"I suppose that's true. So, you got the ovaries to open that envelope?"

She fanned herself, the envelope waving back and forth under her chin as she pondered Jimmy's words. "Ah, so that's why you're hanging around. You've been watching out for me."

His cheeks blushed. "A pretty girl like you…alone here in San Juan poking around, is not really safe."

"Jimmy, I'm genuinely flattered that you care."

Tawny lifted the hotel pen off the pad and ripped the corner of the envelope with it. Separating the seam, she glanced up at Jimmy before looking inside.

"G'head," he encouraged.

She sat on the edge of the bed and carefully emptied the envelope's contents onto the bedspread. One thin layer of bubble wrap. Next, she peeled off the scotch tape and cautiously unwrapped it. Jimmy leaned forward in his chair in anticipation.

"A key?" Tawny held it up between two fingers. "Oh, and there's a note with some letters and a number."

"Let me see that." He concentrated on the note and then he reached over and took the key off the bed. He looked back and forth between them, as if he was making some kind of decision. "This is not Dick's handwriting."

"What does the note mean?"

"Dunno. It just says, 'USC1832'."

"That key must be a public locker key, like from an airport or something. Or perhaps it's a vault box." She stood and walked to the terrace door. "Which means that Mr. Peak was coming here either to drop something off or to pick it up. What do you think this is all about?"

"I don't know. I'm praying it isn't what that caller had said it was. If it is, who knows what's in this box or locker? I'm guessing that USC stands for University of Southern California, where Dick went to school. How you making out on *your* search?"

"I thought you said you already knew how I was doing."

He smiled. "Okay, so I'm a wise guy. I've been trying to keep the media vultures at bay while I attempt to figure out what Dick was up to before he died."

"Died? How can you just assume that, and so calmly? There are bodies missing. And if one of them is your dear Dick, you don't seem too bereft."

"Yo! If that means sad, I'm all tore up about it. But, I'm a realist. Dick and your friend…they're gone," he said, his voice dispersing his grief throughout the room. "Haven't you been listening to the news?"

"You're not a realist, Jimmy, you're a pessimist. I'm not yet convinced that Creama is dead. I have this gut feeling…call it a reporter's hunch, so until I have conclusive evidence, I'm going to remain in denial if you don't mind. What's the *real* reason you're sharing this information with me? After all, I'm the enemy."

"You're not *my* enemy. I don't understand being gay, but you seem like a good person. I can call you a person, can't I?"

She stared at him dead-on. "Don't be a smartass."

"Ha. There it is again. You got a nice smile, Tawny, you know that?" He stood and folded the note around the key and tucked it deep into his inside pocket.

She followed him to the door to see him out and stopped. "What did you mean by keeping the media vultures at bay?"

"It's time I go down the rabbit hole to find out everything I *didn't* know about Dick." He looked into her eyes. "I don't need the press on my back."

She nodded. "And yet, you're talking to me."

"I'm talking to you because I like you. More importantly, I think I can trust you. Watch yourself," he said gently. "Until I know what's behind this, anyone knowing that you're a reporter digging around for information may think that you know something."

"I do know about the key."

He wagged his index finger at her. "Be careful. I'd feel terrible if anything happened to you. I'll be in touch."

"Wait. What if I want to reach you?"

He jotted down his number and left.

She triple-checked the door locks and drifted off to sleep while watching a rerun of *Wonder Woman* in Spanish.

Morning might as well have been there all night long as far as she was concerned. She slept so deeply she would never have known the difference. Barely awake, the quietude of the cool dark room allowed her to hear her thoughts, to feel the longing for what was in her heart. Wishing she could find out what happened to Creama topped the list, and that need overshadowed every other—even the one to miss Chloe. *Finally. It's time to let her go.*

Tawny stretched and yawned and drank her first cup of coffee while listening to a local news piece on the Navy activities on Vieques. "Not the Navy again. Suddenly, everywhere I turn, I hear about the Navy." She paced across her room. "When this is over, I'm treating myself to a whole day in bed." She paused and pushed away the thought of doing it alone. "Culminating in a Thai food banquet spread out before me. Delivered. But right now, I've got me a *dragnet*."

CHAPTER TWENTY-SEVEN

No longer feeling like a lone wolf on a solitary quest, Tawny had a small rag-tag team forming that consisted of a not-so-awful poster thug of the religious right and a gorgeous and sweet straight woman that she liked very much and felt the need to help find closure.

She sat at the third table on the left in the hotel's coffee shop, tapping her foot in anticipation of Kate's arrival. She'd managed to erase the remnants of the B-movie zombie-queen she'd been when she awoke, and now reviewed her research, placing a coordinated "X" next to every map location that had proved to be a dead end.

"Morning, Tawny." Kate took the seat across from her.

She tried not to stare into Kate's Persian-blue eyes when she looked up from her map of Vieques. "Hi."

"You look refreshed. What's your secret?"

"An hour ago I could've been mistaken for the bride of Frankenstein. The secret lies in the third cup of coffee." Distracted by Kate's smile, all she could do was smile back. "Where was I?" she muttered, refocusing on her map and tracing the grid to 'G-8' with her finger.

Kate flipped through the menu. "What's good here?"

Tawny looked up, and on her way back to those bedroom-blues, she took a side trip to drink in the flight attendant's toned and sun-drenched arms. *Right now, everything looks good.* "They make great omelets." *This might be the loneliest moment a gay girl's ever had in a tropical paradise.*

Kate signaled the waitress. "Coffee please, and a veggie omelet." She slid her chair closer to Tawny. "That stray transmission Oliver Greene mentioned last night?"

"You mean that civilian call to the Navy?"

Kate's eyes brightened. "Yes, it keeps coming up for me."

"I've been thinking about that, too. At first I thought I was grasping at straws, but everywhere we turn, I hear something about the Navy." Tawny emptied her coffee cup. "Don't let me have any more caffeine this morning."

"Do I just tell you no?"

The waitress set an espresso in front of Kate.

"You don't strike me as a woman who takes a simple no for an answer, Tawny." She took her first sip. "So, what do you think it all means?"

Tawny tapped G-8 with her manicured red nails. "Have you ever heard of Camp Garcia?"

"Sure. The military base on Vieques. It's been closed for years now, but the government still retains control. Why?"

"Do you think it would be worthwhile to go to Vieques and see what we can find out at that Bahia Mosquito that Greene mentioned? We're certainly not blazing any trails here in San Juan."

Kate's eyes drifted up to the ceiling and then back to Tawny. "I'm remembering something," she said thoughtfully.

While Tawny waited for her to continue, she took a Persian-blue magic carpet ride.

"Once the plane had ditched, the exit door was stuck and I couldn't open it. Carlos pounded on a window with an armrest to break the seal, which allowed the door lock to release. Then he helped me remove the door."

"He actually knew to do that?"

"I guess so. He did it. Once we got the door out of the way and I activated the slide, he asked me what the glow was in the distance—on the water. It was a phosphorescent bay."

"You could see the bay from the plane? Do you think that could have been Bahia Mosquito?"

"I don't know. I guess."

"That's it, Kate. We're not going to one more hospital or talking to one more bureaucrat until we do our due diligence about this bay." She paused to swallow the lump in her throat. "Since the authorities have pronounced both Carlos and Peak dead," she paused again to gather herself, "it's not like we're having any luck with any of the usual avenues. Maybe we need to take another tack here."

Kate stared at her. "So, if Oliver Greene's detailed drawing of an intercepted message means anything at all, you're right." She nodded thoughtfully. "We need to go there in person."

"How do we get there fast?"

"Puddle-jumpers fly there, or we can take the ferry that leaves from Fajardo. I'll ask the concierge after breakfast. Meanwhile, you go upstairs and pack an overnight bag in case we run long. Then, on our way out of town, we can swing by my place so I can grab some things."

"I give you fair warning. In a race I'd lose to a turtle right now."

"Why?" Kate stirred another sugar into her second cup of coffee.

"Remember that guy who followed us to Mayaguez?"

"Yeah, sure…Castilano."

"He was waiting for me when I got back here last night."

"Why?"

"He wanted a powwow, which included two martinis. Hence the three cups of coffee this morning."

"You actually had drinks with him? I thought you couldn't stand him."

"I can't…or couldn't." She spoke in a hushed tone. "There's a lot more to this story, but I'd rather wait until we're alone to share it with you."

"Can't wait to hear it."

The waitress brought Kate's breakfast. "More coffee?"

"Sure, why not. It's going to be a busy day."

Tawny yawned. "Maybe I should have just one more cup."

"No!"

Tawny smiled.

"What?"

"Nothing. Say it again."

"What? No?"

Her smile broadened. "You say it with such command."

"I'm the queen of crowd control." Her eyebrows furrowed. "Too much?"

Too much of sexy maybe. "Finish your breakfast." She signed the check and stood. "I'm going upstairs to pack and I'll fill you in on the details from last night once we're on the road."

CHAPTER TWENTY-EIGHT

Surrounded by an alcove of medical books, Carlos yawned, feeling like the afternoon had lasted two whole days. For the preceding hour, he had progressively slumped deeper and deeper into the armchair in which he sat.

While the psychologist poured a glass of water, he continued to babble on about the process of memory, behavior, and amnesia.

Carlos mentally checked in and out of the session, occasionally drifting off to the garden he missed at the VA hospital. His gaze wandered back to the present. "Doc, you got too many books with the word cognitive in the title."

Dr. Eduardo smiled at him and continued his thought. "Then, if all goes well, we can consider hypnosis as one avenue of exploration."

"I told you everything I can remember, so if you want to put me under, go right ahead." He paused in thought. "Your record of what I say stays confidential, right?"

"Certainly." Dr. Eduardo flipped a page in his book and consulted his schedule. "How about if we set up a session for tomorrow?"

"Okay." Carlos's stomach growled. "Are we done?"

Dr. Eduardo glanced up at the clock. "We have a few minutes left. But I do have one last question, Carlos. If you don't know who Juan is, or how the two of you wound up together, why do you think you feel so responsible for him?"

He contemplated the question. "I really don't know, except to say that you never leave a brother on the battlefield. I have this feeling that I'm supposed to protect him, make sure nothing bad happens to him. Maybe you could ask me that under hypnosis."

Eduardo scribbled in his file. "I don't want you to overthink this. Give it more time. Sometimes, the harder we try to recall something, the harder it becomes to remember. So relax, take solace in the fact that you survived the worst of whatever it was. Like the body, the mind needs time to heal too."

He stared at him. "Does it work the other way around?"

"Meaning?"

"Say there's something I'd want to forget—the harder I try to forget it, the harder it becomes to forget it?"

"Are you referring to something specific?"

"I remember my mother dying when I was young. It's a sad memory and yet I can remember it. I remember her."

Eduardo paused. "Some memories are so deeply rooted, they remain part of us whether we can recall them consciously or not."

"Maybe that's what I feel for Juan, but I just don't know why?"

The doctor nodded. "It's possible. All right, good first session. Get some rest, you look like you can use it."

Carlos found Juan reclining on the patio chaise when he got home.

"How did it go?"

"I can tell you straight up that the chiropractor was a *good* thing. I feel less pain and look, it's easier for me to walk." He crutch-strutted from the patio back inside to the kitchen.

"Wow. You really are moving better."

Carlos reached into the refrigerator and extricated a single bottle of Red Stripe beer from its five siblings. "How did your day turn out?" He hobbled to Juan, handed him the beer, and negotiated with his leg to sit.

Juan shook his head. "Dr. Eduardo said there's a good chance I'll never remember my former life if I have no memory of it at all by now. He suggested I consider hypnosis."

"Same here. Hey, maybe he could hypnotize us together."

Juan took a sip of the Red Stripe and handed it back to Carlos. His brows knitted. "What if I never remember? I'm sure I wasn't some rocket scientist, but how will I know where to live, what to do—or who to be?"

"Do you remember in the hospital when you asked me about your favorite color?"

"You mean when I decided that blue was my favorite?"

"*Sí, Chulito.*"

"It's not blue anymore."

He laughed. "Oh no? What is it?"

"I think it's green. Yes, it's green."

"But you said it could *never* be green."

"That's what I thought too until I sat there in the garden every day and really took time to notice. Do you realize how many shades of green are in that one garden? There can't even be enough names for that many colors. So I wondered, exactly which green did I dislike? Each one had its own beauty. Suddenly the question became 'Which green do I like best?'" He paused. "I wonder if I ever knew there were *that* many shades of green."

"Well, I'm happy that you know it now." Carlos took a swig of the cold, smooth Red Stripe and handed it to Juan. He balanced on his crutch to stand and limped to the living room sofa. "Sometimes I envy you, Juan."

Juan joined him. "You're kidding, right?"

"Hardly. Most of us will never be able to paint our lives the way we really want to because our experiences already color how we see things. But you, my friend…you have no limitations from your past. The way I see it, you have nothing holding you back; you have a second chance to become whoever you want to be. And if it doesn't work out, you can always come home to San Francisco with me, mijo." He stopped mid-breath. "I remember my apartment!"

Juan sat up. "Really? You remember? Well, where is it? What's it like?"

"This is maddening, damn it! I saw my bedroom but I don't know the fucking address. You would think the Navy would clear my ID by now so that I know where the hell I live."

"They'll find it, Carlos. Tell me about your apartment."

He took a breath. "It's Victorian with hardwood floors and an old chandelier in the living room." He sighed. "That's it. That's all I've got." His gaze dropped to his lap.

"It's more than you had yesterday."

Carlos punched the armrest pillow. "I want to go out tonight."

"Out? Where?"

"To a club. With music. And hot men!" He gasped and his eyes opened wide. "Oops."

Juan stared at him blankly.

"I didn't mean to tell you this way. But, I suppose now is as good a time as any. Juan, I'm gay."

Juan continued to stare at him expressionless.

"Do you understand what I'm telling you?"

"Of course I understand. You're…happy."

He shook his head. "No, Juan. I like guys. Do you understand?" He watched his words sink in.

"Oh! *That* kind of gay. So what?" He shifted in his seat to cross one leg over the other. "You know, I knew that, Carlos. I mean I didn't exactly *know*…but I knew."

"How did you know?"

"I can't explain it. Intuition maybe?"

"We call that *gaydar*. Are you okay?"

"Why wouldn't I be? Frankly, I don't know why but I find myself thinking about gay things a lot."

"What gay things?"

Juan gazed up at the ceiling as he mulled it over. "I really liked that boa for one thing. Seems pretty gay to me."

He laughed. "You and every guy in America, straight or gay, likes a boa on the right person."

Juan grunted. "You're right. This is maddening. You know how you keep saying that your mind feels like Swiss cheese, full of holes?"

"Yeah."

Juan flared his arms outward. "Well, all I've got is the holes! I can identify words but have no idea how I know what I do know—and no clue of what I don't."

Carlos stared directly into his eyes. "No one knows what they don't know. Okay, pal, we both need to give it a rest—get some food. Want to eat downstairs?"

Juan nodded. "I agree. But let's have dinner at that little Italian joint around the corner."

"You really like Italian."

"I suppose I do. It might even be my *favorite* food."

"From what I've seen, Juan, *all* food is your favorite food."

"Why don't you go change your clothes and I'll wait for you on the terrace?"

Carlos looked down and examined himself. "I don't look good in this?"

"No, no, you look fine." Juan paused. "I was thinking you might want to change your shirt."

He hobbled to the full-length mirror. "All right, Juan, if you think I should."

"I'm not saying that I think you should. I'm simply saying if you want to change, I'll wait for you on the terrace."

"What's wrong with how I look?"

"Nothing is wrong with it…I just think you look better in that dark blue shirt you bought yesterday."

"Okay," Carlos said sheepishly. "If you like me in blue, then I'll wear blue."

"Don't do it just because I think so."

"Enough already! I'm putting on the blue shirt."

"Well, if you really like that one better…"

CHAPTER TWENTY-NINE

Late the following afternoon, Jimmy emerged from the rabbit hole where he had spent the day chasing down information about his sorely missed friend—the guy he had protected like a little brother, the man he'd followed blindly along every path he had pursued. The one guy he'd always trusted.

He exhaled a sigh of sadness and shifted his thoughts to Tawny. How, even though at first she had presented a tough and determined exterior, through the breached cracks in her shell, the woman beneath the façade was starting to seep through. For the first time, he questioned why Dick had always been so adamant about depriving gay people of equal rights. *She's not any different from any other woman I've known, except that she's gay.*

He admired her strength and dogged determination to find the truth, but mostly he felt grateful that at his lowest moment in this ordeal, she had read him the riot act about giving up. She was the one who had inspired him to keep faith with his hope.

She's one smart chick. If anyone can figure out what happened to Dick, I'd put my money on her.

He scanned the business signs as his taxi rolled slowly along the avenue toward the address on the slip of paper in his pocket. "Here it is. *Aqui, aqui*! You wait here. There's a good tip in it for you."

When he got out of the taxi, he crisped his collar, using the moment to take subtle stock of his surroundings and the passersby. He turned toward the window sign that read *Cerrado*, but the shopkeeper had said he would remain open until Jimmy arrived.

"Sí, señor," said the bent little man when Jimmy entered.

"Are you the man I spoke to about the key?"

"Señor Castilano?"

"Yes. Sí."

"Where is it?"

"Oh, yeah sure." Jimmy reached deep into his inside pocket. He held the key in his palm, and as the locksmith reached out to take it, Jimmy snatched it back in his closed fist. "Nothing better happen to this key."

"Yes sir, it is safe with me."

"How long will it take to identify what it goes to?"

"That depends. Did you say there was a number that came with it? Any information helps."

He unfolded the note that read 'USC 1832' and laid it on the counter. "Does that mean something?"

"I don't know, but with numbers such as that, it could simply be a locker key."

"Can't you tell me specifically what it fits?"

The locksmith pointed his crooked finger to the volumes of dusty books that lined his walls. "I will do my best. Leave me your phone number and I will call you."

"You mean *leave* the key with you?"

"Unless you want to wait. But to do that, you'll have to come back early tomorrow. It could take hours—if I can figure it out at all, that is."

"Shit! Haven't you heard of computers?"

The little man chuckled. "Yes, I've heard of them." He slid a nub of pencil across the greasy register onto a scrap of paper. "Please leave the information and your number."

Jimmy grunted, hiked up his clean sleeve, and copied the note, leaving his phone number at the bottom. He wiped his fingers with his handkerchief, took a step toward the door and turned to the old man. "You have until tomorrow at closing. I'll be willing to pay you for your time." The bell on the door jingled on his way out.

"Back to your hotel, sir?" asked the cabbie when Jimmy got in.

"Yes," he replied. On the ride, he pondered the situation to the exclusion of every distraction. He knew Dick better than anyone ever had—how Dick thought, what he liked and what he didn't. He was privy to every clandestine tryst, every ambition and backroom deal. *So how is it that Dick trusted me enough to send this key but more importantly, why the fuck don't I know anything about it?* He let out a sigh of frustration. *I ain't stopping till I figure this out.*

After leaving a message for Tawny at her hotel, Jimmy closed his eyes until his phone startled him from his trance. He pulled it from his pocket and smiled.

"Hey, Red, nice surprise," he answered.

"How's it going down there?" asked Rita. "I miss you so much, Jimmy. I wish I was there with you."

"It's the farthest thing from a Caribbean vacation as it gets. Maybe when all this is over we could come down here together. You'd love the hotel and the beach."

"Sounds like heaven. Any news about Dick?"

"Nothing worth knowing yet. I been working with that reporter Tawny Beige since her friend is one of the few people still missing."

The call went silent.

"You still there, Red?"

"She's a very pretty woman, Jimmy."

"You mean a very pretty *gay* woman," he teased. "But I gotta say, she's one helluva reporter. I'm glad we met because I think if anyone can figure out what happened to Dick and her friend, my money's on her."

"You mean her friend that's the drag queen?"

"Yeah."

Rita giggled. "I wonder what Dick would think about gay people trying to find him."

He sighed. "Ironically, this is the very example of a moot point."

"I'll never understand why Dick was always so mad about gay people anyway. We're all just people…and Christians are supposed to be nicer than that."

He waited a beat before he spoke. "Christian wasn't his religion, Rita. Politics was."

"Do you have any idea when you're coming home?"

"Not yet. But I'm in the process of tracking down some clues that Dick left behind."

"Like what?"

"It's the craziest thing. The night I took him to the airport, he had asked me about an envelope he had me mail to Puerto Rico. I recovered the envelope here and inside there was a key and a piece of paper with a few letters and numbers written on it."

"That's it? That doesn't sound like something Dick would do without filling you in."

"I know. That's the part that stumps me. Dick and I have always been brutally honest with each other so that I could have his back. This doesn't make sense to me."

"Now that he's gone, does it really matter?"

Jimmy thought of Tawny's reaction when he had resolved that Dick had died. "Don't say that."

"But the media has said…"

"I don't want to hear it. Until I know what happened…"

"I know he was like a brother to you—warts and all."

He teared up. "Yeah. Because of that I can't come home yet. I gotta see this through. For him."

"You're a good man, Jimmy Castilano."

He smiled. "Don't tell anybody. I have a reputation to maintain."

"Your secret is safe with me. All your secrets are safe with me."

"I know I don't say it often enough, but I love you, Rita, and that's only one of many reasons why."

"You sound different."

"I'd be lying if I didn't admit that this ordeal has been a real wake-up call. If something happened to me, I'd want our last conversation to be something worth remembering, you know?"

"You've never been the sentimental type."

"Well, Red, that changes now." He took a breath and steeled himself. "I miss you, honey. When I get home, whadya say we talk about our future—together."

CHAPTER THIRTY

"Follow me, Tawny," said Kate. "I know the perfect place for a break." In the division of daylight, the quotient of sun on Vieques came into her view as a low, round pomegranate. She led her to a cozy spot on the crescent-shaped beach of Sun Bay, in the sleepy fishing village of Esperanza.

Tawny sat and pulled Kate's knapsack toward her. "You mind?"

"No, go right ahead."

Tawny laid her head back on it. "The sand is so toasty," she said, digging her toes down into it.

"This might be the first time since the crash that smelling the ocean doesn't make me want to puke." She smiled at her and took a deep whiff of the ocean breeze.

Tawny closed her eyes and yawned. "Happy to hear that. I'm so loving the inside of my eyelids right now. I swear, I've never met a woman whose promises were emptier than those martinis were last night."

Kate looked down at her. "But someday you'll be old and it'll be one of the few easier recollections of this time." She watched the rhythm of the tide and finally let in its beauty, in the way she once had, before she ever had to pray she'd survive the ocean's cruel and unyielding body.

"You did great finding us that cute inn on the beach," Tawny said, her eyes still shut.

"I stayed there once a long time ago with some flight attendant friends when we had time off and explored the island. Their restaurant's pretty good too." She fixed her stare upward at the palm umbrella canopy. "Call me crazy but I just got a sudden urge for Italian food."

"Who goes to an island and eats Italian food?" Tawny asked sarcastically. She stretched her arms above her head and sighed. "I'm glad you made me pack an overnight bag, but honestly I could fall asleep right here." She turned her head toward Kate and opened her eyes, shielding them from the sun.

"It's in my blood." Kate looked at her, admiring the former newscaster's beauty, wishing she had been born with that nose and those cheekbones. "Flight attendants are always prepared for layovers. Unfortunately, my good case is at the bottom of the ocean along with my favorite makeup." She paused. "Could I sound any more shallow?"

"You look pretty with or without makeup. Just sayin'," Tawny smiled.

Don't get weird. It's just a run-of-the-mill compliment. Her eyes darted away to the far end of the coast and stayed there. "I feel naked without mascara."

"Good thing you're a natural beauty."

She fidgeted and yanked her gaze back from the most distant point she could find. "Um, so…you're good with the dinner reservation I made at the hotel?"

"Definitely. Man, this emotional roller coaster is burning me out."

"No kidding. You're all work and no play, Tawny Beige, and that doesn't help anyone. That sedulous reporter in you is a force to be reckoned with."

Tawny met her stare. "All work? What do you call this lying around on a beach?"

"For a whole ten minutes? I don't know…exhaustion?"

"Smartass."

Kate smiled gently. "The truth is, I'm pretty burned out too. I think I needed more recuperation time than I've taken. But since we met, everything's been a blur."

"I get it. I keep thinking I'm present through all of it, and then I can't remember what day anything happened. Luckily my journalism background forces me to take notes."

"I think it's all finally hitting me. Maybe I should take a day or two to rest."

"Do what you need to do. I understand. But I'm close to something. I can feel it…some piece of the puzzle to help make sense of all of this." She pushed herself onto her elbow. "That reporter inside feels the clock gnawing at time. And the longer that persists, the fewer leads I'll find. All these pieces *must* fit together somehow. They just have to."

Kate touched her arm. "I'm not giving up. I'm riding this out with you."

"No. You're right. You've done enough. I can take it from here."

"Sorry, pal, if you think I'm going to let you get all the glory," she said with a wink.

Tawny paused. "Yes! The answer to your question is yes."

"What question?"

"Remember on the ride to Mayaguez, you had asked me if I thought we'd stay friends after this?"

"That was *how* long ago?"

"You'll have to check my notes."

She admired how comfortable her newly-avowed friend was with herself. *I could use a dose of that confidence.* "So, how do you feel about going back home to San Francisco after this?"

"Hmm. Good question. I haven't even thought about it. It's not like I have anything pressing or any opportunities banging down my door since I left KBCH. I do have my sister and my cat, and my sister is taking care of the cat." She paused. "I can't imagine not having Carlos in my life."

"I overheard that conversation you had with your ex when I stayed over the other night. What's her name again? Zoe? Chloe?"

"Chloe."

"That breakup seemed hard on you."

"You know, when it first happened I cried, I admonished myself, wondered what I had done that was so wrong. I felt so alone and broken. But then the crash happened and now, I'm experiencing some sort of awakening. In a flash, my perspective shifted, and I realize how easy it is to get stuck in the stories in my head. That epiphany turned the breakup on its axis."

"How?"

"This. What I'm doing here—investigating what happened to Carlos is what real love is all about. Loving myself is what real love is about. Suddenly I wondered why I ever cared about what a narcissistic ex thought about me or did to me. Compared to the importance of what I'm doing right now, right here with you, Chloe and her actions are yesterday's news. I dodged a bullet with that girl."

"I have a lot to learn from you."

Tawny continued. "In this moment, I feel resolved about her, knowing that while she's stuck with who she is, I'm not. That leaves me free to be the person I deserve to have in my life. Who knows, maybe someday…"

"Do you think you'll find a deep relationship with someone else? I'm asking because I wonder about that myself, you know, since my ex had cheated on me."

"While I don't know what the future will bring, I realize now that I've spent my life searching for an *incredible* woman when I should've been seeking a credible one instead." Tawny paused. "I wonder what she's doing right now."

"Who? Chloe?"

"No. The woman who actually deserves me."

Kate laughed. "You think she's wondering the same about you too?"

Tawny smiled slyly. "I'll have to remember to ask her if and when I meet her."

"Fair enough." Kate removed her outer shirt, spread it on the sand and leaned back on her elbows. Comforted by Tawny's presence next to her, she listened to the rush of waves. "That's one helluva revelation. What if you're simply distracted and then you feel differently when you get back home and see Chloe again?"

"No, Kate. I'm crystal clear that Chloe was really good at keeping me just insecure enough to fool myself into thinking I wasn't worthy of her. Narcissists are good at that. In reality, she didn't deserve me. I'm not saying that because I think I'm perfect or anything." She scoffed. "Far from it. What I understand now that I didn't then, is that who I am, what I respect in others, she isn't."

"Like what?"

"First off, I wouldn't cheat on my lover. And I would do damn near anything for someone I loved or kill myself in the pursuit."

"Okay, that second one is painfully obvious."

"I don't lie. I don't cheat. And when I give myself to someone, I give genuinely and with the expectation that they know enough to appreciate it and reciprocate. For now, it's good enough to know that I finally get the distinction of character."

"I don't know what I would've done if I hadn't met you, Tawny. I want you to find your friend so badly."

"I feel the same about you. What are the odds that we'd have met in the first place, let alone at a hospital right after the crash?"

"We'll never know. But I know we need to get some answers before we both collapse."

"Really, Kate, you should take a break."

She stared out to sea. "In for a penny, in for a pound, right?" She exhaled sharply. "My life will never be the same after this. Never."

Tawny looked over at her and touched her hand reassuringly. "Something good has to come from this, and we don't know what's right around the next corner. Every time I'm tempted to give up, I think, what if the answer is only sixty seconds away?"

"You wear your dogged pursuit well." Kate slid her hand back to her side. "I've wanted to ask you something for a while. If it's out of line, just say so."

"What is it?"

"Why aren't you on TV anymore? You're a really good newscaster."

"It was clear when Chloe and I broke up that one of us had to leave KBCH. I walked away because I didn't need a daily reminder that she had cheated on me. I certainly didn't need to run into her girlfriend who also works there."

"Ouch!"

"Exactly. How about you? Do you know when you might return to work?"

"Though I know the airline will give me all the time I need, I don't know what freaks me out more—not getting back on an airplane, or getting on one."

"You seemed to do okay on the puddle jumper we took today."

Kate lowered her eyes. "Good to know I can fake it. I was sweating when we boarded."

Tawny chuckled. "Everyone was sweating—it's Puerto Rico!"

Kate dusted the sand from her toes and reached for her sneakers. "It will be dark soon. What do you say we clean up and——"

"Go to the restaurant. We'll start searching again in the morning."

Kate smirked while tying her shoelace.

"What?"

"I know married couples who can't finish each other's sentences."

Tawny raised her right eyebrow. "Meaning?"

"Uh, n-nothing—I…"

Tawny poked her arm. "Lighten up. I'm teasing!"

"Right. You and that mischievous grin."

Kate's eyes drifted the length of the mile-long beach in silence. She inhaled along with the sway of the palm frond guardians of the sea who flaunted the salty breeze. Wedged between cobalt and twilight, her eyes fixed on the Creamsicle swirls that melted into the horizon like hot caramel. She watched Tawny gather her things against the fleeting daylight. "For someone who claims to be burned out, you sure don't look like it."

Tawny stood and Kate followed her to the nearby bench.

"Adrenaline—it's high octane newscaster-fuel," Tawny said. "Probably will sleep for a month when this is over." She sat, dusted the sand from her feet, and put on her sneakers. "How do we get information about Mosquito Bay?"

"We'll ask when we get back to the hotel before we have dinner. We could start out like we did with the Coast Guard and ask about the radio transmissions that night. See if we can find someone who might know."

"But don't you think if there had actually been a rescue at Mosquito Bay that the Coast Guard would have known? Or *someone* would've known?" Tawny asked.

"Not necessarily. Lieutenant Commander Swift told us how chaotic things were. Oliver Greene said he picked up that civilian transmission by accident. We need to go to Bahia Mosquito."

"Right. It's settled then. Tomorrow we'll check out Mosquito Bay. I'm glad you're doing this with me." She glanced over at Kate. "You do realize there's a chance that poking around is dangerous."

"Are you still obsessing about your conversation with Mr. Castilano? In reality, Tawny, why would anyone want to follow you?"

"Because I'm a former high-profile newscaster digging around a high-profile incident. Not to mention I have a horse in this race. If someone wanted to cover up something, from my reputation alone they would know that I'm never going to let that happen. Or maybe I already know something that someone doesn't think I should. Fact is, being a gay activist is probably reason enough for some weirdo."

"I doubt anyone could have followed us here. I'm used to seeing lots of people, and I'm certain that I've never before seen anyone we've encountered today."

"That's a relief."

"Tomorrow will be time enough to get back on the trail. Let's rest and sleep tonight. We can both use it."

They entered the quaint hotel lobby and approached the concierge desk.

Tawny fixed her eyes on the young man's nametag and felt a catch in her throat. "Excuse me, Carlos, do you know Mosquito Bay?"

"Ah. Puerto Mosquito," he replied. "Are you interested in taking the tour tonight?"

"Tonight?" said Tawny.

"Sí. You have to take the tour at night so you can see the water light up. You're in luck. When the moon is full there are no tours, but tonight there's only a crescent, so you'll enjoy it."

"What time do we have to leave here?"

"I'll make a call for you, but you'll have to leave soon."

"Tawny, I'd better go cancel our dinner reservation."

Kate stepped through the balmy evening breeze into the bamboo-decorated restaurant. The shimmering glow from suspended lanterns framed in fire a tableau of black water. As she moved through the space, island music instigated a subtle sway of her hips.

Tranquil evening waves drenched the beach before her and suspended time. She gazed toward the mile stretch of beach where she and Tawny had sat that now sank into obscurity. The crescent moon's slanted glow trickled down in streaks and slivers, its beams wiggling on the surf but never quite slipping back out to sea. She canceled the dinner reservation and found Tawny in the lobby freshening her lip gloss in her hand mirror.

"Let me guess," Kate grinned. "Hibiscus Petale?"

"How'd ya know?"

"It's your go-to shade for evening."

She laughed. "Ready to go?"

"You look tired. Why not stay over another night and we'll go tomorrow night?"

She flexed an eyebrow. "You can wait here if you like but…"

Kate glanced down at her wrinkled capris and smoothed them with her palms. "Should I change?"

Tawny stared at her.

Kate nodded obsequiously. "Or…I can just go like this."

"Are you through?"

"Fine! I'll go get a taxi."

CHAPTER THIRTY-ONE

"We're here," Tawny said, looking out the taxi's window.

"Wait for us please," Kate instructed the driver.

The lethargic breeze off Mosquito Bay strained through the dense night air to lift but one hair from a sweep of Tawny's bangs. She glanced up at the clear, dark sky of a barren crescent moon. Hard as she tried, she couldn't picture this serene setting swept up in a storm so dramatic that it warranted emergency calls and even Coast Guard rescues nearby.

Kate led the way toward the entrance of the small white building bearing a sign that read Mosquito Bay Tour Company. "That was some cool ride to get here, wasn't it?" She held the door for Tawny to enter first.

"If you like jungles," Tawny replied. She smiled at the young woman behind the desk.

"Good evening," said the receptionist. "Do you have a reservation?"

"No, we don't," said Kate, "but we're actually in need of information."

"Is there someone who might be able to answer some questions about an emergency call that came from here last month?" Tawny asked.

The receptionist's eyes drifted beyond them. "Captain Juarez? Do you have a moment?"

Across the lobby, a fortyish brunette in uniform tossed her crumpled water cup into the trash and approached. "I'm Captain Sami Juarez, how can I help you?"

"Hello, Captain," Tawny replied. "My friend and I have come to Vieques in search of information about a missing friend. The Coast Guard in San Juan has confirmed that on April twenty-seventh there was an emergency radio transmission that involved Bahia Mosquito. Would you know anything about that?"

"Ah," she nodded. "The night of Tropical Storm Judy."

"That was a tropical storm?" said Kate.

"No, but that's what I named it." The captain shook her head. "That was a crazy night."

"Can you recall any local emergency radio transmissions during or perhaps following the storm?" asked Tawny.

Captain Sami pulled her long, black hair into a ponytail and put on her captain's hat. "I only remember mine."

Tawny and Kate exchanged a glance. "Yours?" they asked in unison.

"Yes. That sudden storm stranded my boat full of passengers in the bay. We took refuge in one of the coves because the truck to transport the tourists couldn't get back to pick us up until it was almost dawn. We had hovered near the shoreline, but the atmospheric disturbance and downpour caused the bioluminescent organisms to light up the whole bay. It was quite a show." She stared off as though pondering it. "It wasn't until the rain stopped and the water calmed that a passenger spotted the glowing outline of two people on the shoreline."

"*Two* people?" asked Kate.

"Yes. I followed protocol and called it into the Navy. I left my First Mate in charge of getting the passengers back onto the truck to return here while I went to investigate. I found two unconscious men."

"Who were they and what happened to them?" Tawny asked.

"I don't know how they got there. I raced to them to see if they were alive because they weren't moving." The captain paused. "One of them was out cold and totally mangled, and the other one mumbled but he was in bad shape."

"What did he mumble?" asked Tawny.

"It sounded like, 'There's no place like home.' Or something like that."

"Like from the *Wizard of Oz*?" Kate asked.

Captain Sami nodded. "That's why I named it Tropical Storm Judy."

"What happened then?" Tawny followed up.

"I stayed with them until the Shore Police arrived and they took over from there."

Tawny glanced at Kate and then asked, "So the Navy took them?"

"Yes. They medevac'd them."

Kate nodded. "Captain, do you know anything else about them or where they took them?"

"The Shore Police questioned me the next day but they didn't know much more than I did. However, they did tell me that they identified one of the men as a Navy lieutenant, so they transported them to a VA hospital on the mainland. I don't remember the lieutenant's name."

"Stateside?" said Tawny.

"No. In San Juan."

"Did they tell you their names, or if they even made it to the hospital alive?" asked Kate.

"All I know is that they were air-lifted to the VA." The captain looked at Tawny. "Do you think you know those guys?"

"I've been looking for my friend Carlos Benitez, and I keep praying that he's alive. That search has led us here." Tawny scraped back her hair and fought back the tears. "He was in the Trans Air flight crash that occurred that same night."

"Well, I doubt these men were passengers on that flight."

"What makes you say that?" asked Kate.

"There were no life vests on them. Frankly, I don't see how they could have drifted all the way here from where that plane ditched—especially unconscious." She shook her head. "Without a doubt they'd have drowned."

"The Navy sure does keep coming up," Kate said under her breath.

Captain Sami looked at her watch when the truckload of tourists came through the door. "That's really all I know. Are you taking the tour tonight?"

Kate stepped over to Tawny and put her arm around her shoulder. "Thanks, Captain, perhaps another time. Come on, Tawny, it's been a long day." She guided Tawny back outside and into their waiting taxi. "Back to the hotel, *por favor*," she said.

The slow ride back to Esperanza left more questions hanging in the balmy breeze than Tawny would've liked. Questions, she thought, that would have to wait until she could think without the haze of fatigue clouding them. The wind whispered through her auburn locks, blowing a few across her eyes, and the half-open window rattled as the breeze escaped back from where it came. Though the shocks on the old Chevy were bitterly worn from bumps in the road, Tawny laid her head back against the cool vinyl upholstery and closed her eyes.

Kate broke the silence midway back to the hotel. "I could use a drink, and probably something to eat—even though I've lost my appetite." She paused. "How about you?"

Tawny opened her eyes and rolled her head toward Kate. "I guess."

When they arrived at their hotel, they ambled through the couples who were laughing and mingling at the restaurant's bar. What I wouldn't give to have a few moments like that, thought Tawny. Have I ever had that? She continued past them into the restaurant and found a table close to the water.

Kate ordered an Absolut martini, up, with olives, well chilled.

"Make it two," said Tawny. She glanced at Kate and shrugged. "Hair of the dog."

Kate nodded. "It really is the best way to cure a hangover." She smiled.

"Maybe it'll help me to stop obsessing about Carlos for two-and-a-half minutes."

The rush of slippery waves before them filled silent gaps in their fragmented conversation, and Tawny hoped that her candlelit reflection belied her disheartened mood, her haggard face. She took refuge in her martini and closed her eyes to feel it trickle down her throat.

"I thought you said martinis held empty promises," Kate teased with a grin.

"Oh, honey I'm *way* past promises." Tawny looked into her welcoming eyes and lingered in their warmth. She wondered who Kate really was in regular life—if that even existed anymore. In that moment she realized that during their time together, she knew little about what made this woman tick.

Some investigative reporter I am! All she really understood was how traumatized the airplane crash had left her, and how, like her, they shared disdain for unfaithful lovers to whom they'd given themselves over. She watched Kate down her martini and signal the waiter for another. "Careful, Kate, these martinis are strong."

Kate sucked on an olive and stared into Tawny's eyes in such a way that it forced her to fill the silence by changing the subject. "Where do your parents live?"

Kate's eyebrows knitted at the question and a few seconds passed before she answered. "I was raised by a single mother until I was eleven. She worked in manufacturing and suffered an injury on the job. The pain never went away, and so the company doctors gave her stronger and stronger painkillers so that she could continue working. She went into rehab three times and that caused the state to take me away from her." She exhaled. "I went into foster care when she could no longer care for me."

"I'm so sorry. What happened after that? If that's too personal, you don't have to answer."

Kate downed half of the second martini before continuing. She sunk down in her chair and looked out to sea. Low and soft, her voice broke when she answered. "She never recovered, and so I went to three more homes before she passed away. I was in the system until I was eighteen."

"That's awful." Tawny reached across the table and placed her hand on Kate's. "No siblings?"

"No, I was an only child and my grandparents never wanted anything to do with me because they basically abandoned her when she got pregnant. They were religious fanatics and she wasn't married."

"Did they know she was ill? Or that she had passed away?"

"Yes. They knew."

"And still…?"

"Still, their so-called religion didn't call for compassion or empathy, or any of the other loving tenets that religion is supposed to have. They contacted me after she died and asked me if I was willing to repent for being born a bastard so that I wouldn't go to hell."

Tawny choked while swallowing her drink, coughing until her eyes watered. "You have to be fucking kidding me."

"No, but even at the wise old age of eleven, I knew that *they* were the true definition of hell. Suddenly, I understood that I'd be better off bouncing between strangers' homes than I ever would be in their care. I figured out they were the reason my mom had always struggled to survive. She'd been right that we were better off without them."

"So how did you get through school and then become a flight attendant?"

Kate smirked. "The only thing that got me through my childhood was daydreaming about all the places my mom and I used to talk about going. So once I was *expunged* from the system, I worked and took classes at the local college and then applied to Trans Air. Traveling was my tribute to the only good dreams I'd ever had as a kid. I could finally escape—explore the world. I had no roots so it made perfect sense to find a place where I might someday want them. I wanted to do it as much for Mom as I did for myself." She downed the rest of the martini in one long gulp and signaled for her next one.

"Take it easy, Kate, we haven't eaten all day. Damn, these fuckers are strong."

"Yeah?" she smirked. "Well, after having survived a plane crash, they're no match for me."

"Did you ever find that place? To put down roots?"

"San Francisco is the closest I've come so far. But honestly? Sometimes I wonder what it's like to have a family—to be connected to someone." She exhaled remorsefully. "I thought I had that...maybe it's not meant to be."

Their waiter appeared and refilled their water glasses. "The kitchen will be closing soon," he said. "Would you like to order something to eat?"

"I'm drinking my dinner tonight," Kate answered.

The waiter turned to Tawny. "And you, Miss?"

Tawny considered the question. "No thanks. I'm too tired to eat."

When Kate was halfway through her third martini, Tawny signed the check and stood.

"Hey," Kate elongated the word and then slurred the remainder of the sentence. "I'm not exactly finished, Tawny."

"Yes, you are." Tawny slid Kate's glass to the other side of the table. "Trust me, you'll thank me in the morning." She laced her hand around Kate's arm and guided her to a standing position.

Kate laughed. "This is the best I've felt in a long time!"

"Come on, we need sleep. Mornings are coming earlier and earlier these days."

Kate stumbled. "Wow. Okay. Glad you're hanging on to me."

They ambled down the dimly lit path toward their beachside cottage, with Tawny gently holding Kate's arm.

"How is it possible that you're single, Tawny?" She stopped and looked at her. "Honestly, look at you! You're smart—no, wait," she pointed at her, "smart...and beautiful. You know that?"

She snickered. "That's the martini talking."

After a few more steps, Kate stopped again on the path and turned to her. "No. It isn't," she said emphatically.

"Okay, I'm wonderful."

They began walking again and Kate said, "Yes, you are wonderful. Screw that Chloe-Zoe...Chloe who...who cheated on you. She didn't and doesn't deserve you. You need someone who will love you right."

Her body weaved. *And…and,*" she swayed slightly then straightened up to make her point, "cherish you."

"I agree. But that sounds like a wedding vow. Stay right here." Tawny leaned Kate against the doorjamb and fumbled in the dim light to insert the key into the lock.

"Tawny?"

With the key finally in the lock, Tawny looked up. "What?"

Kate nailed her with the Persian blues, leaned in, and kissed her.

Tawny recoiled. "What are you doing!"

Kate snickered. "It's called kissing."

Tawny turned the key, reached for the doorknob and opened it. "I don't take advantage of women who've been drinking," she said, guiding Kate into the room. "Nor do I sleep with straight girls. You're welcome!"

Kate fell facedown on her bed and passed out after one huge yawn. Tawny removed her shoes and covered Kate with a blanket, staring down at her tempting companion, thrilled that her Persian blues were on lockdown—at least for now. She'd done well hiding her attraction, but sabotaged by fatigue, her defenses were weakening. *That kiss didn't help! I need a curious straight girl like I need a hole in my head!*

Tawny changed and brushed her teeth, then climbed into the bed opposite Kate's and turned off the light. She closed her eyes and tasted the kiss again, for however brief it was, it still tasted good on her lips.

Tawny awoke in the fog that she now simply called morning. With one eye barely open, she realized Kate was spooning her. She jolted toward the edge of the mattress, patting her body to make certain she wasn't naked. The jolt woke Kate.

Kate stretched and yawned. "Wait. What? What am I doing over here in your bed?"

"Ask your martinis. I'm as surprised as you are. The last time I saw you, you were two sheets to the wind—maybe three—and passed out on *your* bed."

Kate groaned into her pillow. "Did we…?"

"No! God no!"

"Well, you don't have to be so emphatic about it."

"Yes, I do—so that there's no doubt in your mind. Whatsoever."

Kate covered her eyes, then peeked through her fingers and groaned. "Oh, I *do* remember you telling me that you don't take advantage of women who've been drinking. Did I make a total ass of myself?"

Tawny chuckled. "It's about time you let loose a little." She stood, headed toward the bathroom, and turned to Kate. "Don't worry about it. Why don't you order some coffee while I grab a quick shower?"

She closed the bathroom door, turned on the shower and got in, letting the cool water cascade through her hair onto her scalp and down her backside. She could still taste the kiss.

CHAPTER THIRTY-TWO

Carlos double-checked the address on the scrap of paper he pulled from his pocket for the Copacabana nightclub. He turned to Juan. "Are you sure you don't mind going to a gay bar?"

Juan shrugged. "How would I know?" The taxi rolled to a stop. "Besides, isn't it a little late to be asking?"

Carlos paid the fare, stuffed the change into his pocket and grimaced when he slid out. Juan waited patiently for him as a group of young people flowed around them toward the entrance.

One young man in the group stopped and stroked Carlos's beard. "Hola, Papi!" he said.

"Hey!" said Juan, staring him down.

The young man flitted past. "Sorry, I didn't know he was your boyfriend."

Carlos nervously reached behind him and took Juan's hand. "Okay, Juan, let's go shake what the mamis gave us." He limped into the club, his crutches providing little protection for his battered leg.

The main disco room pounded and thumped and pulsed; at first Carlos felt it in his chest, then in his throat. The bass from the dance floor made his leg momentarily throb as it sponged up the beat. Music sparked a direct line of energy through his upper body to the twirling disco ball above. Something about this sensation seemed familiar, inevitable, and all at once he felt alive. It felt like home—whatever that meant.

Juan tapped Carlos on the shoulder. "Nothing about this is familiar, but I like it; I *really* like it."

"You look like Dorothy when she got to Oz, Juan."

"Oz?"

"Yes. *The Wizard of Oz*?"

Juan wagged his head back and forth. "Comin' up empty. I've *still* got nothin'." He glanced over his shoulder and then leaned to Carlos's ear. "That guy behind us is staring at me."

Carlos checked out the man behind them whose elbows rested on the bar, a beer bottle dangling from his fingers, and his bare chest smooth and toned. "He's cute. Go for it."

"But I'm with you."

"This isn't a date."

"It isn't?"

"No. Wow, to think I worried about taking you to a gay bar."

Juan bounced to the beat and stared at the man dancing in front of him.

"Oh my god, I love this song and I hate this cast!" said Carlos.

"Would you like to dance?" the beer-man asked Juan.

"Go ahead." Carlos nodded. "Go." He shooed Juan toward the dance floor. Although comforted by the blur of bodies moving to the beat, the *Eau de Beer* wafting up his nostrils, and the mindless daily chatter of which he caught snippets, he still wondered about who he had been before he had amnesia. Why no one from his life had tried to find him. He thought about how much he missed Tawny, then wondered what else he'd forgotten about her besides her last name and phone number. Suddenly, he realized how much he needed her, not knowing exactly why, but deeply saddened that he didn't know how to find her.

He hobbled to the crowded bar in search of a seat when someone tapped his back. "You and your crutches can squeeze in here," a man said. He whipped around and stared into his eyes. "Chulo! Chulo is that you?"

"Carlos? Jesus! I meant Lieutenant?"

He grabbed Chulo and hugged him for dear life. "Chulo! What the hell are you doing here?"

"I'm on leave—here in San Juan to visit my cousin. But you! What happened to you, and what's with that beard—and the crutches?"

"I could say it's a long story, but I don't know the whole story myself, which is also a long story. I can't believe I recognized you!"

"Why wouldn't you recognize me?"

His eyes opened wide. "I have amnesia." He grabbed Chulo and hugged him harder this time. "Oh my god, I actually *know* someone!" He wouldn't let go.

"You what?" Chulo pulled back to look into his eyes.

"I think I was in some kind of accident and then a coma. I woke up at Buchanan."

"If you have amnesia, how did you recognize me?"

"I don't know, man. Can we go sit somewhere quieter? I need to ask you about…me."

Interrupted by the sight coming toward them, they both paused to gawk at the spindly drag queen as she sauntered past, dressed in a ball gown and a pasty purple wig. Carlos's mouth hung open on its hinge. "Ow, she looks like a Mrs. Potato Head gone bad."

Chulo nodded. "Sad she has no prom corsage. You want a beer?"

"Sure."

He pointed to the far end of the bar. "There's an outside deck in the back. I'll meet you there."

Carlos hobbled back through the muscled brown men who gyrated on the dance floor. He watched the sweat glisten on sculpted chests as he worked his way toward Juan. "Ugh, I just want to dance!"

Juan spun around when Carlos tapped his arm. "Hey!"

"I'll be out on the deck!"

"What?" Juan yelled over the music.

He pointed across the bar. "The deck!" As he pried his way through the crowd and the blaring music, he wondered if he'd always been overwhelmed by crowds, or if this was his new landscape. He finally caught his breath when he neared the softly lit patio and aimed for its subdued ambiance.

Chulo waited for him and carved a path to an empty wooden bench against the wall. "Here," he said, handing Carlos his beer.

"I don't know how long it's been, Chulo, but you look good—I think." Carlos swore he heard the hiss of rising steam when the cold beer met his parched throat.

"So do you…minus the beard. What possessed you? The beard is *so* not you." Chulo sipped his cocktail.

He stroked his chin. "It isn't?"

"No. What happened to your leg? Did you get hurt on maneuvers?"

He shrugged. "I don't know. There seems to be a blackout of information on what happened to me or how I wound up where I did."

"Where did you wind up?"

"On Vieques."

"Vieques? Well where are you staying?"

"We just got released from the VA and we…my friend Juan and I, are at the Santa Clara Rehabilitation Center."

"Who's Juan?"

"I don't know. But they found us unconscious together and we've stuck to each other like glue ever since we woke up from our comas."

"Comas! Jesus, Carlos. That's awful. Is there anything I can do to help?"

He sighed. "Tell me a little about myself. Do you know my address?"

Chulo shook his head. "No. Sorry. But do you remember that time on shore leave in San Diego?"

"San Diego?"

"Yeah! The two guys we met?"

Carlos stared at him blankly.

"Come on. Seriously? Nothing?"

"Sorry." He fixed his gaze on the ground.

Chulo paused. "Oh wait, I know! The weekend we went to Gay Pride in WeHo? You must remember that."

"What's WeHo?"

"West Hollywood."

He shook his head. "I've been to West Hollywood? My mind is like Swiss cheese and it's really weird. It's like I'm never really…me." He wiped the beads of sweat from his forehead.

"Hunk alert." Chulo's eyes fixed on someone behind him.

"Where?"

"He's handsome." Chulo pointed. "Over there with the sideburns."

Carlos turned his head to look and then turned back to Chulo as the hunk approached.

"There you are, Carlos. I got worried," Juan said. He eyed Chulo warily.

"He's yours?" Chulo pouted.

"Juan, this is my friend Chulo. We served together in the Navy and I recognized him."

"No kidding?"

"For real."

"That's great. Does he know where you live or about us?"

"What 'us', Juan?"

"Hi." Chulo extended his hand. "I'm Chulo and sorry but I've never been to Carlos's place."

At that instant, a half-drunk, pint-size man staggered up to them. He bobbed forward and backward in front of Chulo. "Hola, sexy. You want some Chunky Monkey?"

"Go away! I told you earlier, I'm not interested," Chulo said.

"I thought you were faithful to me," the drunk replied.

"I don't even know you!"

"Well, that's the whole point," the drunk slurred.

"The only thing this fag is faithful to is his options—and honey, you are *not* an option."

Juan stepped in. "My friend said he isn't interested."

The drunk shrugged and staggered on.

"So macho," Chulo said. "Thanks, Juan. But I *am* Navy, you know. This helpless sissy thing is only an act."

"Now now, Chulo, Juan was just being helpful."

Chulo laughed. "I know. Thanks, Juan."

Juan continued to observe him. "So what exactly do you know about Carlos? Were you two involved?"

"No! We're shipmates."

Carlos scoffed. "I wasn't cute enough for you?"

Chulo whipped around to face him. "Don't be a diva, Carlos. You think you're RuPaul or Creama LaCroppe or somebody like that?"

"What did you say?" said Carlos.

"I said, 'Don't be a—"

"No. That name. What was that name?"

"RuPaul."

"No. The other one... *LaCreep*. Who is that?"

"You're kidding, right?"

"No. Who is Creamy LaCreep?" he said, frustrated.

"That's *Creama LaCroppe...*" Juan ridiculed. "Puerto Rican...Drag Queen Diva... Extraordinaire." Juan's hand gracefully whisked the imaginary hair off his face.

Carlos stared at him, his eyebrows hiked up higher than Joan Crawford's. "You know this Creama person, Juan?"

"Know her? Sometimes I think I *am* her. I told you I think of drag queens a lot...it's one of the few things I kind of remember."

Carlos's face twisted. "Of all the things you could remember—a drag queen? Seriously, dude!"

CHAPTER THIRTY-THREE

From inside the club a siren blasted and the disco ball twirled, flecked with kaleidoscopic reflections that Carlos could see from the patio.

"What the hell is that?" Juan said.

"Come on, you two, it's time for Ruby Wails and her Tropical Sails. It's the hottest show in town. I'll go grab us a table before they're all gone. Here." Chulo handed Carlos his crutches. "I have your beer." Chulo raced inside and Carlos sat there, stunned, staring at Juan with a scrunched forehead.

"I'm having fun, Carlos. Hey, are you okay?"

"I'm not sure. My brain is misfiring again. Why does the name Creama LaCroppe sound familiar?"

"For me too. Gosh, what if I was a drag queen?"

"You! A drag queen? *Hahaha.* You're giving me a headache."

"Me? What did I do?" He bent forward and pulled him to his feet.

"Go ahead, I'll follow you," said Carlos.

Juan stepped in front of him to clear the way. "Come on, Chulo's over there." He guided Carlos the rest of the way, held his chair and secured the crutches between their seats. He looked up at the stage. "Who is *she*?"

"I told you," Chulo answered, "it's Ruby Wails. He's a local boy."

Juan's mouth fell open. "That's a boy?"

"What did you think?"

"She's gorgeous," Juan confirmed.

"Time to rethink that beard, Carlos. I think Miss Ruby is more your boyfriend's type."

"Juan is *not* my boyfriend."

"Good, can I have him?"

"Chulo, if I say you haven't changed, would I be right?"

"Maybe. But you lack credibility. You don't even remember your favorite drag queen."

Carlos stared up at Ruby Wails. "I have a favorite?"

"You really do have amnesia. Jesus, Carlos, are you all right?"

"Cher. I like Cher." Juan elongated the name the second time it rolled off his lips.

Ruby Wails belted out, "At first I was afraid, I was petrified."

"I know I've heard this song before! I know I have," Juan said.

"Great, Juan! That makes two things you remember. We'll just *stay* at the *bar* 'till it all comes back to you."

"Everybody knows this song," Chulo said.

"Juan also has amnesia, but his is worse than mine."

"What is this, an Amnesia Anonymous meeting?" asked Chulo.

"Don't be ridiculous!" Carlos retorted. "That would make no fucking sense. It's like…redundant. You wouldn't know anybody there or even why you went."

"True."

Carlos continued. "And then at an Amnesia Anonymous meeting you would have to share things you can't remember with a bunch of people who can't remember why they're even there."

Chulo laughed. "What would the first step of the twelve steps be?"

Carlos thought. "I am powerless over my powerlessness to remember."

"Powerless squared! Love it. What would be the second step?"

"I am powerless over my powerlessness to remember."

"I thought that was Step One," Chulo said.

Carlos threw him a sidelong glance. "Amnesia—it's a bitch."

One of Miss Ruby's 'Sails' made her way toward Juan and pulled him onto the stage as a prop. Juan posed for louder applause.

"He's a real ham, your friend Juan."

"So I see."

When Miss Ruby segued into Cher's "Believe," Juan took his seat next to Carlos.

"She's doing Cher," yelled Chulo.
"Cher," Carlos repeated.
"Yes, but don't start," Chulo warned. "No one does Cher better than Creama LaCroppe. Not even Cher does Cher as good as Creama does her." Chulo held up a five-dollar bill for Miss Ruby and stashed it in her fake cleavage.

When the show ended, Chulo turned to Carlos. "How long will you be at that rehab?"

"I don't know. We just got there."

"You said the name of the place is Santa Clara?"

"Yes."

"Okay. I have to report for duty very early tomorrow so I have to get a cab to the airport right now. I'm on a red-eye back to the mainland, but stay in touch with me." Chulo took a bar napkin and wrote down his phone number. "Call me and let me know how things are going or if you need anything."

Carlos tucked the napkin into his pocket and hugged Chulo. "I will," he smiled.

When last-call ended, the house lights came on. "Come on, Juan, we need to get a taxi. I'm exhausted." Carlos hid the grimace from his leg pain and Juan's jaw dropped open on its hinge when the spindly drag queen with the pasty purple wig staggered by.

"Carlos, she's hurting my eyes."

"Let's get out of here."

The late-night stragglers staggered toward the exits while Juan waited patiently and let Carlos lean on him. The crowd outside had all but dissipated by the time Juan and Carlos reached the street. They quietly waited for a taxi in the late humid air when two policemen drove past. Juan lit a cigarette and watched them slow down to scrutinize the gay people.

"Since when do you smoke, Juan?"

"Since now."

"Don't do that, it's bad for you."

"So is almost dying, only to recover and not know who I am. Seriously, what are the odds I would have survived some terrible trauma—followed by surgery, a coma, amnesia. Shall I go on?"

"I fail to see the logic."

"The point is that I'm a lucky guy."

"How do you figure?"

Juan smiled. "The way I see it, life or God must have something left for me to do or I wouldn't still be here."

"That's the first time I've heard you mention God. Do you think you used to be a religious person?"

"Hmm, I suppose I'm *spiritual*." Juan tried it on for size. "Yes. Spiritual. Carlos, that's the third time those cops have gone around the block." He puffed on the cigarette.

"So what." He waved away the smoke. "You can put that out now."

"They're giving me the creeps."

Carlos looked down the street. "A taxi should be along soon. The bartender said that we should wait right here."

Juan and Carlos watched the police car roll to a slow stop. Two officers exited the vehicle and waited in the path of the tall drag queen with the purple wig.

"Here comes a taxi," said Carlos.

"What do you suppose those cops want with that drag queen?"

"I don't know. It's very late and our ride is here." He held up his crutch to flag down the cab. The taxi pulled over and Carlos slid in first. "Come on, Juan."

Juan waited. "Something isn't right, Carlos. I don't have a good feeling about those cops."

"The drag queen can take care of herself, Juan. She's a big girl—a *real* big girl. Come on, let's go." He leaned out the door and tugged on Juan's arm. "It's her purple wig. It stopped traffic."

Juan reluctantly climbed into the backseat next to Carlos. "Go around the block please," he said to the driver.

"What?" asked Carlos.

"Remember when you told me, 'Do the right thing and the right thing is bound to happen'?"

"Now? You're going to quote me *now*?"

"We can't just leave."

"It's not our problem."

The cab cruised around the block, and by the time it had come full circle, a whole vignette had taken place. "Carlos, look! The tall cop is pushing that poor drag queen around. Oh my god, the short cop just punched him."

"Leave it be, Juan, you don't want to get involved."

"Are you crazy? We already *are* involved—we're here! What if that were you or me?" Juan flung open the door. "Someone needs to stop this right now." He raced out of the car before Carlos could respond.

"Hey! Hey what are you doing?" Juan yelled. "Wait a minute! Leave him alone."

"Sir, stay out of this," said the tall cop.

Carlos exited the taxi when the short round cop stepped menacingly toward Juan.

"What did he do wrong, Officer?" asked Juan.

"None of your business," Patrolman Shorty's partner said.

Juan turned to the purple-haired queen. "Are you bleeding?"

"I was standing here waiting for a taxi when that one hit me."

"You're under arrest," the cop said to the drag queen.

Juan stood firm. "I asked you nicely what he did wrong?"

The short cop pushed Juan. "Get out of the way, faggot, or I'll beat the crap out of you too."

"Like hell you will!" Juan spat.

Shorty's partner took a swing at Juan and Juan sidestepped it. Carlos hobbled toward them, flailing a crutch overhead. "What the hell do you guys think you're doing?"

"Great, we got another one," Patrolman Shorty taunted. "How many fags you think we can arrest tonight?" he asked his partner.

"What charges?" Juan barked.

"Drunk and Disorderly, indecent exposure, public nudity…"

"No one here is any of those things!" Juan protested.

"What are you, the daddy?" Shorty asked facetiously. "A girl with sideburns?" He laughed. "Move on!" The cop shoved Juan.

Juan shoved back harder.

"Let's add assaulting an officer and resisting arrest to those charges."

"You smug bastard!" said Juan. "I want to smash this guy's face, Carlos!"

"That sounds like a threat." The cop latched onto Juan's arm.

"Take your hands off him, Officer," Carlos demanded. "Violence doesn't solve anyth…"

Shorty lunged at Carlos and knocked him to the ground.

"Ow! My leg!" Carlos screamed. He looked up at the instant before Juan landed a one-two punch on the cop who threw Carlos down. "Juan, no!"

CHAPTER THIRTY-FOUR

The flagpoles' grommets clanged each time the offshore breeze sailed through the proud flags outside Buchanan VA Hospital. Flanked by rows of starched palms, Tawny and Kate marched in lockstep toward the visitor's sign.

Tawny glanced at Kate as they neared the entrance. "I can't wait to get this over with."

Kate stopped before entering. "Wait."

Tawny turned and ran smack into Kate's Persian-blue stare. "What?"

"About last night…"

"Let's not do this right now."

"I think we should talk about it."

"Nothing happened, Kate. There's nothing to talk about." She opened the door.

"Yes, there is."

Tawny let go of the door and scraped her waves off her face. "Can we talk later? I'm very nervous about walking into this place."

"But things have felt different between us all day."

"No they haven't."

"Well, then it's felt different for me."

"One drunk kiss is not going to change anything."

Kate stiffened. "What? I *kissed* you?"

"Nice to be so memorable."

"Oh, god, and then I woke up in bed with you!"

Tawny glanced around to see who else had heard that. "Look, I need to stay focused on what we're doing here. Like I said, I'm nervous about walking into this place."

"Why?"

"Surely you've noticed we're running out of options. I'm afraid even *I'm* losing hope."

Kate took her hand. "Look at me. It's going to be all right. I'm here for you no matter what."

"Thanks," was all she could muster under the influence of the Persian blues.

"Are we good?" Kate asked.

"Yep."

"Even though…?"

"Yes. It was a drunk moment and we don't need to talk about it."

Kate looked away and then back at her. "What if I need to talk about it?"

Tawny exhaled hard. "One thing at a time. Right now, we need to do this."

"So I *did* make an ass of myself. Nice," Kate groaned. "Are you ready to get what we came for?"

"You bet your ass I am."

Kate smiled. "Atta girl. Come on." Tawny followed her inside and up to the directory on the wall by the elevators.

They scanned the departments that were listed on the framed felt board with the white plastic letters. Kate read them aloud. "First Floor: Acute Care Clinic, Emergency Department, Surgery Clinic, Chief of the Day's Office, Information Desk? Hmm."

"What about that one there?" Tawny pointed to the listings on the second floor. "Social Services."

Kate thought about it. "Let's go with the obvious."

"Information Desk," they said in unison.

"Welcome Aboard," said the young and cheery receptionist. "How may I help you?"

"I'm trying to locate one or two men who were medevac'd here either on April twenty-seventh or April twenty-eighth."

"Are they active military or military family?"

Tawny hesitated. "Umm, I don't know."

"April twenty-eighth was a while ago. Are you sure they were brought here? This *is* a military hospital."

"Is there someone I could speak with?" asked Tawny.

"Ma'am, we have a 400-member staff, and more than 230 enlisted corpsmen, not to mention 100 in Civil Service. Who exactly would you like to speak *with*?"

"Good question. Could you tell me if the patient I'm looking for is still here?"

"What's their name?" The millennial's fingers poked a few keyboard letters.

"Benitez," said Kate. "Carlos Benitez."

"B-e-n-i-t-e-z, Carlos," Information Girl repeated while her fingers bounced off more keys than were necessary to type the name. "I don't see him listed here, but that doesn't mean he wasn't here. He could have been released by now."

"Is there a way for us to find out if he *was* here?" asked Tawny.

"Sorry, ma'am, that's not my job. Unless you're family, I can't give you any more information."

"Thanks," Kate said. She tugged on Tawny's arm. "Come with me."

"But, Kate…"

Kate pulled harder. "Let's go, Tawny." She nudged her away from the Information Desk and whispered. "Forget her. She's just the first stop on this train."

"You're getting to know me a little too well."

Kate snickered. "How well did I get to know you last night?"

"We're back to that again?"

"Let's go with your first guess. Social Services. Second floor."

Kate and Tawny waited for twenty-two minutes in the Discharge Planner's office before the nondescript mousy-haired bureaucrat returned.

"The man that I told you about?" he said. "He was Navy all right. Reserve Lieutenant Carlos Benitez." He dropped the file on his desk.

Tawny leaned forward in her chair. "Are you certain? Oh my god… he's alive?"

"If this in fact is him, Miss Beige. I hate to crush your hopes but the name isn't exactly uncommon here."

"I don't know how Carlos could be in the Navy without me knowing about it. But that doesn't mean it's not him."

The Discharge Planner glanced again at the file. "I signed this man's discharge papers which means I might have met with him briefly. Your friend, what does he look like?"

Tawny fumbled for the picture of Carlos that she had in the zipper compartment of her purse. "Here, this is recent."

The planner glanced down at the photo and back up at the desperation in Tawny's eyes. "It's not turning on any lightbulbs. Then again, I process a lot of people that I never meet. Do you have another picture?"

She pulled out her phone, scrolled through photo after photo of Carlos dressed as Creama, and found the one selfie with Carlos out of drag that they'd taken before he dressed for the DRAG interview. She handed the phone to the man behind the desk.

He studied it for a moment and then quietly shook his head. "Sorry."

"The one you discharged," said Kate. "Where did you send him?"

"Sorry, ma'am, I can't divulge that information."

"Let me guess. It violates HIPAA laws?" Kate said softly.

The planner nodded.

"But you don't understand," Tawny began. "I've been searching for weeks since the night of the crash; I'm a nervous wreck. He's my best friend and I must know what happened to him," she said with a break in her voice.

The bureaucrat's sigh did little to soften his tight military expression. "Look, I have to step out for about, say, a few minutes, but I can't tell you where Benitez was shipped." He opened up the file and placed one of the pages from the middle of it on the top.

"Oh, come on!" Tawny fired back.

Kate grabbed her hand and squeezed it.

The planner continued. "I'll be returning Lieutenant Benitez's records when I get back from the head. I wish you luck finding your friend. Good day." The Discharge Planner stood and left Kate and Tawny alone in his office.

Kate lunged from her chair and picked up the top page on the file. She pulled out her new iPhone and snapped a photo of it. "Got it. Tawny, I can't believe you got through to him but here it is." She showed the photo to Tawny.

"Santa Clara Rehabilitation Center, San Juan," she read out loud. "Let's get out of here."

They left the Social Services office and waited for the elevator. "Kate, if Carlos had been here, maybe someone remembers him."

"Okay, but where do we go to find out?"

"Let's look at the department list again."

They stepped into the elevator and Kate pressed L.

"I'm going to every floor in this hospital to interview everyone I can find." While Tawny tapped her foot waiting for the door to open onto the lobby, she broke a sweat.

Kate held the door open for her. "Hold on. You don't look like you feel well."

"I don't." She stepped out and teetered toward a chair in the lobby but stopped to lean against the wall. "I'm dizzy."

Kate caught her. "Let's go. I'll drop you off at the hotel to eat and rest. We can come back later."

"But we're here now! If I collapse, isn't it better to do it in a hospital?"

"Come on. You need a time-out." Kate held her arm and led her outside to a bench, where she placed her head between her knees. "Do you want me to get you a nurse?"

"No! The dizziness is gone."

"Then I'm driving you to your hotel."

"But we're here now and what if this is really my Carlos?" She sat upright. "We may be so close! Remember what passenger Benitez told us when we visited him in Mayaguez? He said that when he and his wife were treated for their injuries, the authorities kept asking him if he was in the Navy. What if *my* Carlos *was* in the Navy and he was here?"

"Then we can ask when we come back." She escorted Tawny to the car and they got in. Before starting it, she looked at Tawny. "Let's be realistic. We're talking about Creama LaCroppe, Puerto Rican Drag Queen Diva Extraordinaire. The Cher of Chers." She paused. "Do you really think that Creama LaCroppe could be a Navy lieutenant?"

"You're probably right." Tawny retreated for only a moment. "But what if you're wrong? He fooled you, Kate. And if he really was in the Navy, then he fooled me too. I wasn't only his best friend, I'm an investigative reporter by trade—who feels better now. Let's go back inside."

"No, you're going back to the hotel. You're faint because you haven't been eating, you're tired, and rightfully upset. Take a breath, then take a break. We'll come back."

Tawny deadlocked in Kate's Persian blues again and released a sigh. "All right. But first thing in the morning."

"First thing," Kate conceded. "I'll pick you up any time you say and we'll come back here or we can go to that rehabilitation center."

She pouted. "Any time?"

"Just name it."

"Even if you change your mind?"

"Even if."

"I could talk myself blue in the face with you, Kate Taylor."

"Yeah, but you look good in blue." She smiled.

Tawny shooed the Jeep with both hands while trying to conceal a grin. "Drive."

"Who are you—Miss Daisy?" Kate flipped the stick shift into reverse. "Lookin' more like Miss Lazy to me."

"Lazy!"

"Sheesh. Lighten up!"

CHAPTER THIRTY-FIVE

"Ahh." The relief of her arctic abode blasted Tawny the instant she opened the door. *Kate was right to bring me home!* "So freaking hot—humid," she bitched while ripping off her sweaty T-shirt. As she stripped and dropped the clothes into a pile on the floor, the blinking red light on the hotel phone by the bed caught her eye. She lifted the receiver and pressed the button to retrieve her voice mails.

"Not now, Chloe," she said to the recording that droned on. "Let me see," Tawny mocked. "I can have a date with Mr. Bubble and a club sandwich from Room Service—or an edgy, annoying conversation with you. That's a no-brainer. Calgon, take me away." She hung up and started toward the bath. *What if she learned something I need to know? Ugh.* "Later."

Revived from her bath, Tawny tore into her sandwich like a condemned prisoner. Between bites, she pulled out the clasped envelope from her locked valise in the closet and brought it back to the dining table. She removed the papers she'd brought from Creama's desk and sorted through them with one hand while holding her sandwich with the other.

At the bottom of the stack, Creama's Visa bill was paper clipped to something. "Here it is! The picture—the one I've been looking for!" She licked the mayo from her finger and flipped on the reading lamp behind her. Tilting the photo for the best light, she studied it. "Three sailors. Why *these* three sailors? Who are these guys? I wish this picture wasn't blurry." She reached for her reading glasses and tilted the photo for better light.

The neurons in her brain fired up into a frenzy. "Wait. What?" She rubbed her eyes to make sure she wasn't hallucinating. "Well—I'll be straight without a date! If it isn't a young pre-LaCroppe sailor named Carlos *I'm-in-the-Freakin'-Navy* Benitez!" She dropped the sandwich onto her plate. "Sonofabitch!"

She stood and paced across the room, fanning herself with the photo. "Creama?" In disbelief she bent down to look at the picture again under a brighter lamp. "We were best friends. We shared all of our secrets! At least I thought we had." She thought it through. "All those weekends when you told me you went on a spiritual retreat, you must have been in," she bounced when she sat on the bed, "in the Reserves?" She reached for the phone.

"You're already asleep, Kate?"

"Um-hmm."

"Sorry to wake you but I had let you know you that I finally found that photo of the three sailors."

"The one you've been searching for?"

"Yes, the one from Carlos's apartment. It looks like my best friend was a closet seaman."

"Did you say semen?"

"No! S-e-a-man. He's one of those sailors!"

"Are you stoned or something right now? 'Cause you sound a little delusional."

Tawny rolled her eyes. "No, I'm not stoned and I'm not hallucinating." She picked up the picture and stared at it again.

"Maybe it's just a drag costume."

"Huh? I guess it *could* be a sailor drag, but it sure looks authentic." She glanced down at the photo again. "Go back to sleep and I'll see you in the morning."

"You need to get some sleep."

"Yes, I will. I know we start early tomorrow—I'll sleep fast."

She hung up the phone and took another bite of her sandwich, laying the other papers out on the table and running her fingers over the envelope that she found stuck to the table at Joe's. She pulled out the note inside and stared at it for the umpteenth time. "What the hell does it mean? Strait Bahama Hold Swiss. Ugh, I'm fucking exhausted."

Too tired to finish the food on her plate, she left a message for Jimmy and passed out within seconds of her head meeting the pillow.

An hour later the peal of the telephone smacked her awake, shattering her dreamless sleep.

"Sissy? It's Mary!" Larry joked. "Where the hell have you been?"

"Ah shit, I forgot to call you back," Tawny moaned.

"Ah shit is right. I've been trying to reach you for two days."

"Larry," she said quietly, "I may have found Creama." She yawned hard enough to make her eyes water.

"What? Are you serious? Oh my God! Is she alive?"

"Slow down. Have you ever seen Creama do any routines with sailors or maybe seen her in sailor drag?"

"No."

"Well, if, and it's a big if, Creama turns out to be Naval Reserve Lieutenant Carlos Benitez, then we might be in luck."

"What are you talking about? Knock, Knock, hel-lo, are you dreaming or are you awake?"

"I'm awake *now*, Larry."

"Did you say Navy? *Hahahaha!* Creama in the armed forces? What's her rank? Little Commander Mermaid? Oh wait, did you say Lieutenant LaCroppe?" He guffawed. "Captain Creama reporting for duty!" He snorted. "I said 'duty'."

"Jesus, Larry!"

"I'm sorry, but that's just too funny."

"If the guy I've located is him, he's alive, and he's a Lieutenant in the US Navy."

"No way! Our Creama? What's her specialty? Sharpshooter of pointed remarks with nine-millimeter sarcasm?"

She chuckled. "Geez, it's such a long story, but Kate and I found evidence of a rescue and a Carlos Benitez that led us to Buchanan Military Hospital."

"Kate," he mused. "The cute but straight Kate?"

"What has gotten into you? Have you been drinking?"

"Only a teeny-weeny bit—plus three shots for Coco's birthday. Tawny, if Creama's alive, why the hell hasn't she contacted us?"

"Honey, I don't know anything for sure yet. It may not even be her. But there sure does seem to be a run on Carlos Benitezes down here. I spent last night on Vieques checking out a big lead, and it took forever to get back to the VA hospital in San Juan to follow up on the lead. That's where I got this information, but I'm drained. I haven't slept much, and I won't know anything until tomorrow at the earliest. I promise I'll call the moment I know something."

"I'm sorry, kitten. We're all rooting for you here, and I'm very proud of you. Tell Kate to take care of you for me."

"I'm finally getting closer to finding some answers. Can you do me a favor?"

"Name it."

"Relay the information to Chloe. In fact, I got a message from her but fell asleep before I could call her back. Any idea if she has anything new to report?"

"I guess you haven't heard the latest?"

"Only her voice mails. What *latest*?"

"You didn't hear it from me, and of course I can't tell you who I heard it from, but rumor is she left her girlfriend because—and she was quoted on this. Chloe said the biggest mistake she ever made was leaving you."

She sighed. "I'm over it, Larry."

"What? Yeah right."

"No, I mean it. These past weeks here have given me some distance, and a different perspective—on everything. Faced with life and death, Chloe and relationship drama are unworthy of my time. Life is too damn precious to get stuck in *that* story."

"This Kate woman is sounding more and more interesting."

"What does she have to do with anything? Besides, she's straight and we're friends. It's not what you think it is."

"Don't be so quick to judge, kitten. Maybe it's not what *you* think it is."

CHAPTER THIRTY-SIX

At the Central Jail early the following morning, the Public Defender interviewed Juan and Carlos separately and then together. Under the late night fluorescent lights of the jail cell, Carlos had likened the purple-haired drag queen to a radioactive runaway Crayola crayon that managed to escape from the *big* box.

In the interrogation room, Carlos sat across from his lawyer with his hands folded on top of the gouged wooden table. "Why do I have to repeat the whole story? I told you before, Juan and I were leaving the club. We got into a taxi and after we drove around the block, we saw the purple Mrs. Potato Head getting beaten up by the cops—for what turned out to be absolutely no freakin' reason." Carlos's blood was percolating. "Then without provocation, the short cop threw me and my pinned leg onto the ground." He slapped the table and leaned back in the nicked-up wooden chair, his leg aching now more than ever.

"You, Juan, and the drag queen relate the exact same story," said the attorney, "and it's been corroborated by the taxi driver." He leaned on the table and looked directly at Carlos. "But, Lieutenant Benitez, surely you recognize the gravity of the situation. You realize that an infraction of the law with an ensuing arrest may have military repercussions? Now, if we can get the charges dismissed—"

"Dismissed?" Juan interrupted. "We should be filing gay harassment and assault charges against those officers."

"He's right, Juan. It's Conduct Unbecoming," Carlos said. "The military may have tossed out, 'Don't ask, Don't tell,' but they ain't gonna like this. Depending on the charges, the bottom line is I could be dishonorably discharged."

"That's insane, Carlos. What gives them the right to harass us?"

"Look," said the lawyer, "all the cops want is an apology for Juan's punch and you're free to go. It's a small price to pay. According to them," he read from a sheet of paper, "there was due cause for them to search the drag queen, and the one who knocked you down, Lieutenant, thought you were a threat because you came at him with your crutch."

"Oh puleeze," Juan said. "A man on crutches in a cast is a threat to armed police officers? You insult our intelligence by asking us to apologize for being gay bashed." Juan tapped the table with his index finger to make his point. "If somebody doesn't stand up and do the right thing here, we won't have any rights left! This will keep happening until we purge this disgusting behavior. It's simply unacceptable."

"Give it a rest, Juan," said Carlos. "You're starting to sound like—like a politician."

The attorney stood and paced to the other side of the room and then turned. "Lieutenant. I understand what happened. If you pursue this, the consequences will most likely be a stain on your career, if you still have one."

Carlos sneered. "So what are you saying, huh? Are you saying, oops our resident homophobes got a little cranky last night and we just happened to be lucky enough to get in their way? That's punishing the victim."

"Lieutenant, the police captain promised me that the officers will be dealt with appropriately. Are they really worth your career? Your pension?" The attorney glanced at Juan. "Your relationship?"

"Juan is my friend, not my lover."

Juan bent down near Carlos's ear. "Carlos?" he whispered. "We don't exactly know the nature of our relationship."

"Oh Jesus!" Carlos blurted. "Fine! I'll say whatever, just get me the hell out of here!"

The lawyer turned to Juan. "So you'll apologize, Juan?"

Juan leered at the lawyer. “Yeah, fine, I’ll apologize. When do we get out of here?”

“You’ll be taken back to lockup now. I’ll begin the paperwork and you should be home by dinnertime.”

“Dinnertime?” Juan scoffed. “It’s eight o’clock in the fuckin’ morning.”

CHAPTER THIRTY-SEVEN

Tawny stood on her terrace and inhaled the salty breeze, waiting for the second cup of coffee to hit her veins. Plagued by the montage of the past few weeks' events, none were more vivid than that one unexpected moment with Kate in Vieques. While she could no longer taste the vodka-kiss that Kate had bestowed upon her, the moment had yet to fade. It ghosted her with feelings of longing.

Grateful that the ring of her hotel phone interrupted the recollection, she reentered her room to answer it. "Kate?" she said when she picked up.

"No, it's Jimmy."

"Oh. Hey."

"Where ya been? I was worried," he said.

"Kate and I went to investigate on Vieques."

"What was you *in-vest-igatin'* on Vieques?"

"Don't act like a six-year-old. Did you know that two men were rescued from Vieques the morning after the plane crash?"

"No, I didn't. Did you know that the key from the envelope goes to a safety deposit box?"

"No, *I* didn't."

"Who were the guys?"

"Whose safety deposit box?"

"Tawny, let's talk in person. How about later on?"

"Sure. I have some potentially exciting news."

"Really? Did you find something?"

"I'm not sure, but you're right. We need to sit down and go over this. Listen, I'm about to walk out the door. Will you call me later?"

"You got it, kiddo."

She hung up and stared long and hard at the crystal blue ocean. The phone rang again and she let it. *Just one more deep breath.* "Hello."

"I'm on my way," Kate said.

"I'll wait for you out front."

Breathe, she reminded herself. *You'll know soon enough.* She left immediately and paced outside the hotel while watching for the Jeep.

Kate pulled up to the curb with a sudden stop. Her long blond hair was anchored by the ponytail hole of her baseball cap, and she flashed her fresh and bright smile when Tawny got in.

"We're heading to the rehab first, Kate."

"No coffee?" Kate said with an air of desperation.

"We'll get some on the way. You know the way, don't you?"

"Won't matter till I get some coffee."

Tawny pulled her sunglasses down her nose just far enough to see Kate from above the frame. "Okay, Princess, make a right up ahead. There's a coffeeshop on that block."

They grabbed two menus as they came through the door and took the nearest free booth. A minute later, the waitress came to their table.

"One espresso for my friend and a regular coffee for me, please," said Tawny.

"And I'll have the Number Nine, eggs scrambled," Kate added. "Aren't you having breakfast?"

"No, I'm too jumpy to eat."

Kate handed the menus to the waitress and waited for her to leave. "Did you bring the picture?"

Tawny took the photo from her purse and handed it to her.

Kate studied it intently. "That's him in the middle, isn't it? Blurry or not, you can't miss those eyes."

"Yes."

The waitress brought their coffee and Kate downed the espresso shot.

"Looks real to me." Kate handed the picture back to her. "So, are you ready for whatever we find or don't find today at the Santa Clara rehab?"

She put down her coffee cup. "I hope so. But the truth is, I won't know the answer until we get there."

"Remember, no matter what happens, I'm here for you."

"My emotions are all over the map. On one hand, I'm pissed off that if Carlos was in the Navy, why didn't I, his BFFFF know about it? I feel betrayed. And...and if he's alive, why hasn't he contacted me?"

"BFF...*FF*?"

"Best *freakin'* friend *freakin'* forever...freakin'!"

Kate placed her hand on Tawny's arm. "With a little luck, you may learn the answers to those questions today."

"I don't know. While I really need some sort of closure—I'm frightened of what I might find out. During this whole journey, as hard as it's been not knowing what happened to him, at least I had some hope. But if Carlos is really gone, that's not the kind of closure I'm prepared to live with."

"If that's the case, remember that you're the best *freakin'* friend he could have ever had."

She paused, then sighed at Kate's Persian blues. "Carlos wasn't my friend. He was my family."

"Sounds to me like you have a case of good old-fashioned cold feet." Kate smiled. "Have something to eat. It'll steady your nerves."

"No food when I'm this nervous. I can't." She took a moment to gather herself. "I spoke with my friend Larry last night. The messages I keep getting from Chloe are more than concern for Carlos."

"Really? Does she want you back?"

"I've been avoiding her so I'm not sure, but according to Larry, she left her girlfriend and things are pointing in that direction."

"I know you said you were over it—over her. But really, Tawny, deep down is that what you honestly want? Isn't there some small part of you that wishes she'd finally come to her senses?"

"No. Because I've finally come to mine. I'm holding out for the right woman this time—if I ever find her. If she even exists. And if not? Well, I'm never going to settle again for the wrong woman, even if that means I remain independently owned and operated. These past few weeks have been a real wake-up call—and you've had a lot to do with that."

"Me?"

"Don't take this the wrong way, Kate, but being with you has been a revelation. I feel closer to you as a friend than I ever did to Chloe as a lover *or* as a friend."

Kate's eyes darted away and then back to Tawny when she spoke again.

"This quest to find Carlos has shifted me, transformed my thinking—opened up some chakras or moonbeams or something."

"Tawny?"

"Huh?"

"What's the *wrong way* to take that?"

Forty minutes later, Kate made her final turn onto the wide avenue. "It should be on this block." She slowed down and coasted.

Tawny pointed to the sign. "There it is—up ahead on the right."

Kate rolled the Jeep to a stop and set the brake in front of the Santa Clara Rehabilitation Center.

Motionless, Tawny stared at the entrance.

"Come on, one foot in front of the other."

"Huh? Yeah. I'm right behind you."

CHAPTER THIRTY-EIGHT

"Chow time, *girls*." The jail guard's antagonism dripped from his mouth each time he'd had to address Carlos, Juan, and the purple-haired drag queen throughout the night. The drag queen moved close to Juan while the guard placed their sandwiches on the cot.

Carlos stroked his beard and stared him down, but the guard scoffed as his flat-footed waddle carried him back out of the cell.

"He looks like a bulldog," Carlos muttered.

"Hey, Papi, listen, I'm really sorry I got you and Juan in trouble. But thank you for standing up for me. I owe you everything for that." The drag queen crossed the cell and sat on the cot next to Carlos. "How's your leg?"

"Listen, my purple prom queen, Juan was right. We have to do the right thing and stand up for each other. What's your name, anyway?"

"I'm Miss Chi Chi Rivera." The drag queen shook his hand. "Pleased to meet you." She stood from the sagging cot. "I would like to repay you both. So, Juan, let me see your palms and I'll give you a reading."

"Chi Chi, you can read palms?" Juan asked excitedly.

She straightened her wig. "I can do much more than that, but first let me have a look." Chi Chi stepped across the cell and sat on the other cot next to Juan.

"Give him your hand, Juan," said Carlos before he took a bite of his cheese sandwich.

She traced the lines in Juan's hands.

Juan giggled. "That tickles."

"I see a long life—and great things that await you, my friend." Chi Chi studied Juan's hands, turning them obliquely to better examine the fingers in the light. She brought the hands closer to her and then looked back and forth between them. "You have the ability to move mountains, Juan."

"Nah…" Juan blushed. "Really?"

"Sí, sí *amor*, I don't know if you know this, but you're a powerful man. You could easily hold a position of authority with many people hearing your words and following your example." Chi Chi stopped abruptly. "May I see your palms, Carlos?"

Carlos put down his sandwich, wiped his hand on his pants and held out his palms. "Do me, Chi Chi."

Chi Chi crossed to him and examined his palms while he chewed. "Hmm."

"What? What's with the 'hmm'?"

"I see you're very artful. You and Juan have unusual compliments. Cup your hand." She examined his palm's landscape. "You both have very developed mounts."

"Developed what?" asked Juan, crossing the cell to look.

"The mounts. See? This fleshy part represents fame, charisma, and art. And this one here shows Carlos's strong leadership." She looked up at Carlos. "Charisma and art." She paused. "Have you ever thought about going into entertainment or politics?"

"Entertainment," Juan mused, trying it on for size.

Carlos nodded. "Politics. Hmm."

Chi Chi continued. "Maybe something involving large groups of people, but you both show a major shift around the same time. Some big event is about to come into your life." Juan stretched open his hand and studied it. Chi Chi continued. "Whatever this big event is, it will happen soon. There's a twin nature between you two that until now was split." She traced the same set of lines in each of their palms. "Here's where the lines converge. Think of it like twins who are separated at birth, then meet as adults and discover they have the same interests. It's fate. Very interesting!" Chi Chi closed her eyes and put her hand on her forehead.

"So what does all this mean?" Carlos asked.

Her eyes popped open. "It means a death!"

Carlos gasped.

"*Not* a physical death. More like death of old ways—a rebirth."

"Can you tell if I'm going to meet the love of my life? No offense, Juan."

"None taken. But that's partly true, Chi Chi. We had a bad accident and I almost died. But we don't remember it."

"You have a rare twin nature. I never get psychic impressions this strong in a first reading. How long have you two known each other?"

"I don't know," Carlos answered. "That's part of what we're trying to figure out."

Chi Chi traced another line in Carlos's palm. "Here's the big event crossing your life line. Something beyond this accident you speak of, and it happens soon after. Pay close attention, Carlos, because what you do with this opportunity will affect the rest of your life, and who knows, maybe the lives of many others."

Carlos looked up from his palm into Chi Chi's eyes. "For the better, or worse?"

Chi Chi folded his fingers into his palm and looked deep into his eyes. "That, my friend, is up to you."

CHAPTER THIRTY-NINE

Santa Clara Rehabilitation Center wore its Sunday morning like a siesta. Tawny held the door for a resident who tried to maneuver through it in his wheelchair, and even with a few residents milling about in the lobby, the place was serene.

She tapped her fingers on the counter, waiting for the manager to return. Kate gently placed her hand over hers and stopped the tapping.

"Sorry. The suspense is killing me. They said they would notify this Benitez guy that we're here and that was twenty minutes ago."

"Relax, Tawny, the staff is obviously a skeleton crew on Sundays."

"I'm sorry it's taking so long," the manager said when she took her seat behind the computer. "I rang Lieutenant Benitez's room but there was no answer, so I had the security guard check the apartment. No one's there."

"Thanks," Kate said. "We'll wait here in the lobby if that's okay."

"*Momentico*, let me make another call." She picked up the phone and pressed two digits. Tawny listened to the conversation even though she didn't understand Spanish. The manager raised her voice before hanging up.

"Señorita, it appears that Juan and Lieutenant Benitez didn't return from their outing last night," she said sheepishly.

"What's an outing?"

"We have a curfew, but the lieutenant called last night beforehand to say that he and Juan would be back after curfew. The night manager just informed me they never returned."

"Who is this Juan person you keep mentioning?" asked Tawny.

"The lieutenant's roommate."

"Oh. How about if I leave a message for him?"

"You're welcome to, but it might be better if you call or simply come back later. I can't tell you where they are or when they'll check in, or if they'll get your note right away."

"Thank you," said Kate. "Tawny, we can come back."

"Oh man," she groaned. "More waiting?"

They got back into the Jeep.

"What if...?"

"What if what?" Kate started the car and pulled out onto the Calle Esperanza.

She sighed. "I've been foolish to think that Carlos could've survived that crash and be in some rehab with a guy named Juan. We're really reaching for straws here. I think I need to prepare myself for the fact that he's gone."

"We've come this far because of you, and one way or another, we're seeing this through. It's the only solid lead we have left so I'm not letting you give up now."

"It's a dead end."

"We don't know that for sure. Hey, how about we go to the beach and decompress for a little while."

"I'd rather go to my room and wait for Jimmy's call."

"Why?"

"Dick Peak had him send an envelope to Puerto Rico before he left San Francisco. When Jimmy came down here, he tracked down the envelope and there was a key inside with a number written on a piece of paper. He's been researching what the key belongs to and he called me this morning with some answers. Anyway, I want to update him about Vieques."

"What would Dick Peak's key possibly have to do with Carlos?"

"Nothing. But if we can identify it, it may provide clues about Peak's intended trip here, which may have to do with why I've been looking over my shoulder since this ordeal began. As a reporter, I have to pull the thread. Andy, the *Chronicle* reporter was beaten up after attempting to pass information to Jimmy and me on the same night. In the same place at the same time! And that may have something to do with that key. Jimmy and I need to have a face-to-face to make sure neither one of us is missing anything. I don't have a good feeling about it and neither does he."

"I thought you didn't like Jimmy."

"He's not such a bad guy. A little limited perhaps."

"It was only a few weeks ago that you called him the poster thug of the religious right."

"That was before I knew he was watching my back, and yours… and before I knew he had a sense of humor. Truth is, I think he's a decent guy, and I feel safer with him around believe it or not."

"You really think we can trust him?"

"I do. My gut tells me he wants to make sure we're safe."

Kate dug into her knapsack at a red light. "Good," she said, "I have a swimsuit with me. Why don't you leave a message for Jimmy to meet us on the beach? Come on. A dip in the ocean will melt away your stress. It's so fucking hot and humid today."

"*Every* day. I find it hard to believe you'd willingly go back into the ocean after your ordeal."

Kate pulled into the hotel's parking garage. "I can't let the plane crash win. Simple as that. Until that event, I always loved the ocean. But I'm afraid to go in alone. Please come in with me?"

"Okay." Tawny smiled. "Come up to the room. We'll change and I'll leave Jimmy a message."

The crystal-clear baptismal font was locally known as the beach at Isla Verde. To those who would leave their troubles ashore, the salty aqua surf promised to cleanse them in every curl and trough. Tawny allowed the waves to rock her while she kept an eye on Kate. She watched her dive into the water and then stand in the thigh-deep ocean.

The flight attendant's streaky blond hair fell to her shoulders, the salty water dripping down her bikini cleavage. *What was I thinking that night in Vieques? No, I did the right thing, fending off a pass from a drunk straight girl—that I'm terribly attracted to! Awkward!*

She floated on her back, cradled by a wave that let her stretch out her arms and watch Kate swim to her.

"Hey, I think I see Jimmy walking onto the beach."

"Where?" Tawny let her feet sink to the sandy ocean floor as she focused in the direction Kate was pointing. "That's him. I have to go."

"Don't you want me to come with you?" Kate dunked her head and slicked back her hair.

"Give me a head start," she said. "See you upstairs."

Kate reached for her hand under water and squeezed it. "Hey. We okay?"

"Yeah, I've gotta go," she said before quickly turning away and riding the surf to shore.

"Nice scenery," Jimmy teased when she came dripping out of the ocean.

"Meet me at my room in ten minutes."

He stood, dusted himself off and left the beach, veering onto a frond-lined path.

She retrieved her beach towel from a chair and wrapped it around her goose bumps. While blotting her hair dry, she spied a woman who watched her every move from above a magazine. Tawny turned away and covered up in her sari, but when she turned back around, the woman had vanished—the magazine still on the chair. She felt a chill race down her spine, clutched her beach bag, and dashed toward her room.

A minute after she got there, there was a knock at the door. "It's me," said Kate.

Tawny opened the door. "Jimmy is on his way up." She tried not to stare. *Great. She just* had *to bring the cleavage.*

"You mind if I rinse off in your shower?"

"Help yourself but hurry up—he'll be here any minute."

"Save water, shower with a friend?" Kate laughed.

"Very funny. Still not letting it go?"

"Hey can I ask you a question?" Kate called out from behind the closed bathroom door.

"What's up?" Tawny flipped her sandals off her feet, stripped and stepped into shorts and a T-shirt.

"Are you going back to Chloe?"

She pretended not to hear her. "What'd you say?" There was another knock at the door. "Jimmy's here."

Kate turned off the water. "I'll be right out."

CHAPTER FORTY

Tawny let Jimmy in and then locked and chained the door. He stood in the entryway, his hands clasped in front of him.

Kate exited the bathroom clothed and smiled at him. "Hi."

"Hey," Jimmy answered, quickly averting his eyes.

Kate fidgeted and put her hand on her hip. "We sort of met in Mayaguez. I'm Kate."

"Yeah, I remember. How you doin'?"

"Good."

"Come in and have a seat," Tawny said to him.

"Thanks." Jimmy strolled over to the window. He first peered down at the beach and then surveyed the terrace before sitting. "So you were on that flight that crashed," he said to Kate.

"I was the congressman's flight attendant."

"He musta liked that."

"Jimmy," Tawny began, "I think someone was watching me on the beach."

"Who?" asked Kate.

"Was it a dark-haired woman about thirty with a straw hat, reading a Spanish magazine?" Jimmy asked.

"Yes! You know her?"

"No, but I saw her watching you when you got out of the ocean."

"Who could she be?" Kate asked.

"I don't know. The better question is why was she watching me?"

Jimmy smiled. "Maybe she liked you."

She dismissed the notion with a wave of her hand. "So, what have you got?"

Jimmy glanced at Kate and then Tawny.

"It's okay," Tawny said. "There isn't anything you can't say in front of Kate."

"You first," Jimmy said.

Tawny took a cigarette out of the pack in the night table drawer.

"Since when do you smoke?" asked Kate.

She looked up. "Since now. Who are you, my mother? I'm just so frustrated."

Jimmy snickered. "She smoked while she drank martinis the other night."

"Thank you both but I already have a mother and a father." She lit the cigarette and reached into the closet for her locked valise. She dialed the combination, opened the black case and extricated the chubby file before setting it in front of him.

"What's all that?"

"In there is evidence that Creama LaCroppe is a Navy lieutenant, for starters. There's also a note I haven't yet shared with either of you..."

"What note?" Kate asked.

"A note from who?" asked Jimmy.

Tawny leaned over the table. A delicate trail of exhaled smoke wafted toward the now open terrace door. She opened the file, reached to the back of it and pulled out an envelope. "I don't know who wrote it and I don't know what it means, but..." She clamped the filter between her teeth and slid the note out of the envelope. "Here." She handed it to Jimmy. "You're both right," she mumbled while crushing out the cigarette.

Kate moved behind his chair to look over his shoulder.

He took the note but stopped cold. "Did I hear you say that you believe Creama LaCroppe was an officer in the United States Navy?"

"No, I said he *is*, not was."

"No. You did *not* just say that Creama La..."

"Yes, Jimmy. That's exactly what I said."

He pulled his reading glasses from his inside pocket, flicked them open, and turned the note around and then upright. "Strait Bahama Hold Swiss. Where'd you get this?"

"Believe it or not, I found the envelope stuck with chewing gum to the underside of the same table at Joe's, where you had sat with Andy."

"Who's Joe?" Kate asked.

"Joe's is a what, not a who," Jimmy explained, using his open hands as punctuation. "A coffee shop."

"Jimmy, do you know what it means?" asked Tawny.

"My guess is it's a sandwich hold the cheese."

She struck Creama's hand-on-hip pose. "You're joking, right?"

He laughed. "Maybe you're carrying around somebody's lunch order."

She shook her head. "In a sealed envelope! Bubble-gummed to the underside of that particular table the day after?" She shrugged him off. "Forget it. What did you find out about that key?"

"It belongs to a security vault box that I assume is number 1832, but only because the note says 1832. I don't know where to find the box except I *did* learn that it's not at an airport or any public place. It's a private series—like a bank maybe."

Kate reached over his shoulder. "Can I see that note?" She studied it and read aloud. "Strait Bahama…Hold Swiss…Bahamas Swiss. Hold. Bahamas Swiss Holding?" she mused as she moved toward the nearest night table and reached for the drawer.

"What is it, Kate?"

"Where's your phone book?"

"Other side of the bed."

Kate pulled out the San Juan Yellow Pages, sat on the bed, and flipped through the bank section. "San Juan Savings…." Her voice trailed off into a mutter as her index finger scanned the pages. "Here it is in black and yellow." She turned the phone book toward Tawny and pointed to the ad on the middle of the left page.

"Strait Holding Company?"

"Read the bottom," Kate said.

"Branches throughout the Caribbean and…"

"Go through the list."

Tawny scanned the ad. "Bahamas. Strait Holding Company Bahamas?"

Jimmy stood and crossed the room. "And in the Bahamas there's off-shore money and access to Swiss accounts." He took the note back from Kate and read it again. "A Swiss account at the Strait Holding Company Bahamas? This is totally possible! Ladies, I believe we may have found a clue to where the box is that fits this key!"

"Jimmy," Tawny began, "who was the third guy with you and Andy that night at Joe's?"

"He's a source—a Silicon Valley dude. Works for one of the big software companies in Mountain View."

"Was he the one who had information that would damage Peak's career?"

"There were rumors. Andy called me that night and told me to meet him at Joe's at one a.m. to make a deal. I never found out what it was, though, because that guy was already there."

"So then Andy wanted to trade information? For what?" asked Tawny.

"Yeah, for an exclusive interview with Dick. But me and Rita—that's my girl," he explained to Kate, "we were, ya know…busy. I got to Joe's late. When I arrived, I saw Andy sitting in the booth having what looked like a heated discussion with this guy. I walked over and that's when I heard this joker laying out claims about Dick that were disastrous. So I sat down and tried to straighten him out. He was trying to extort Dick for something that didn't happen. At least I think it didn't happen." He paused. "I hope it didn't happen."

"Claims such as?" Tawny asked.

"He accused him of laundering campaign money."

Kate interjected. "Tawny, who do you think left the note under the table?"

"I don't know but it makes sense that Andy did. I know he thought he was in danger, especially by the way in which he ushered my friend Larry and me out of there so fast. He slipped Larry a note and practically pushed us out the door." Something in Tawny's brain clicked when Jimmy zeroed in on her.

"Andy slipped you a note?" he verified.

Tawny nodded. "Shit, maybe Andy wrote both notes and this one was meant for you, Jimmy."

"But why?" he asked. "That note Andy gave you and your friend—where is it?"

"Ohmigod, it's probably still in my purse." She grabbed her purse and dumped its contents onto the bed.

He leaned over and picked up the photo of Chloe and Tawny. "Is this your girlfriend?"

"Not anymore."

He glanced over at Kate and smiled. "You're doin' better now anyway."

She snatched the photo from his hand and dropped it into a pile of purse litter. "Stop picking at my belongings."

Kate stepped over to the bed and stared down at the photo.

"Do you or do you not have that note?" he asked impatiently.

"Hold your horses." Tawny searched the compartments. Then she reached deeper and felt along the bottom lining. Soft and crinkled, a dirty piece of paper was stuck there. "Here it is," she said, handing it to him. She followed him to the terrace door and looked over his shoulder while they compared the handwriting of the note that Andy had handed to Larry against the one that Tawny had found stuck to the table.

"No doubt," he said when he handed both notes back to her. Kate came over to look.

"One and the same," Tawny agreed.

"So then, assuming that Andy wrote both notes, he was already afraid he had incriminating information. That must have been his bargaining chip when he called you, Jimmy."

"Boy, you automatically assume that Dick Peak was guilty of somethin'." He pleaded his case with Italian-hands that opened for punctuation. "No evidence. No trial. Just guilty because of who you *think* he was."

"Dick was guilty of being exactly that—of being Dick Peak. That was offensive enough. Don't you think all this evidence is pointing to a dirty political deal?"

"No, I don't. It's all circumstantial."

"You've been in politics too long," Tawny said.

"No, I believe in Dick."

"Switching teams?" she teased.

He raised his arms like a conductor. "Wow, and here I was just really starting to like *yous*. Ya know, when you think of Dick Peak, I know you see a bigot. But I've known Dick since he was a kid. Under all that political façade, he was just a good and decent old-fashioned guy. At least his legacy won't be a wig and lipstick."

"Maybe he was a decent kid, but the world has news for you. As a man, he was a greedy, womanizing, mean-spirited homophobe."

"He didn't hate gays. Let's say his attitude was…strategic."

"Jimmy, homophobes don't hate gays. They're afraid of them."

Kate stepped in between them and whistled. "Okay, you two, back to your corners! Jesus, enough ideological bickering. In case you've forgotten, we're trying to find out the truth about that fateful night when the two people you each love were probably killed in a plane crash." She turned to Jimmy. "I was there and I can tell you, Jimmy, that Carlos 'Creama LaCroppe' Benitez was as brave a hero as you will *ever* see. Sadly, Mr. Peak met his fate looking after himself. Now, both of you snort, groan, have a pissing contest, do whatever you have to do…but get it over with already." Kate picked up the phonebook, pointed to the listing, and stared down Tawny and Jimmy. "We're going to the Strait Holding Company to find that box. They have limited Sunday hours."

Tawny conceded. "She's right."

Jimmy cleared his throat. "I apologize."

"Me too. All right, Kate, let's go so maybe Mister Jimmy Ostrich can take his head out of the sand long enough to see the writing on the wall about his friend."

"What's that supposed to mean?"

"A self-righteous, egotistical…" Tawny started.

"Enough!" said Kate. "I'm not ready to be a mother. Now let's go."

On the way to the elevator, Tawny whispered to Jimmy, "She sounds like a *mean* flight attendant."

"Yeah, on a flight to hell maybe," he whispered back.

They both snickered.

"Catch. You're driving." Kate tossed Tawny the car keys when they exited the hotel. "Now both of you get in the car and no fighting."

Jimmy sat in the back of the open Jeep that bounced with each pebble in the road. "Why do you keep looking in the rearview mirror, Tawny?"

"I want to make sure we're not being followed."

He grinned. "I thought maybe you was admiring me in my Foster Grants. Ya know, in all probability no one is following us and nobody cares."

"Then why are you being so careful?"

"Occupational hazard."

"How can you say that?" she asked. "What about that woman on the beach earlier?"

"Like I said, maybe she liked you."

"You're just trying to ease my mind."

"Is there something wrong with that?"

Kate faced Jimmy. "I hate to interrupt your little cloak-and-dagger repartee, but have either of you thought about what you're going to do to get into that vault box?"

Tawny's and Jimmy's eyes met in the rearview mirror. Neither of them answered.

"I didn't think so," Kate said.

"Ladies, I think we can assume that if Dick mailed the key to himself, that the box is in his name. Knowing him well, I think the reason he mailed it was because he didn't think it was safe on his person. I can do his signature real good. Do it all the time."

"Unless they know he's listed as deceased and they have the box frozen or whatever," Kate said.

"Or," Tawny blurted, "he knew that if something happened to him, you would find the key, Jimmy! Seriously, why else would he have asked you over and over if you knew where you'd mailed it?" Jimmy nodded. "If he didn't want to tell you about the key but he wanted you to know about it, he could have you send it, knowing that you were going to look at the addressee."

"If that's true, then Dick might have put my name on that vault box authorization card. I'm authorized to do a lot of things for him."

"Exactly."

"To answer your question, Kate, I'm going to walk into Strait Holding and sign the old J.C."

"Jimmy," Tawny said, "you may not want anyone to know what's in that box."

"You gonna sell me out, Miss Lancôme of Paris Matte Crimson?"

"What do you think?" she asked, turning into the palm-lined parking lot at Strait Holding Company.

"While I'm not a gambling man, I still think I can trust you."

Tawny parked and killed the engine. She unfastened her seat belt and turned to face him. "Do you want me to go with you?"

"Yes," he said. "It always looks better if you got a broad—sorry, a *lady* with you."

"How *ever* did you learn to be so charming?" Tawny asked.

He sat up straight. "I come by it naturally."

CHAPTER FORTY-ONE

As their taxi pulled away, Juan handed Carlos his crutches and helped him negotiate the curb. Exonerated men, they entered Santa Clara, checked in at the desk and aimed for their apartment.

"Carlos, look at the bright side. At least we got out of jail hours before they said we would. Oh, I also got Chi Chi Rivera's number in case we want to call her."

Carlos shot him a sidelong glance. "Terrific, Juan. Exactly why would we want to call her? Never mind, all I can think about is a hot shower and my bed."

Juan followed Carlos into the apartment and plopped down on the couch. "I'm numb! Good thing it's Sunday—no appointments." He leaned his head back on the throw pillows. "Ahh," he moaned.

Carlos stripped off his crumpled shirt, gulped down two glasses of water and called out from the kitchen. "Is it okay with you if I shower first?" He waited but there was no reply. "Juan? Juan." He limped over and saw Juan's eyes on lockdown, already asleep. "I'm right behind you, my friend," he said as he hobbled off.

Within minutes of his one-legged shower, Carlos drifted off, praying he'd feel better when he awoke.

Two hours passed before Juan's growling stomach woke him. He groaned and stretched out the painful kinks that had nested in his neck, then shielded his eyes from the angled late-day sun that breached the slats in the blinds and painted a warm streak across his chin. He scratched his stubble on his way to the shower and smiled when he heard Carlos snoring.

Leaning into the cascading water, he washed the pungent smell of jail out of his hair and then shaved. "What a difference," he said to the man in the mirror, whose face he was finally accustomed to seeing.

Refreshed and clean-shaven, except for the long sideburns that he considered a badass way to cover the scars there, he wrapped the damp towel around his waist and found Carlos sitting on a chaise on the terrace. "Good morning," he said.

"Good morning? How could you let me sleep till four thirty in the afternoon, Juan?"

"I just woke up myself and took a shower. Besides, you were blowing 'Zs'—snoring."

"Was not."

"Were too. Hey, let's go eat. I'm starving."

"If you're dressed for dinner," Carlos began, "I think you look better in the purple towel."

Juan scoffed. "You do not find me even remotely attractive, do you?"

"Can we save this conversation for later? I'm hungry too."

"Yes. I'll get dressed."

"While you do that, I'll hang and water the plant we bought yesterday. How about this corner right here in the late day sun?"

"That's nice. But don't you think it would look better in the other corner? Is this music playing the CD you bought?"

"Yes. Do you like it?"

Juan listened for a minute. "I do like it."

"Go! Get dressed so that we can go eat."

Jimmy and Tawny left the bank and got back into the Jeep.

"So? What happened in there?" Kate asked.

Jimmy snapped his seat belt together. "There was no box number 1832."

"You're kidding."

"He's not," said Tawny.

"Got any other ideas?" he asked.

Tawny laid rubber pulling out of the parking lot. "As a matter of fact I do."

He smiled. "Why am I not surprised?"

"Kate and I are going back to Santa Clara Rehabilitation Center. Would you care to join us?"

"Seriously, ladies, you honestly think Creama LaCroppe is this guy who wasn't there this morning? It sounds to me like you're chasing your tails."

"You weren't there at the VA hospital. Everything points to this person being my Carlos." She made a left at the light. "Either way, I have to know."

"You mean Ensign Drag Queen?" he chided.

"Very funny," Tawny shot back. "FYI, that's *Lieutenant* Drag Queen to you, pal."

Kate wagged her head. "Please, the two of you are becoming a chore."

"What did we do?" Jimmy asked innocently.

"Yeah," Tawny added. "What's wrong?"

"You both need therapy—the long, drawn-out kind. So, if there was no box number 1832, then what does 1832 mean? What does it have to do with the Strait Holding Company?"

Jimmy shrugged. "Adjusted for inflation, that's the 128,000-dollar question, isn't it?"

For the next several minutes, only the rumble of the Jeep's suspension interrupted the silence.

"Jesus, we've been driving forever. Where the hell is this place?" asked Jimmy.

Tawny pulled up in front of Santa Clara and brought the Jeep to a sudden halt. "Here." This time she didn't need to be prodded. Jimmy and Kate trailed into the lobby in her wake and joined her at the front desk.

"We were here earlier to see Lieutenant Carlos Benitez," Tawny said to the manager. "You told us to come back?"

"Ah, sí, sí, the lieutenant has returned…"

Tawny's pulse quickened.

"Apartment 209." She pointed beyond her. "Down that path to the right, take the first stairwell up one flight. You can take the elevator, but it's slow."

"Gracias," Kate said. "Tawny, wait up."

Tawny's heart pounded harder, and although she led the pack, her legs felt like cellophane noodles in gooey brown sauce. *What if this isn't him? Oh no, what if it is? Oh God let it be him so I can thank him for taking ten years off my life! On top of it, I've spent a minor fortune!*

"Whoa, Tawny!" Kate said.

Tawny halted and pivoted 180 degrees. "Huh?"

Jimmy pointed to his right. "The stairs?"

"Oh, yeah," she said doubling back. She took the steps two at a time and found the apartment—impatiently tapping her foot until Kate and Jimmy closed ranks. She exhaled a nervous breath.

He placed a comforting hand on her shoulder. "Calm down, you're going to give me a heart attack."

She tried for a deep breath. *Tap tap*. "This can't be right. I hear Judy Garland singing 'Somewhere Over The Rainbow.' Creama hates Garland."

"Knock louder." Jimmy prodded her but she was frozen still. He reached across her and gave the door a solid *rap rap rap*. In a New York second, Kate glanced at Tawny who glanced at Jimmy who glanced back at Kate. No one breathed.

The door opened. "Yes?" said the tall handsome man with the long sideburns and bangs.

"Hello," Kate said sweetly. "We're looking for Lieutenant Carlos Benitez. Is he here?"

The man crossed his arms and looked at them askance. "Are you from the Navy? Is this about last night?"

"No," Tawny jumped in, "we're not from the Navy. I'm sorry to disturb you but I'm searching for Carlos Benitez. Do you know where we can find him?"

"Come in, I'll get him for you."

Kate and Jimmy nudged a stiff Tawny into the small foyer.

"Please wait here," the man said politely. He turned the corner and disappeared.

CHAPTER FORTY-TWO

Carlos glanced over his shoulder when Juan came out onto the terrace. "I'm almost done," he said.

"Some people are here to see you."

Carlos turned to him. "People? Here to see me? What people?"

"Some man and two women. They're not from the Navy."

Carlos laid his garden glove on the table next to his bullet shell.

Juan picked up the bullet shell and examined it. "Where did you get this?"

Carlos frowned. "It was with my personal effects at the hospital. I keep staring at it hoping it'll jog my memory, but so far, nothing." He grabbed his cane and winced as he limped into the apartment with Juan following. Carlos turned the corner of the living room and moved toward the three people in the foyer. The blond woman looked straight at him.

He caught a flicker of something, but it was too brief to capture any images. The blonde nudged the other woman whose back was to him. She turned around in what seemed like slow motion.

Carlos gasped. "What the…" A flood of dismembered memories rushed his brain all at once, overloading all of the circuits but one. His voice shook. "Tawny?" he said in disbelief.

"Tawny's eyebrows arched and wrinkled her forehead. *Gasp*. Jimmy caught her when she teetered to the side. "Creama? It *is* you!"

"Tawny?" Carlos said again, more sure this time.

"Creama?"

"Tawny!"

"Creama! You're alive!" She stepped closer.

"Ohmigod, ohmigod, ohmigod! Tawny!"

She embraced him and kissed his cheeks relentlessly. "I can't believe I've found you."

"Tawny!" Carlos held on to her for dear life. "Jesus! It's *Beige*, Tawny *Beige*...*not* a shade of lipstick! Let me look at you." Carlos leaned back to get another view.

"Creama, where the hell have you been? I've been searching for you since that awful plane crash. Why haven't you called? We've all been worried sick about you and," she grabbed him again, "oh thank God you're alive!"

Carlos glanced at the man who wiped a tear from his eye and then blew his nose in his handkerchief.

"Tawny?"

"Yes, Creama?"

"Did—did you say plane crash?" Carlos's face twisted. "Why are you calling me Creama?"

"Uh-huh, I said plane crash."

Carlos began to hyperventilate. "I think I'm going to faint."

"Steady, Carlos." Juan edged Tawny out and gently guided him to the sofa. "Sit here and put your head between your legs." Juan paused. "Come in," he said without turning to the three.

When Tawny raced to put her arm around Carlos, he sat up. The other woman took the armchair on the far side of the room, and the man nested in the closest location to the door.

"Ow!" Juan squeezed his own forehead as he stood fully upright.

"Juan, what is it?" Carlos asked.

"I don't know. My head hurts where that cop hit me."

"Sit here on the floor in front of me and I'll massage you," Carlos said. He stared at the blonde while he rubbed Juan's temples. "I get flashbacks every time I look at you," he said. "Do I know you?"

"Yes and no," she answered. "I'm Kate Taylor, and I was your flight attendant on Trans Air 44...the plane you were on that went down in the ocean."

"I know that I've seen you before but I have no memory of this crash. Tawny, why did you call me Creama? And why did I answer to it?"

"You're joking, right?"

"I have amnesia. I don't remember. I remember you, though…kind of."

Juan moaned when Carlos squeezed his neck muscles. "Are you going to introduce me?"

"I'm sorry. Tawny and Kate, this is Juan." Carlos saw the flashback again. This time some of the images stuck. "Yeah, the flight attendant," he mused. "And you, you look familiar," he said to the man. "Are we friends?"

"Not exactly. My name is Jimmy Castilano and I lost my friend, Congressman Dick Peak, on that flight."

"The news." Carlos nodded. "That's right, they said Congressman Peak was on that plane."

"Yeah," Juan added. "Don't you remember that night in the hospital when they showed his memorial on TV?"

"Creama, are you telling me you don't remember anything?"

"I remember you, Tawny. I know I live in San Francisco. But the Navy screwed up my identification and lost it, so I'm still waiting for them to release my address." He stared at her dead-on. "Would you please tell me why you keep calling me Creama?"

"Honey, you're Creama LaCroppe, Puerto Rican Drag Queen Diva Extraordin*aire*." Her hand floated up and away with the elongated exaggeration of the 'aire' in 'extraordinaire.'

"What's wrong with your arm and hand?" asked Carlos.

"Nothing. That's the famous Creama introduction move."

Juan glanced at Tawny. "Dream-crusher. I had hoped *I* was Creama."

"Seems everybody's got a leg up on this Creama LaCreme but me. After last night, I don't think the Navy would be happy about it."

"LaCroppe," Tawny corrected him. "I wouldn't worry about that. Now that I've found you, I'm taking you home."

"Please tell me you know where my apartment is."

"I not only know where you live, I have a key to your place and your rent is up to date. I even have your credit card. Oh, Creama! I'm so sorry. This was all my fault."

"It was? Tawny, do you know if Juan and I were lovers?"

"Sorry, Creama, I don't know Juan. You've been single for a long time."

"Oh." Carlos frowned.

"My head feels better. Carlos, you're my guardian angel." Juan stood and kissed him on the forehead.

"Sheesh," Jimmy muttered under his breath. Tawny shot him a look.

"Would anybody like a beer?" asked Juan. "It's my new favorite beverage."

"Definitely," Jimmy said, following Juan toward the Red Stripe oasis.

Carlos squeezed Tawny's hand. "Tawny, I kept trying to call you, but it was a nightmare. Each time I picked up the phone, I'd forget part of your number. I couldn't remember your last name…I didn't know how to find you!" He grabbed her and held on for dear life. "Oh, mija. I can't believe you're here."

Tawny gazed into his eyes and welled up. "Oh god, look at you," she said, tears streaming down her face. "What happened to your leg? You have a cane…and with that beard you look so…so…" She sobbed leaning into his shoulder. "Butch." She gathered herself, sniffled and looked up. "Is that a scar near your eye?"

"It's a miracle that you're alive, Carlos," Kate said. "You're a *very* brave man. You personally evacuated several passengers, some of whom were injured and unconscious, even a mother and her baby. They're all alive and well because of you. Quite frankly, until now I didn't think you could have survived because you stayed behind to help others. Thanks to Tawny, we found you. She's been relentless, day and night since it happened."

In the kitchen, Juan's hand trembled causing him to drop the bullet shell.

"I'll get that," Jimmy said, bending down. He picked it up, inspected it and handed it to Juan. "Where'd ya get that?" he asked as they walked back into the living room.

"It belongs to Carlos." Juan laid the bullet shell on the coffee table and retreated to the armchair. Nervously twirling the quarter in his pocket, he gulped his beer.

"I did all that?" Carlos asked Kate.

"Did all what?" asked Juan.

"Kate was recounting the plane crash I was in," Carlos explained. "She said I rescued people but the lifeboat disappeared before I could evacuate the plane."

"Carlos, if you were in that plane crash, what about me?"

"Huh? Yeah, Kate, so what about that?" Carlos said. "Do you know Juan? Well Juan's not his real name; he has amnesia too."

"The only thing I can tell you is that I thought I heard you shouting that someone was still in the aircraft, but then the lifeboat drifted away. But since the authorities are still gathering data, the National Transportation Safety Board hasn't formally released any information. I'm sorry, Juan. I don't believe I've seen you before."

Momentarily distracted, Juan watched Jimmy eye the bullet shell. Thinking that the man might steal it, he reclaimed it. A vague memory stirred when he heard the *chink* of the bullet shell hit the quarter in his pocket. He observed Jimmy again.

"Is there a reason you keep starin' at me? 'Cause I ain't no fag."

Something in the timbre of Jimmy's voice woke another layer in Juan's sleeping memory. "Jimmy?" he said.

"Yeah."

"Nothing," said Juan. He studied Jimmy when he spoke, and when he listened to the others. There was something about him that he couldn't quite put his finger on.

"You mind if I get another beer?" Jimmy asked.

"No." Juan followed him into the kitchen, watched Jimmy lean into the fridge and observed his mannerisms; even took a whiff of his cologne.

"You ready for another?" Jimmy popped the top and offered the first cold one to Juan.

"No. Why does this feel familiar?" Juan thought out loud.

"Hey listen, I'm sorry about callin' you a fag. That was *in-sens-i-tive*. I'll try to do better."

"Fag? Really? The word is 'gay.' Remarks like that only perpetuate fear and hatred, you know." He paused before continuing. "Carlos is gay and evidently he's not only my hero. He rescued lots of people. Would you call him a *fag*?"

"Okay, okay, I get the point. I'm sorry."

Juan led Jimmy back to the living room and turned to look at him again. "Are you sure I don't know you?" he asked.

"Doubtful," Jimmy replied. "Highly doubtful."

Carlos was in the midst of recounting the tale of his ordeal to Tawny and Kate. "So when I woke up from my coma, they told me about Juan and that he was still in a coma." Carlos looked downward. "No one expected him to pull through—even I had my doubts. Then I made it my personal mission to make him wake up."

Juan sat and listened, twirling the coin in his pocket. He fidgeted with the bullet shell and kept an eye on Jimmy.

"So, you were right, Tawny," Jimmy said. "I gotta hand it to ya. You are really something. You set out to find your friend and Bing Batta Boom you found him!"

"What?" said Juan.

"What what?" Jimmy replied. Tawny, Carlos, and Kate went silent.

"What did you say?" Juan asked.

"I said, Tawny was right—"

"No," that funny word…bing something."

Jimmy chuckled. "Yeah, Bing Batta—"

"Boom." Juan wasn't sure if the flash of lightning he saw was from where the cop had hit him in the head or if it was a flashback. Remnants of images imploded in his psyche. Ordered fragments collided like a thousand-piece jigsaw puzzle blown across a room by a stiff wind before they coalesced. He stood and lunged toward Carlos. Light-headed, he staggered, nauseated from the saltwater he could almost regurgitate.

"Juan! You okay, man?"

Judy Garland's CD was still playing. She sang: "Ding, ding, ding went the bell."

"Carlos, I need to talk to you."

"Now, Juan?"

"Yes, now."

"Can't it wait?"

"No, Carlos. Now."

"Right now?"

"Yes, right now!" Juan said indignantly. "I feel like I'm going to be sick."

Jimmy shook his head. "Geez. Fags. They're so temperamental."

"Go ahead, Juan, I'm listening."

"Here? In front of all these…people?"

"Why not? Tawny is my best friend. Kate and Jimmy are her friends and they've all been looking for me."

Juan broke a sweat. "Carlos, the plane crash."

"Yes. What about it?"

"Carlos, think! Your arms had to be pried off me when they found us."

Carlos stared at the floor, his brows furrowed. "The inside of the plane," he mumbled. "Water! The water is filling the plane. Lightning." He grabbed his leg. "Ugh! That's when my leg cracked. I jumped into the ocean. My leg!" He hyperventilated. "The salt stung my leg so bad." He paused and closed his eyes. "No, wait. I pulled someone out on top of me. I can almost see it. Jesus! I think I'm having amnesia and déjà vu at the same time."

"What?" Kate asked.

"I think I've forgotten this before." He stared pointedly at Juan. "Juan, are you thinking what I'm thinking?"

"What the hell are you thinking?" Jimmy interrupted.

"Carlos, I think I'm…"

"You're what, Juan?"

"Carlos, I…"

Carlos stared at Juan wide-eyed. "Oh God!"

"I really think I'm—"

"Carlos, are you not saying what I think you're not saying?" Tawny interjected.

"Would somebody finish a goddamn sentence around here?" Jimmy shouted.

Tawny stood and stared with her mouth agape. "Er, uh…" she muttered but no words came forth. "Uh."

Jimmy scratched his head. "Would somebody please tell me what the fuck is going on?"

Juan walked over to Jimmy and took the quarter out of his pocket. He tossed the coin up in the air with his left hand and caught it with his right hand, twirled it between his knuckles and slipped it back into his pocket.

"Hey, where'd ya learn to do that?" Jimmy asked.

"You taught me, Jim. In your backyard when I was eleven years old."

Silence crashed the party.

"Anyone else suddenly able to see pigs fly?" said Kate.

Jimmy's jaw dropped open. "Holy freakin' shit! Dick? No. No, you can't be…no, you ain't Dick!"

"Well you ain't *dick* either, Mister!" Juan retorted. He spun around and undid his belt and pants.

Tawny covered her eyes. "Oh, I don't think I want to see this."

"Hey, what are you doin'?" Jimmy said.

Juan pulled down his pants just far enough to expose the tiny scar on his right buttock. "Remember your BB gun, Jim? You shot me in the ass! I remember that." He pulled up his pants.

"Dick! It's really you?" Jimmy sprang to his feet. "Wait a minute. How come you don't look or sound like you?"

Juan lifted his bangs. "Those scars are from reconstructive surgery and my face is still a little swollen. They had to repair my airway, but honestly, I don't know what my voice was like before."

"Sonofabitch, Tawny, you did it!" said Jimmy. "This is unbelievable. I'm so freakin' glad you're alive, Dick!" He pulled Dick into a bear hug and patted him on the back. "Hey, buddy." He pulled away and lowered his voice. "Uh, did you switch teams? What are you doin' livin' with a fag?"

Dick gave Jimmy a stern look. "Did you learn *nothing* from our little talk in the kitchen? You can't talk about my best friend that way."

"I'm so glad you're alive! So, what are you doin' livin' with a *gay* guy? Especially one that you hate? Wait, I thought I was your best friend." Giddy, he patted Dick on the back again and wagged his finger to reprimand him. "You got some 'splainin' to do, Dick."

Carlos intervened. "Who do you think you are—Ricky Ricardo? Wrong Latino island, dude!"

"Hate?" Dick chimed in. "How could I hate Carlos? He saved my life, took care of me in the hospital. Then, when they were ready to leave me in the street, Carlos made sure I was safe and had the best care available. If it weren't for Carlos, I would be dead, or at best, wandering the streets of San Juan injured and alone."

"But, but, he's your nemesis. Him and that DRAG organization. Don't you remember them picketing you?"

"I… I don't remember." Dick massaged his right temple. His hands started to shake and he hyperventilated, his chest heaving to get a full breath.

"You're a United States Congressman for chrissake! A bastion of the Religious Right."

"No, they're the nasty people. The fanatics. I'm *not* one of them!"

Jimmy paused, stared into his eyes and spoke softly. "You're right, Dick. You're not *one* of them—they are many of *you*. Maybe you want to review your voting record against gay marriage, or on hate crimes legislation, religious liberty…"

"No! No, I couldn't have done that. Only a total asshole would do that!"

"Dick Peak? You?" Carlos stared in disbelief. "Why were we on the same plane?"

"Because we learned he was up to no good, and you were following him to get dirt on him," answered Tawny. "You were going to expose him. Don't you remember the candlelight vigil? The Dawn Chang television interview for DRAG, the Diversity Rights Activist Group?"

Carlos shook his head. "It's all jumbled in my mind."

Tawny grabbed his hand and stared into his eyes. "You, Creama LaCroppe, were the spokesperson for Diversity Rights Activist Group. You were following Dick Peak to Puerto Rico because he was up to something slimy."

"Hey!" Jimmy protested.

Carlos shook his head in denial. "Not Juan. Juan is good—and sweet. He's so caring and—"

"And Juan is Dick Peak," Tawny said.

"Carlos, I can't get over that you're Creama LaCroppe, Puerto Rican Drag Queen Diva Extraordinaire. You realize what this means, don't you?"

"What, Juan? I mean…Dick."

"Now you *have* to shave off that beard." Dick laughed. "I can just see Creama LaCroppe in a Cher gown with that beard. *Hahaha*."

Carlos laughed. "Wait. How about Miss Chi Chi Rivera with that purple wig and my beard?" Dick and Carlos shared a fit of nervous laughter.

Jimmy scratched his head. "Chi Chi who? Never mind, I don't wanna know. Man, this is crazy. I need a time-out." He sprinted toward the terrace.

Carlos and Dick gawked at each other, and Kate gave Tawny a gentle nudge. "Come, Tawny. Let's get some air and give these two a minute."

CHAPTER FORTY-THREE

Tawny followed Kate out onto the terrace to find Jimmy sitting on the edge of the striped ottoman with his head hung and his lit cigar dangling from his left hand. She stopped and rested her hand on Jimmy's shoulder. "Are you okay?"

His gaze drifted slowly upward to meet hers. "No. I don't freakin' believe this. They're clueless…they don't realize…You know they're in for a serious reality check once they remember how they *really* feel about each other."

Tawny groaned. "I know! Who would have ever thought that those two could ever—would ever…"

"Aw shit. You don't think they been…been, you know, *together*, do ya?"

"Don't put that image in my head!"

Kate spun around, leaned against the railing, and folded her arms across her chest. "Listen to the two of you." She scoffed. "First of all, it's not the end of the world! Stranger things have happened than those two making nice."

"Yeah? No!" Tawny mocked. "You don't understand, Kate. You don't know what it's like to be discriminated against, to have people constantly trying to convince you that you're less than human; that you don't deserve equal rights. Let alone when people with a public platform mount campaigns against you and come gunning for you. You don't get it."

"Yes, I do!" Kate shot back.

"I appreciate the straight solidarity, Kate. Really, I do. But you don't understand. Growing up knowing you can't marry the person you love, or being hated because of how you're born. Being constantly vigilant so that you don't get attacked."

"I do get it, Tawny. More than you think." Kate looked away and then back at her. "Believe me, stranger things than Dick and Carlos making peace have happened."

"Really! Like *what*?"

"Like, I get it because…because I'm gay. We went through all of this together, became good friends and all this time you never suspected that *I'm* gay."

Tawny's glance blossomed into a full-on stare, no blinking. "What? No—you're not."

"Yes, I am."

Stupefied, she stared at her. "How is it I'm just finding this out?"

"I like you."

"I like you too, Kate," she said innocently.

"No, Tawny, I *like* you."

Tawny paused. "You mean you *like* me like me?"

Kate smiled at her.

Startled, Tawny raked back her wavy mane. "That's it! I'm a complete failure as a homo. If there was Gay School, I—I would flunk Intro to Homo 101." Her jaw hung open.

"Ha! This day just keeps on giving, doesn't it?" Jimmy stoked his cigar. "Hey Tawny, this is the first time I've seen you truly speechless. So Kate," Jimmy exhaled the smoke, "what other strange things have happened? Respectfully, I really want *yous* both to know I am thoroughly loving this."

Kate evaded Tawny's stare. "Well, maybe I thought you'd figured it out and weren't interested. After all, you're an investigative reporter for god's sake. But back to the present. Tawny, look at you and Jimmy, becoming friends, out here together—commiserating."

"Don't look at me," Jimmy said. "Tawny is the expert on *commiserating*. Just ask her."

"I don't believe you. How could you do this to me? After all the time we've spent together and you never said a word!"

"Hey, I never said I was straight, you assumed it. Told ya' I wanted to talk about our night in Vieques."

"At least what happened in Vieques makes sense now."

Jimmy sat upright like a hungry puppy salivating for scraps. "What happened in Vieques?"

"None of your business," the women snapped in stereo.

"Kate, do you think you could have picked any other time to tell me? I mean like *any* other time?" She sat on the ottoman next to Jimmy. "Gimme that." She swiped the cigar from his fingers and puffed on it. "How could you do this to me? You lied by omission."

"You're right. I picked a bad time. But when you made it pretty clear in Vieques that you weren't interested, I decided to wait until this ordeal was over and behind us. You didn't need any more on your plate." Kate hesitated. "For the record, I remember the kiss."

"Kiss?" said Jimmy.

Tawny met Kate's gaze. "I feel betrayed."

"That was never my intention. I didn't want anything to get in the way of our friendship or our search. I'm sorry, but I can't help how I feel about you. I'm seriously attracted to you."

Tawny stared at her and shook her head. "I've been fighting my feelings for you all the way through this because I thought you were straight."

Kate's Persian blues smiled at her. "You have feelings for me?"

"You want to know what I think?" Jimmy began.

"No!" they barked.

"We need to talk about this, Kate."

"I know."

"As soon as we figure out what to do about Carlos and Dick," Tawny added. "Jimmy, got any ideas?"

Kate answered first. "You two don't have to do anything. They're fine. Look at them." Jimmy and Tawny stood, and the three of them peeked into the apartment and eavesdropped.

"Carlos," Dick was saying, "if what they told us is true, we not only weren't lovers, we hated each other's guts."

"Juan, I mean, Dick, how can that be? We've been through life and death together."

"You know how I feel about you," said Dick.

"How?"

"We're best friends. I love you, man. I owe you my life."

"You don't owe me anything…Dick. That sounds so weird, Juan." Carlos closed his eyes, shook his head, and then looked at him. "Listen. Now that your friend Jimmy is here, he can take you home and you can get back to your life. He'll take good care of you."

"Carlos, how can you say that? We're a team. You can't abandon me now! You can't send me back to that unconscious vacancy that I used to call a life. Not that I can really remember any of it except for Jimmy shooting me in the ass. But come on. You've seen that Peak guy."

"Juan. You are that Peak guy." Expressionless, Carlos lowered his voice. "So, what do you propose? Do I join an ex-gay ministry or pretend I'm the straight guy who rescued you, or are you coming out? Are you even gay?"

Dick fell back onto the sofa and expelled an exasperated sigh. "Are those my only choices? Because if they are, I'm so screwed."

"You got any other suggestions?"

Dick sat upright. "I'm in shock. I need time for this to sink in—to get used to the fact that I'm Congressman Richard Peak." He paused in thought. "From now on, maybe my nickname should be Rick instead of Dick. Or how about Rich?"

Carlos sat next to him and patted him on the knee. "I'm going to need time to get used to this, too, mijo."

Dick sighed. "Between us, Carlos, if I had known who I would turn out to be, I'd have tried harder not to remember."

"Juan-Dick-Rick-Rich, however narrow-minded and mean-spirited the former Dick Peak was, Juan more than made up for him. What you did for Chi Chi Rivera was no small thing. Juan is part of you; Juan is the best part of you. He's your second chance. This guy, the one you are now—he could set a lot of things straight." Carlos paused. "Bad choice of words. You know, make it right. Shit, you know what I'm trying to say."

"Boy, Chi Chi Rivera was right! This must be that big change she saw coming for us."

"No joke. Tawny?"

Tawny poked her head in from the terrace. "Yes, Creama?"

"You can all come in."

She led Jimmy and Kate back into the living room.

"Dick and I have discussed it. Jimmy, I think it's best if you take him home."

"What?" Dick protested. "Carlos…"

"Actually, there's a little problem with that," Jimmy interjected.

"A problem?" said Dick.

Jimmy glanced at Tawny and Kate. "I think maybe we should all take a seat," he said calmly.

Tawny stared into Kate's eyes with disbelief as she sat on the couch next to Carlos, who took her hand.

Jimmy held Dick's gaze and spoke softly. "Brace yourself, buddy. There's more to this than your brain might be able to accept right now. This is the story of how you got here and not all of it will be easy to hear." Jimmy spoon-fed him the events starting with the ROAR rally in San Francisco and the envelope Dick had given to him. With forthcoming allegations against him, he reminded Dick to consider that Carlos had been his nemesis.

The only time Dick interrupted him was to react to his political record on his fight against equality. "No! That's not who I am!"

Jimmy caught Tawny's glance.

"I've got this," she said. Tawny chronicled the rest as a seasoned journalist trained to lay out the facts.

After hearing about the note under the table, the incidents culminating in Andy's assault, and the man at Joe's Diner who was threatening to expose him, Dick stood and paced across the room.

"Expose me?" Dick lamented. "What kind of rogue was I?"

"Did...did you say *rogue*?" asked Jimmy.

Carlos confirmed it. "He said rogue."

"Fine. What kind of *scoundrel* was I? Is that better?"

Together, Jimmy and Tawny concluded by telling him about the key and their search to find the box that it fit.

Dick looked at Carlos. "So you were following me in order to hurt me."

"Seriously, Juan? I know as much about this as you do."

"But, Carlos, I trusted you."

"We trusted each other."

Dick turned to Jimmy. "Did I do whatever it is they're accusing me of?"

"That remains to be seen. Think, Dick. Can you remember anything at all?"

Dick shook his head slowly. "Nope. How will I ever remember where this box is?"

No one answered.

"Aha! I've got an idea," Carlos blurted. "Dr. Eduardo could ask you about it under hypnosis, Juan. You have a session in the morning."

Dick sighed. "Carlos, you're brilliant. Perfect. Then it can wait until morning."

Carlos nodded. "So that's settled for now."

"Carlos?"

"Yes, Juan, I mean, Dick."

"I'm still starving and I could really go for some Puttanesca at that little Italian joint. Are you still in the mood for Italian?"

"Well, Dick, it is your favorite food—*today*."

"I don't believe these guys," Jimmy sneered.

"Give us a break, will you, Jim?" said Dick. "We spent last night in jail for being gay bashed by cops while attempting to defend the honor of a psychic, palm reading, purple-haired drag queen named Miss Chi Chi Rivera. Frankly, I've discovered that can give a guy quite an appetite."

"Yeah," said Carlos. "Nothing gives you a heartier appetite than defending a drag queen's honor."

Dick snickered. "Good one, Carlos."

"Gay bashed?" said Kate.

"Jail?" added Tawny.

"Hold on!" Jimmy interrupted. He turned to Dick. "Did you say Italian?"

CHAPTER FORTY-FOUR

Dr. Eduardo pulled his chair closer to the couch in his office. "Very good, Juan. That's right," he said in the soothing tone of a trained hypnotist. "Continue to relax and breathe with your eyes closed."

Jimmy stared down at his friend—or the guy who had once been.

Eduardo continued. "You're going deeper now than you were before."

"Doc, you've been at this for a while," Jimmy whispered. "When are you going to ask him? You gotta get him to remember—"

"Quiet please. Continue to go deeper and focus on my voice, Juan." Eduardo eyed Jimmy. "Only *my* voice. Can you tell me your name again?"

Dick sighed. "Juan."

"Is Juan your only name?"

"No."

"What's your other name?" asked the doctor.

His face twitched. "Dick."

"Who are you more comfortable with right now?"

"Juan."

"Why are you more comfortable as Juan?"

He smiled. "I like Juan."

"That's fine. You can go back to being Juan in a little while. But for now, I need to speak with Dick. May I talk to him?"

"Yes."

"Very good. Dick, are you with me?"

"Yes."

"Thank you," Eduardo continued, "do you remember your life as Dick?"

"No." He paused. "Not really." He sighed. "Maybe."

"Let's focus on that time."

"Okay."

"Dick, you left San Francisco to come here to San Juan, Puerto Rico. Do you remember that?"

"No."

"That's all right. Do you know Jimmy?"

"Yes."

"Is he your friend?"

"He's my brother."

Jimmy smiled.

"Jim is here trying to find an envelope you gave to him. I want you to picture a white envelope. It looks like any other envelope, and it's addressed to—"

"Me."

Jimmy stepped closer.

"So you remember the envelope?" Eduardo asked.

"Yes."

Jimmy handed the key to Eduardo.

"Good. Inside that envelope is a key with a note. This key that I'm placing in your hand right now fits a lock box."

"I know."

"Yes, you do. Can you tell me where that box is located?"

Jimmy paced to and from the window four or five times, waiting for what felt more like minutes than seconds. "It's Jimmy. Where's the box, Dick?"

"Shh." Eduardo glared at Jimmy and then resumed his methodical ritual. "Continue to relax and breathe, Dick. You're going deeper now." He waited several seconds. "Where is the box that this key fits?"

A silent minute prevailed. "At the hotel," Dick answered in a subdued tone.

"Thank you, Dick," said Eduardo.

"Number 187."

"1-8-7," Jimmy whispered into Eduardo's ear. "Doc, that can't be right. The note says 1832."

"Dick," Dr. Eduardo began, "are you sure the box number is 1-8-7?"

"Yes."

"Then what does the note with the number 1832 mean?"

"I didn't…"

"You didn't what, Dick?" asked Jimmy.

Dick punched the couch on which he was lying. "No! No!"

Dr. Eduardo patted Dick's shoulder to comfort him. "It's not important, Dick. Take a deep cleansing breath and relax." Eduardo waited. "We're done for today. You're safe and more relaxed than you've ever been. I'm going to count backward from twenty now. When I reach number one, you'll awaken refreshed from a long peaceful nap. Twenty, nineteen, eighteen…"

"Tawny, what could be taking this long?"

"Relax, Carlos. Dick's in good hands. I don't believe I care—worse yet, I don't believe you've been shacked up with Dick Peak. Creama! Dick Peak?" She wagged her head like a disappointed mother. "Where did I go wrong?"

"I wasn't. I was living with Juan." He exhaled hard. "I can't believe that Juan is Dick Peak." He scoffed. "Maybe it's a good thing that I can't remember everything he's done."

"It looks to me like you two are an item."

Carlos's jaw dropped. "What? No!"

"Come on. The kiss on your forehead? He called you his guardian angel."

"Tawny, there will be no Juan-bashing. Juan's a great guy. Somebody you can look up to, and not just because he's tall. He's loyal…and sweet, and attentive."

"You had a Cocker Spaniel that fit that description."

Carlos laughed.

"Creama, I can't take you seriously with that beard. It's like you're in drag."

"I hate to break it you, but as it turns out, I'm not only an accomplished sissy, I'm also pretty macho. And macho sissies like me sometimes have beards. Deal with it."

"I don't care if you look like Sasquatch—which you do! Maybe I can finally get a night's sleep now that I know you're alive and coming home." She hugged him. "You're the part of me that I've missed most."

"Tell me you're not getting any sleep because of me when you have that cute blond girlfriend."

"Kate's not my girlfriend. Until yesterday I'd have bet everything I own that she was straight."

"Uh-huh. I assumed..."

"I honestly didn't know that she was gay until she told me yesterday."

"What!" he said. "How could you miss it? I'm gonna revoke your gay card."

"Ugh. I really don't need any reminders of what a failure I am as a gay girl. For the record, we've spent every waking minute since we met looking for *you*. Kate was so persistent. Fact is, there were times I might have lost it were it not for her."

"You never noticed how she looks at you? 'Cause I've certainly noticed!"

"I've been so busy hiding how I look at her, it never occurred to me to notice how she looks at me."

"I like the two of you together, mija."

"Stop." She flushed. "The point is, finding you would have been infinitely easier if I'd known from the start that you were in the Navy." She poked his arm lightly. "How is it you never told me that?"

He shrugged. "I dunno."

"It's okay. At first, yeah, I'll admit I was crushed because I thought we knew all of each other's secrets. But I'm not mad. You can tell me why you kept it from me."

He stared at her. "I *honestly* don't know."

She studied his eyes. "Do you really not remember or are you conning me?"

"That's what I'm saying, mija. All I know is that I panicked when I couldn't find you." He batted his eyelashes at her. "So now you have to forgive me."

She smiled and checked the time on her phone. "I thought Kate would be here by now."

"Uh-huh. So, she's staying with you until we leave?"

The door opened and Dick entered followed by Jimmy.

Carlos pushed himself off the couch and balanced on his cane.

"Hi, Carlos. Tawny," Dick nodded.

"My heart is racing, Juan. How did it go?"

"I don't think you should call him Juan anymore," said Jimmy.

"It's all right." Dick placed his hand on Jimmy's shoulder. "Carlos and I know who we are—kind of. Since our trip to hell and back, we don't have any secrets."

"So that makes you and the entire Navy," Tawny quipped.

"We're good friends and I owe him my life."

Carlos stepped toward them. "We didn't come this far to not see it through. If Juan is in trouble, I want to help him."

"Creama, that's very sweet," Tawny said. "But think about what you're saying. You'll be helping to exonerate someone who has potentially committed a crime. A man that you've protested against—vehemently."

He looked into Juan's eyes. "He would do the same for me."

"You know it," said Dick.

Carlos reached for Tawny's hand. "Tawny, however strange it seems to you, for me and Juan, life as we knew it is some far away dream. I don't remember exactly who I used to be, but I'll bet I've never been more sure of who I am, or more certain of who I want to be. Like it or not, fate has played its hand. Fate *always* wins."

"Carlos," Dick began, "remember what you said the day we left the VA? You told me, 'It's not as important to be, as it is to become.' It's about the process, isn't it?"

Jimmy groaned.

"Knock it off, Jimmy," Tawny reprimanded.

Dick sat in the armchair and Jimmy hovered nearby. "The vault box is at the hotel where I was supposed to stay," said Dick. "Box 187."

"Box 187?" asked Tawny. "So it isn't 1832?"

There was a knock at the door. "I'll get it," said Jimmy.

"No, it isn't," Dick said.

"Then what's 1832?" asked Tawny.

Dick shrugged.

Tawny looked past him. "Hi, Kate. Are you moved in?"

"Certainly am. What did I miss?"

"I think we're going to the lock box we've been searching for," Tawny replied. "Dick knows where it is."

Kate's eyes opened wide. "You know where it is?"

"Hold on, girls." Jimmy scratched his day-old stubble. If there's something in there that could implicate Dick, then I can't let you see it. That goes for you too, Carlos."

Carlos sat down on the couch. "You can't do that. Juan, tell him."

"Whoa, wait a minute, Jimmy," Tawny protested. "I've been with you all the way through this and so has Kate. You wouldn't have even found Dick if it hadn't been for us." Tawny did her impression of Italian-hands, Jimmy-style. "What happened to, 'You're a loyal person, and loyal people can be trusted'?"

Jimmy chuckled at her impression. "We *are* loyal people, Tawny. But we have different allegiances now. I'm sorry, but that's the way it is."

"No, Jimmy," Dick interjected. "Things *are* different now. Carlos and I trust each other."

"That's right," Carlos affirmed. "Like it or not, we're one big happy dysfunctional family."

"Tell that to Ellie Brisbane," Jim said.

"Ellie." Dick paused. "Ellie?" he repeated.

"Yes, Dick, your sister Ellie."

"I remember her—kind of. Tall? With dark hair?" Dick thought for a moment. "My sister. How is she?" he asked sweetly.

Jimmy exhaled. "When you found out she was gay, you kinda disowned her. But get this, she's Tawny's old girlfriend."

Kate shot Tawny a glare. "Tawny, I should write them all down, you know, so that you don't forget."

Carlos laughed. "Duck, Tawny. Incoming!"

"Oh no," Dick moaned. "Not Ellie. How could I have hurt my sister like that? My own flesh and blood."

Tawny tapped her foot. "Folks, we're getting off topic here. Well, Jimmy?"

Jimmy stroked his chin and thought about it. All eyes rested on him and silence prevailed. "On one condition, Tawny. Anything that we find in that box stays strictly confidential. I want your word."

Tawny nodded eagerly. "Agreed. Everything will be off the record. Kate, are you in?"

"Are you kidding? I want to know what's in the box as badly as you do."

"We can't have five people traipse into a vault box," said Carlos. "What do you wanna do, Juan?"

"You and me, Carlos," Dick replied.

"What?" said Jimmy.

"Carlos is my emotional support drag queen." He stared at Carlos. "We need to get you one of those little vests like they had on the emotional support dogs at the VA."

Carlos laughed. "No! Mine's blue. With sequins."

"I need him with me, Jim. You three wait for us in the hotel lobby and I'll let you know what we find as soon as we come out. Fair enough?"

CHAPTER FORTY-FIVE

Kate sat in the Jeep in front of Santa Clara waiting to load her caravan for the trip across town. "Do you need help, Carlos?" she asked when they arrived.

"No, I've got it." He slid in next to her with his cane.

Tawny grabbed onto the roll bar and climbed into the backseat where Jimmy and Dick flanked her.

Kate peeled out and hung a quick right. Her eyes met Tawny's in the rearview mirror.

"I'm getting smushed on the turns, Kate," Tawny complained.

"Better slow down," Carlos sang. "What I *do* recall is, if Mama ain't happy, ain't nobody happy."

"Oh, so you see it too," Kate quipped.

"Tawny, if you can't have a good time, then you're not really trying," said Dick.

Tawny sneered at him. "Oh, shut up."

"Don't bite *my* head off. I'm just quoting Carlos."

"Yeah, well, just because I'm moody, it doesn't mean you're not irritating."

"One big happy supercalifragilistic dysfunctional family," said Carlos.

"Thank you, Mary Poppins." Kate cranked up the radio. "Perfect! Now I can't hear any of you!" She sang along to Cher's, "If I Could Turn Back Time."

"You have a great voice, Kate," said Carlos. "You should do Creama LaCroppe's backup vocals."

Jimmy joined in, enthusiastically belting out the lyrics and bopping to the beat.

Tawny turned to him and laughed. "*You* know the words to a Cher song?"

"Hey! Hey, I love Cher!" Jimmy poked her arm lightly in time to the beat and sang to her.

"Creama," Tawny called out, "I think Jimmy should sing backup."

Carlos turned to watch him. "Jimmy."

"Yeah, Carlos."

"You do the white man's hustle like nobody's business, man."

"Thank you, Carlos."

Tawny stared at Jimmy. "It wasn't a compliment."

"I don't know the words," Dick shouted. "I'll hum. Great hand choreography, Carlos."

"Gracias, Juan."

After Cher, Kate changed the station and they crooned to Ricky Martin's, "La Vida Loca," all the while seat-dancing and laughing. Kate turned at the hotel driveway and killed the radio when she let everyone out at the entrance. "I'll meet you after I park."

Once Carlos vacated the passenger seat, Jimmy climbed into it.

"What are you doing?" asked Kate.

"I'll go with you," he answered. "I don't like the idea of you going solo into the garage."

Kate smiled at him. "Here I thought chivalry was dead."

"Nope," Jimmy smiled back. "Not in Castilano Country."

"I'll be sitting over there when you're done," Tawny said to Carlos when he and Dick veered toward the front desk. She ambled to an elegant armchair in the seating alcove across the open-air lobby. Orchestrated by the indolent flow of a mermaid-sculpture fountain, lush tropical foliage yielded to tiled patios and manicured gardens that hugged the winding path toward the beach. She sighed away the thought of having to return to the bustling chill of San Francisco with its fog and rain. Tawny closed her eyes and inhaled, savoring the tropical punch breeze and even the muggy air that coated her skin.

"Pardon me," a woman said.

Startled, Tawny's eyes popped open. "You! You were on the beach at my hotel."

"I didn't mean to alarm you. I'm a reporter from the RGN."

"RGN?"

"Yes, The *Rainbow Gay News*. May I ask you a few questions?"

"Me? About what?"

"Aren't you that TV newswoman?"

"Former newswoman."

"Word on the street is you're in San Juan investigating the Trans Air flight that crashed last month."

"Actually, I'm on vacation. I no longer investigate."

The woman met Tawny's bluff with a polite smile. "I have friends in the gay community who told me you were looking for a passenger on that flight."

"Wow. Gay news sure travels fast down here."

The reporter nodded. "Can you tell me the name of the person you're looking for?"

"Hold on, how did you find me here?"

"Pure coincidence."

Tawny raised an eyebrow. "Right. I didn't catch your name…"

"Sorry." She handed Tawny her business card. "I'm Adriana Rodriguez."

"Adriana, as a journalist I'm sure you can appreciate that I have no comment at this time."

"For the record, you have no comment, Miss…?"

"Tawny Beige." *Nice looking up close!* "I wish I could help you, but this isn't a good time. I'm waiting for friends."

"I understand. You have my card so give me a call at your convenience." Adriana held her gaze. "Maybe you'd like to have dinner sometime? I can show you a great time in San Juan."

Tawny looked beyond her to see Kate and Jimmy stopping behind the reporter, Jimmy's hand resting on Kate's shoulder. When Adriana pivoted to leave, she ran smack into Kate's folded arms and a dead-on glare.

The reporter waited a beat before speaking. "Don't hate me because I'm cute, mami. Hate me because your girlfriend thinks I am." She smiled and left.

"Hey, Tawny, wasn't that the broad from the beach?" Jimmy asked.

"Yes." She stared at the business card. "She's a gay reporter."

"What is it with you lesbos? I can't tell who's who anymore." He watched Adriana walk away. "Les-bo-riffic!"

"Nice to see you expanding your vocabulary, Jimmy. But I'm really tired of you thinking we're *all* from the Isle of Lesbos," Tawny grumbled.

"Are you going?" Kate asked Tawny.

"Going where?"

"Are you going to dinner with her?"

"Uh-oh," Jimmy teased.

"Please, Kate, don't encourage him."

Tawny stood when she saw Dick and Carlos walking toward them. "Here they come."

"That was quick," Jimmy said. "We just parked the car. Well? What was in there?"

"We haven't opened it," said Carlos.

"Keep it down until we get back to my hotel room," said Tawny.

"*Our* hotel room," Kate corrected her.

"R-right." Tawny held up the reporter's card. "The less we're seen together right now, the better."

Kate looked at the card in Tawny's hand. "Would you like me to hang on to that for you?"

Tawny winced and slid it into her back pocket. "Come on, guys, let's order room service and look things over."

"Room service?" Dick pondered it. "I know I'm going to *love* something called room service."

Carlos play-slapped Juan's arm. "What do you think you had every day at the hospital?"

Juan stared at him. "*Not* hotel food?"

Once they were back at the hotel, everyone surrounded the envelope sitting on the dining room table. Motionless, they stared down at it like a wake of turkey vultures waiting for dinner to die.

Kate looked up. "Are we all just going to stand here?"

They each scrambled into a seat.

"Big improvement," said Jimmy. "Now we're sitting and staring at the damn thing."

Dick reached for the envelope and picked it up.

"Wait." Carlos placed his hand across Dick's forearm. "Whatever's in there, I'm here for you, mijo."

Dick looked into his eyes. "Carlos, if there's something bad in here, I can't obligate you. The man I used to be doesn't deserve to have you as a friend."

Tawny and Jimmy locked eyes.

"But you're not the man you used to be, Juan."

Dick continued. "I appreciate that, but if there's a score to be settled, then like you taught me, it's up to me to do the right thing so that the right thing happens. Remember that?"

"Sure, I remember. Under normal circumstances that's how things go. But we've been through everything *except* normal circumstances. We're going to do whatever we need to do. Just know I'm here for you."

Jimmy steadied Dick's trembling hand and then Dick severed the tattered seal of the generic white envelope. He patted Dick's shoulder. "No one knows you're alive, so if it's that bad, you can just stay dead."

Dick looked at him. "Live a lie?"

"Seriously? In law school you majored in lying, buddy."

"As a politician you lived in six degrees of separation from the truth," Tawny chimed in.

"You *did* make an art form out of saying one thing and doing another," Carlos agreed. "You were slicker than lube."

"Okay, all right, I get it!" Dick said. "Thanks a lot, guys."

"Give me that!" Jimmy snatched the envelope from Dick's hand. He turned it over and let the contents fall onto the table. "You gotta be kidding me. That's it?"

"It's a thumb drive," Tawny said.

"That's all that's in there?" said Carlos.

"Yes," Jimmy replied. "How are we going to see what's on it?"

Kate stood and went to the phone. "I'll call the concierge. The hotel has a business center."

A minute later, the entourage left the room and followed Kate to the elevator.

"What's up, Tawny?" asked Jimmy while they waited.

"What do you mean?"

"I've seen that look on your face before."

"What look?"

"The look you had the night that we opened the first envelope in your room. Like something doesn't add up."

"What's the number 1832 about? It wasn't the vault number. It's too short to be an account number. Could it be an area code, 1-832?"

They entered the elevator and Kate pressed "2".

"Let's wait until we see what's on the thumb drive," Carlos said.

They all gathered around Kate who sat at the computer. She slid the thumb drive into the USB port, and the four stood behind her with their eyes fixed on the screen. The little green task light flickered.

"Okay," said Kate. "We have files coming up. Shit, they're all protected."

"Protected?" said Dick.

"Yes, we need a password to open them," Tawny said. "When is your birthday?" she asked.

"I don't know."

"November twenty-first, 1985," Jimmy offered.

Kate typed the date. "No, that's not it."

"Mijo, you're a Scorpio."

"Oh god, I'm older than I thought."

"Try Lester," Jimmy said.

Dick's voice cracked when it jumped up an octave. "Lester?"

Jimmy shrugged. "It was your nickname during your awkward years."

Dick shook his head. "A potential criminal, over thirty I might add, with a nickname of Lester. This *is* bad."

Kate typed it in. "Nope."

"1832," Tawny blurted. "Try 1832."

"Yeah, do 1832," Jimmy echoed.

"No go," said Kate.

Tawny nudged Kate from behind. "Try USC1832."

"USC," Carlos said. "Isn't that where Dick went to college?"

"Yes! We're in," said Kate. "Brilliant, Tawny." Everyone bent toward the monitor.

"What are those?" asked Dick.

Tawny read the screen. "I think documents from some company and lots of numbers. I wonder what those numbers mean."

Kate clicked on the first folder. "Can anybody here translate legalese?"

"So that was the big deal about USC 1832?" Jimmy said. He turned to Dick. "You put the key to the vault box in with a note that had the password? I guess that makes sense." He pointed at the screen. "Kate, what's that company file? The one labeled, CC."

Carlos rested his hand on Kate's shoulder and leaned closer. She clicked again and read the title. "Cosmopolitron Corporation."

"Cosmopolitron Corp?" said Jimmy. "Yeah—open up that one. Let me see that."

Tawny focused on the screen. "What is it, Jimmy?"

"That Silicon Valley source guy—the one who said he had dirt on Dick? That's who was with me and Andy at Joe's the night of the crash. That whack job works for Cosmopolitron. His name is Fay, Izadore Fay. They call him Izzy."

Dick traced the scar on his temple. "So, if this Izzy Fay was trying to expose me, was it because I stole something and have his company's documents in my possession?"

"I have a different question," Carlos said. "Why is the only other file on this disk a bunch of numbers—and legal mumbo jumbo?"

"Maybe I was researching my crimes," Dick lamented.

"Or…" Carlos countered, "maybe you got somethin' here on somebody else. Never show a fool an unfinished job. Let's not rush to judgment, Juan Dick Rick. Um—Rich? Which name are we on now?"

"Dunno," Dick shrugged.

"There's a lot here," Kate said. "For starters, I can print out some of it and we can go through it in the room."

"Sure," Tawny chimed in. "If need be, we can come back down here and print out more."

"Do it," said Dick. He turned to Carlos. "You say I attended this USC that was part of the password?"

"Yes, University of Southern California. Third in your class, mijo."

Dick's jaw dropped open. "How do you know that?"

Carlos stared at him. "How the hell would I know? The better question is, how can I remember where you went to school when I don't know my own damn address?"

Dick shook his head. "You know more about me than I do, Carlos."

Jimmy laughed. "That ain't saying much, boys."

CHAPTER FORTY-SIX

"Jesus, it's about time." Jimmy answered the knock on Tawny's hotel room door and held it open for the waiter to wheel the dinner cart inside.

"Bring it on, I'm starving," said Dick. "Hey, Tawny, it's dinnertime. Put your papers down."

"I will."

"I'll wait for you," said Dick.

She looked up. "You can start without me."

"No, I can't."

"Why?"

"Because you've barely eaten."

Tawny scoffed. "Like you care."

"I do care," he stated sincerely. "Don't you get that you're my family now?" He paused. "You're all my family."

Tawny laid the papers on the bed and smiled at him before she took a seat at the table. She was only beginning to understand that he was no longer the man she had once despised. Of the two of them, only she remembered the hate speech and smug ignorance. She watched how he and Carlos cared for each other—Dick rearranging his chair so that Carlos could get his leg comfortable and the way Carlos listened to Dick and waited patiently when he struggled to find the right word.

Once everyone dug into their meal, the conversation drifted back to the lighter moments of their day. Jimmy spoke of Rita and how glad she was to learn of Dick's survival. Dick responded with an eagerness to meet her again. Then, Dick and Carlos shared their experience of jail and described Chi Chi Rivera in such stunning detail that even Jimmy couldn't hold back his laughter. Kate invited the gang to her place in San Francisco once this was all behind them, and she told Jimmy she looked forward to meeting the woman who had stolen his heart.

"You're awfully quiet, Tawny," said Jimmy.

"Huh? Sorry. I'm sitting here wondering how Izzy Fay orchestrated this and how he actually framed Dick. We need to find that body of evidence that opens the door, and we need to understand what placed Dick at risk in the first place. If we can find the risk, then we'll know which money to follow."

"Kate, is she always like this?" asked Carlos.

Kate glanced at him. "Yes. Always the dogged reporter. She hasn't come up for air since we began searching for you."

The dinner conversation crashed into a wall of reality and silenced the room.

Jimmy sighed then stood and dropped his napkin onto his plate. "I guess we'd better get back to it then." He picked up a stack of papers, sat on the bed, and began to read. One by one, the group followed his lead and retreated to their assigned tasks.

Stacks of paper and rows of printouts on the bed separated Tawny and Jimmy, and Kate slumped in the armchair with a short stack on her lap.

The second wastebasket was already full as the team finally narrowed down the pages to any information that looked remotely important.

"Tawny?"

"Yes, Jimmy."

He glanced up from reading. "You realize, now I can technically say I've spent an evening in bed with you."

"As if," she retorted.

"What's a matter? You losing your sense of humor, woman?"

"Sorry, Jimmy. It's more like I'm losing my mind, which is starting to feel like mush."

"What do you make of this, Dick?" Carlos handed him a sheet of paper and Carlos continued to sort and organize by subject matter.

"These are…wait. I know that I know what these are." He stared harder, as if the intensity would force instant recall. "Damn it. I can't remember."

"Let me see that page," Jimmy said, leaning off the bed to reach for it. He studied it. "This is marketing data. In fact, it looks like two sets of marketing data with very different costs."

"How do *you* know?" Tawny asked.

"Marketing was my major in college."

"You. You have a degree in marketing?"

"I didn't say I graduated. Nevertheless, this is marketing meta data."

"What's meta data?" asked Carlos.

"It's data about data," Jimmy replied.

"So, two sets of data. What am I missing?" said Kate.

Jimmy turned to her. "It's one way to embezzle a lot of money, for one thing."

"What else could it be?" asked Tawny.

Jimmy thought for a moment. "My guess? If it's important enough to be on a password-protected thumb drive, it's either a shady deal or confidential movement of money. Ladies and…" Jimmy glanced at Carlos, "…ladies, keep your eyes open for a deal gone bad. I think Carlos might be right about Dick having the goods on someone. Dick, if you'd suspected that Fay was coming after you, it woulda been just like you to beat him at his game." He addressed everyone. "We've got to follow the money by starting with the numbers listed in those columns."

"I'm on it," said Kate.

Jimmy winked at Dick. "The best defense is a strategic stealth offense," he said. "I learned that from you, Dick."

Carlos sat there with his mouth open. "Wow, Jimmy. You're good, man."

Jimmy snickered. "I am good, aren't I?" He paused and looked around the room. "Look at us." He tried to hold back his chuckle like a muffled brain-imploding sneeze in a crowded theater; the chuckle percolated into a laugh that boiled over into a belly-rolling guffaw. "Have you ever seen a group less likely to have this much going for them?"

Tawny laughed. "Right?" She laughed harder.

Jimmy continued. "I'm in freakin' Puerto Rico! Trying to resurrect Dick Peak—conservative Republican religious right congressman—

with liberals and gays over club sandwiches and Coca-Cola, while in bed with the *ultimate* lesbotron." His words slammed into a brick wall. "Hey. Hey, why am I the only one still laughing? Why are you all staring at me?"

Tawny shook her head. "Liberals and gays? Jimmy, do you ever hear yourself? By the way, we're *on* the bed, not in it." She paused. "You really think I'm ultimate?"

"Yes. No, no. You're taking it all wrong. I mean come on, what are the odds we would all end up here together trying to do the right thing—the *same* right thing?"

Tawny sighed. "He's right. Dick, I don't—well I didn't—like you… ever. What you stood for, what you did about it. I'm doing this for Carlos."

"Tawny," Dick began, "I feel ashamed of who I used to be. I promise that I'm no longer that guy. I'm not wasting this second chance in my life. With your help, I might be able to do the right thing here. First, I need to know what the right thing is, but I understand if you need to bail out."

"Bail? Who said anything about bailing? I guess deep down if I didn't believe you, Dick, I wouldn't be here."

"Thanks, Tawny. That means so much to me and I won't forget this. At least I'll try not to."

Kate slapped the stack of papers. "I've got it! Sonofabitch. Got it."

Jimmy spun around. "What? What?"

"1832. It's right here under our noses. United States Code. USC 1832." Everyone sat up straight. "U.S. Code Title 18: Crimes And Criminal Procedure. Section 1832, Theft Of Trade Secrets."

Jimmy looked over Kate's shoulder. "USC! Sheesh, it's the U.S. Code of Justice! So, along with that marketing information, I'll bet there's at least one count of embezzlement—probably some theft of confidential information. Whatever the hell is involved, money is on the move—I can smell it."

"So what does all this mean?" Tawny asked.

Dick sighed. "I really hope it doesn't mean I stole from this Cosmopolitron Corporation."

"Like I keep telling you," Carlos said, "someone else did and you were about to nail them for it. Why else would that Izzy guy try to eliminate Andy the reporter? Wasn't he trying to give information to Jimmy that would help you out? Andy was trying to warn you that Fay was setting you up."

"Carlos," said Tawny, "we're talking about Dick Peak here. Pre-Juan Dick Peak."

"Hold on, Tawny," said Jimmy. "What if Carlos is onto something? Dick, what if you did all this cloak-and-dagger shit with the key and the box because you were afraid someone actually *was* trying to set you up—or worse—like what happened to Andy? You sent the thumb drive to a place where no one but me would know to look for it."

Kate nodded. "But how do we find out the truth?"

"Keep readin'."

"I can't, Jimmy." Tawny's eyes watered when she yawned. "I need sleep and my brain feels like playdough. The exhaustion from searching for you, Creama, has finally hit me. I'd pawn my lipstick collection for a hot soak and a facial right now."

"Your *whole* lipstick collection for just that?" Jimmy teased. He perched his hand on his hip. "Come on, Tawny, your *entire* collection?"

"You're right, add a massage to the deal."

Carlos rubbed his eyes. "I'm pretty wiped out myself, guys. We really need sleep; my leg is aching something fierce. Come on, Dick, let's go."

"Sure, Carlos. Like you always say, tomorrow's another day."

"Listen up," Carlos started, "since Dick and I have therapy tomorrow, how about if we all get together afterward for dinner?"

"Sounds good," Jimmy said. "Come on fellas, I'll drop you off at the rehab on my way back to my hotel. I'm so tired I have to remember which floor I parked my car on."

"Everyone get a good night's sleep," said Tawny. "I have a feeling we're just scratching the surface here."

Each member of the untidy band of sleuths hugged and said goodnight.

Kate set the remaining room service trays outside the door while Tawny ran a bath.

"I'm going to soak for a while," Tawny called out from the bathroom. "I'll try not to wake you when I get out."

"I'm so tired, Tawny, I don't even think sleeping on a sofa bed can wake me." She sighed. "Look, I don't want anything to feel awkward between us until we can talk. Are we good?"

"We're fine. See you in the morning."

Kate scrunched her pillow in the dimly lit room while listening to CNN. She was drifting off to sleep when the phone rang. "Hello," she answered softly.

"I'm sorry, the hotel must have given me the wrong room," said the female caller.

"Who are you trying to reach?" asked Kate.

"Tawny Beige?"

"This is her room, however she can't come to the phone right now. Would you like to leave a message?"

Click.

CHAPTER FORTY-SEVEN

After their long and tedious day of therapy, Dick held the door for Carlos to step outside the rehab and wait for their ride.

"Physical therapy made me really hungry, Juan."

"Me too." Dick looked at him. "But I do *not* want to eat Italian again tonight under any circumstances."

Carlos chuckled. "Oh no? I thought Italian was your favorite food."

Dick frowned. "Keep up, Carlos. That's so three days ago. Actually, it was my favorite—until I remembered Chinese dumplings." He paused. "I remember dumplings. I want dumplings *now*."

"Here they come," Carlos said as Jimmy pulled the car over to the curb.

Kate hopped out. "Take the front seat, Carlos. I'll get in the back with Dick."

"Where's Tawny?" asked Carlos.

"She's meeting us at the restaurant," Kate answered.

"Are you comfortable, Carlos?"

"Yes, Jimmy, thanks."

"Sure." Jimmy smiled.

"Where are we going for dinner, Jimmy?" asked Dick.

"Chez Wong. It's Chinese, if that's all right."

"Oh good, Chinese food!" Dick turned to Kate. "It's my favorite."

Tawny stood from her chair and hugged Carlos first when the group arrived at Chez Wong. "Hi, Creama. Hello, Dick."

"Hiya, Tawny!" Dick clutched Tawny and squeezed her tightly, gently lifting her off the ground.

"Oh! Okay—now we're hugging." With her arms forced around him, her flailing wrists settled on cordial pats on his back until he set her feet back on the ground.

Kate snickered, found a seat and took a menu from the stack while everyone else took a seat.

"I spent the day reading everything I could find on that thumb drive," Tawny began. "I think Jimmy and Carlos nailed it. This Mr. Fay seems pretty unsavory."

"How so?" asked Dick.

"I had to read between the lines to bridge some gaps, but if I'm piecing this together correctly, Fay has been selling proprietary information to a rival company by the name of Link Inc, here in San Juan." Tawny looked across the table at Jimmy. "Do you have any knowledge of this?"

He shook his head. "None."

Tawny continued. "Whether Fay was recruited by Link Inc or he brought the information to them remains to be seen."

The waiter came to the table with his pen poised. "Do you need a few more minutes?" he asked.

"Are you the actual Keeper of Time?" Carlos quipped.

"I'll come back," replied the waiter.

"So," Tawny resumed, "to try to understand this deal, I called San Francisco today and spoke with Andy at *The Chronicle*."

"No shit?" said Jimmy. "You spoke to Andy?"

"Yep."

"How's he doin'?"

"He's okay. And he felt a whole lot better by the time our conversation ended. Andy said when he was at Joe's, he *was* trying to pass the envelope to you under the table, but only because you had arrived late. He wanted you to have it for the very reason Carlos said. It was proof of Fay selling out Cosmopolitron. His aim was to broker a deal between you and Fay. But since he couldn't give you the note with Fay there, he stuck it underneath the table. He thought you knew about it when he made some remark about 'getting paid under the table'?"

Jimmy smacked his forehead with his palm. "Is that what the hell he was talking about?"

"Yes." She took a breath. "Here's where we are. Andy confirmed the amounts we uncovered last night, and he was able to tell me when Fay had skimmed from those marketing contracts. Fay filtered that money into Dick's Senate campaign through Link Inc. His goal was to frame Dick for accepting rival bribes and for conspiring against his constituent—Cosmopolitron. Fay made it appear as though Dick was stealing proprietary information from his constituents at Cosmopolitron, in exchange for big campaign donations from Link Inc.

"Link Inc was all in because they wanted Dick out of the way. They were backing his opponent and implicating Dick would have sunk his Senate run. I'm guessing Fay received a big payday from Link Inc."

Dick squeezed Tawny's hand. "So I was being honorable?"

Tawny nodded. "It appears that way. After the call, when I ran Andy's information against the customer lists, then compared that to the marketing campaigns that Jimmy found last night...well, I'm no forensic expert, but it looks like a classic setup to me. And get this. All of that money was sent through the Strait Holding Company, Bahamas branch."

Four speechless souls gawked at her.

"Tawny," Jimmy sighed.

"Yes, Jimmy?"

"Those ovaries? They're fuckin' amazing."

Kate choked on her water and coughed. "How's that?"

"Private joke," Tawny replied.

"In more ways than one," noted Kate.

"You're still a *great* investigative reporter," said Jimmy, "even if you don't wanna be on TV anymore."

"So, I'm innocent," said Dick.

"Yes, you are." Tawny smiled.

"Oh Tawny! You're like—my *best* friend!"

"Hey!" Carlos and Jimmy protested in unison.

"I thought I was your best friend!" said Jimmy.

"I thought *I* was your best friend!" said Carlos.

"Can I take your order?" the waiter said.

"I'll have the Number Two, Wong Foo on the side," Carlos said.

"The what?" said the waiter.

"Just the Number Two, hold the Foo."

"We'll take a bottle of your best wine to celebrate," added Jimmy.

"Do we have enough proof to clear Dick's name?" Carlos asked.

Jimmy nodded. "I have someone I can call who might be able to answer that question. I'll call Senator Tate first thing in the morning."

"A.C. Tate?" Tawny cringed. "Eech, 'Tater the Hater'? That pathetic, Far-right, anti-gay, keep 'em barefoot and pregnant schmuck?"

"But he loved Dick!" Jimmy explained.

Tawny tapped her finger on the table vigorously. "You know, maybe if he did love dick, he'd be a better human being."

Kate and Carlos laughed and Jimmy's face flushed.

"Ha, ha. Very funny," Jimmy said snidely. "Just for that, Tawny, I think I'll place the call to the senator *tonight*, from *your* room."

"Isn't it too late in the day to be calling a senator?" Carlos asked in a transparent attempt to ward off World War III.

"Carlos, don't even try," said Kate. "They've been this way since the day they met."

"What way?" Tawny spat.

"Yeah," said Jimmy. "What's wrong with you, Kate?"

After dinner, comfortably seated on Tawny's bed, Jimmy waited for Senator Tate to come on the line. He glanced at Tawny.

"What's that grin?" Tawny asked him.

"Kicking back on your bed is like the dessert I never got to have tonight."

She wagged her head. "I'm telling Rita."

"G'head," he dared her, "she already knows that men are dogs when it comes to beautiful women."

Tawny smiled. "Thank you, Jimmy."

"I'm only stating the obvious," he replied. "Yes, hello." He sat up. "Senator? You heard my message correctly, sir." He paused to listen. "Yes, that detailed message I left you doesn't seem real, I know. But it's the truth." He paused again. "For real. Dick's here, live and in person. Yes, sir, one moment."

Dick hesitantly took the phone from Jimmy. "Hello? I wish I could say I remember you, sir, but the truth is I can't even remember me. Yes, I'm listening carefully." Dick's expression was stern as he concentrated intently without interruption. "Then, Jimmy will explain the rest?" Pause. "Thank you very much, Senator. I look forward to meeting you—um, meeting you again." Dick placed the phone back on the receiver. "Jimmy?"

Jimmy stood and patted Dick on the shoulder. "So, you want I should explain it?"

"Yes."

"Okay, kids, it's goin' down like this. Senator Tate is arranging for us to bring Dick home anonymously on a private plane. The good news is that since we're in Puerto Rico, we don't need any documents, passport or anything like that for him or for Carlos. In the meantime, the senator is having Fay's computer confiscated by none other than his old friend, who just happens to be on the Board of Directors at Cosmopolitron Corp. Tonight, I'm emailing a copy of the thumb drive with the evidence on it to Senator Tate. By the time we get Dick back to San Francisco, they should have Fay in custody, and Tate will break the news of Dick's rescue to the media."

"Wow. He's doing all of that for *me*?" Dick said.

"He owes you, Dick. You scored him a lot of votes with the Right Of America's Religious. Right before you left for the airport after the ROAR rally, Tate told you he'd back your run for the Senate." Jimmy stared at his friend. "What's wrong, Dick?"

"It's so foreign, Jim. All of it. I can't even imagine it."

"When do we leave?" asked Carlos.

"Tomorrow," Jimmy replied.

The following morning, the lemon sun had yet to fill the sky and steam the air.

"Is that the last of it, Jimmy?" Kate asked while packing the Jeep.

"Yes. Hey let me get that for you." He lifted the last of the luggage into the back. "*Umph*. Whadya got in here, rocks or somethin'?"

"It's Tawny's case."

He glanced at Kate. "Probably extra lipstick."

"Hey Jimmy," Dick said. "I was hoping we'd hear some news before we got on the plane."

Jimmy wiped the sweat from his brow. "Patience. It's all happening as we speak. We'll know when they arrest Fay."

Carlos hobbled out of Santa Clara Rehab urgently flailing his cane. "Dick. Dick! Everybody get in here!"

Dick, Kate, and Jimmy ran inside as Tawny was raising the volume on the lobby TV. They huddled together and watched CNN's breaking news.

"Look!" said Jimmy. "It's Senator Tate."

They listened as the senator spoke into the bank of microphones and addressed the cameras.

"Once again, I urge all Americans, especially those in the great state of California to honor Congressman Peak for his fastidious and successful efforts to crack down on the worst of white-collar crime and economic espionage. Had the accused succeeded, it would have cost thousands of jobs held by hard-working Americans, and would have destroyed Cosmopolitron Corporation, a great innovative American company. To that end, I'm grateful to share with America that I've learned Congressman Peak has been found, having miraculously survived the Trans Air plane crash." Several reporters vied to get their questions through the cacophony of reactions.

The senator raised his hands. "Please, everyone." He waited for the crowd to quiet down. "I have no information beyond what I've told you. But I promise that as soon as I do, I'm sure the congressman will let me know when to share it."

Carlos smiled. "Guess that means it's time to go home, Dick."

Dick looked around. "This *is* my home."

CHAPTER FORTY-EIGHT

Throughout the ensuing months in San Francisco, Dick tried to reassemble the roughly-carved puzzle of his former life. Old friends visited, introduced themselves, and infused him with their versions of what might have once been *his* memories. He researched his history on the Internet, reading his own story with the solemnity of a never-ending obituary. At times he stopped reading to take in the enormity of his former beliefs and subsequent actions that now only made him angry or want to cry. In those moments, he wondered if he was even worthy of redemption.

Dick concluded that he'd been both hated and loved for what felt like all the wrong reasons. But in the end, he knew that the causality for those reasons rested squarely with him. Unable to reconcile being the source, as well as the object of vitriol, he felt a deep need to retake the playing field and level it. He decided it was time to try to undo some of the hateful policies he had once championed.

While there remained plenty of loose ends in his mind—missing reasons for who he had been—having his sister Ellie, Carlos, Jim, Tawny, Kate, and now Rita, became his universe. He seized every opportunity to let his new family know the depth of his gratitude for having them to rely on.

As he was unpacking some plates, he heard the knock on his door. "Just a minute," he called out from the kitchen. Dick set down the plates and answered the door of his new Victorian apartment in the Castro. "Hiya, Jim! Come on in."

Jimmy panned the room, nodding in approval. "It's looking more like home, Dick."

"What do you think? Should I leave the couch where it is or face it toward that other window?"

Jimmy mulled it over. "Personally, I like it where it is, but you need something on the end—like that table over there, and maybe put that lamp on it."

Dick turned to fetch the table and lamp, set it up and then stepped next to Jim to study it. "You're right. How did I not see that? You've got a real eye for this decorating stuff."

"Here," Jimmy said. "I received this envelope in the mail today. It's addressed to you."

Carrying another end table across the room, Dick glanced down at the oversize envelope in Jimmy's hand. "Open it for me, would you?"

Dick set the table down and fetched two beers from the fridge. The shimmer of the gold foil envelope liner caught his eye when he sat next to Jimmy on the couch and handed him his beer.

Dick took a swig and set the bottle on the newly placed end table. He slid the invitation out of the fancy square envelope, stared down at it and read out loud. "The Right Of America's Religious requests your presence as the guest of honor at the ROAR Welcome Home Event." He looked over at Jimmy. "It's in two weeks."

Jimmy remained silent as Dick stood and drifted toward the window, a bare hardwood floorboard creaking beneath his step. His boots made a solid clop when he halted.

"How can I be the guest of honor to something I want to spend the rest of my life forgetting, Jimmy? Actually, I have forgotten it, haven't I?"

Jimmy smiled. "Yeah, *you* have, but the rest of us remember."

Dick looked back to the invitation in his hand. "A special honor will be given to the man responsible for your rescue, US Naval Reserve Lieutenant Carlos Armando Jose Benitez. Oh my god, Jimmy. They have no clue about Carlos, do they?"

"I guess not. What do you want me to do with this?"

Dick stroked his five o'clock stubble and met Jimmy's stare. "RSVP, of course. I'll be there."

"Dick, are you sure you can handle this?"

"Absofreakinlutely. The one lesson I've clearly learned is that with Carlos by my side, I can literally handle anything."

"True that, my friend," Jimmy answered. "He's a good guy."

"Besides, here's my opportunity to start undoing some of the damage I created."

"How?"

Dick recalled something Jimmy had repeatedly said since Puerto Rico. "Adjusted for inflation, that's the 128,000-dollar question."

Down the hill, Carlos grabbed his phone and tapped Tawny's number. It rang once. "Pick up."

It rang again. "Come on, Tawny, pick up!"

Fourth ring. "Pickuppickuppickuppickup."

"Hello?"

"Jesus, were you down by the river washing your clothes with a rock?"

"Creama, something is fundamentally wrong with you."

"Honey, there is nothing fundamental about me. Are you sitting down?"

"No, but I'm standing over a soft chair in case I keel over. What's up?"

"Are you ready for this?"

"What? What?"

Carlos exhaled hard. "In two weeks, I'm receiving an award from the Right of America's Religious."

"Whaaat?"

"They're honoring me for rescuing that loveable little bastion of the religious right, our dear Juan-Rich-Rick-Dick-Peak. It's a big event."

Tawny laughed.

"Not funny! Scary."

"You're seriously considering this?"

Carlos paused. "You don't think they'd try to turn me into a straight zombie, do you?"

"Creama, honey, your chances of turning straight are nil. Not sure about the zombie thing. Have you spoken with Dick?"

"Not yet. You're my first call! You know what that means, don't you?"

"What?"

"I'm Diva. That makes you Vice Diva. You have to go shopping with me for this event."

"You're really going?"
"I wouldn't miss it!"
"Ball gown or suit?"

In the days leading up to the ROAR event, Jimmy, Carlos, and Dick met a few times to discuss what they would say and they strategized how they would navigate the very organization whose last rally with Dick at the helm had led to his life-threatening awakening and his allegiance to Carlos.

"I really think I can reach them," said Dick. "I know I can make them see what they're missing—how spreading bigotry and hate is leading them in the wrong direction."

"Mijo, you really think they'll change their minds? Especially once they learn that I'm gay?"

Dick looked into Carlos's eyes. "I don't want to change their minds. I want to change their hearts."

Jimmy shook his head. "You're being idealistic. For years, you led the way to convince these people that their bigotry was not only right, it was required. I know you hate to hear this, but you gave them the idea and then you empowered them. They're not going to change just because you had a revelation, because *we* had a revelation."

Dick bit his lip and paused. He searched Jimmy's eyes. "I have to try, Jim. I *have* to try."

Jimmy waited a moment and then said, "I've been with you since the day you started, and although you don't remember all of it, I do. I don't want you to get your hopes up. Prepare yourself for the worst."

"I hope you're wrong," Dick sighed.

He nodded. "I hope so too. I know one thing is for sure. If you can't change their minds, no one can."

"If a person can't change their mind, maybe it's because they don't really have one," said Carlos.

CHAPTER FORTY-NINE

With the night of the event finally upon them, Jimmy led Dick down the hallway to his dressing room. "Where did the last two weeks go? I feel like you just got the invitation to this shindig." He stopped and looked left. "Follow me, I think it's this way."

"I'm glad you said it, Jimmy. I thought I was the only one who felt like the time flew by."

When Jimmy opened the door to the dressing room, Dick saw Senator A.C. Tate puffing on his cigar.

Jimmy shook his hand. "Nice to see you, Senator."

"Hello, Jim. Dick, glad to see you, son," he said in a warm Southern drawl. "You look better than the last time I saw you." They shook hands.

"Thank you again, sir," said Dick. "For everything."

Tate nodded. "I should be the one thanking you. Do you have any idea how deep that corruption went?"

"I've tried not to follow it in the news. It's very upsetting."

Tate continued. "Thanks to you, I look like a hero—and my poll numbers are through the roof." He paused. "Terrible thing that happened to ya, Dick. Just terrible. But there are still plenty of opportunities waiting for you—when you're ready."

"I'm speechless, Senator. I can't thank you enough for all your help. If you hadn't had Mr. Fay's computer confiscated, I might never have been able to prove my innocence or come home."

"Well, I definitely owed you one, Dick. And now we're even. Mr. Fay is going away for a long time, and in the process you managed to save a huge company from crumbling. A lot of people who would have lost their jobs are in your debt, from the line workers right up to the C-Suite. Are you certain I can't convince you to jump back into the arena soon? Man, your approval ratings are higher than mine. Jesus, even the Democrats suddenly like you."

"I'm flattered to receive the offer, A.C., but it's going to take time to get my head straight. Really, I can't take the credit here. Jimmy was as persistent as a bloodhound, working with the reporter, Tawny Beige. She's the *real* deal. Tawny is the genius who found me and put all the information together. Well, her, Kate Taylor, the flight attendant, and of course Lieutenant Benitez. Without Carlos, I'd probably still be sick, wandering aimlessly and living on the streets of San Juan, never to be found."

Tate nodded. "He's a fine example of American military. Makes me proud to be on the Senate Arms Committee, knowing there are men like him serving."

Jimmy and Dick glanced at each other and smiled.

"Yes, sir," said Dick.

There was a knock on the dressing room door. "Ten minutes, Mr. Peak."

Senator Tate moved toward the door. "I'll let you get ready, son. Good to see you up and around." His hand reached for the doorknob and stopped. He turned to Dick. "Speaking of the lieutenant…one last thing."

Dick hesitated. "Yes?"

"Too bad he's reserve. Do you think he'd like a promotion and a more prestigious job?"

Dick exhaled. "I can't speak for him but your confidence is well placed. We could definitely use a lot more like him."

"Good luck out there tonight."

"Goodnight, Senator."

Jimmy, Dick, and Carlos peeked out at the audience from the wings.

"This is a smaller venue than ROAR normally picks," Jimmy said. He gave Carlos the once-over. "You look mighty spiffy in that uniform, Lieutenant Benitez."

"Too butch, Jimmy?"

Jimmy laughed.

"I figured if I had to wear pants, they should be, you know—official pants. You ready, Dick?"

Dick felt shaky and his hands suddenly went cold. "I guess I'm about to find out."

"My little spiel on stage went fine," said Carlos. "Yours will too. I'll wait for you here."

Dick nodded nervously, flipped his lucky coin from his left hand to his right, twirled it between his knuckles and slipped it into his pocket. Jimmy and Carlos flanked him as they listened to the emcee's introduction.

"And now, please welcome former Congressman Dick Peak!"

Carlos smiled and patted him on the back. "Go get 'em, Juan."

The antithesis of every video he had watched of his formerly smug self, Dick stumbled on his first step. Sweat trickled down his back from lights hot enough to bake a cake, and everything he saw appeared to move in slow motion. He took five tentative steps to the microphone, fighting the urge to shield his eyes from the bright stage lights.

Clenching his speech with clammy hands, he tapped the microphone twice and glanced down at the damp pages he placed on the lectern. "Friends. Um, friends. I appreciate you all coming tonight and I want to thank you all for your kind words and prayers. They've helped me greatly. There are so many people and things I wish I could remember, and in time perhaps I will.

"But my purpose tonight is to share with you what I *do* know and what I've learned from my death-defying experience." He gazed out to the far reaches of the room and leaned into the mic.

"I stand before you tonight a humble man who is born again. But not born again in the way I used to mean it. For whatever reason, I've been graced with a second chance." He coughed, took a sip of water from the bottle on the lectern and glanced side stage at Carlos before continuing. "God gave me a rare opportunity to step outside myself and my life, long enough to really appreciate and understand it. Long enough for me to see who I really was before the crash." He took a deep breath and popped the mic with his exhale. "I have to be honest with you; I don't much care for the guy I used to be." He gazed down into the near rows and tried to steady himself before continuing.

"You see, something really strange happens to you when you don't know who you're *supposed* to be. You find yourself being who you were intended to be—who you really are. It's a mighty gift, my friends. A mighty gift. In those moments of clarity, you no longer get to define yourself and others with labels that come from all the chatter you hear and the bias in your head. Stories that tell you who and what to like or hate. Freeing yourself from all that is...well, it's salvation in its purest form. My salvation meant learning to love people for who they are, without judgment, without the hate I used to hold in my heart for people who were different from me—for those I didn't understand. Ironically, the result was discovering what real love and meaningful change are all about."

He glanced into the wings again and this time he saw Jimmy nodding.

"What I'm sharing about this convoluted journey may or may not make sense to you, but I can sum it up." Dick stood tall and scanned the faces watching him. *It's now or never.*

"Here's what I've learned: Life itself is *the* treasure and it's beyond measure. There are no luggage racks on hearses for good reason, and the gestures we make in this life *do* matter. To that point, were it not for the selfless and fearless action of a highly principled Navy Reserve Lieutenant, I wouldn't be alive today. This man knew me before. He hated me and the things I stood for, yet he literally risked his limb and his life so that I might survive. Yes, gestures *do* matter. Humanity and kindness *do* matter—above all else."

"Benitez. Benitez!" the audience chanted. Whistles rocketed forth from the back of the room. Dick bent his left leg and leaned forward, resting his elbows on the podium. "That fearless lieutenant is perhaps the most righteous man I may ever know. He's also a gay man."

Dick ignored the groans but he felt the collective disapproval wafting through the heavy air. Two people in the front row stood and walked toward the exit, so he spoke with greater command.

"People, wait. You can walk out on me, but realize this: you're just walking out on yourselves. If you love God, then join me in the fight for equality and fairness..."

"Hey, Peak!" an old guy heckled from the front row. "You didn't lose your memory. You lost your mind!"

Dick zeroed in on him.

"I was wrong. Wrong to lead you down a path of hate and fear. Don't you get it, man? Don't you *all* get it? When you have all that fear and hatred in your heart, God has no place left to live. Prayers then become hollow because you're praying for the demise of others. I'm asking you to find it in your hearts to take a step back, to give *yourselves* that second chance to let love live." For a moment, he felt a glimmer of that formerly charismatic congressman he had watched on the videos.

"I'll pray for you," someone yelled.

"Prayer is great," Dick countered, "but actions are what matter. Courage is what matters. Loving your neighbor—is what matters."

The emcee hustled across the stage and whispered, "Thank you" in Dick's ear as he eased the microphone from his fingers. He smiled broadly and spoke into the mic. "Thank you and welcome back, Congressman Peak. Let's give him a hand."

The applause fell short of anemic and Jimmy led Dick offstage.

Carlos waited for them just beyond the curtain. "You okay, Dick?"

"No."

"Jimmy, we've got to get him out of here. *Now*."

"Okay, you take him to the stage door and I'll get his gear from the dressing room. Go! I'll meet you at the back door in two minutes."

As their limo inched toward the stage door, it separated them from the rabid pack of protestors who vehemently dissented—who closed in and shouted inflammatory epithets.

"Hey! Hey! Back off," Jimmy hollered as he ushered Dick and Carlos into the limo and slammed the door shut behind them. "I got to tell you, Dick. It's super weird being picketed by ROAR."

"Follow my lead, Jimmy. I'm used to it," Carlos said.

Dick slumped forward with his hands covering his eyes.

"What is it, mijo?"

Dick looked up at Carlos and then turned to Jimmy.

Jimmy smiled. "You knew this wasn't going to be easy, Lester."

"Lester?" Dick laughed. "I don't know how you do that, Jim. Were you always able to make me laugh at the worst possible moments?"

"Wha?" Jimmy said with his wise-cracking grin.

"How can you make me smile when I feel this bad? That's *wha*. What am I going to do now, Carlos? My life is over."

"*Now* who's being the drama queen, Juan-Rich-Rick-Dick? Huh? I can tell you who it's not. It's not Juan being a drama queen. Nope, it isn't Juan. And you don't see Jimmy sniffling in his hanky, do you? No. And there's no Miss Creama LaCroppe, Puerto Rican Drag Queen *Victim* Extraordinaire in this limo, is there? You've already come back once from the dead. You've got this!"

"You think so?"

"Me and Carlos already know so, don't we?" Jimmy agreed.

"Sure do, buttercup."

Jimmy winced and then laughed. "Hey Carlos, you hungry?"

"Yeah, man, I'm starving. You want to go Italian?" He put his hand on Dick's shoulder. "Dick, it's going to be okay."

"Dick, look at me," Jimmy said gently. "At least you were exonerated of all wrongdoing and you're a true hero to American business. Think about how many jobs you saved! You'll find your way again. In the meantime, you have plenty of starting over money from the airline. Be patient and give it some time."

"You really think that's all there is to this?" said Dick. "Time?"

Jimmy sighed. "I see it as a great start. You got a second chance at life. Don't be a schmuck, take it. Make a clean break from all-a-this. The dirt, the national and state politics." He paused and glanced at Carlos. "Carlos?"

"Yes, Jimmy."

"That was a dumb question. Of course I wanna go Italian."

"I shouldn't even bother asking."

They both laughed while Dick stared at them wagging his head. "Oy! If I can survive the two of you. Sometimes I want to click my heels three times and say 'there's no place like home'."

Jimmy shrugged. "Go ahead, if it'll make you feel better."

CHAPTER FIFTY

With summer come and now almost gone, the temperate late day October sun waned through the storefront window on Castro Street. The shards of stained glass high in the transom window over the shop's door refracted the light, slicing it like prismatic ink on the opposite wall of the "Dick Peak for Mayor" headquarters.

It had been months since Dick mused over the conversation in the limo that night after the ROAR fiasco.

"Hey, boss," Jimmy said as he came through the door. He organized the stack of papers he was holding and tapped the packet on the desk until all the pages lined up and then placed them in a folder. "Are you ready? We need to leave now if we're going to walk to the LGBT Community Center."

"I'm as ready as I'm going to get, Jimmy." Dick tossed his lucky coin, caught it and twirled it as usual before slipping it into his pocket.

"Stay calm, Dick, it'll be fine." Jimmy handed him his suit jacket. "Looks like it's going to be a helluva turnout. We were supposed to have the Ceremonial Room, but they had to move us to their biggest room because the turnout is greater than we imagined. It's sold out."

"That's great news, Jim. Who would have ever thought that this is where I would wind up?"

Jimmy laughed. "Certainly not me."

"Is Rita able to make it?"

They walked onto Castro Street and headed toward Market Street.

"She's gonna try but she's been having a lot of morning sickness with the pregnancy and all. She says she feels better when I rub her feet; it's some reflexology shit or somethin.' Anyways, I've been doing it twice a day because she likes it."

"You're a good husband and you're going to be a great dad."

"You think so?"

"I know so." Dick stopped in front of the iconic Castro Theater. Weathered by history, Dick took the present moment to appreciate anew how the art deco facade glistened when the sun was low in the sky. He grinned at Jimmy.

"Wha?" Jimmy's hands completed the syllable.

Dick laughed. "You're quite a renaissance man, Jim. A family man. Tell me, is it because of all those family values speeches I gave when I was the *evil* Dick?"

They passed Cliff's Variety store, the only iteration of gay Home Depot that had occupied the block for almost as long as the theater had.

"Funny thing is, Dick, after I saw you were alive, man, it really hit me—how the only thing we ever have is the present moment. It was a real wake-up call. I figured, I love Rita and she loves me. But what struck me was that I'd better make her my family before somebody else got her! I realize now that family is what you make it. Like you and me—and Carlos, Tawny, and Kate." He chuckled. "And what a family we've become, huh?"

"Thanks, Jimmy. No one in my own family will speak to me except for Ellie." After what I'd done to her in the old days, that, my friend, is a damn miracle."

"Ironic, isn't it, Dick?"

"Really. Ellie is now speaking with me for the same reasons that the rest of the family won't. It's like it all flip-flopped."

"Just the same, give it time, they're not bad people."

"Misguided, Jim. Severely misguided."

"So were we." They crossed Market Street and picked up the pace until they reached the community center.

Carlos barreled into the private room in the back of the venue. "Finally! You're here," he said to Dick.

"Something wrong?"

"Some guy is upstairs who wants to speak with you. He says he worked with you at ROAR."

"You want me to handle this?" Jimmy asked Dick.

"No, but I need you with me to tell me who he is and how I know him."

"You mean tell you if you liked him," Jimmy added.

"Where is he, Carlos?" asked Dick.

"He's with your sister in the room upstairs."

Dick nodded. "Okay, call Ellie on her cell and tell her we're on our way up."

Dick and Jimmy took the stairs up one flight and opened the office room door where Dick's sister was waiting.

"You wanted to see me?" asked Dick.

The man in the dark blue suit pivoted to face him.

"What do *you* want?" Jimmy said defensively. "Dick, this is the guy who tried to oust you from ROAR when you were Executive Director."

"So then, you tried to do me a favor." Dick stepped forward and shook the man's hand.

"No, Dick, he's Granger Madsin, one of *them*."

"That's only partially true, Jimmy. I am Granger Madsin, but I'm no longer one of them. I'm here to help—to join your campaign."

"Why?" asked Dick.

Granger looked him in the eye. "Last year, what you said in your ROAR welcome home speech was pretty hard-hitting. You were right, Dick." He paused. "It's time for me to do the right thing—to come out of the *right* closet, so to speak. I've been thinking about it ever since that event, and while I may be bullheaded, I'm not a hateful man. I believe this is the first stop on my train to salvation station. Can you use me? I do great fundraising work and you got through to more people than you realize. People I know we can solicit."

"Seriously? I can use all the help I can get. Glad to have you aboard, Granger. I have to get downstairs, but go down to the VIP check-in and ask for Larry or my Personnel Manager, Miss Chi Chi. Leave your number and I'll call you tomorrow. We'll talk."

"Thanks, Dick, you won't regret it."

Dick smiled. "Thank you, Granger. I promise you won't regret it either."

When Granger left the room, Ellie put her arm around her big brother's waist and laughed. "*You* are the one who hired the purple-haired Latina drag queen as a personnel manager?"

Dick shrugged. "Well…yeah! No one has a knack for reading people quite like Chi Chi Rivera. She's got like this psychic palm-reading thing goin' on. In my experience, she's eerily accurate."

"Psychic? Palm reading? Uh-huh. Are you sure you're still my brother?"

"Still? I never *was* a brother to you, Ellie. But, I'm determined to make that up to you." He kissed her on the forehead. "We'll see you after. Come on, Jimmy, we better get back down there."

CHAPTER FIFTY-ONE

"Ladies and gentlemen," the announcer said into the microphone. "We hope you're enjoying this terrific community event. Now I know we promised you headliner entertainment, but I'm sorry to say that there's been a slight delay. Bear with us because you'll hate yourself if you leave. And then all your friends will make fun of you. Have a cocktail. Have several!"

The audience laughed, but backstage, Tawny scrambled down the hall and picked up her phone on the first ring.

"What! What? No! Creama is stuck in the elevator?" she yelled at her sister. "No, Scarlett. She can't be stuck now! Where's Larry? He was supposed to escort her."

"Calm down," Scarlett replied. "It's still the dinner hour and someone's working on it now. Larry and Dick are on the landing where it's stuck, calming down an elevator full of Cher posers."

"Oh my god! Oh my god! Creama is stuck in the elevator with Cherapalooza—the All Cher Revue? What are we going to do?"

"Tawny, chill. It's all under control."

"You call this *under control*?"

"You all look so gorgeous," Creama said to the All Cher Revue in the elevator. "If I didn't know I was me, which I didn't for a while, I'd think I was you."

"Oh thank you, La Diva," said the Cher facsimile in the back row of the elevator.

Creama smiled. *La Diva, once again.* "You're welcome, my little Cherayna."

Creama took in the breadth of the drag troupe she had long ago created. "I can't tell you how it warms my heart that in my absence you kept Cherapalooza-The All Cher Revue alive and well. So while we're stuck here, let me just say: Cherella, Chermiqua, Cherlonda, Cherayna, Chergarita, Cheramina, and Toots. Thank you!"

Gasp. Cherlonda broke a sweat. "I can't breathe! Can't stand closed-in places. There's no air. We're going to die! *Gasp.*"

"Honey, honey. Calm down!" said Creama. "The nice man on the other side of that door is fixing it right now. Don't pass out. Come on, you're a big strong…Cher. Show some decorum, Cherlonda. Ask yourself: how would Cher react to this crisis? With decorum." She sighed. "That's right. Yes she would."

"Cherella, give me your top," said Chermiqua.

"Chermiqua!" Cherella snapped, "Are you crazy? Do you know what I paid for this Bob Mackie designed for Cher? I bought it on Cheraphernalia."

"I don't care where you bought it, give it up, Cherella," Chermiqua bellowed in her deep baritone. "We need to fan Cherlonda so she knows there's enough air."

"Wait," Creama interrupted. "What the hell is a Cheraphernalia?"

"Cheraphernalia.com. It's like eBay only it's all about Cher."

"That's not Mackie," declared Creama. "And one of you could have told me about that site while I was getting my memory back! Do you have any idea how much I paid for this gown, Cherella?"

"Are you sure Cher never wore this, Creama?"

"I may not remember everything…but *Queen* Diva's wardrobe?" Creama scoffed.

"Dammity! I was scammed on Cheraphernalia? Here take the damn thing."

"I can't breathe," Cherlonda sniveled.

Creama rolled her eyes. "Well, snap out of it!"

The 'All Cher Revue' froze. Spontaneously, the minions burst into applause.

"Brava!" Cherlonda gasped from the floor. "Like in the movie *Moonstruck*. Oh you sounded just like Queen Diva, Creama."

"Aah," cooed the chorus as they applauded.

Creama struck a pose. "All right, Mister Sisters, let's rehearse, "If I Could Turn Back Time." She set the beat with a clap and a tap of her pointy-toe heels, and then sang, "If I could turn back time."

Cherapalooza answered. "If I could find a way."

Tawny's heels clacked up one flight of stairs to where she found Dick and Larry standing in front of the stuck elevator door. "Larry, what the hell?"

"Don't panic, kitten, the elevator guy said he should have them out in a few minutes."

"What the hell is that music?" asked Tawny. "Is that…is that 'If I Could Turn Back Time'?"

"Sounds like it to me," said Larry as he tapped his foot to the melody seeping from the elevator shaft.

"Oh my God! I was in the coma so long that Cher is already gay elevator music?" asked Dick.

"No, Dick, I think it's Creama."

Jimmy called out as he came down the hallway. "Hey, Dick, you need to go."

Dick checked his watch. "Okay, Tawny, we'll see you backstage." As Jimmy led him down a separate hallway on their way back to the fundraiser, Dick slowed and reached for a terrace door. "Hang on, Jim."

"Something wrong?"

"No, I need some air." He and Jimmy stepped onto the terrace and Dick stared into the distance. The sun had barely set before the East Bay snuggled into the blanket of hills for the night, the twinkling only outdone by the sparkling span of the Bay Bridge. Dick took a deep breath and let the cool evening breeze sigh on the nape of his neck. "I hope I'm ready for this, Jim."

"Don't worry, you've been ready for this for a long time."

"Okay then, let's do it," said Dick, reaching for the door.

"Don't you want to flip your coin?" Jimmy asked.

"You know, I always look to see whether I've flipped a heads or a tails. But I realize that it doesn't matter. Like me, they're simply two sides of the same coin." Dick smiled and held the door. "After you."

"Wait, do you have your speech?"

Dick tapped the suit pocket over his heart. "Right here."

Once backstage, Jimmy reached out and touched Dick's arm. "Last check."

Dick turned around to face him and Jimmy straightened his tie and crisped his collar. “Okay, looks good.” He winked and tapped Dick’s arm. “Knock ’em out, Lester.”

Dick made an unannounced entrance onto the stage and picked up the microphone. “Good evening, everyone! Welcome to Diversity Rights Activist Group’s Community Benefit.” He smiled. The room became instantly still as he gained his audience’s attention. “Thank you all so much for coming tonight. My name is Dick Peak, and I’m here to fight to advance equality.” He left his speech in his coat pocket and walked to the front of the stage.

“I know this is the first time many of you have seen me up close, and you’re probably wondering where the *evil* Dick Peak went. You’re not alone.” He gazed out across the faces, grateful for the moment. “That’s what I wondered too—after that macho *shero* Creama LaCroppe did her Wonder Woman act and rescued me from that sinking plane. I’m happy to report that *that Peak guy* is long gone.”

Laughter erupted and broke the remnants of any tension that Dick felt in his limbs. He chuckled. “Oh, I see most of you have heard that story. Believe me when I tell you that there are no firsts quite as powerful as those you get after having amnesia.” He took a few steps across the stage while reflecting, then pivoted to face the audience.

“‘Dick Peak, Pariah of the Religious Right!’ At least that’s how it reads on the cover of Time magazine. Inside that issue are excerpts from some of my past speeches. I have only one word to describe almost all the poo I used to spew. *Not*!”

Dick shared the laugh with his audience. “Now that we have *that* out of the way. Seriously, though, some people are skeptical about my change of heart, but I have news for them. I didn’t change my heart. I got one. This fight,” the timbre of his voice warmed, “this fight for equality has been the fight of every American since our great experiment began. Historically, discrimination has been the price of entry for almost every ethnicity and community at some point, and now it’s *our* time to take that bold step forward to claim the economic and social equality that the LGBTQ community so rightly deserves. Equality that’s long overdue.”

As he finished the sentence, he realized how quiet the audience had become and he looked up to find that all eyes were on him. “As Supreme Court Justice John Paul Stevens once said: ‘At stake in this case is nothing less than the essence of a free society.’ And while that’s so true about many issues in our country, it’s never been more relevant than right here. Right now. Equality is the heart of the matter and

I'm here to help silence the hate and ignorance." As an afterthought, he added, "I mean, seriously, people, who would know more about ignorance than I do?"

The audience laughed spontaneously, but for Dick, it was another of many revelations that were coming to him almost daily now.

"But the point is—what's important is what *you* think, and what *we* do about it. I asked myself, 'Do I have what it takes? Do I have the drive, the determination, and most importantly the dedication to fight this good fight?' The answer is simple. Yes. I can fight; only *this* time I'm not fighting *for* the right—I'm fighting for *what* is right."

Tawny came out onto the stage and whispered in Dick's ear.

"Well," said Dick, looking out at the house. "I've just been informed by the lovely network newswoman Tawny Beige that there'll be a slight delay in tonight's spectacular entertainment. You're not going to believe who's here. Really. You won't *believe* it."

"Well, where are they?" yelled the blond woman seated in the front.

"Stuck in the elevator. Still—better than being stuck in the closet. But they'll be out soon. Well, not *out*…I meant out of the elevator."

CHAPTER FIFTY-TWO

"Finally!" said Tawny as the elevator door opened onto a tableau of Chers. She looked Creama up and down when she stepped out onto the landing. "Love. The. Gown. Blue is so you."

"Juan picked it out. Can I wear it to your wedding?"

"No." She laced her arm around Creama's as they began walking. "Are you okay?"

"I'm fine, mija, but Cherlonda wilted under the pressure."

"Please. She's been auditioning for the drama-queen-cotillion since she snagged her first pair of fishnets. Come on, honey, everyone is waiting."

Dick had the audience in his pocket by the time he saw Creama standing stage left. "Once again, everyone, thanks for your incredible support. Together, we will stand united in the fight for equality. I'm going to stop here and turn you over to our emcee; you all know her and love her, the amazing Puerto Rican Drag Queen Diva Extraordinaiiiire, Miss Creama LaCroppe!"

The audience applauded and whistled when Creama sashayed onto the stage alone and took the mic Dick handed her. "Boys and Girls are you ready?"

"Yes!" came the audience's reflexive cry.

"Are you ready for the famous San Francisco treat and I don't mean Rice-A-Roni?"

The audience cheered.

"You're the treat!" a young man called out.

Creama zeroed in on him. "No, I didn't mean me, you cute thing in the front row. Do you have an older brother? All right, everyone, you know them and you love them. Let's hear a big welcome for "Cherapalooza-The All Cher Revue."

A medley of Cher tunes burst forth from the speakers, providing accompaniment for Cherapalooza. Choreographed and narrated by Creama, they toured the stage like Olympic synchronized swimmers—in drag.

"It's a Cher for every era!" announced Creama. "Or, as I call it, a *Chera*. Show the girls some love. Here they are: Cherayna, Cherella, Chermiqua, Chergarita, Cheramina, Cherlonda, and Toots! Give it up for Cherapalooza. Thank you, you bunch of Cher wannabes."

The audience laughed and applauded as Creama crossed the stage and took her place in front of the Cherapalooza lineup. A prop person ran onto the stage and placed a bejeweled headdress on top of the Cher wig on Creama's head. The stage gels focused in on the troupe as the houselights dimmed. The bejeweled headdress sparkled almost as brightly as Creama's eyes. Music blared through the surround system, and Creama's voice rang out in every direction as she sang lead to the Cher song, "Believe."

Cherapalooza performed the backup, and when they reached that part of the chorus where Cherayna, Cherlonda, and Chergarita performed their dance routine, the entire audience stood and danced with them in the aisles.

Backstage, Jimmy and Tawny danced to almost the whole performance together.

"You sure have come a long way, Jimmy," said Tawny.

"Geez, I was just thinkin' the same thing about you. I told you that day in the Jeep in San Juan, I love Cher. Guess we'd better get used to being the well-oiled machine that we are," Jimmy teased. "After all, we each have someone special to watch over, and those dudes are pretty tight." He paused. "In case you haven't noticed, so are we."

"You mean 'tight' until the campaign is over?" Tawny teased.

Jimmy took a long smooth puff of his unlit cigar. "The way I see it, when our candidate gets elected, we're going to be spending *lots* of time together. Like Carlos said, we're one big happy family."

"I believe he said we're one big happy *dysfunctional* family."

Jimmy smiled at her warmly. "There are worse things."

"Did you just say there are worse things?" Tawny smiled back.

"I did."

"Careful, Jimmy. Your old crowd will think you're a *fag*."

"Yeah, well…fuck 'em. Besides, it would make Rita and me very happy if you would finally say yes already to being the baby's godmother. She already has a godfather and a godperson."

Kate came toward them and placed the latest arrangement of congratulatory roses on the prop desk. "What are you two plotting now?"

"Nothing," Jimmy said with childlike guilt.

"I should know better than to ask," said Kate. "You two should be supervised. By the way, Tawny, your ex is looking for you. She asked if you would give her an interview about the campaign."

"Chloe's here? What did you tell her?"

"I told her that I handle all the PR and that I'd be happy to answer any questions she might have."

Tawny lifted an eyebrow. "Did she have any questions?"

"Only one," Kate replied. "She wanted to know when she could get her jazz CD collection back."

"And you said…"

"That we packed it up for her months ago, and she can pick it up tomorrow at noon."

Tawny frowned. "Tomorrow? I thought you were taking me to Big Sur for the weekend since it's our last getaway before our wedding."

Kate put her arms around Tawny and smiled before she kissed her. "Would I break my promise or ever miss an opportunity to have you to myself? Scarlett said she'll stay at the apartment this weekend and handle it. You can thank your sister now," Kate said, looking beyond Tawny.

Tawny turned. "Where ya been, sis?"

Scarlett held up a bottle of Dom Perignon. "Handling the *important* things." She placed the Dom on the table next to the champagne glasses.

Creama hustled off the stage to where Tawny, Kate, Jimmy, and Scarlett greeted her with open arms.

"Oh my, Tawny. I don't remember all of my past performances, but I'll bet tonight was up there with the best of them."

"Creama," said Jimmy, "I swore I was dancing to Cher. I fucking kid you not!"

"Thanks, buttercup."

"Hey, guys," Dick said when he arrived.

"Dick, did you hear that we got more endorsements?" said Kate.

"No, who?"

"Willie Brown, Governor Newsom, and State Senator Wiener. And the Human Rights Campaign has just made their support official."

"Really?" said Creama.

"That's wonderful news!" said Dick.

"Congratulations," Tawny added.

"Does anybody know that cute tall guy at that table near the stage?" asked Creama.

"Which guy?" asked Tawny.

Creama took her hand and they peered out at the audience beyond the curtain. "That one," she pointed.

"That's Senator Wiener," Tawny said.

"Is he single?"

"I'll find out for you," she answered as they returned to their circle of friends.

Ellie exited the stairwell and joined the group. "Incredible show!"

Dick kissed her on the cheek. "So? How did we do tonight?"

"Donations are through the roof, big brother," she answered. "Wait until you see for yourself."

He pulled her close and gave her a big hug. "Thank you for everything, Ellie. You're amazing."

Scarlett gently twisted the bottle of Dom Perignon away from the cork.

"Good timing, Scarlett." Dick gave her a double thumbs-up.

When Cherapalooza left the stage, everyone applauded and Creama reached out with open arms, returning each of their air-kisses to her cheeks as they passed her on the way back to the dressing rooms.

The group showered them with kudos and heartfelt thanks.

"I love you, girls!" Creama called out down the hall.

Cheramina turned back to face her. "Welcome back, La Diva Creama!"

Ellie was already handing out the champagne glasses.

"Scarlett," said Dick. "Why don't you pour?"

Scarlett poured everyone enough for a toast.

"Viva La Diva *Extraordinaiiiire*. To Creama," Dick toasted.

"Here! Here!" said the group.

Dick tapped his glass to get everyone's attention. "Before we get barraged by the press and our backstage guests," he began, "I want to take a moment to toast you all, my very special team. Without Creama, I wouldn't even be alive, and without each of your unique talents, I wouldn't be where I am. I promise to do my best to always deserve you."

"To the soon-to-be Mayor Dick Peak." Creama tossed back the champagne and looked into Dick's eyes. "You know, Juan, I hope all those people out there appreciate what you're doing to spearhead their fight for equality."

"It's not just *their* fight, Creama. It's ours too. All of us."

"Hmm," said Kate, jotting something into her phone. "We should work on that line for our next mailer, Dick."

"By the amount of contributions, I can tell you that you got the point across just fine, big brother."

Back in the dressing room, Carlos peeled off Creama layer by layer, and lovingly placed her back into her stage box. He scrubbed his face and dressed in a white formfitting T-shirt with jeans and boots, then left the dressing room to find Dick. He entered the now empty, dimly lit ballroom where Dick sat alone in the quiet.

Carlos straddled the chair facing him. "Well, Papi, you were quite the talk of the town tonight."

"You know, Carlos, it's probably going to be a long bumpy road."

"So what." Carlos raised his arm and gave the proletariat-fist-of-resistance. "Power to the people—*Umph*!"

Dick smiled. "I love you, man, but you're no Che Guevara."

"You're right. I'm more like *Cher* Guevara."

Dick laughed. "Where is everybody?"

Carlos looked past him. "Here they come now."

"Hey, Dick, are you ready? Rita just called and I need to get home," Jimmy explained.

"Is she okay?" asked Carlos.

"The hormones are tough on her right now. Oh," he rolled his eyes, "and I'm not allowed to go home until I find mint chocolate chip ice cream at this hour—and it has to be the green kind—with the *tiny* chips, not the white kind with big chips."

"Jimmy," Kate began, "you need to go home to your wife. We'll take Dick home."

"Come on, Jim, let's go get the coats," Tawny said.

They strolled arm-in-arm down the corridor.

"What a night, huh, Jimmy?"

He wiggled his hips. "Les-bo-tronic."

Tawny laughed. "You are so weird."

"Weird enough to be the father of your godchild? Come on, you know she's gonna need someone like you. I mean Creama can't be her only role model for a godperson!"

"God*person*?" said Tawny.

Jimmy exhaled. "This gender pronoun thing still trips me up, so for now I've chosen to remain gender neutral where Carlos is concerned…whenever possible. Come on, Tawny, say yes. It'll be fun. You two can undo whatever I teach her."

They stopped in front of the side-by-side closets at the end of the corridor.

Tawny grinned. "Yes."

Jimmy's eyes opened wide. "You mean it?"

She kissed his cheek. "I do."

"All right!" He returned the peck on the cheek. "Rita will be so happy you said yes." They turned back to the side-by-side closets.

Jimmy yanked open the door to the right closet and laughed. "Surprise! Ain't nothin' in *this* closet!"

Bella Books, Inc.

Women. Books. Even Better Together.

P.O. Box 10543
Tallahassee, FL 32302

Phone: 800-729-4992
www.bellabooks.com

CPSIA information can be obtained
at www.ICGtesting.com
Printed in the USA
LVHW110715240921
698607LV00001B/1